LOVE CHILD

LINDA KAVANAGH

POOLBEG

This novel is entirely a work of fiction. The names,
characters and incidents portrayed in it are the work of the
author's imagination. Any resemblance to actual persons,
living or dead, events or localities is entirely coincidental.

Published 2005
by Poolbeg Press Ltd
123 Grange Hill, Baldoyle
Dublin 13, Ireland
E-mail: poolbeg@poolbeg.com

© Linda Kavanagh 2005

The moral right of the author has been asserted.

Typesetting, layout, design © Poolbeg Press Ltd.

13 5 7 9 10 8 6 4 2

A catalogue record for this book is available from the British Library.

ISBN 1-84223-223-1

Typeset by Patricia Hope in Palatino 9.7/13.6
Printed by
Litografia Rosés S.A., Spain

www.poolbeg.com

About the Author

Linda Kavanagh has worked as a journalist for several Irish newspapers and magazines, and was a staff writer on the *RTÉ Guide* for fifteen years. She lives with her partner in Dun Laoghaire, Co. Dublin. Her first novel, *Love Hurts*, was published by Poolbeg in 2004.

In memory of my dear Father,
a lifelong trade union activist.

Acknowledgements

Sincere thanks to the Poolbeg team, especially editor Gaye Shortland for her eagle eye and amazing patience, to Mike for all his support and advice, to Matt Merrigan, national industrial secretary of SIPTU, for information on trade unionism, to John Synnott of John Synnott and Co. Solicitors, for patiently answering all my legal queries. Many thanks also to others who provided valuable information and insights. If any mistakes have occurred in interpreting any of this information, the fault lies entirely with me.

PROLOGUE

The prison warden silently slid back the tiny viewing hatch to Cell no. 47. Inside, a body was still twitching as it hung from the overhead beam. Gently, the warden closed the hatch once again. Too early to raise the alarm. Better make sure that the job was well and truly done. Another five minutes and he'd pull the emergency switch. By then, the bastard should be well and truly dead. Smirking, the warden walked away from the cell. Yes, five minutes should do it. That would be just long enough to ensure that the prisoner couldn't be revived, that the perpetrators had time to disappear, yet not so long that it would wreck his own career. He didn't need a disciplinary enquiry deciding that he hadn't checked the prisoner often enough. He patted the breast pocket of his uniform gleefully. Soon, it would be bulging with lots of lolly. A warden's salary wasn't great, but it was nice when there were occasional perks like this one . . .

CHAPTER 1

Joanna looked around her new office with a broad smile of satisfaction. Having moved in less than a week ago, the upstairs premises in Dublin's Dame Street was still a novelty. Her own office, in the best part of town! She could hardly believe it. She grinned at the mirror on the wall opposite her desk and saw a pretty, red-haired woman in a dark suit grinning back at her. Well, she thought ruefully, the rent on this place will soon wipe the grin off my face. But hopefully she'd soon have a long list of clients.

Sitting down at the large desk, she listened to Mary, her secretary-cum-telephonist, bustling around outside, making tea for them both. Her *own* secretary – she could hardly believe that either! Here she was, a fully qualified solicitor, starting her own business! Really, so much had happened in so short a time.

She sighed. What a pity that her dear old mum didn't understand how well she had done – now in a nursing home, her mother, Catherine, wasn't even aware that she was opening her own practice. Early onset Alzheimer's disease had by now led to the disintegration of the mother Joanna loved so dearly.

Mary, a bubbly woman with her hair in a blonde ponytail, arrived with two cups of tea, and the two women sat drinking in companionable silence. Joanna marvelled that until two weeks previously, she hadn't even known Mary existed. But she'd chosen her instinctively from the batch of applicants sent round by the employment agency – Mary wasn't as well qualified in legal and secretarial duties as some of the other applicants, and she came with the baggage of a broken marriage and two difficult teenagers. But the two had instantly established a rapport, and Joanna respected Mary's honesty and directness, especially when she'd admitted that she really needed the job and would work hard and study legal jargon to bring herself up to date.

Joanna didn't want a frosty automaton sitting in the outer office – she wanted a warm human being, who could deal with whatever sort of crises cropped up. And Joanna knew that a solicitor had to deal with all the vagaries of human nature. Mary had dealt with lots of crises in her own life, so she'd instinctively know what needed to be done, rather than having to be told.

"I didn't nip out for any buns, in case the phone rang," Mary said apologetically. "Maybe in the mornings I could call into the café next door?"

Joanna smiled. "Surely we should start as we mean to go on?" She appraised her secretary. "What size would we both be at the end of a year of bun-eating? But maybe we should invest in a few packets of biscuits – have you any favourites?"

Mary's face brightened. "I love Mikados – with all that fluffy coconut, marshmallow and jam – "

"So do I!" said Joanna, marvelling at the number of things that they had already found in common. "So Mikados it is – at least until we get tired of them! Take the money out of the petty cash tin when you need it."

Suddenly the phone rang, and the two women looked at each other in expectation. Could it be a possible client? Or just the telephone people checking the line, or a friend of Joanna's ringing to wish her well in the new office?

Mary hurried outside to the phone as Joanna picked up the tea mugs and carried them out to the small washroom off the reception area.

"Good morning, Joanna Brennan Solicitors – how may I help you?"

Joanna waited expectantly at Mary's side now, raising her eyebrows in query as the other woman listened in silence to the caller at the other end.

"Yes – just hold on – I think her current client is just leaving . . ."

The two women grinned at the small deception, and Joanna hurried into her office and sat down at the big desk to take the call.

"It's someone ringing on behalf of an old friend of your mother's!" Mary called in, before putting the call through.

"Hello, Joanna Brennan speaking."

"Good morning – you don't know me, but I'm one of the nurses at St Mary's Hospital. I know you're a friend of the family so perhaps you already know – Agnes Kilmartin was admitted here after a heart attack and is in intensive care."

4

Agnes Kilmartin had been Joanna's mother's closest friend, and Joanna was seized by guilt as she remembered that she hadn't called or contacted her in months.

"No, I didn't know. How is she?" she asked.

"She's stable at the moment and quite lucid. In fact, she wants to sort out some legal matter, so she asked one of us to contact you."

"Of course," said Joanna. "I'll call around as soon as she wants me to."

The nurse thanked her, suggesting that a visit sooner rather than later might be appropriate. "With heart-attack cases, it's hard to know what will happen during the next forty-eight hours. Some pull through, others don't. But she's a very determined old lady."

"I'll call around this afternoon," Joanna told her. "How's Tom, her son, coping with the situation?"

Tom was Agnes Kilmartin's beloved son, a quiet, gentle man in his mid-thirties – just a few months older than Joanna herself – and Joanna had always felt a deep affection for him. During her childhood, whenever she and her mum visited the Kilmartins, she would follow Tom about the large house and gardens – opulent by the Brennans' standards – and he would eventually yield to her pestering and take her to see the wonders at the end of the garden, where a small pond made the area home to a myriad animals, insects and birds. Together, they'd lie on the mossy bank, while he pointed out the different creatures and explained about their habitats. That had been a magical time for Joanna and had instilled in her a lifelong love of nature and an interest in conservation issues.

"Tom's obviously crazy about his mum," answered

the nurse, "and he's spent as much time as possible with her since the attack."

Tom was a science lecturer at University College Dublin, and apart from the time he devoted to his students, he was involved in a series of wildlife research and conservation projects, which took him to Africa, South America or the Antarctic during the university recesses.

"Well then, I'll probably see him this afternoon," said Joanna. "I'll be there about two thirty."

Replacing the phone, Joanna sat lost in her own thoughts. Poor Agnes, she thought. Her mother's friend would die with grim dignity, trying to maintain control even until the very end.

It had always puzzled her how her own warm, cheerful and impecunious mother had been a friend of the austere and wealthy Agnes Kilmartin. They were as unalike as chalk and cheese! Joanna's mother, Catherine, had been a woman in love with life, determined to extract every ounce of joy from it. Joanna had adored her scatty mother, but what she and Agnes Kilmartin had found to talk about she would never know. How could such opposites have anything to discuss? But obviously they had found *some* traits and characteristics to admire in each other.

"Well?" said Mary, appearing at the door. "Do we have our first client?"

"Yes, I think so," said Joanna. "My mum's old friend has just had a heart attack, so I'll call to see her in hospital this afternoon. I suppose she wants me to draw up a will for her, or maybe add a codicil to an existing will." She grinned at her secretary. "So you'll have to tell all our prospective clients that I'm inundated with work and can't return their calls until tomorrow morning!"

CHAPTER 2

Joanna made her way along the hospital corridor towards the Intensive Care Unit where Agnes Kilmartin was being treated. She felt guilty for not having been in touch with her mother's old friend for ages, and she was dreading seeing a proud Agnes reduced to needing round-the-clock medical attention. Agnes hated any fuss, and she'd probably be in foul temper at being confined to a hospital bed!

As she hurried along the corridor, lost in her own thoughts, she almost collided with Tom Kilmartin, who was just leaving the Intensive Care Unit.

"Oh, Tom – I'm so sorry to hear about your mum," said Joanna. "I'd no idea she was ill until one of the nurses rang on her behalf earlier today, saying she wanted to see me about a legal matter."

"It was very sudden, Jo – I've had no time to inform anyone yet." Tom gave a gentle, wistful smile as they hugged each other. "So you've started out in private practice! Congratulations!"

"Thanks, Tom – but tell me about poor Agnes. She just doesn't seem like heart-attack material."

"Well, no one is more surprised than her that this happened. In fact, she's absolutely furious! I think she's always believed she's immortal."

"But there's no chance she's going to die – is there?"

Tom shrugged his shoulders helplessly. "No, but apparently the first forty-eight hours after a heart attack are critical."

"So the nurse told me. Well, Agnes was always a determined woman, so I'm sure she'll get through this setback as well. Did you know she'd sent for me?"

Tom shook his head. "No. She didn't mention you or any legal matter to me. But before the ambulance arrived, she insisted on searching for some document and bringing it to the hospital with her – even though she was clutching her chest and gasping for breath at the same time!" He grinned impishly. "Maybe she's going to disinherit me – and leave everything to some cult, or maybe even the Cats' and Dogs' Home!" His face took on a serious expression. "Actually, I wouldn't mind at all if she left everything to an animal welfare organisation. I earn a good salary – I don't really need anything more." He touched Joanna's arm and smiled. "So don't feel bad if she asks you to make any changes like that!"

"But the house and garden in Ballsbridge – surely you'd miss that?" Joanna asked impulsively.

"Yes, I really do love the house – I'd hate to have to leave the garden and the pond – remember when we used to sit out there for hours watching the frogs, insects and birds?"

8

Joanna nodded, pleased that he hadn't forgotten.

"But as far as I'm concerned, everything is Mum's to do what she wants with. So you just do whatever she asks you to do."

Leaving Tom, Joanna headed into the Intensive Care Unit, where Agnes Kilmartin lay propped up by numerous pillows. The woman looked only a shadow of her former self, and Joanna tried not to let her dismay show too obviously on her face.

"Agnes," she said, grasping her hand and kissing the gaunt, sunken cheek. "I'm so sorry to hear that you're ill."

"Don't bother trying to dress it up in nice language," said Agnes, her voice stronger than Joanna expected it to be. "I'm dying, and that's all there is to it. We all have to go sometime, and it looks like my time is up." As imperious as ever, Agnes turned towards the nurse who was hovering in the background. "Listen, my dear, go and make yourself a cup of tea, and leave Joanna and me alone. I have something to say that is for her ears only."

The nurse nodded and whispered to Joanna that she should call her immediately if there was a change in Agnes's condition.

"Go on – get out!" said Agnes hoarsely. "I haven't got much time left, and I don't need it filled up with your inanities. I have important business to conclude!"

The nurse hurried outside, raising her eyes to heaven as she did so, and Agnes and Joanna shared a conspiratorial smile.

"They all drive me crazy," said Agnes impatiently. "A woman can't even be left to die in peace!"

LINDA KAVANAGH

Joanna smiled. Agnes would end her life as she had
lived it – imperiously!

"How is your poor mother?" Agnes asked, her voice
softening.

"Same as ever," said Joanna sadly. "I try to see her at
least once a week in the nursing home, but often she
doesn't even know where she is."

"I used to visit her regularly too, you know, and
sometimes Tom came with me."

"I know you did, Agnes," said Joanna gently. "Mam
couldn't tell me herself – but the nurses used to tell me
when you'd been in." Joanna wondered again about the
bond that had kept these two unlikely friends together.

As if she knew what Joanna was thinking, Agnes said:
"She was my closest and dearest friend. There was nothing
we wouldn't have done for each other. Your mother was
my rock of strength."

Joanna nodded. "I know what special friends you were."

"And now we can't even say goodbye to each other,"
said Agnes bitterly. "Life's not easy, is it, my dear? And
death can be such an untidy, long-drawn-out business.
Though not in my case, it seems."

Suddenly, groping under her pillow, Agnes tried to pull
out a document.

"Here, Joanna, I want you to have a look at this."

Joanna reached across, took the document and sat
down on the side of the bed, close to Agnes so that she
wouldn't have to use up her fading energies by having to
talk out loud.

"I've been a stupid, self-indulgent woman," Agnes said
bitterly. "I made this will just after Ivan died. It was only a

10

stand-by, in case I was run over by the proverbial bus. I intended writing a proper, more detailed one, when the time was right – but I kept putting it off. I was always going to sort things out tomorrow. It's so easy to put off the things you fear, but in my case, those tomorrows are looking decidedly less likely by the minute." Agnes pulled herself up on her pillows. "At the time, I was trying to protect people – innocent people who could get hurt if its meaning was too clear." She coughed. "But the cover-ups are no longer necessary. Those who needed protection back then no longer need it now."

Joanna smiled. "Sounds very mysterious, Agnes."

Quickly, Joanna ran her eyes over the document. It contained all the usual legalese – until she reached the part about bequests. There, she discovered that Agnes Kilmartin was leaving the Ballsbridge house to her son Thomas Kilmartin and the remainder of her estate to be shared equally between "the offspring of Ivan Kilmartin and the offspring of Harry Sweeney".

Joanna looked up in surprise, to find Agnes Kilmartin's rheumy eyes watching her carefully.

"Well?" said Agnes. "What do you think of that?"

"It seems a bit odd, but it's really none of my business –"

"I'm afraid, my dear, that it *is* your business – in every sense of the word. I want you to help me write a new will. None of the bequests in it will change, but now, with the passage of time, I can at last put actual names to these bequests. The truth finally needs be told." Agnes pursed her lips. "Although I deliberately made this will ambiguous, Joanna, your mother knew all about the contents of it, and as my executor she was going to ensure that my exact

wishes were carried out when the time came, assuming
I should die before her." A tear formed in the corner of
Agnes's eye, but she brushed it aside angrily. "But Catherine
can't help me now, although she'd agree, if she could,
that it's time to tell the truth." Agnes gazed at Joanna.
"There's also something I need to tell you, Joanna – since
your mother's no longer in a position to do so."

Joanna nodded. It all sounded very mysterious.
Quickly, she scanned the final part of the will – the part
that referred to Agnes's instructions regarding her burial.
Her instructions were bizarre, to say the least.

"This man Harry Sweeney – who is he?" Joanna asked.

Agnes coughed, and her thin frail body was suddenly
racked with spasms of pain.

Joanna heard someone running along the corridor as
though galvanized by the sound of the coughing.

"One of those damn-fool nurses again!" said Agnes, in
between coughs. "Joanna, Harry Sweeney was on remand
for murder back in 1970. He died in Mountjoy prison
without ever – " She went into a spasm of coughing just
as the nurse entered the room.

Hurrying to Agnes's side, the nurse placed an oxygen
mask over her face, and gradually some colour returned
to it, and her breathing became more normal.

"I really think Mrs Kilmartin's had enough excitement
for today," said the nurse gently.

"Yes, OK," said Joanna, gathering up the will and
placing it in her briefcase.

Then Agnes weakly pushed aside the oxygen mask
and struggled to speak again. "Joanna . . . could you come
back . . . tomorrow . . . please?"

Joanna looked down at the frail figure of her mother's friend. That plea must have been one of the few times in Agnes Kilmartin's life that she had ever asked for something, instead of demanding it as her due.

"Yes, I'll come back tomorrow morning – early," said Joanna gently, leaning forward and kissing the old woman's cheek. "Then we'll make out the new will, and you can tell me what's been on your mind."

Agnes nodded, the coughing having subsided. "I'll tell you the whole story then – it's one I should have explained a long time ago. And Tom deserves to know the truth too – but I took the easy way out, always putting it off until the following day. Which never came. I suppose I was always worried about what he'd think of me. I've been downright cowardly, you know."

"I could never think of you as a coward, Agnes," said Joanna, squeezing her hand.

"Well, I *have* been an old fool, and you'll probably be shocked at what I have to tell you, Joanna." She smiled whimsically, then continued weakly, "But then, solicitors are a bit like doctors and priests, aren't they? They're privy to people's most intimate secrets." She clutched Joanna's hand. "And you *are* my solicitor now, aren't you?"

Joanna nodded. The two women smiled at each other in a sudden surge of affection, and Joanna felt a lump in her throat as she gazed at her mother's proud friend, only now understanding some of the qualities that had drawn them together.

Then just as quickly, the benign expression on Agnes' face was gone, replaced with a scowl, as though she considered the smile a sign of weakness. "But I'll tell you everything in private – without any of these nurses listening in!"

Sensibly, the nurse pretended not to hear and continued plumping up Agnes's pillows and smoothing the covers.

Joanna had trouble swallowing as she said goodbye. Agnes really was an admirable woman – still fighting, right to the very end.

* * *

As Joanna got ready for bed that evening, she was still puzzling over Agnes's strange bequests. What on earth could a wealthy property developer's widow have in common with a man on remand for murder? And what on earth was Tom going to think when he discovered that he, as "the offspring of Ivan Kilmartin", had to share his mother's assets with this unknown "offspring of Harry Sweeney"?

Padding out to the kitchen in her dressing-gown and slippers, Joanna opened the back door and called the cat in. She was relieved when a tiny streak of black fur charged through the door. There were evenings when Devil wouldn't come in at all, despite cajoling and promises of exciting and tasty cat delicacies. Although still a kitten, she was already exerting her feline independence! Joanna preferred Devil to be in at night. Apart from her advantage as a surrogate hot-water bottle, the kitten had yet to be spayed, and Joanna didn't want any marauding toms getting in on the act before she could be taken to the vet.

Spooning out some cat-food into a dish, Joanna thought again about her first professional client. She readily admitted to herself that she was looking forward to learning more from Agnes the following morning. Why would anyone not name the beneficiaries in their will? And make such bizarre funeral arrangements? And then there was the "something" that Agnes needed to tell her personally. Joanna stroked the kitten as the little creature gobbled her food. Would all her future clients offer such interesting commissions? She doubted it. She'd probably spend most of her legal career doing conveyancing, sorting out landlord and tenant agreements, closing house sales and settling petty disputes between neighbours.

It had also been great to see Tom again, after all these years – he really was a very attractive man. She wondered idly why he'd never married – probably because he was far too interested in his career. After all, couldn't people say exactly the same about *her*? Here she was, already nearly thirty-five and not a man in sight. Joanna sighed. Maybe being an only child had something to do with it. Maybe that was why Tom hadn't married so far either . . .

Joanna looked sadly around the empty house in Blackrock. There was only herself and the cat living there now. But once, the house was filled with laughter, back in the days when her parents had both been healthy. Those had been the days that stupidly she'd never expected to end. She hadn't noticed that as she herself grew older, so too did they. Then illness had quickly taken its toll on both of them. Now her beloved father was dead, and her mother in a nursing home.

Firstly, her father had suffered a heart attack and became an old man almost overnight. Gone was the jolly, easygoing man who had been a companion as well as a father, the one who had introduced her to museums, art galleries, and had instilled in her the lifelong love of learning, simply because he made it all seem so much fun.

Then, in the aftermath of his heart attack, her mother began behaving strangely. She went from being a fun-loving, active woman to one who was confused, who couldn't remember things, who forgot where she was going, and became irrational, paranoid and temperamental.

It was only when Agnes intervened, advising them to contact their doctor, that the sad truth came to light. A house visit was arranged, and Joanna and her father explained Catherine's increasingly bizarre behaviour to their family doctor when he arrived.

"Let me have a little chat with your mother," said their doctor. "Does she know I'm here?"

"That's part of the problem, doctor," said Joanna anxiously. "Mam doesn't seem to be aware of anything any more. She seems to be living in a little world of her own."

They found Catherine in the kitchen.

"Oh hello, " she said smiling. "Who are you, and what brings you here today? Do I owe you some money?"

As Catherine started fumbling for her purse, the elderly doctor gestured for Joanna and Bill to leave them alone together.

It hadn't been long before he joined them in the drawing-room.

"Hrrrmph, I'd like Catherine to go for a few little tests," he gravely told Joanna and her father. "I can't really be certain what the problem is – "

"But you have a pretty fair idea," finished Joanna.

The doctor looked troubled. "Well, let's just wait and see," he said. "No point in anticipating the diagnosis, is there?"

But after a series of tests at St James's Hospital Geriatric Department, the sad diagnosis had been confirmed. Catherine was suffering from the early stages of Alzheimer's disease.

Joanna's dad had died not long afterwards, of a second heart attack. After his death, her only option was to move her mother to a nursing home, where she would no longer be a danger to herself. Now, all Joanna had left of her family was a kitten and an empty house that had once been filled with chaos, fun and laughter.

Joanna made herself a cup of tea before heading to bed. She didn't really want it, but her mind was racing and she wasn't quite ready to sleep yet. She was intrigued and flattered that Agnes had chosen her, rather than a more experienced firm of solicitors, to draw up and administer her new will.

She thought again about the friendship between Agnes and her mother, a friendship spanning over half a century. Joanna sighed. She was overdue a visit to her mother. Lately, with setting up her new office, she'd missed a few visits. She'd definitely go within the next few days . . .

Just as she was getting into bed, the telephone rang. Since she lived alone, Joanna was always wary about answering the phone late at night. It was invariably some drunk dialling a random number, or some pervert asking about the colour of her knickers. She hesitated, but curiosity got the better of her. Anyway, she could always hang up if it was a pervert . . .

"Joanna – "

At first she didn't recognise the muffled voice. Then suddenly, she knew who it was. "Oh Tom – sorry, but I didn't realise it was you – "

"That's OK, Jo. I shouldn't be ringing you so late. But I thought I could save you a journey."

"W-what do you mean?"

"There's no longer any need for you to call to the hospital in the morning – Mum passed away half an hour ago."

CHAPTER 3

The following morning, before she left for the office, Joanna telephoned the house in Ballsbridge. She'd hardly slept all night, worrying about Agnes's strange will. She was also dreading Tom's reaction when he learned about his mother's choice of burial plot.

"Tom," she said hesitantly, "regarding the funeral arrangements – your mother made a rather strange request in her will . . . "

"Go on . . ."

"She wants to be buried in Glasnevin Cemetery in the same grave as a man named Harry Sweeney."

"*What?* Are you sure, Jo? That can't be right. Who's Harry Sweeney? Surely she'd want to be buried alongside my father?"

"I'm sorry, Tom – but that's what she requested. I don't know much about this Harry Sweeney yet."

"Are you sure she wasn't hallucinating, because of the drugs she was on?"

"No, Tom – definitely not. As I said, it's in the will. So, I'm sorry, but we really do have to carry out your mother's wishes. There's no law that says a person has to be buried with their spouse. And your mother's made it clear that that wasn't what she wanted."

There was a pause.

"So what do you know about this Harry Sweeney?" Tom asked

"Well . . . only what your mother told me yesterday."

"Come on, Jo – you're hardly going to tell me he was a rapist or a murderer, are you?"

"Well, actually . . . your mother told me he was on remand for murder when he died."

"W-what? You're joking, aren't you? Jo – I'm uptight enough as it is."

"Tom – that is honestly what your mother told me."

"But who did he murder?"

"I don't know any more than that, Tom."

"Jesus, Jo – I can't let my mother be buried with a murderer!"

Joanna felt awful, but she had to defend Agnes's dying wish. "It's what she wants, Tom. And besides, this man was only on remand – he's never been proved guilty in a court of law."

"Well, there's never smoke without fire, is there?"

"Tom, I know you're upset, but a person is innocent until proven guilty. Obviously, this man meant something special to your mother. And you have to respect her wishes." This was so difficult!

"Oh God, Jo – what on earth was my mother thinking of? I mean, she led a quiet, sheltered life – never really did anything very exciting. Occasionally, she'd go to a lunch or function with Dad, go to bridge or visit your mother in the nursing home – that was all. Why on earth would she want to do something like this? It's totally out of character!"

Joanna sighed. She could understand Tom's anguish but felt helpless to do anything about it. "I don't know why, Tom. Look, I'll do my best to find out all I can about Harry Sweeney – then you may feel happier about fulfilling her wishes. There's bound to be some valid reason why she's chosen to take this course of action."

Tom's voice shook. "Why on earth would she deliberately choose not to be buried with her own husband? I know they didn't always get along, but surely . . ." His words trailed off.

Joanna wished she could provide some explanation, but she was as much in the dark as he was. If only Agnes had survived a little longer! "Maybe Harry Sweeney was a long-lost brother of your mother's?"

"I doubt it. Mum's only brother was called Joseph, and he's been dead for years now. Although after this other surprise, I'm beginning to wonder . . ."

* * *

"Any phone calls?" Joanna asked, as she arrived at her office.

"Yes," said Mary. "Your old friend Freddy O'Rourke wants to offload one of his clients on you. Someone whose dog bit a neighbour. The Gardaí were informed, so there's a court case in the offing."

Joanna wrinkled her nose. She and Freddy O'Rourke

had been through law school together, then both of them had joined his older brother's practice, which had already built up a reputation for being at the cutting edge of Irish compensation cases. But the kind of cases they handled were ones where huge money was involved – this brief was obviously too small for them to be bothered with.

It also offered Freddy another excuse for getting in touch with her. For Freddy O'Rourke had a big crush on Joanna – which she didn't return. Otherwise, she might have stayed on at Michael O'Rourke's firm when he'd offered her a more senior position there. But the thought of having to continue fending off Freddy's advances and attempts to date her on a regular basis was just too awful to contemplate, and she'd turned the offer down in favour of starting up her own practice. Which she'd always wanted to do, anyway.

"Is that all we've got?"

"'Fraid so," said Mary cheerfully. "But at least you now have the time to get going on Mrs Kilmartin's will. Next week, we'll probably be inundated with business, and you won't have a spare minute. Just you wait and see."

Joanna grinned in spite of her apprehension. Mary was determined to be cheerful! But there was only enough money in the kitty to pay the rent, and Mary's wages, for another two months. By then, hopefully some serious business would have come in. Otherwise, she might have to take out a bank loan to tide them over . . .

"OK – so we'd better take the dog case. Beggars can't be choosers."

Soon, Mary was on the phone, getting the details of the case from Freddy O'Rourke, who was thoroughly disappointed that Joanna was too busy to speak to him personally.

"I'm afraid Joanna is with a client at present," Mary lied.

Well, it *is* partly true, Joanna told herself, reaching for the phone. Her client was the late Agnes Kilmartin, and she'd better start her research on the woman's very confusing will. First, she'd better find out who Harry Sweeney had supposedly murdered, and why. Perhaps that information would supply some link to his relationship with Agnes Kilmartin. And allow Tom to feel happier about burying his mother according to her wishes.

Quickly, she dialled the newsroom of the *Evening Dispatch*, where her closest friend, Orla Rogan, worked as a journalist.

"Orla, glad I caught you. I have a big favour to ask you."

"Well, I'll consider it, as long as you're free to meet me tonight."

Joanna grinned. "Hang on – I don't want to be dragged into one of your usual hare-brained schemes – "

"How does dinner at the Promenade sound?"

"Now you've got me interested. But what's the catch?"

"There's none at all, my dear friend. I've got to do a bloody restaurant review and write it up for tomorrow's issue."

"Why aren't you taking Declan?"

Orla and Declan had been engaged for the previous six months. They both worked in the newsroom of the *Evening Dispatch*, and they were planning to get married the following spring. Joanna had already been lined up as Orla's chief bridesmaid.

There was a moment's silence before Orla replied. "It's a long story. So are you coming or not? Don't dare tell me you've got a better offer! Besides, you'll have my full attention for the entire evening. Then you can tell me about this favour you need."

"OK!" said Joanna, laughing. "You're on!"

The two friends arranged to meet at the top Dublin restaurant later that evening. Joanna spent the rest of the afternoon reading up on the precedents regarding injuries by dog bite, which were covered by the 1986 Control of Dogs Act. Under the relevant Sections 22 and 26, if it could be demonstrated in court that the dog was dangerous, the judge could either fine its owner, insist it be kept under tighter control – or order it to be destroyed.

Joanna bit her lip. If they had the misfortune to get Judge McGrath in court, he was known for invariably ordering that the offending dog be put down. Amusing rumours circulated among the legal profession that the judge had once lost a vital part of his reproductive anatomy to a dog and that this resulted in his prejudiced pronouncements. But what was amusing over a cup of coffee in the Law Library was far from funny when there was a devastated client involved.

If there were tears and trauma, and a dog that had to be put down, Joanna knew that she was just as likely to end up in tears herself. Maybe after a few more years' experience, she'd harden up. But she knew that if her own beloved kitten had to be put down, she would be distraught.

She massaged her temples and checked in her briefcase for some Paracetamol tablets. She didn't have any. Another stock item needed for the office! And maybe they should get in some boxes of tissues, for all the emotional clients who would be lining up to tell them all their problems!

"Make an appointment for me with the owner of the dog, will you, Mary?" she said with a sigh.

After that, she decided that it was time to go home, soak in a bath and get ready for her evening with Orla. She felt a little guilty at leaving the office so early, but she justified it by reminding herself that she'd actually be working that night. She wouldn't just be stuffing her face, free of charge, in one of the country's top restaurants – she'd be doing research on the Agnes Kilmartin case. Besides, as Mary had said so often during the past week, soon they'd be inundated with work, and they'd never be able to get out of the office!

"I'm heading home, Mary. Sorry to run out on you like this, but I've got a rotten headache, and I just want to go home and soak in a bath – though I must call into the nursing home to see my mother first."

Mary studied her face. "Do you think that's wise? You look all done in."

"I am – but I'll go and visit Mam," said Joanna resignedly. "I'm already feeling guilty about missing two visits to her lately." Then she felt even more guilty at sounding as though visiting her mother was a chore. Which was true sometimes, she had to admit . . .

CHAPTER 4

Catherine O'Brien looked at her watch and grimaced. She was waiting for her friend Agnes, who was giving the senior hockey team a pep talk about tomorrow's away game. Catherine smiled to herself. Agnes took everything, including school sports, very seriously, but they were all boring as far as Catherine was concerned. As friends, they were so different in every way: Agnes was tall, dark and elegant, and a stickler for time-keeping, whereas Catherine was small, bubbly and red-haired, and would probably be late for her own funeral. Which was why everyone found it strange that she and Agnes were so close.

It hadn't always been that way. When Catherine had started at the school, Agnes Cashen was regarded as future Head Girl material. She was autocratic, dogmatic and hadn't approved of Catherine or her laid-back approach to life at all. In fact, she'd taken a distinct pleasure in rebuffing Catherine whenever she got the opportunity.

Nor had Catherine liked Agnes either – she'd considered her a snooty, self-opinionated cow, until she'd learnt the true story from other classmates. Then she realised that it was just Agnes's way of compensating for her fear that she could never fulfil her wealthy father's expectations. Not only did he expect her to excel at sports and in the classroom, he'd also taken it for granted that she'd be Head Girl, just as her brother Joseph was already Head Boy at his exclusive school.

But Catherine hadn't realised the pressure that Agnes was under until the day she tried to cheat in a maths exam. Agnes had brought in a piece of paper with maths formulae written on it, which she'd tucked up her sleeve, but due to her nervousness, she'd let it fall to the ground – and the supervising teacher pounced on it.

"Someone is trying to cheat!" the teacher shrieked, with the barely suppressed glee of one anticipating a showdown. Holding the offending piece of paper aloft, she announced: "I expect the guilty party to own up at once – or you will all be penalised!"

This meant detention for the whole class, or even a resitting of the exam. All the pupils looked around, shaking their heads exaggeratedly, as if to show that it wasn't them.

But Catherine had seen Agnes drop the piece of paper. Knowing the pressure Agnes was under to achieve excellence in every subject in order to please her father, Catherine now watched the struggle that took place within her classmate. She saw the misery on Agnes's face as she contemplated how her admission of guilt would rule out her chances of ever being Head Girl. And she saw dread in the slump of Agnes's shoulders as she contemplated the punishment her father would mete out to her, coupled with the humiliation of being a star pupil fallen from grace.

As Agnes began to push back her chair to stand up, Catherine's kind heart came to a swift conclusion.

"I did it, Miss," she said, standing up.

"You —?" said the teacher, clearly disappointed, and her surreptitious glances at Agnes told Catherine she'd been positive it was that brazen hussy who dared to think she was Head Girl material. She had clearly been looking forward to taking her down a peg or two. As for little Catherine O'Brien — well, she wouldn't have expected any better.

After she'd been severely reprimanded by the Head Nun — such chastisements rolled off Catherine like water off a duck's back, since they happened so often — she left the Head's office, only to be accosted by Agnes.

"Why on earth did you do that?" Agnes demanded.

"I don't know," said Catherine meekly. "I suppose I realised that you had far more to lose than I had."

Anger and gratitude fought for domination on Agnes's face. She was angry that someone was able to spot the vulnerabilities she took such care to hide, yet grateful for Catherine's timely intervention which had saved her from humiliation, punishment and, worst of all, her father's wrath.

"Well, thank you," said Agnes stiffly to Catherine, having never had to thank anyone for anything in her life before. "I won't forget it – ever."

And she hadn't. That day had been the start of a lifelong friendship.

"You know," Agnes had said, as she'd surveyed her new friend, "with your red hair and green eyes, you look just like a cat. So from now on, that's what I'm going to call you – Cat. Anyway, it's short for Catherine, isn't it?"

Catherine nodded, smiling. Typically, Agnes hadn't asked if she'd mind being called Cat, but in fact Catherine was quite flattered. It wasn't everyone who was awarded a special name – and certainly not by Agnes Cashen.

Of course, Catherine would never have called Agnes by any diminutive of her name! Fortunately, the name Agnes suited her new imperious friend and was short enough not to require any abbreviation. But even if it had been ten syllables long, Catherine couldn't imagine anyone ever having the nerve to shorten it!

CHAPTER 5

"Mmm – this food is yummy," said Orla, licking her lips as she finished a large gooey dessert. "I was worried in case we were in for an evening of nouvelle cuisine – you know, a main course of half a designer lettuce leaf, with a blob of something unmentionable in the middle."

"Well, you couldn't call any of this designer food," said Joanna, in between spoonfuls of lucious creamy pudding. "The portions are enormous!"

"Thank goodness for that!" said Orla, pushing back her long blond hair from her freckled elfin face. "I was so hungry that if we'd been fed that kind of crap, I'd have had to drag you round to the nearest fish and chip shop afterwards!"

"But I'll bet you the bill will be designer-style!"

"Yeah – but at least the newspaper is paying for it." Orla looked around for a waiter so that she could order two Irish coffees. "Anyway, I'll probably never be back here again – unless you bring me here when you're one of the country's wealthiest solicitors!"

"Don't hold your breath," said Joanna, laughing. "I have only a dog-bite and a will as yet! Which reminds me . . . the favour . . ."

"Oh, yes – so what did you want to talk to me about?"

The Irish coffees ordered, Joanna told her friend about Agnes Kilmartin's will, of her unfinished conversation with Agnes, of Tom's concern, of her own mother's involvement and of her need to find out exactly who Harry Sweeney was – and any other details of the case that Orla could uncover in the newspaper archives.

"I went to see Mum earlier this evening," Joanna explained, "but I couldn't get any sense out of her. She became very agitated when I asked her about Agnes's will."

"Well, I suppose she doesn't fully understand any more," said Orla, looking sad. "Poor Catherine – and poor you! I can't imagine what it must be like – to watch your mother go slowly downhill like that."

Joanna felt sad, but didn't want the evening to descend into melancholy. So she changed the subject back to the business in hand.

"So you'll do your best to get me that info?" she asked.

"Yeah, sure – that shouldn't be a problem. How soon do you need it?"

"ASAP?" said Joanna, grinning.

"You're a slave-driver," said Orla, as the Irish coffees arrived. "But for you, I'll pull out all the stops. Just pray that tomorrow is a reasonably quiet day – if the government falls or a major scandal breaks, your query will go right to the back of the queue."

Joanna grinned. "This is a lot more urgent than any

31

political shenanigans, my dear friend. If the government falls, you'll just have to ignore it, or you'll have me to deal with!"

Orla's face took on an expression of mock horror. "Ooh, you have me terrified!" Then she added, "But you must admit – it's a very odd situation. What on earth can a rich property-developer's widow have in common with a probable criminal? I wonder if Harry might have been her long-lost brother? Tom's mysterious, long-lost uncle who's been living as a hermit on some remote island, or with a tribe of pygmies in the rain forests, and known to no one but Agnes . . ."

Joanna grinned. "I suggested that already – but Tom says he never heard of any uncle other than Joseph, who emigrated to Australia."

"Well, stranger things have happened. Didn't you tell me once that Joseph was the disgraced brother? Maybe he changed his name to Harry and sneaked back to Ireland under this new alias . . ."

Joanna smiled. "You have a wonderful imagination, Orla."

The two women sat in silence for a few minutes.

"Does Tom know about the rest of his mother's will yet?" Orla asked at last.

"No – I thought that the bit about her burial arrangements was enough to begin with! As for the rest of the will – I'm dreading having to tell him. I wish Agnes had managed to hang on for another day, so that she could have explained exactly who this other person is. It's weird, isn't it? Why leave a huge chunk of her fortune to a child she didn't even seem to know?"

"It's weird, I agree," said Orla. "But, you know, the word 'offspring' could also be plural, couldn't it? So Harry Sweeney could have had more than one child."

"Yes, you're right – I hadn't thought of that."

"Well, it or they won't be in their infancy any longer . . ."

"That's right – and this 'child'or 'children' could be anywhere in the world! How on earth am I ever supposed to find out where they are?"

Orla frowned. "I wonder how Tom will react? I don't think I'd feel too happy if I was in his position, and suddenly found out that my inheritance was being carved up between me and some unknown kids. And, apart from the Harry Sweeney issue, the will is rather strangely worded, isn't it? Tom is only named in regard to the house – but I presume he's also the one listed as 'offspring of Ivan Kilmartin'?"

Joanna looked worried. "That's what I've been assuming. What else could it mean? Agnes and Ivan didn't have any other children."

"I don't know. It's odd, isn't it? Sooner you than me telling Tom about all that!"

"I'm not looking forward to it," said Joanna. "I feel guilty that I know more about his mother's private affairs than he does. And now, you do, too."

Orla grinned. "My dear friend, I'm privy to so many secrets that yours is actually very minor. Did I tell you who the Minister for Finance is having an affair with? Now, that's a secret worth knowing . . ."

Joanna grinned as she took a sip of her Irish coffee. "Don't even bother to tell me unless I get to handle his divorce."

"I doubt if he'll be divorcing, my dear. Don't you know, the little woman will hang in there, and it will all blow over."

"The bastard!"

"The sleazebag!" Orla finished off her Irish coffee, then wiped the cream from her mouth. "Anyway, back to our Tom – you're quite fond of him, aren't you?"

Joanna nodded. "Well, yes, I've always been, since the days we used to – well, not exactly play together – but he used to teach me about nature and point out the different animals and insects that were found down by the pond at the bottom of their garden."

"Sounds very intimate!" said Orla, with a wicked grin. "Did he show you anything else?"

"Orla!" Joanna blushed crimson. "For heaven's sake, we were only kids! Well, I was a kid, but he was nearly a year older – "

"All the better to teach you with, my dear! You've gone all red, Jo, so there must be more to this than you're telling me. Do you fancy him? People don't go red if they're not interested in a guy."

"I'm not interested in Tom!" Joanna exclaimed, then realised that what she'd just said wasn't strictly true. There was definitely something special about Tom Kilmartin.

Orla, satisfied that she'd uncovered a chink in her friend's armour, decided to drop the subject – at least for the present. "Mmm – those Irish coffees were gorgeous. Could you manage another one?"

Joanna nodded, glad to have the subject changed from Tom. Now that Orla had forced her to examine her feelings about him, she hoped that she could behave professionally at their forthcoming meeting and not start blushing as soon as he appeared.

"So – how is the wedding dress coming along?" she asked, keen to get the spotlight away from her own personal turmoil.

"It's not," said Orla, waving to the waiter and ordering two more Irish coffees. "Declan and I are finished."

"Finished! But I thought . . ." said Joanna helplessly. "What's happened?"

Orla's face darkened, and Joanna could see that tears were now starting to form at the corner of each eye. But since Orla hated sentimentality, Joanna pretended not to notice.

"This is for your ears only!" said Orla fiercely.

"Of course!" Joanna replied, reaching for her friend's hand. "You and I know that everything we tell each other is strictly off the record."

"Remember I told you that Declan was going on a press trip to Spain?"

Joanna nodded.

"Well, the bastard got friendly with one of the other journalists – a little floosie from the *Trident*, who wears her skirts up to her arse – and they've been having an affair ever since. Apparently everyone in the newsroom knew about it, except me!"

"Oh God. So how did you find out?"

Orla mopped her eyes with a napkin. "At least *someone* had the decency to tell me. You know that nice photographer, Eoin – the one I sometimes work with? Well, yesterday, when we were out on a job together, he

35

said that he felt he ought to tell me. Needless to say, I was dumbstruck. But I'm very grateful that he did, because that made me realise why all the people in the newsroom stopped talking every time I walked in!"

"You poor love – but what did Declan say about it? I mean, are you really sure it's true?"

"Oh, it's true all right – at first he denied it, then he confessed. Said it was just a brief fling – that he wouldn't be seeing her any more. But I kicked him out of the apartment. And I'm pretty sure he's moved into her place already – the scumbag!"

"Then you're well rid of him," Joanna said firmly. "There are plenty of decent men out there. What about the photographer – Eoin?"

"He's married. Anyway, I wouldn't fancy him, even if he was available. But he's a good mate, and I'm grateful to him."

Joanna patted her friend's hand encouragingly. "Don't worry, love – you'll soon find someone worthy of you." Suddenly, an image of Tom Kilmartin appeared in Joanna's mind. Why was it that as soon as she thought about a worthy example of manhood, an image of Tom forced its way into her consciousness?

"I don't really want to go home yet," said Orla sheepishly. "Would you mind if we went somewhere else – just for a little while?"

All Joanna wanted to do was go home to her bed and her little cat, but who could let down a dear friend in distress? "Of course not! Let's go to that new nightclub – I think it's called The Blue Onion," she said brightly. "After a few more bottles of wine, you'll feel like a new woman!"

"Great!" said Orla, brightening up. "Then we can drink to Declan's downfall – hopefully the bastard will fall and break his neck. Or his prick will fall off!"

After Orla had paid the bill, the two women left the restaurant and made their way down Leeson Street, the site of many of Dublin's nightclubs. Soon the duo were settled in comfortable seats at the bar of The Blue Onion.

"Cheers!" said Joanna, clinking her glass against Orla's, as they prepared to demolish the first of several bottles of wine. "Here's to your new and wonderful *après*-Declan life!"

CHAPTER 6

Declan Dunne was feeling very pissed off. What had started off as a wonderful fling with Sasha Miller had turned terribly sour, terribly quickly. Even the name Sasha annoyed him. Was it made up? It sounded Russian – maybe that explained why she was able to down neat vodka by the double measure. Or maybe she just used the name for professional reasons – that is, if you could apply the word "professional" to the crap she wrote!

And for this he'd lost the only woman he'd truly ever loved! Orla wouldn't take him back, and he couldn't take much more of Sasha's inane whinings. While they'd been having rambunctious sex, it had all been wonderful, and he hadn't noticed how really boring she was. There was something really exciting about doing it with a new body – or maybe what he really meant was a different body? God, maybe by association he was becoming as illiterate as Sasha! Anyway, another person's different sounds, different techniques and different way of reacting made the act a lot more titillating. And Sasha's arse really was exciting – it almost had a life of its own. And she certainly knew where her best asset lay and wore really short skirts to show it off. It swayed and wiggled and drove him demented with lust – at least it had previously done so, until he realised that there wasn't a brain to go with the arse. How on earth did she ever get to be a journalist? Probably some editor or senior sub had fallen for her arse the way he had, and got conned into giving her a job before he came to his senses.

Declan scratched his head. What on earth was he going to do? He'd already moved into Sasha's apartment – which was full of appalling pink, frilly, girly things. There was no room for a fellow to put his football boots, his general paraphernalia and, most important of all – his precious autograph album, with autographs and photos of him with all the famous people he'd interviewed over the years.

He sighed. Even Sasha's bloody dressing-table had a frill around it – like the Barbie-doll furniture set his sister had once owned. He'd never thought that real people could actually *live* like that. Maybe Sasha saw herself as Barbie – which left him playing the role of wimp-doll Ken. No way – he'd have to get out of here fast!

He heard the door of the apartment opening.

"Hi, sugar!" said Sasha, sidling up to him, her swaying bum still causing his prick to harden. *Sugar!* What the hell did she think he was? Anyway, he didn't really care at that moment, because she was fondling the front of his trousers, opening his zip, and suddenly they were on the floor and he was tearing off her postage-stamp-sized skirt and tiny knickers.

Afterwards, Declan felt disgusted with himself. Her big voluptuous bum had made a fool of him again. And he was the laughing stock of the office. Everyone thought it was so funny that the great Declan Dunne had succumbed to the Bummer! And he hadn't even known, when they'd gone off to Spain on the press trip, that Sasha had been awarded that moniker years before, when she'd used her prized asset to break up the marriage of the newspaper's senior science editor. *Science* editor! What on earth was an intelligent guy doing with such a pea-brain? Possibly trying to explain Einstein's Theory of Relativity to her, he thought dryly. Back then, that science guy had been a source of amusement and gossip throughout the office. Now *he* was the patsy they were all talking about.

Now that the sex was over, Declan looked at Sasha Miller with distaste. Maybe he should give Orla another call and see if she'd mellowed at all. He didn't really blame her for being furious – he'd behaved like a cad. Was *still* behaving like a cad. Maybe if he told Sasha that he needed time to think – that it was too early to think about a serious relationship between them – he could get out of her apartment and back to the relative safety of – where? Home to his parents? Orla had kicked him out of *their* apartment. But maybe if he called round there, with a bunch of roses, she'd see that he was really sorry. Surely she couldn't want to throw away those two happy years they'd spent together? Just because he'd made one silly mistake? Yes, he'd go round there, let himself in and wait for her when she returned from work. Besides, she still had that expensive engagement ring. It had cost him a fortune – in fact he was still paying for it. That was another good reason for them getting back together!

Sasha, still lying on the floor, saw him smiling and assumed that it was because of her. "Did you enjoy that, sugar?' she whispered, in her most seductive voice. "You're such a big sexy boy – why don't we slip into bed," she made a purring tiger sound, "and go for a repeat performance?"

God, she sounds like a bad imitation of a gangster's moll in a 1940s movie, Declan thought. Nevertheless, he rolled over on his back and allowed her to begin working on him again. And before long, they had made their way into the bedroom.

Tomorrow's another day – I'll phone Orla in the morning, thought Declan hazily as Sasha started doing remarkable things to him with her tongue. That's *two* remarkable assets she posesses, he told himself happily.

CHAPTER 7

Catherine O'Brien met the gentle and affable Bill Brennan at an evening class on antique restoration. Bill, who bought and sold books from his little shop on one of the city quays, was fascinated by the petite and bubbly redhead, who was now a qualified jeweller. She, in turn, was captivated by his passion for old and rare books and the lengths to which he would go in order to find a sought-after tome for a client.

Amid the remnants of old chairs, writing boxes and miscellaneous items that the students brought in to restore, romance blossomed between them. The two exchanged hints on restoration, and before long they could be found in a nearby café after class, discussing what they'd just learnt in the classroom. Gradually the conversation turned to discussing how well their beautifully restored pieces would look in their first home together . . .

Before long, Catherine was also helping out in Bill's bookshop at weekends, where students and professors gathered, all anxious to discover what treasures Bill had acquired during his midweek book-buying expeditions around Ireland and abroad. Within six months, Bill and Catherine were engaged, and Catherine designed – and made – her own engagement ring.

"I'm so happy for you, Cat," said Agnes as she surveyed the engagement ring her friend had made. It featured a single tiny diamond, and it looked exquisite on Catherine's slender little hand. Agnes knew that the tiny diamond was all that Bill could afford, but its size didn't matter to Catherine. And Agnes was thrilled to see her dearest friend so happy and excited about the future. Bill and Catherine would never be rich, but between them they posessed a wealth of love and companionship, and they found delight in everything the other did.

"When we find somewhere to live, I'm going to open my own workshop," said Catherine enthusiastically. "Then Bill and I will both have our own businesses – isn't it exciting, Agnes? Then when we have kids, I'll be able to continue working from home. Not many women are that lucky."

"That's wonderful, Cat," said Agnes, hugging her friend, "and I intend becoming one of your first customers!"

Agnes, of course, was not expected to have a career. Her wealthy property-developer father, Phelim Cashen, had educated her to become the wife of an equally powerful businessman. But Agnes insisted that she was having a career of her own, and her father reluctantly agreed that she could do a secretarial course and work in his office until he found a suitable husband for her. Of course, these were not his exact words to Agnes. Her father cleverly allowed his daughter to think that the decisions she was taking were entirely hers.

"What I'd really like to do is study science at university," Agnes confided in Catherine. "I was good at it when we were at school, wasn't I, Cat? And I got honours in Biology in the

43

Leaving Certificate! But of course, Dad won't hear of it. When I suggested going to Trinity or UCD, he nearly hit the roof! He said women should know their place, which was staying at home and producing children for their husbands. When I pointed out that I wasn't married yet, he said he'd soon sort that out too!" Agnes sighed. "Oh Cat – I really envy you! You're free to do what you want with your life. Dad will probably expect me to marry some awful old fuddy-duddy whom I'll hate."

"Well," said Catherine, smiling wanly, "being penniless doesn't give you many choices either. I wanted to go to art college, but since my parents had no money, I had to do an apprenticeship in a manufacturing jeweller's instead. Besides," Catherine patted her friend's hand, "whoever you marry should be your choice, Agnes. Your father can't bully you into marrying someone you don't love."

Agnes nodded. "D'you know, Cat, I really miss poor old Mum. I wish she was still alive – maybe she'd have supported me against Dad. Although she was always terrified of him too."

"Agnes," said Catherine crossly, "you don't need anyone else to fight your battles. You must learn to make your own decisions – you can't let your father decide how you'll live your life!"

"I don't have your guts, Cat," said Agnes sadly. "I've always had the comfort of money, and I don't think I could survive without it. And I know that Dad would cut me off without a penny if I went against his wishes."

"Welcome to the real world," said Catherine tartly. "Money isn't everything, Agnes. Happiness is what really matters."

Later that year, Agnes met her future husband in the head office of her father's company. Ivan Kilmartin had recently joined Cashen Construction Ltd as a senior partner, and his own company, Kilmartin Construction, was in the process of amalgamating with Cashen Construction. Henceforth, the company would be known as Cashen Kilmartin Construction.

"It's a good move for us," Agnes's father told her. "Kilmartin is a fine young lad. A bit of a hothead – that's how he got himself into a bit of financial trouble – but buying him out and clearing his debts gives me the expertise and young blood that this company needs." His brow darkened. "Especially since that upstart brother of yours took himself off to Australia!"

Agnes bit her lip. Her brother Joseph, whom she loved dearly, had been unable to submit to his father's domination. After completing his engineering degree, he had been given a place on the board of Cashen Construction, but father and son found themselves constantly at loggerheads. Eventually, after a blazing row, Joseph resigned from his seat on the board, packed his bags and left the country.

Since Joseph left, Agnes had felt the extra pressure to be the kind of child their father wanted. As a female, her father would never allow her to sit on the board, and this annoyed Agnes greatly. While she sat taking the minutes at their meetings, she often felt that her own ideas were as good, if not better, than those suggested by the board members. But, of course, she was too timid to ever say so.

But Ivan Kilmartin was quick to spot her potential. And to realise that marrying the boss's daughter would be a sure-fire way of eventually getting control of the entire company. He got on well with Phelim, and he knew that if he showed interest in Agnes, his future wealth and success would be assured. Besides, Agnes was a reasonably attractive woman, of the type he liked – tall, slender and with a bit of class. She was well educated and would be an asset at important functions and social events.

Initially, he sought Phelim's approval, since he didn't want *to jeopardise his career by making the wrong move. But Phelim heartily approved, and Ivan asked Agnes out on their first date. When he brought her home that night, he merely kissed her on the cheek before departing. Agnes was impressed. Any other men she'd dated had had their tongues halfway down her throat before they'd even settled into their seats in the cinema! On their second date, he brought her a tiny posy of flowers. He looked so sheepish and embarrassed that Agnes felt her heart flip over. She was so impressed that a man who was a powerhouse in the boardroom could be shy in the company of a woman he clearly wanted to please. As he drove Agnes back to her home after their second date, once again he just kissed her on the cheek. Agnes was amazed – and pleased.*

But little did she know that after Ivan dropped her off home, he'd retired to a bawdy nightclub in one of the city's backstreets, where his lust had later been satisfied by a young prostitute in an upstairs room.

Agnes enjoyed being courted in such a gentle, old-fashioned way, and she was quick to realise that her father approved of her relationship with Ivan Kilmartin. For the first time in her life, Agnes found that she was actually pleasing her father, and it was a delightful feeling. She'd always felt that she'd disappointed her father by not being a boy, and when Joseph had left for Australia she'd felt the weight of his disappointment even more.

Now, however, her father was warm and outwardly caring, whereas previously she'd merely felt like a nuisance whose life needed sorting out. Now, he was asking her opinion on the décor for the new office layout, and consulting her on where he should locate the kitchen in the new office extension.

Unfortunately, Catherine didn't share Agnes's rosy view of Ivan Kilmartin. "Are you sure you know what you're doing?"

she asked Agnes several times. "I'm worried that you'll marry a man because your father approves of him, not because he's the right one for you."

"Don't be ridiculous, Cat," said Agnes hotly. "You don't really know Ivan – when he's around, you avoid him like the plague, so how could you know how he treats me? He's kind and gentle, and he's never tried to push himself on me. He respects me, Cat."

Catherine had said nothing more, but Agnes was aware that her friend continued to be unhappy about her relationship.

Yet when Ivan proposed several months later, Agnes accepted immediately. And Catherine was there to offer her congratulations.

In Agnes's mind, Ivan was somehow linked to the change in her father's attitude towards her, and she wanted it to continue. Besides, Ivan was everything a woman could possibly want – he was tall, handsome and charming. And he clearly respected her – he had never even tried to consummate their relationship. The most he'd attempted was a gentle grope of her breasts, for which he subsequently apologised, although Agnes had been longing for him to continue.

But while Agnes continued to be impressed by Ivan's restraint, the truth was more sinister. Through his association with several prostitutes, he'd picked up a venereal disease, which prevented him making any more intimate advances to Agnes, at least until he was cured. After all, if he gave the boss's daughter VD before the wedding, he'd probably find himself out of the company in double quick time! And that was something that Ivan Kilmartin wasn't prepared to risk.

Ivan wanted to buy the engagement ring from a "proper" jeweller, but Agnes insisted that Catherine would make her ring. "Cat knows what I like," she said firmly. "Wait till you see, Ivan – it'll be gorgeous!"

Reluctantly, Ivan had agreed, with the proviso that the ring would be large and ostentatious and set with at least a two-carat diamond. A man in his position had to ensure that his fiancée sported an impressive rock on her finger. He needed to impress his father-in-law-to-be, as well as the society pages of the newspapers.

The friends' weddings were, of course, very different. Catherine and Bill opted for a small, intimate wedding, attended only by their immediate families and close friends. After all, they needed to save their money to put a deposit on a house, and they'd just seen a dilapidated old place in Blackrock that might just fit their budget. Agnes gave Cat and Bill a beautiful bronze sculpture of cows grazing in a field, which Cat had so admired in an antique shop one day when she and Agnes had out been window-shopping. And to the base, Agnes had attached a generous cheque, which would more than cover a deposit on a house.

In contrast, Agnes's father pulled out all the stops for her wedding, inviting hundreds of guests – most of them his own business acquaintances, politicians and celebrities – and Agnes was paraded like a prize mare. Nevertheless, she basked in her father's approval. It seemed that, at last, she was doing something right. Her father heartily approved of her choice of husband – and Ivan knew only too well that he'd made the biggest career move of his life the day he married Phelim Cashen's daughter . . .

CHAPTER 8

Orla had promised to meet Joanna for lunch the day after their night out on the town and to accompany her to the Ilac Centre, where she would give her honest opinion on a lime-green dress that Joanna had spotted a few days before. If it was still there and Orla approved, she would buy it. After all, she'd need to look good when Tom Kilmartin came to her office. Then, if the day was reasonably warm, the duo were planning to buy sandwiches at a delicatessen in Westmoreland Street, stroll up Grafton Street and eat their lunch in nearby St Stephen's Green, where they would sit beside the pond and watch the amusing antics of the ducks.

And hopefully, Orla would have managed to get some more information on Harry Sweeney by then.

However, mid-morning, just as Joanna was drawing up a particularly tricky landlord and tenant agreement, Orla phoned.

"Hey, kiddo – sorry, but I won't be able to meet you

today. That bitch Julie-Anne Jones is out sick again, and I've been asked to take over some of her assignments for today. And I've got to finish off my own stuff as well. So I'm afraid I'll have to eat lunch at my desk."

"Oh, OK. Poor you!" said Joanna. "Oh, Orla – I suppose you haven't had time to find out anything about Harry Sweeney?"

"'Fraid not. Sorry. But I'll try to get the information for you this afternoon."

"OK, thanks, Orla."

Joanna was disappointed but knew the pressures that Orla had to cope with. If her friend had no time this afternoon, she'd get on to the Department of Justice herself and make enquiries.

It would also have been nice to have Orla's honest opinion on the dress, but she'd already made up her mind to buy it anyway.

At lunchtime, Joanna made her way to the Ilac Centre and bought the dress in ten minutes flat. It had stood the test of time – it was just as gorgeous as she'd remembered it, and it fitted beautifully when she tried it on. Then, on impulse, she bought some matching satin underwear. Hopefully, it might come in handy, if she ever got up close and personal with Tom Kilmartin . . .

It was a fine day, and Joanna walked through the city centre with her purchases, thinking ruefully that she'd really have enjoyed sitting out on the Green with Orla. She was also worried that she had no information for Tom yet. She felt restless and unwilling to go back to the office – besides, she hadn't eaten anything since breakfast-time. On cue, her stomach gave a gentle grumble.

50

Popping into a takeaway on O'Connell Street, Joanna ordered a big salad sandwich. Now, all she needed was a place to eat it. Maybe she'd walk up Findlater Street and sit in the Garden of Rememberance on Parnell Square.

Just then, a bus came around the corner, slowed down and stopped at a bus stop she was passing. One of its listed destinations was Glasnevin Cemetery. If that wasn't an omen, what was? Suddenly, Joanna knew where she was going to go. She would visit Harry Sweeney's grave! Quickly, she joined the queue of people who were boarding the bus, and soon she was on her way.

Alighting at the bus stop in front of the cemetery, Joanna crossed the road and made her way through the gates. At the cemetery office, an elderly man looked up the site number of Harry Sweeney's grave and gave her directions for finding it, then Joanna proceeded down the main tree-lined avenue, pausing briefly as she passed the graves of Charles Stuart Parnell, Michael Collins and Eamonn de Valera, men who had shaped Ireland's history. The cemetery was a surprisingly beautiful and soothing place, and Joanna felt relaxed as she wandered through the groves, past rows and rows of graves, pausing occasionally to read an epitaph or to study a particularly elaborate headstone. She was surprised to discover that she was enjoying herself. What a pity, she thought, that cemeteries are associated only with sad occasions, because then we lose sight of their historical and architectural significance. In fact, Glasnevin Cemetery had a perennial beauty, which brought her a strange inner peace.

At last, she came to Harry Sweeney's resting place. It was an impressive grave, with a magnificent headstone, bearing the words *Harry Sweeney 1935–1970*, accompanied by an inscription which read: *May he find in death the peace that was denied him in life*. Care and attention had clearly been lavished on the grave – but by whom? There were fresh flowers on the grave, so someone was still mourning Harry Sweeney.

Joanna sat down on a nearby edging stone and contemplated the mound of earth that was Harry Sweeney's final resting place. "Oh Harry," she whispered softly, "can you tell me anything about your life? You were only thirty-five when you died – the same age as I am now. What was the connection between you and Agnes? And who is keeping your grave in such beautiful condition? Obviously, you're still deeply loved by somebody, Harry – but who?"

But there was only the buzz of an insect flying by and the faint sound of buses and cars passing by on the distant road. Mind you, Joanna thought with a wry smile, if anyone *had* replied, she'd have been terrified!

Yet despite the fact that he'd been on remand for murder, Joanna felt a strange affinity for this man. Harry Sweeney was an enigma. She wanted so badly to unlock the door to the mystery of Agnes Kilmartin's will and to discover what role Harry had played in Agnes's life.

Joanna could feel the pleasant warmth of the sun on her back. It was a beautiful day, and she felt no inclination to rush back to the office, so she took out her sandwich and proceeded to eat it. She didn't feel that she was being in any way irreverent – wasn't it the Mexicans who took picnic baskets to the graves of their loved ones each November, to celebrate the Day of the Dead?

Anyway, she didn't think that Harry would mind if she enjoyed her lunch in his company.

As she chewed her sandwich, she wondered why Harry would have killed someone and why Agnes Kilmartin would have been friends with a murderer. Then she reminded herself that he was still technically innocent, since he was on remand when he died. Was he really innocent, and would she ever find out the truth? The mound of earth, and the fresh floral arrangement, told her nothing. All they revealed was that someone still cared about Harry Sweeney.

And *I* do, too, Joanna thought suddenly, surprising herself with the vehemence of her feelings. Now that the last of her enormous sandwich had been consumed, she stood up and dusted the crumbs off her clothes. "I'll be back soon, Harry Sweeney," she said, "on the day we lay Agnes beside you."

After leaving Harry's grave, Agnes went back to the cemetery office near the main gate, where the old man still sat, surrounded by huge ledgers.

"Hello again," she said, smiling. "I wonder if you can tell me anything about that grave – Number 127m. Who owns it and keeps it in such good condition?"

The old man beamed at her. "Ah yes – that one's owned by Mrs Kilmartin. Lovely lady. She pays to have the grave tended to regularly, and she sends a floral tribute every week. Nice headstone, isn't it?"

Joanna was astonished. "Yes – it's beautiful," she said. "But I don't think there'll be any more flowers arriving – Mrs Kilmartin died two days ago."

The smile didn't leave the man's face. "Aah – then we'll be expecting her soon," he said, as though death was simply another rite of passage in the scheme of things.

"Expecting her? What do you mean?"

"Well, Mrs Kilmartin always made it clear to us that she intended to be interred in that grave herself," said the old man.

"Then do you know who Harry Sweeney is?" Joanna asked eagerly. "I mean, was he a relative of hers?"

The old man inclined his head. "I'm sorry, my dear, but I have no idea. Obviously, he was very important to her, because she'd been visiting his grave for . . ." he scratched his head, "it must be nigh on thirty-five years. I'm working here for the last thirty years, and I know from the previous clerk that she was coming here regularly before then." He looked directly at Joanna. "Aren't you one of the family?"

"I'm a friend of the Kilmartins."

"Well, surely the family must know who he is?"

Joanna hesitated. The truth would sound ridiculous. "I – I – yes, I suppose they do."

"Well, then, do you happen to know who the undertakers for Mrs Kilmartin's funeral are? I'll need to make immediate arrangements to have the grave opened and ready for her." He made it sound as though Agnes would be attending a party rather than coming to her final resting place.

"Thank you," said Joanna, smiling. "I'll ask the undertakers to phone you as soon as possible."

Leaving the cemetery, Joanna didn't have long to wait before the arrival of another bus, which would take her back to the city centre.

Then, she walked the rest of the way to her office, still

clutching the bags containing the new lime-green dress, the satin bra and knickers.

Once in the office, she rang Tom on his mobile. Since the new university term hadn't started yet, he could be anywhere. If he didn't answer his phone, she'd leave a message. However, he answered his phone immediately.

"Hi, Jo – any news?"

"Hopefully, Orla will have some additional information this afternoon," she told him, "but I've just been talking to the man in the office at Glasnevin Cemetery. He's told me that your mother owns that grave and regularly visited it over the last thirty-five years. She also told them that she intended being buried there herself."

"Oh my God!"

"Yes, I'm afraid so, Tom – your mother clearly wanted to be with Harry in death. Now we have to find out what the link was between them in life."

CHAPTER 9

Catherine sat in her armchair in the nursing-home day room. All around her, old dears were sleeping after their midday meal, and the TV droned on although no one was watching.

She had the distinct feeling that something was very wrong. People didn't tell her things any more, but that didn't mean she was unaware when something bad had happened. Sometimes, her own words wouldn't form themselves into articulate sentences, but that didn't mean she couldn't feel and understand at a deeper and more meaningful level. She definitely knew that something of monumental importance had just happened. Something sad, something that made her very worried. Was someone she loved in danger?

Catherine sighed. There were so many secrets to keep, so much information to hide. And now, she sensed, whatever had happened would bring people to her, people who were looking for information and who would be asking all sorts of awkward questions.

Catherine was deeply worried, because she knew that her own thought processes were not as agile as they'd once been. Keeping secrets had been easy then. And she'd known clearly who the enemy was. Now, people would be trying to wheedle the information from her, trapping her with their smooth words and indirect questioning. But she must stay silent at all costs. People had to be protected.

Catherine shuffled over to the big window and looked out. It was a bright cloudless afternoon, so she decided that it was an ideal day to go into town and do some shopping. She would get new slippers for Bill, since his old ones were worn out and his toes were already sticking out of them. Now where had she left her purse?

Leaving the day room, she reached her own room and set about searching for her purse. Suddenly, she wondered who on earth Bill was. And why was she going to buy him slippers? Sighing, she abandoned her search. She would go to Agnes's house instead. Agnes was bound to know who Bill was.

Catherine walked out through the nursing-home front door, but since the gates were kept permanently locked, she was unable to leave the grounds. So she sat on one of the garden benches, thinking that she was waiting for a bus to take her to Agnes's house – or maybe to the city centre to do her shopping – she wasn't sure which. She would get on the first bus that arrived.

Catherine felt distinctly agitated. Somewhere in the back of her mind was the nagging feeling that she needed to speak to Agnes urgently. Joanna had been asking her questions – about secret things that only she and Agnes knew. How much did Joanna know? And had Agnes finally decided to break her years of silence? Oh dear, if only her friend would tell her what to do. Where on earth was Agnes?

Catherine thought about her lovely daughter, whom she adored. Joanna had told her that she had her own solicitor's practice now, and Catherine was very pleased, she and – now who was her husband? Why, it was Bill – that's why she was buying him slippers! She and Bill hadn't been able to afford to send Joanna to college, but she'd obviously got there somehow . . . Catherine wrinkled her brow in concentration. Hadn't Agnes had something to do with it? Ah, yes! She remembered it all now . . .

Catherine sighed and shifted in her chair. It was strange how she could remember the past quite clearly, yet she couldn't remember the names or identies of the people who now visited her. Of course, she remembered Joanna, her daughter, and Agnes, her dearest friend. Yet at other times, when she and Agnes were in the classroom together, she knew that logically she couldn't have any daughter. Oh dear, it was all so confusing!

And once again, she couldn't remember who Bill was . . .

CHAPTER 10

"I'm not happy about this at all!" Tom Kilmartin muttered, his eyes filled with tears.

"I know, Tom, I know," said Joanna soothingly, as she held his arm. They were walking at the head of the funeral procession leading to the opened grave where Harry Sweeney lay. Now, Agnes Kilmartin was about to join him. Tom was doing his best to stay in control, but Joanna could feel his whole body shaking. He had loved his mother deeply, and he was having great difficulty in letting her go. Especially to a grave where a man other than her husband was buried.

"I just don't understand why Mum wanted to do this. I mean, there's a perfectly good grave over in the next aisle where Dad is buried – "

"Tom, you're doing what your mother wanted."

"But what will I say if people ask me why she's being buried here? I don't even know why myself!"

Joanna looked around. Only a few dozen people had

come as far as the graveyard. Earlier, there had been at least a thousand people in the church, but most would have been acquaintances rather than friends, people who'd done business with Ivan Kilmartin over the years. As such, they would never intrude on a family's private grief by coming to the graveside. Besides, most of them were happy to escape as soon as the obligatory respects had been paid.

"There's no need to worry, Tom – only friends have come as far as the graveside," Joanna assured him. "I'm sure most of them won't even notice and, if they do, they'll be too discreet to confront you about it."

"But what about the press? I saw several photographers at the church – "

"You don't need to worry about them. Orla told me the newspapers would only be taking pictures of prominent people attending the church service." Joanna linked her arm in his. "Look, you've got to expect some media coverage – your mother was the highly respected widow of a millionaire businessman – her funeral, and those attending it, are bound to attract some interest."

"I'm sure there'd be a lot more media interest," said Tom, with a wry smile, "if they knew that my mother chose to be buried with a man who wasn't her husband!"

Joanna tried to smile back, but she was filled with dread of the following day, when Tom was due at her office, and she'd have to tell him about the strange bequests in his mother's will.

* * *

As Agnes's coffin was lowered into the grave of Harry

Sweeney, an elderly woman blessed herself, brushing away the tears that had formed in the corners of her eyes. She stood apart from the group of mourners around the grave, partially hidden behind a convenient yew tree. Poor Agnes, she thought. Poor proud, decent and generous Agnes. And poor Harry. They were together at last, and she was pleased that she'd been instrumental in helping them to have some time together. After all, she'd got what she wanted too.

The woman pulled the brim of her hat down over her face. Just in case. There was only one person at the graveside who might recognise her, and she didn't want to take that risk. No one else knew who she was or why she was there, and that's the way she wanted it to stay.

She watched as Joanna Brennan held Tom Kilmartin's hand while the coffin went in and the prayers were said. Had Agnes told her son the truth before she died? If not, the will was going to come as a big shock to him. And to others too, when it was time to tell the truth herself.

As the prayers came to an end, and the mourners began leaving the graveside, the elderly woman slipped quietly away.

* * *

The following morning, not long after Joanna arrived at the office, Orla rang. "Got you some info on Harry Sweeney," she told her friend. "He was on remand for murdering a young woman called Colette Devane, back in 1970. There's a picture of her here – she was aged nineteen at the time. Unmarried."

"Wow, tell me more!"

"She was his wife's sister."

"What!"

Joanna heard the rustling of paper at the other end of the phone.

Then Orla resumed. "Hmmm – our Harry looks quite attractive in these old newspaper photographs – gorgeous dark hair – I'd say he was probably in his mid-thirties at the time. But it's hard to tell with old newsprint. Anyway, Harry was on remand in Mountjoy, then one day, before the case ever got to court, he topped himself – hanged himself with the sheet off his bed."

"Not very nice. Almost seems to confirm his guilt, doesn't it?"

"Well, he always protested his innocence. But according to this report, he didn't have an alibi for the night the woman was murdered. And there was a witness ready to testify in court that he'd seen him strangle Colette Devane in the Phoenix Park." There was more rustling of newspaper. "Looks like he left a cigarette butt at the scene of the murder, as well as some documents in Colette Devane's apartment – so it all seems to confirm his guilt, doesn't it?"

"It certainly looks that way. Anything else?"

"There's also a mention of a wife – well, it states in one of the newspaper reports that Harry Sweeney's wife disappeared some weeks before he was arrested."

"Does it give her name? First name?"

"No, actually – just Mrs Sweeney. But at least, because of Colette, we know her maiden name must have been Devane."

"Maybe he murdered her too. Do we know what Harry did for a living?"

"Hold on a minute. Yeah – he was some kind of trade union official. That's all that's written here. But I'll keep on digging."

"Do we know anything about the witness for the prosecution?"

"No. Maybe they were under protection or something of that sort."

"And could I have photocopies of all that stuff?"

"Listen, slave-driver – I actually have to do a day's work in between my hangover and doing your bloody research!" said Orla, laughing. "I know I'm a genius, but even *I* can't work that fast! OK, I'll photocopy this stuff for you. But I also have to write up that restaurant review from a few nights back. Remember?"

"Sorry! We had a great night at the restaurant , didn't we? Thanks a million," said Joanna. "But how are you feeling?"

"I'm OK," said Orla gruffly. "At least one person's delighted that I've finished with Declan – I rang my mother today and, when I told her, she cheered!"

"How is she?" asked Joanna, who rarely saw Orla's mother nowadays, although she'd known her since the two girls had been at school together.

"She's fine – but she's still nagging me to come and visit her."

"That seems perfectly reasonable to me," said Joanna, laughing. "At least you can have a decent conversation with your mother – that's more than can be said for mine!"

"Sorry, you're right. OK – I'll go and see her soon."

"So are you definitely finished with Declan?"

"That bastard's history," said Orla firmly. "I'd never feel confident that he wouldn't run off again as soon as some cute-assed popsie appeared on the scene. A weak guy like that I don't need. So I'm going to play the field for a while – maybe you'll come pubbing and clubbing with me?" Orla laughed. "After all, your own private life isn't all that hectic, Ms Serious Solicitor. You know what they say – all work and no play makes Jill a dull girl!"

"Jesus Christ, Orla – I'm getting too old for all this carousing!"

"Huh! I'm a whole year older than you – you're just a wimp!"

Joanna smiled. Socialising might help to take my mind off Tom Kilmartin, she thought. "OK, you win, Orla. But I can't afford to be hung over every morning! Every time I've been out with you lately, I've ended up that way! I need my wits about me if I'm to build up a strong client base."

"Well, you won't find any clients by sitting home alone with your cat each night," said Orla matter-of-factly. "Who knows – if you come out socialising with me, you may find loads of clients in the pubs and clubs. They'll be out there drowning their sorrows because of their legal problems – and you'll reap the benefits when you can offer them a professional shoulder to cry on!"

"I doubt if it's my *shoulder* they'll be after," said Joanna dryly. "Still, there *is* a grain of sense in what you say, O Wise One. What plan of action do you have in mind for us?"

"Well, I have to cover the first birthday party of that dreadful magazine, *Celebrity*, next Monday night – it's the kind of job I just hate, but Julie-Anne Jones, the silly bitch who usually covers that kind of stuff, claims to have the flu this time, but I don't believe a word of it. Anyway, it's quite a big bash, and it's being held in that new hotel on the quays. It's bound to be as boring as hell, but there might be a few interesting people there."

"By people, I presume you mean men," said Joanna, laughing.

"Of course!" said Orla, sounding surprised. "I haven't turned to women yet – although they might be a good deal more dependable!"

"What time do we need to be there?"

"Eight-ish should be fine. Then if it's boring, or we haven't met any interesting *people*, we can head out to the Burlington Hotel for a nightcap."

"Sounds great," said Joanna. Maybe it *was* time that she started having a decent social life. She'd spent so many years studying that she'd lost contact with many of her friends. Of course, there was Freddy O'Rourke, who still kept annoyingly in touch – but she needed a wider base than that. Maybe she'd become a livewire socialite – one of those people who was regularly invited to all the best bashes in town, and referred to the gossip columns as "the well-known Dublin solicitor, Joanna Brennan".

"Joanna *Kilmartin*" came a whisper from somewhere deep inside her, and she blushed. Why was she wasting so much time thinking of that man? He was just a friend from her childhood days. Anyway, Tom was a serious academic and didn't seem to be the marrying kind or – suddenly she gasped – maybe he was already *in* a relationship! Her heart took a sudden dive down into her boots as she considered that possibility. She knew Tom liked her, but probably just as a friend. And if he *did* have a special person in his life, wouldn't she be a fool to hang around hoping, like a lovesick teenager? She'd have to find out!

"Joanna! Are you still there?" said Orla, interrupting Joanna's reverie.

"Sorry, yes."

"In the meantime, how about a drink this evening? I can't believe how much spare time I have now that I've got rid of that asshole Declan! Why don't we meet in the Morrison Hotel at eight?"

"W-what? Oh, no, I can't – Tom Kilmartin is coming into the office on Monday morning, and I need to get things organised before then."

Orla laughed. "There's a whole weekend between now and then, Jo – there's no need to put your life on hold in the meantime. Who knows what exciting adventure we could have tonight? Or tomorrow night, or on Sunday night! C'mon – say yes!"

"Oh, alright. See you at eight."

Putting down the phone, Joanna got up and went out to the reception area.

"Mary," she asked humbly, "could you add a supply of painkillers to our shopping list? I have an awful feeling that I may need them again soon . . ."

CHAPTER 11

It was the first time that Catherine had ever seen Agnes cry. She'd hurried to Ballsbridge in response to a distraught phone call from her friend, and now the two women were sitting in the large basement kitchen in Agnes's house.

"Now start at the beginning, Agnes. What has got you into such a state?" Catherine asked anxiously.

"Oh Cat, if only I'd listened to you!" her friend sobbed. "You were right all along about Ivan. He only married me for the family money and to get a foothold in my father's business!"

"Are you sure?" said Catherine, who'd been sure all along. But like a true friend, having initially voiced her concerns when Agnes and Ivan started dating, she'd then kept her counsel when Agnes angrily brushed her fears aside.

"Yes, I'm sure," said Agnes, wiping her eyes. "I was a fool not to listen to you – a romantic fool who couldn't see any further than the big wedding day and the chance to finally do something right in my father's eyes. Oh Cat – what am I going to do?"

Agnes dissolved into tears once more, and Catherine put her arm around her.

Then Agnes dried her eyes and made an attempt to compose herself. "Before Ivan went out, he was talking to someone on the phone in his office in the house. I don't normally listen in – I mean, they're usually business calls – but he was whispering angrily to someone." *She sniffed.* "I was just about to go into the room when something stopped me. Call it instinct or self-preservation, I don't know. But Cat – " *Agnes started to cry again at the enormity of her discovery,* "It was obvious he was talking to a woman, and saying that he really loved her – that he'd only married me because of the career prospects my father could offer him. He told her that since there was no divorce in Ireland, he'd set her up in an apartment. As long as she was willing to keep seeing him, he'd give her all the material things she wanted." *A fresh wave of weeping ensued, as Catherine held her friend tightly.* "And, Cat – I now realise she's not the first woman Ivan's been involved with." *She looked bleakly at Catherine.* "There were other phone calls in the past, but I fooled myself into believing they were wrong numbers, or business calls from women who worked in the company's offices. But now I have to face the truth."

"Does Ivan know that you overheard his phone call?"

"No, I just crept upstairs, locked myself in the bedroom, stayed there until he left, then phoned you. Oh, Cat – what will I do?"

"Well, it's probably better if he doesn't know that you know – at least until you've had time to digest the information and decide what you want to do."

"Well, I don't have many choices, do I?" *said Agnes bitterly.* "There's no divorce in this country, and my father thinks that the sun, moon and stars shine out of Ivan's backside, especially because of Joseph leaving for Australia. Ivan's become Dad's surrogate son, so even if I told my father about his philandering, he'd just tell me that men are like that and to make the best of it." Agnes's eyes darkened. "In fact, my father might even consider Ivan's philandering a mark of his virility!"

"Yet both of them will be in church on Sunday, craw-thumping as usual," Catherine added.

Agnes nodded, and the women looked at each other in despair.

"Well, at least I still have you, Cat," said Agnes, suddenly smiling through her tears. "If only I'd listened to you in the first place!"

"You nearly killed me when I offered my opinion of Ivan," Catherine said, smiling back.

Agnes laughed guiltily. "Sorry, Cat – maybe I was just protesting too much. Deep down, I probably guessed that there was some truth in what you were saying. But Daddy was so pleased that I was seeing Ivan, and I was so pleased to be pleasing my father at last . . ." Her voice trailed off.

"You'll get through this, Agnes," said Catherine staunchly. "You'll find other ways of getting joy out of life. Who knows what good things the future will bring?"

* * *

And Catherine had been right. A few months later, Agnes met trade union official Harry Sweeney at a charity ball, and the attraction between them was instantaneous. Just weeks before, Harry had been instrumental in getting increased pay and better conditions for the workers at Ivan's building sites, much to Ivan's chagrin and Harry's delight. As a result there was no love lost between the two men. Harry was accompanied to the ball by his wife Maura, and to both couples' initial dismay, they'd been seated beside each other for the meal. Ivan, with typical rudeness, ignored Harry and ensured that he was seated as far away from the trade unionist as possible, ignorantly plonking himself between Harry's wife and another guest sitting further up the table.

"I won't be seated near that bastard," Ivan muttered angrily as he changed places. "If he had his way, he and his trade union would wreck all my businesses."

That left Agnes and Harry sitting beside each other. Initially, Agnes tried to make polite conversation to cover up her embarrassment at Ivan's behaviour. But before long, she was laughing at Harry's jokes, and they were chatting animatedly to each other.

"Oh Cat, he's really nice – we spent the whole time talking ninety to the dozen," Agnes told her friend the next day, her eyes sparkling. "He has a lovely self-mocking sense of humour – I could hardly believe that this was the demon Ivan is always ranting on about!"

"People are rarely as bad as Ivan makes out," said Catherine dryly.

"He has the most gorgeous brown eyes, too," Agnes continued, "and I felt myself melting as I looked into them. Oh Cat, I really like him!"

"But he's married . . ."

"Yes. Maura, his wife, was very quiet – she hardly said a word all night."

Catherine sighed. "Well, it's hardly surprising, since you seem to have monopolised her husband!"

Agnes looked chastened. "Oh Cat, I didn't mean to do that – I hope she wasn't upset. It's just that he's such fun, and he's gorgeous!"

"Well, I'm glad you enjoyed yourself. Maybe you'll see him at the ball again next year."

Agnes beamed. "Well, it just happens that we're both attending a fundraising dinner next week, without our partners, and he's going to ensure that we're seated at the same table. Oh Cat – he's so nice!" Agnes did an out-of-character pirouette around the kitchen. "Do you know what he said to me when we were introduced? He said: 'I don't think I'm your husband's favourite person.' It was so ironic, I had to smile – and I never stopped smiling all through the meal!"

"Agnes, please be careful," said Catherine. "He's married and you're married – nothing good can come of it."

Agnes looked horrified. "Cat, you do think I'd have an affair with him, do you? I'm just enjoying his company, for God's sake. Ivan doesn't even put up a pretence of making polite conversation, so it's nice to have someone to chat to for a change."

"I hope that's all it is," said Catherine, "because both of you have too much to lose."

"Well, while I certainly wouldn't care what Ivan thought," Agnes retorted, "I'm well aware that Harry does have a wife, and she seems very nice. But why does everyone assume that a man and woman can't just be friends?"

"No reason at all," said Catherine.

"Good. So just accept that that there's nothing more to it – I'm enjoying a man's company, and he's enjoying mine. That's all there's to it, Cat."

"Well, I'm glad you're enjoying yourself," said Catherine, who was genuinely pleased to see a glow of happiness on her friend's face. Ivan's infidelities had lowered her friend's self-esteem, and of late, there hadn't been much joy in Agnes's life.

But she also feared for her beloved friend's naïvety – despite Agnes's wealth and comfortable life, she was unworldly in matters of the heart.

"But please be careful," Catherine added yet again, fearing the inevitable outcome. Because she recognised that look on Agnes's face – the look of a woman who was falling in love.

CHAPTER 12

"Oh God – my head hurts like hell, and Tom Kilmartin is due in twenty-five minutes!"

"Here – take these," said Mary, leaning across Joanna's big desk and shoving a packet of Paracetamol and a glass of water under her nose. "What on earth happened to get you in this state? You look as though you've spent the entire weekend on the tiles!"

"I went out drinking with Orla again last night." Joanna looked up blearily at Mary. "That's the umpteenth night in the last week that we've ended up in a nightclub afterwards – ugh, I feel so bad that I wish I could die this minute!"

"Well, you can't die until you've returned your phone calls. Three potential clients phoned on Friday afternoon – and each of them swears that their problem is in need of urgent attention!"

"Oooh – I think I'm going to be sick!"

"Stop being so melodramatic," said Mary briskly. "You're a professional businesswoman, and you can't allow yourself the indulgence of a hangover. I'm going to stand here until you take those tablets."

Groping for the tablets and glass, Joanna gagged several times before she managed to get the tablets down her throat. This hectic social life was more than her system could cope with. Now that Orla was single again, her friend was determined to live life to the full. And drag Joanna along with her!

"Now the next thing you're going to do," said Mary, "is get up off your arse and take it next door to the café, where you'll order a full fry, with tea and thickly buttered toast. But absolutely *no* coffee. The greasy food will line your stomach, and when you come back to the office, you'll feel like a new woman."

"I couldn't possibly eat anything –"

"Listen," said Mary, "you employ me to run the office, and part of that job description – as far as I'm concerned anyway – is to make sure that you're in a fit state to deal with your clients. Now please go and do as I ask. I'm an expert on hangovers – I drank like a fish after Leo left – so I guarantee that this cure really does work."

Obediently, Joanna rose to her feet, checked her pocket for money and headed out the door. Twenty minutes later, she arrived back at the office, smiling. "You were absolutely right!" she told Mary gratefully. "I feel an awful lot better."

Mary smiled. "You'll probably have bouts of nausea during the day, but we'll keep them at bay with more tablets and plenty of liquids. Now get into your office, get your documents organised and I'll let you know when Tom Kilmartin arrives."

"You're a treasure!" said Joanna gratefully.

Mary turned slightly pink with pleasure, and the two women smiled at each other. Then Joanna headed into her office and closed the door, while Mary took up her position in the outer office, surrounding herself with ledgers and a desk diary to make the place look busy and more businesslike.

Just then, as Mary heard footsteps below, she had a brainwave. She grabbed the phone and began talking to a non-existent client at the other end of the line. "Of course, Mr O'Neill, I'll get Ms Brennan to ring you as soon as she's free. She's rather busy at the moment, and she has a client arriving just now – " Mary looked up and gestured a greeting as Tom Kilmartin arrived at the top of the stairs and made his way into her outer office. "Alright, Mr O'Neill, I'll ask her to ring you back later."

Putting down the phone, Mary greeted Tom Kilmartin with just the right amount of cool professionalism, accompanied with appropriate pleasantries about the weather. "I'll tell Joanna you've arrived," she then told him, hoping as she stood up that the pleat at the back of her skirt was straight.

In Joanna's office, she briefly closed the door. "Tom Kilmartin's here – and he's stunning! You didn't tell me that he was such a fine thing!"

Joanna laughed. "Do you really think he is? I never really noticed."

Mary gave her a knowing glance, then stepped outside again and ushered Tom in, miming silent kisses behind his back. Joanna could barely keep a straight face, and Tom looked surprised to find her grinning as he entered the room.

Joanna quickly changed her expression to one more suited to a formal occasion. After all, the poor man had just lost his mother, and she was now going to have to deliver another bombshell.

"Tom – good to see you. How are you feeling?"

Tom smiled his slow, gentle smile. "OK, Jo – I suppose I still can't believe that Mum has finally gone. It was so sudden – one day, she was in good health, the next day she's gone." He smiled sadly. "And she died still being the tough old boot she'd always tried to be."

Joanna was quick on the uptake. "Do you mean that at heart she wasn't really as tough as she seemed?"

Tom nodded. "I think Mum wanted everyone to think she was as hard as nails. But I saw the soft side – and so did your mother. I think that was one of the reasons why they were such good friends."

"Friendship is a strange thing, isn't it?" said Joanna, thinking briefly of Orla. "Sometimes you think a friend is really tough – and you conspire with them to let them preserve that image of themselves. Then it all crumbles some day when you or they need support, and the friendship moves on to another, deeper, level."

Tom nodded. "And how is poor Catherine?"

Joanna grimaced. "She's OK, Tom – well, as OK as she *can* be, given her condition. I went to see her a few evenings ago, and I mentioned your mother in a roundabout way. But she got all agitated. It was almost as though she knew that something had happened to Agnes, although there's no way anyone could have told her that your mother had died. Or that she'd even understand if they did."

Tom nodded. "Maybe at some level we don't yet fully comprehend, people who are close develop a special bond, and she *does* know something. I'll go and visit her again soon – I haven't been there in a while. Do you think she'll still remember who I am?"

Joanna sighed. "Who knows, Tom – I'm just waiting for the day when she no longer knows who *I* am."

For a few moments, they both sat in silence.

Then Tom sighed and looked directly at Joanna. "Now, what have you got to tell me about this will, Jo? I have a terrible sense of forboding – I suspect we're talking about other things so that you can avoid breaking the news to me." He laughed. "Has Mum really left everything to some religious temple in Hindustan?"

"It's not quite that odd – but there is a strange bequest in the will. Maybe you yourself can throw some light on it."

As briefly as possible, Joanna told Tom about the existing will, how his mother had intended explaining the specific bequests to her but had died before she could and how she had promised that she would also reveal information to her and Tom that she said finally needed to be told.

Tom's face was ashen as he absorbed this latest bombshell. He opened his mouth to speak, but no words came out.

"I've no idea what she was going to tell us," Joanna added, "but your mother assured me that the bequests themselves wouldn't change. Assuming that you're 'the offspring of Ivan Kilmartin' referred to in the will, we now need to look for a son, daughter or several children of Harry Sweeney. But without any background information to go on, finding this other beneficiary – or beneficiaries – is going to take a little time."

Tom nodded, and Joanna watched his face anxiously but it remained blank with shock.

"At least you've still got the house you love," she said softly, as the silence in the room lengthened. "Your mum obviously knew how much it meant to you." She paused. "But are you still certain that the name Harry Sweeney doesn't ring any bells?'

Tom shook his head, speaking at last. "I'd never heard of him until my mother died. Have you found out any more about him, Jo?"

"Well, as a matter of fact, I have," said Joanna, giving Tom a brief summary of the information she'd received from Orla.

There was silence for a few moments before he spoke. "I don't understand any of this," he said at last. "My mother never mentioned this man, yet every week she sent flowers to his grave. Then he hanged himself – which seems to prove his guilt, doesn't it? And now, his child or children – whoever they are – are to be beneficiaries of her estate?" His voice trembled. "I don't begrudge them anything – as I told you before, I'm well paid and there's more than enough money in Mum's estate for all these people. But . . ." He left the word hanging in the air.

Perfectly on cue, Mary arrived with two mugs of tea and a plate of Mikado biscuits. "Everything OK?" she asked sweetly, giving Tom the benefit of a radiant smile before she sashayed out of the room.

"You must feel gutted, Tom," said Joanna softly. "I mean – it must be quite a shock. You know, finding out that there's another beneficiary – and a very strange one at that."

Tom nodded, then smiled. "To be honest, Jo, I'm gobsmacked. And a bit confused as to why Mum never explained to me that her will wouldn't be a straight-forward one. Why on earth didn't she say anything during all those years we lived together in the same house?"

Joanna nodded. "I agree, it's odd. But from what she said, I think that if she hadn't died that evening, she intended to tell both of us everything the next morning." She hoped her words might ease his obvious pain and confusion. "Look, Tom . . ." she said, reaching out her hand to touch his, "I'm sorry about all this."

Tom reached across and grasped her outstretched hand. "Thanks, Jo," he said softly. "I really appreciate your concern."

Joanna withdrew her hand, which was now tingling pleasantly. "Does your mother have any papers or documents at home? There might be something there that could throw light on this situation. Maybe letters from this Harry Sweeney?"

He nodded. "There are tons of papers belonging to Mum and Dad, and lots of old books and stuff, in the room that used to be Dad's office at home. As far as I know, nothing's been touched in there since he died, but you never know, do you? This afternoon, I'll start going through them. Maybe some information on this man will turn up."

They both stood up, since the meeting seemed to have reached its natural conclusion.

"Thanks for everything, Jo," he said, taking her hand, then suddenly raising it to his lips.

Joanna felt a tremendous sexual frisson run through her body – she felt as though she was going to suffocate with excitement. "No problem, Tom," she said, relieved that her voice sounded reasonably normal.

He paused at the door. "I'm honestly not aggrieved about the will, Jo. If that's what Mum wanted, then fair enough. She obviously had her reasons. But I suppose I'm worried in case . . . " He left the sentence hanging, gave a whimsical smile, and Joanna's stomach turned over.

Which wasn't the ideal thing for someone suffering from a hangover.

"Thanks for everything, Jo," he said again, then he was gone.

Joanna sat down at her desk, feeling weak at the knees, as she heard him saying goodbye to Mary and making his way down the stairs.

"What a gorgeous man!" said Mary, bouncing into Joanna's office. She stopped short as she saw Joanna with her head in her hands. "Time for more tablets?" she clucked sympathetically. "Oh well, that's what you get for staying out all night carousing. Now if *I* had my way, I'd prefer to be snuggled up in bed with someone gorgeous like your last client – "

"He's not a bloody client – he's a friend!" said Joanna, annoyed. "And I couldn't take another of those awful tablets – I'm going out for lunch!"

Mary kept a straight face until she heard Joanna clumping down the stairs and out into the street. Hmmm, she thought, so it *is* the way I suspected. Ms Joanna Brennan *does* have a soft spot for Professor Tom Kilmartin. She grinned wickedly to herself. And I think that Professor Tom Kilmartin has a hard spot for her!

CHAPTER 13

"Good morning, Dr Culhane, I'm Joanna Brennan."

"Please – call me Gary."

Joanna was sitting in her office, facing her new client – the young man whose dog had allegedly bitten chunks out of his neighbour's arm.

She studied her client and liked what she saw. He was a good-looking man, probably in his mid-thirties, with dark blond hair and a pleasant smile

"So, Gary – can you tell me exactly what happened?"

"I'm afraid not – for the simple reason that I wasn't there when this 'alleged' offence took place. Secondly, I don't believe that anything like she claims ever happened. Bruce wouldn't hurt a fly!"

"But this next-door neighbour of yours is saying that your dog attacked her when she leaned over to pat it." Joanna studied the document that Freddy O'Rourke had forwarded to her. "This summons from the Gardaí says that Mrs Ellen Byrne has sustained 'severe bite-marks on her arms'. That's quite a serious charge for us to deal with, Gary."

"I don't believe a word of it," said Gary Culhane indignantly. "Bruce would never bite anyone – not even that miserable cow next door! In fact, if anything, Bruce is afraid of *her*, because she and that husband of hers are always having screaming matches, and he shouts abuse at poor Bruce every time he passes in or out of his house."

"What type of dog is Bruce?"

"He's a ten-year-old boxer. A big, gentle dog – I swear, Joanna, he wouldn't hurt anyone!"

Instinctively, she believed him, but her faith in Gary – or in Bruce – was not going to solve this problem. Mrs Ellen Byrne was clearly out for blood – Bruce's blood.

"So – how did it all happen?" she asked. "Do you know anything about the – alleged – sequence of events?"

"Well, this bloody woman claims that she was coming out of her house and walking down the path, and she stopped to pat Bruce – which is a total fabrication, since all she ever did was avoid him – and she claims that he turned on her and bit her on the arm. She then went to her GP, who treated her and gave her a tetanus injection. I presume he'll be called to court in her defence."

"Not necessarily, but he'll probably need to send a letter, detailing her injuries and the treatment given."

"They only went to the Guards because I wouldn't pay up!" said Gary angrily. "After she'd been treated, she and her husband were standing on the doorstep, and he approached me and suggested that I should pay something for his wife's suffering and her medical expenses."

Joanna was surprised.

"But I told him to get stuffed," Gary continued, "since I was positive Bruce had never touched his bloody wife! Then Jackie Byrne stormed off, saying that I'd regret not being more 'cooperative'! The next evening, just as I arrived home from work, a Garda appeared on my doorstep and told me that my next-door neighbour had filed a complaint against Bruce!" As he spoke, Gary looked near to tears. "Look, Joanna, I'd pay anything to save old Brucie – I've had him for years, and he's very special to me. But paying the Byrnes would have looked like an admission of guilt, wouldn't it?" He rubbed his nose. "But maybe I should have paid them off – I think I *would* have, if I'd known what was going to happen next."

"Well, we can mention the bribe as part of our defence, but it comes down to your word again his in court," said Joanna sadly. "But tell me a bit more about these neighbours of yours – they sound like revolting people."

"They are!" said Gary angrily. "Ever since I bought the house next door to them a few years ago, there's been nothing but fights between the two of them. Jackie Byrne, the husband, is away quite a bit, and it's peaceful then. But when he's there, he's always shouting at his wife – I can hear stuff being thrown around and her crying. This can go on for hours, but the next day they'll be all lovey-dovey in public."

"Have you ever tried to do anything about the situation?"

Gary nodded. "I was worried in case his wife was being beaten – and one night, when he was giving her a really hard time, I knocked at the door to see if she needed any help. But *he* answered the door and told me to mind my own business. The next day, they told me that if I interfered again, they'd report me to the police." He looked totally exasperated. "After that, I decided to have nothing to do with them. So any time the shouting and crying starts, I just put on a CD or turn up the television." His face darkened. "Until now, that is. Now, I'm so angry that I want to go next door and murder both of them."

"I can imagine how you feel. Now, Gary, if the court does award your neighbours damages, you can claim it through your house insurance policy," Joanna informed him. "I suggest you notify your insurance company immediately."

"I don't care about damages – I'd gladly give them everything I own if I could just save Brucie!"

"Leave it with me for now," said Joanna, patting his arm. "I'll find out exactly when we're likely to get into court. One thing you can do, Gary, is ask your vet to give you a letter saying that Bruce doesn't have any propensity towards viciousness."

Garry nodded. "Will that help our case?"

"It could do – it's important that we collect as much ammunition as we can. Then I'll need a little time to prepare our defence."

Gary looked bleakly at Joanna, and her heart went out to him in his obvious distress. "Please, Joanna, do whatever you can," he entreated her. "I don't care what it costs, as long as I can save poor old Bruce."

When Gary had left, Joanna got up, went to the tiny kitchen and made tea for herself and Mary. Then she took her cuppa back into her office and sat down again at her desk. She'd really liked Gary Culhane, and she understood his pain. But she wasn't too hopeful of the outcome, especially if Judge McGrath was sitting on the bench the day they went to court. The success of the case would rest on which side was the most believable. And a plaintiff with visible injuries and medical records was difficult to counter, no matter how confident the defendant was of the animal's innocence.

Joanna sighed. She also had to keep up the search for information on Harry Sweeney! Suddenly, she had an inspired thought. Quickly she dialled Orla's number.

"Hello – Newsroom."

"Hi, Orla – could you do me a big favour? You have a good contact in the Gardaí, don't you? I'm getting bogged down in Agnes Kilmartin's will, so I've decided to get a private detective to do some of the digging for me. Would you ask your friend to recommend a good one? Money isn't a problem, and I want the very best."

"Hold on – am I on some kind of retainer? Or should I leave the newspaper and work fulltime for you as a researcher?"

Joanna laughed. "My dear Orla – you're useful to me *precisely* because you're a journalist and have access to all those lovely newspaper files, microfiche and contacts. Besides, you'd be a disaster as a researcher – you'd wither and die if your by-line and photo wasn't displayed on everything you write!"

"So I'm a bloody egotist now, am I?" said Orla, laughing. "That's hardly the way to get a friend to do you a favour!"

"Go on, Orla – soon, I'll be inundated with wealthy and influential clients and you'll be coming to *me* for tip-offs.

Aready, I've got a dog-bite case and several conveyances lined up – and I won't give the exclusives to anyone else."

"Very funny. Hold the front page for a dog-bite story! OK, I'll ring my old pal Mick McHale – but just remember, you owe me big-time. And I'm still working on the Harry Sweeney case – it's a wonder I have time to do any newspaper work at all."

"Thanks, Orla – I presume tonight's big outing is still on?"

"Yeah – I'll pick you up around seven thirty. If I ever get out of the office, that is. With all *your* work to do as well as my own, I could be here till midnight!"

Joanna chuckled. "See you at seven thirty," she said, as she put down the phone.

CHAPTER 14

"Maura – I need to talk to you."

Maura Sweeney looked up and saw the pained expression on her husband's face. At last he was going to confirm what she'd already suspected. In some ways, it was almost a relief. At least now, it would be out in the open.

"What is it, Harry?"

"Maura, I'm sorry to do this to you – but I want to be honest with you."

Maura sighed. "It's OK, Harry – I've suspected for a while now. You've met someone else, haven't you?"

The relief on his face was almost comical and for a moment she almost felt like laughing hysterically. Then her eyes filled with tears. Although she'd always known this day would come, it hurt like hell now that it had happened. Nothing had prepared her for the intense pain, and she was finding it difficult to breathe.

"Look, I'm sorry, Maura – I never meant to hurt you. I didn't go looking for anyone – it just happened."

Maura stifled a sob. "It's all right, Harry. I'm just glad you told me."

Harry was surprised at Maura's mildness. "You're not going to throw things at me? Or call me a bastard?"

Maura smiled wanly through her tears. "What would be the point, Harry? It was inevitable that one of us would meet someone else eventually. For some time now, there hasn't been much to keep us together, has there?"

"No, and I'm sorry – it's my fault, I know that. I've been spending far too much time working, and that hasn't been fair to you. And lately, well, I've been spending the time with someone else. But I'll make it up to you as best as I can, Maura. I'll sign the house over to you, and the insurance policies too. Along with your own job in the Civil Service, you should be financially secure."

A deep sigh escaped from her throat. It didn't help that she'd rehearsed this day many times in her own mind and planned to deal with it calmly and reasonably when it happened. Now she longed to cling to him and beg him to stay. But she had always known that she wasn't the kind of woman who could hold such a charismatic man – Harry was the total opposite of her own plodding, shy personality. And she recalled the night of the charity ball, when she'd watched her husband's eyes twinkle with delight at the comments made by Ivan Kilmartin's wife. And she'd known then that it was only a matter of time before this day arrived.

She gave a deep sigh. She and Harry had been happy in their own way. Maura recalled the early days, when they'd held mock fights to determine which of them loved the other most. And Harry had surprised her by insisting that he share the cooking, cleaning and washing-up. "Well, we're both working, aren't we?" he'd said reasonably. "Besides, as a trade union official, it wouldn't be right to promote equality in the workplace but not at home, would it?" But the spark had gradually died, and they'd each stopped claiming to love the other more a long time ago. Gradually, they'd become like two polite strangers sharing a home.

Maura now put her arms around her husband, possibly for the last time. "Thank you, Harry," she said, blinking the tears from her eyes. "What are you going to do now? I assume you intend moving in with this woman?" Although she guessed who it was, Maura couldn't bring herself to use the woman's name. But she wondered briefly how Harry and Agnes were going to deal with Ivan Kilmartin's wrath when he found out that his wife was leaving him for his arch-enemy.

"It's not that easy – she's married too," said Harry, returning his wife's embrace. "So we're planning to move abroad – that's why I want all the legalities sorted out in your favour before we leave."

Maura withdrew from Harry's embrace and sat down. As the impact of Harry's departure registered with her, she also had to accept that his departure would also end her own dream – of ever having a child of her own. While she couldn't conceive naturally – numerous tests had confirmed that – she'd been planning to broach the subject of adoption with Harry. If only she'd got round to discussing it earlier, then at least she might have been left with a child to love . . .

"How soon do you intend leaving the country?"

"In the next few months."

"Colette's going to be devastated when she finds out you're going, Harry."

"I know," Harry sighed.

"And I really worry about her being with that horrible Kilmartin fellow."

"So do I – but your sister won't listen to anyone. She loves living the high life."

"I've tried to make her see sense, but it's no good. Maybe you'd talk to her again – that's the only thing I'll ask of you before you go."

"Of course I will, Maura – you know how fond of her I am. But don't expect me to have any better luck – Colette is besotted with Kilmartin."

As I am with you, Maura thought sadly. Perhaps loving the wrong man runs in our family.

CHAPTER 15

Although it was only half past eight, *Celebrity* magazine's first birthday party was already in full swing, with every wannabee, hanger-on, minor celebrity and ligger in attendance. Orla had already interviewed the publishers of the magazine, got the inane comments and gushing congratulations of the minor celebrities in attendance, mug-shots had been taken by Eoin, the photographer on duty for that night's "About Town" column, and now, at last, Orla was free to rejoin Joanna and enjoy the party on her own terms.

Joanna had been standing with – and listening to – a bunch of know-it-alls who were competing with each other to hog what they perceived as the limelight in their particular group. "As I was saying –" intoned one particularly boring chap, and Joanna looked around to see if deliverance, in the form of Orla, was yet at hand. Thankfully, she could see her friend heading in her direction.

"See that little bitch, Sasha Miller, over there," Orla

muttered under her breath, as she took Joanna aside, "the one in the skintight skirt – if you could call it a skirt, that is! I don't think any Trade Descriptions Act would pass it as such!"

"So that's her?" said Joanna, astounded. "But she's a tiny, insignificant little thing! I don't know what any man could see in her," she added loyally. "I mean, her arse is out of all proportion to the rest of her – it's *huge*!"

"Well, that seems to be part of her charm," said Orla. "She's got half the men on the Dublin newspaper circuit panting over her and her arse. Including Declan Dunne."

"I don't see Declan here tonight – do you think he'll turn up?"

"I have no idea," said Orla haughtily, "and I really don't care. I just hope that if he does appear, I won't go puce with embarrassment, because everybody will be watching the two of us, to see how we're both dealing with the situation." She sighed. "I wish I'd thought of asking some guy to come along tonight – you know, as a prop. Maybe even that fellow I met in the nightclub the other night."

"But I thought he was just a one-night stand?"

"Yes, I know he was," said Orla testily, "but I don't want to look as though I can't get a man's attention, while all the guys in the newsroom are hanging around bloody Queen Bee Sasha Miller!"

Joanna giggled, thinking of the wild bees' nest that Tom had once shown her at the bottom of his garden and how he'd explained to her all about the gigantic queen inside, with a huge pulsating rear end full of eggs, to whom all the bees were giving their full attention.

"That's a very apt description," she replied. "That

arse of Sasha Miller's almost pulsates like a queen bee's!"

The two women dissolved into a fit of giggling, and Orla almost spilled her drink over Joanna's dress.

They were still giggling when a male voice said: "Hello! That sounds like a great joke – any chance I could hear it?"

Joanna swung around. "Gary!" she said, giving him a big smile. "What a lovely surprise! I certainly wasn't expecting to see you here!"

"I'm here with a friend of mine, but he appears to be chatting up some woman already, so I don't want to cramp his style!"

Joanna hastily introduced Orla, explaining: "Gary is a client of mine."

"Oh," said Orla, pretending that she knew nothing about the dog-bite case. She and Joanna always ensured that no one else knew they sought help or advice from each other, since client confidentiality was regarded as the cornerstone of both their professions.

However, Gary was so wound up about his problem that he soon found himself explaining it all to Orla. And she found herself studying his expressive face and gorgeous brown eyes. Seeing how well they were getting on, Joanna excused herself and headed off to the women's toilet.

All the cubicles were full, so Joanna found herself waiting in a queue until one of the cubicles became available. Why oh why, she wondered, were there never enough toilets for women? Maybe she should suggest to Orla that she do a feature on the subject – maybe talk to architects and planners . . .

Suddenly, Joanna realised that a conversation was taking place between the occupants of two cubicles.

"So how do you like living with Declan?" one occupant asked.

"Oh, it's wonderful," came the wispy-voiced reply. "He's such an adorable man! We're having such fun! We just can't keep our hands off each other – I'm even trying to change my work hours so that we can spend more time together."

"You *do* know that he was engaged to Orla Rogan from the *Evening Dispatch*?" said the occupant of the second cubicle.

"Oh that – it meant nothing," came the scornful reply. "They were childhood sweethearts, you know – poor Declan felt that she *expected* him to marry her. But now that he's found *me*, that relationship is well and truly over. This time, he's found a *real* woman!"

Joanna was incensed. Childhood sweethearts indeed! Declan was in his mid-thirties, and he'd only met Orla two years before! Trust that bastard to try and trivialise their relationship!

The sound of flushing toilets alerted eveyone in the queue to the fact that the occupants would soon be emerging. Everyone started adjusting their position and trying to look as bored as possible, and Joanna realised that every other woman in the queue had been listening intently too!

Sasha Miller and her friend emerged from the cubicles and proceeded to the sinks, where their conversation continued without interruption as they washed their hands. Joanna was glad that she wasn't among the first two in the queue, so that she could stand and observe Sasha as she preened herself in the mirror over the sink. Obviously, Sasha had no idea that Joanna was a friend of Orla's. But then, thought Joanna, a woman like Sasha was so self-absorbed that she didn't see anything or anyone outside of her own little world.

"So you two are really serious about each other?" asked Sasha's friend.

"Oh yes!" said Sasha, in her breathless little-girl voice. "We can't wait to get a bigger apartment – or maybe even a house in the country! We'll probably get engaged next Christmas."

It was clear that Sasha was in love with love – and with herself.

"Is Declan coming to the party later?" asked the friend.

"Ooh, the poor dear is working a late shift tonight!" said Sasha. She pouted at her reflection in the mirror, then gave a little lascivious laugh. "On the other hand, I have my hands full right now with darling Seamus McGrath, the managing editor of the magazine – such a charming man!"

The two left the women's room, and the buzz of conversation began once again. One woman made a derogatory remark about Sasha to her companion in the queue, and several other women joined in, adding their own pithy comments. As Joanna's turn arrived and she headed into the next available cubicle, she heard one woman say to her companion: "Whoever bloody Declan is, he deserves her!"

As she left the women's room, Joanna made her way through the groups of party guests, on her way back to join Orla and Gary. Suddenly, she noticed that a team of waiters was carrying out a huge gooey birthday cake and placing it on a low central table in the conference room. Needless to say, Sasha Miller was standing alongside the table, clearly hoping to be at the centre of things and maybe even get her picture in the "About Town" column. Moving in directly behind her, Joanna eyed Orla's rival with distaste. What on earth could Declan have seen in her? And more to the point, what had Orla ever seen in Declan?

Then the lights were dimmed, there was a sudden hush and people began singing "Happy Birthday" in honour of the magazine. Sasha Miller was in her element, smiling sexily at Seamus McGrath, the managing editor of the magazine, who was standing beside her.

Clearly, the managing editor was impressed by Sasha too, for he invited her to blow out the single birthday candle.

As she leaned forward, lips pouted sexily and her scrawny little breasts hanging provocatively out of her skintight top, Joanna suddenly had an idea. Quick as a flash, she pushed Sasha's big bum with her knee.

Within an instant, Sasha had fallen forward onto the cake. With barely suppressed glee, Joanna watched as Orla's photographer friend Eoin snapped away, taking pictures of Sasha as she tried to extricate herself and wipe off the cream that now covered the front of her dress and her face. Grabbing Seamus McGrath to steady herself, Sasha only succeeded in spreading the cream onto his clothes too. Seamus was livid at having his big occasion spoiled and was cursing as the catering staff tried to wipe the cream off his clothes.

Grinning to herself, Joanna slipped away and headed back to where she had left Orla and Gary. She found them still engrossed in each other.

"What's going on?" asked Orla. "I thought I heard singing – have they brought out the birthday cake yet?"

"What? Oh yes, I think the birthday celebrations have already taken place," said Joanna, trying to look disinterested. "Sorry I was away so long, but the queue for the toilets was really long. Orla, why don't you do a feature on the lack of adequate toilet facilities for women?"

Orla promised to think about it, but Joanna could see that her friend wasn't even considering her suggestion. She had eyes only for Gary, and Joanna wondered if this could be the beginning of something special for the two of them. Gary was so nice, Joanna thought, and Orla certainly needed an ego-boost right now. Mind you, she thought, chuckling to herself, I think Orla will get quite an ego boost tomorrow, when she sees the photos that Eoin has taken of tonight's event!

CHAPTER 16

"You're becoming very popular," said Mary approvingly, as Joanna took two Paracetamol tablets, washing them down with her morning cuppa, followed by a Mikado biscuit. "There have been three calls for you this morning. One landlord-tenant lease problem, one conveyancing job and another solicitor wanting your advice on some legal point."

"Not Freddy O'Rourke, I hope," said Joanna fervently.

"No, it's not," said Mary cheerfully, "but I can't help feeling sorry for that poor fellow. Don't you feel anything for him at all? He did refer that dog-bite case to you, after all . . ."

Joanna said firmly, "No, Mary, I don't feel anything for Freddy – except annoyance every time he rings up. Anyway, I imagine he was quite happy to offload the dog-bite case onto us – it wouldn't be regarded a big enough case for Michael O'Rourke & Company."

Mary went back to the outer office, leaving Joanna to mull over the events of the night before. She'd been more than pleased with her handiwork at the party – seeing Sasha Miller suffer had given her a great sense of satisfaction. Hopefully, there would be further satisfaction when the newspaper hit the streets in the afternoon.

But now, there was work to be done. And top of the agenda was the administration of Agnes Kilmartin's will. Joanna sighed. The task Agnes had set her seemed more suited to a private detective, and soon she'd have one, if Orla's friend came up trumps. But first, she'd make an appointment with Harry Sweeney's trade union. Maybe someone there could shed some light on the enigmatic Harry, or at the very least provide her with some personal details, such as his last known address.

Lifting the phone, Joanna made an appointment to meet George Mullan, the current branch secretary, at the union's headquarters in Liberty Hall.

As she replaced the phone, she heard the other phone ringing outside, and Mary answered it in her usual bright and cheerful manner. "Hello, Joanna Brennan Solicitors – how may I help you?" She then put the call through to Joanna.

"Have you seen the evening newspaper yet?" shrieked Orla, at the other end of the line. "If not, can you go out and get a copy quickly? You're not going to believe what's on page 5!"

"OK, OK! Will do."

"Call me back."

"OK."

Grinning, Joanna put down the phone.

"Mary, I'll be back in a minute! Just going out for a newspaper!"

She rushed down the stairs and out to the local newsagent's, which fortunately was only a few doors away. Within minutes, she was back with two copies of the *Evening Dispatch*.

"Page 5!" she said to Mary, handing her a copy.

Each of them tore through the pages to get to page 5. They both reached it simultaneously and, after a sharp intake of breath, there were shrieks of delight as they gazed at a full colour picture of Sasha Miller's big backside. The caption underneath Orla's report of the party read: *Taking the plunge – journalist Sasha Miller created quite a stir last night at* Celebrity Magazine's *first birthday party.*

Another photo showed a dishevelled Sasha, with cream in her hair, alongside Seamus McGrath, who was wiping cream off his sleeve, and neither of them looking very happy about what had happened.

Joanna grabbed the phone and rang Orla.

"Orla?"

"Well?" Orla could hardly contain her anticipation of Joanna's reaction.

"It's fantastic!" shrieked Joanna.

"I wish I'd seen it happening last night," said Orla, giggling gleefully. "It must have happened around the time you went to the loo, Jo, and while I was talking to Gary. But the place was so crowded that I never even saw the birthday cake! How on earth do you think it happened?"

"I've no idea," said Joanna, "but who cares? It's wonderful, isn't it?" Joanna smiled to herself. She'd tell Orla all about her little prank at a later date. When they could both drink a toast to Sasha's downfall and fully savour it all!

"Thank goodness Eoin was in the right place at the right time," said Orla fervently, "and I hope Declan is hugely embarrassed by the whole thing too!"

"It was a great night, wasn't it?" said Joanna happily. "I enjoyed myself, anyway! And you seemed to be having a good time too – with my client! How did you and Gary get on last night?" She was hoping that he had asked Orla for a date.

The night before, Joanna had left the party early and taken a taxi home soon after the excitement of the Sasha incident. Apart from wanting to give Gary and Orla a chance to be alone, she'd been feeling genuinely tired by then, and worried about Devil, who'd refused to come in before she left for the party. Of course, when she'd arrived home, Devil was waiting for her on the doorstep, looking totally innocent. "It's the vet for you, my girl – you need spaying pronto!" she'd told the little cat, as it purred loudly, rubbing against her leg and affectionately sticking its tiny claws into her expensive tights.

"Nothing happened with Gary," said Orla forlornly. "He had every opportunity to ask me out – and I was hoping he would – but although we got on great, he just said goodnight and that he hoped he'd see me again sometime."

"Oh well," said Joanna, trying to sound positive, "you can't win 'em all. At least you got your revenge on Sasha Miller."

CHAPTER 17

"Agnes – what's the matter?" whispered Catherine.

She and her friend were sitting in Bewley's Café on Dublin's Westmoreland Street.

Agnes's hand shook as she tried to hold her coffee cup. "I'm pregnant, Cat," she said. "Harry and I never intended this to happen, so what on earth am I going to do now?" Catherine was stunned. She had watched her friend's friendship with Harry Sweeney gradually ripen into love, and she had desperately feared the outcome. Harry was a wonderful man, and she knew he adored Agnes, but what future was there for them in the Ireland of 1970? Catherine knew that Harry's wife had accepted the situation, but Ivan Kilmartin never would – she shivered – if he ever found out. As far as Ivan was concerned, there was one law for him and a different one for everyone else.

But she reached across and took her friend's hand. "Oh God, Agnes – does Harry know?"

"Not yet."

"Look, if you want to go to England – you know, for an abortion – I'll come with you," said Catherine. "We can say that we're going to London for a few days' shopping, or to visit a relative of mine. I don't know much about how to get an abortion, but we'll soon find out."

Agnes looked bleakly at her friend. "Cat – I love Harry. I couldn't get rid of his baby. I didn't intend to get pregnant, but now that it's happened, I want to have his child." She gripped Catherine's hand tightly. "Besides – Maura, Harry's wife, isn't able to have children, but Harry's always wanted kids himself. How could I deny him this chance?"

"But how – I mean, what about Ivan?"

Agnes grimaced. "Well, there's no future for Harry and me here, is there? Since there's no divorce in this country, it looks like we'll have to leave Ireland if we want to be together. Especially now that I'm pregnant with Harry's child."

"Well, you certainly can't stay here with Ivan."

"We've talked about going to Australia – what do you think?"

"Well, you have your brother Joseph over there," added Catherine, smiling. "He'll be thrilled to have you near him."

"And he'll be able to help us settle in, advise us where to live, help us to get work."

"I'm sure Harry will have no problem getting a job over there – he'll have all the workers organised into trade unions in no time!" said Catherine, smiling.

"I'll miss you, Cat," said Agnes, a lump in her throat. "Promise that we'll always stay in touch?"

"Of course we will – you're my dearest friend, and we're not going to let a few oceans keep us apart! Now let's start getting you organised. If you and Harry are going to emigrate, *you're going to need some help. Bill and I will do all that we can, although we don't have much money to give you –* "

"I'll go to my father," Agnes interrupted, grinning suddenly as she saw the incredulous look on Catherine's face. "Don't worry, Cat, I'm not planning to tell him about Harry and me! But I'll drop hints about what I'd like for my birthday next month – maybe a new car – and see if he takes the bait. He can be quite generous, you know, as long as he feels that he's controlling the situation. Then I can sell the car and use the money for our new life in Australia!"

"I presume your father will cut you out of his will when you run off with Harry?"

Agnes grimaced. "I guess so. Dad idolises Ivan, so he'll be livid that I've left him for Harry. He also shares Ivan's view of trade unions and trade unionists."

"But you're going to have his grandchild – I'm sure he'll eventually come round."

"Well, maybe eventually, Cat. But I don't actually care. I'll have Harry, and that's all that matters."

"Well, he can hardly cut off both his children, can he?"

"I don't know – poor old Joseph certainly won't get a penny. But at least I'll be with the man I love. We'll survive somehow."

"Well, the first thing you've got to do is tell Harry that you're pregnant," said Catherine.

"Thanks, Cat," said Agnes, smiling through tears, "I don't know what I'd do without you! I came in here a nervous wreck – now I can see a real future ahead for Harry, me and the baby!"

CHAPTER 18

Declan Dunne whistled as he locked his car door and walked along the road. He was carrying a large bunch of red roses and was en route to Orla's apartment. Correction, he thought, *our* apartment. Because, pretty soon, he hoped to be reinstalled there, with Sasha Miller and her big arse just a distant memory.

Declan intended letting himself into the apartment, since he still had his key. He intended to surprise Orla when she arrived back from work. Maybe he'd even get into their bed and be waiting naked for her when she arrived – he used do that in the good old days, and it always made her really horny. Combined with the roses, hopefully it would do the trick for him again.

The apartment block, where he and Orla had lived together, was situated on the outskirts of the city, along a small road adjacent to the M50, the city's main ring road. Effectively, they lived out in the country, yet with the M50 close by, they could be in the city centre within twenty minutes. They both enjoyed being able to look out over green fields and country roads, and since they'd been saving for their own house, they'd scour the local countryside at weekends and days off, looking for a suitable site on which to build their dream home.

Declan paused, drawing the fresh country air deep into his lungs. He sighed happily. This was definitely the life – he hated living in Sasha's cramped city-centre apartment, where the only smell that assailed your nostrils was either the local rubbish bins or car fumes. Here he was, back where he belonged – back where you could watch lambs gambolling in the fields and sheep grazing peacefully throughout the summer months, hear the gentle hum of the hay-baler in late summer and smell the freshly cut grass as the local farmers made up their silage bales for the winter months.

Declan sighed happily. He loved working in the city. He loved the excitement of being a news journalist because no two days were ever the same, but he also loved the tranquillity of rural Ireland, and he figured that if he could just get back with Orla, he'd have it all. Well, he'd *had* it all once, but unfortunately he hadn't realised how important it was until too late. Hopefully, he'd soon have it all again.

Their top-floor apartment was in one of five three-storey blocks, and Declan was of the opinion that theirs was the nicest block, since it was farthest away from the main road and overlooked beautiful green fields. He recalled how sometimes he and Orla would gaze out over the countryside in the evenings, watching the setting sun and being driven to a frenzy of lust by the sheer beauty of their surroundings. Yes, he thought happily, I can't wait to see Orla's face when I present her with the roses. Initially, she'll pretend to be tough and put on a brave face, but it won't be long before she'll be sobbing in my arms and welcoming me back into her life again. He would let her have her pound of flesh by grovelling and confessing that he'd made a terrible mistake, but once he told her he loved only her, and couldn't envisage life without her, it would be plain sailing.

Letting himself in the main door of the apartment block, Declan bounded up the stairs, feeling excited and pleased as he thought of the night of lust that hopefully lay ahead of him. At the door of the apartment, he fumbled for his key – dammit, he was like a child, he was so excited! Eagerly, he pushed the key in the lock and turned it – or tried to turn it – but nothing happened. Puzzled, he put down the bunch of roses on the floor and gave his full attention to turning the key. Still, nothing happened.

Suddenly, it dawned on him. The bitch had changed the locks! Furious now, he stabbed the key into the lock again, but still nothing happened. By now, he was purple with rage – how dare she think that she could do this to him! He'd been prepared to tolerate some initial anger when she saw him – after all, he'd behaved very badly on that press trip – but this business of changing the locks was just going too far!

Picking up the bouquet, he stomped down the stairs angrily. She certainly wasn't going to get these expensive bloody roses now! He felt livid at the injustice of it all – he'd had to borrow the money for the roses from one of his colleagues because he was skint until the end of the month. Bloody Sasha Miller and her demands had drained him financially. Since she couldn't – or wouldn't – cook in the evenings, they'd had to eat out or send for a takeaway every evening. And he'd had to foot the bill! Women – who needed them!

Leaving the building, Declan checked all around him to ensure that no one was present to witness his humiliation, then he sneaked behind the apartment block and flung the bouquet of roses over the hedge into the adjoining field. This made him feel marginally better – although he was still smarting over the injustice of it all – then he hurried back to his car and zoomed out of the complex and onto the M50 sliproad, nearly causing a collision with a truck in his haste to get away from the area. The truck driver blasted his horn and Declan gave him the single-finger salute, which so incensed the truck driver that he sat menacingly on Declan's tail until they reached the city centre. Shaken, Declan managed to lose the truck at a set of traffic-lights, which fortuitously changed to red just as he shot through them, but a garda saw his reckless action, and he was hauled over to the side of the street and given a ticket and a lecture on dangerous driving. To add to his humiliation, the truck driver went past, blowing his horn and gloating happily.

Back at Sasha's apartment block, Declan climbed the stairs wearily. At least he could depend on Sasha to give him a massage – as a preliminary to sex, of course – and that would help to relax him a bit. He certainly needed relaxing right now. A night in with Sasha was exactly what he needed.

But Sasha was not in the mood for doling out sympathy to anyone else. In fact, she was furious.

"Have you seen this evening's newspaper?" she screamed at him the minute he entered the apartment. "I've been totally humiliated – and I'm sure that bitch Orla Rogan had something to do with it! She and that fucking photographer – look what they've done to me!"

Declan was hardly in the mood to reciprocate, but since he didn't want to end up sleeping rough that night, he decided that he'd better try to placate Sasha. "You look great in those pictures," he said lamely, realising as he said it that it wasn't what Sasha wanted to hear.

"I look t-terrible!" she wailed. "How could anyone publish these pictures?"

"But you look as though you were having lots of fun!" said Declan desperately. All he wanted to do was get into the shower and let the scalding water take away his own pain and humiliation.

As Sasha sat weeping, Declan racked his brains to think of some way that he could end this horrendous scenario. I suppose I could just go out to the pub and leave her, he thought. But then he remembered that he had no money, and secondly, the door to Sasha's apartment would undoubtedly be barred against him when he returned – and even he couldn't face the thought of two evictions in the same evening.

Suddenly, he had a brainwave. "I had a lovely surprise for you this evening," he told her, smiling. "I bought you a lovely bouquet of red roses – to show how much I care about you."

Sasha stopped crying. "Oh Declan!" she whispered.

"You're wonderful! But where are they? Can I have them?"

"Unfortunately not, my love – you see, I called to a friend's place and left them there by mistake," he lied. "I was afraid to leave them in the car in case they wilted – so I brought them into –" he thought rapidly, "John Boyle's house." Declan named a colleague that Sasha wasn't likely to know. But then he wondered: was there any male journalist in Dublin that Sasha *didn't* know? He looked at her sadly. "I was in such a hurry to get back to you, that I completely forgot to take them with me. They're still in a vase of water, in John's pad. But I'll get them for you tomorrow."

Shit, Declan thought. Now he'd have to borrow more money from his sub-editor colleague. A complicated love life was turning out to be very expensive.

Suddenly, Sasha began to cry. And her sobs became louder and louder. "I don't want my roses tomorrow!" she howled. "I want them *now*!" She began battering his chest with her tiny fists. "Why did you tell me you've got roses for me if I can't have them now? You're cruel, Declan, you're so cruel! You know how much these photographs in the paper upset me – now you're making it worse! Can't you go round and collect my roses from this friend of yours?" She pouted through her tears. "If not, I'm going to go out – I can't stay in any longer, I'm so upset! I'm going to go out clubbing!" She gave him a malevolent stare. "And you needn't think that you can stay here, living it up in *my* apartment while I'm gone. If you don't care enough about me to go and get my flowers, you can get out of here and go to hell!"

Visions of a night spent sleeping in a cardboard box loomed up before him, and Declan shivered. "OK, OK – I just thought you'd prefer me to stay here and rub your back – help you relax –" Maybe, he thought in desperation, if I can get her turned on, she'll forget all about the flowers until tomorrow. "C'mon, baby – let me ease those shoulders with a nice massage. Here, let me take off your bra – "

"Get away from me, you – you – bastard!" shrieked Sasha. "Go and get my fucking roses!"

Declan realised that he had finally run out of options. "OK," he said in defeat, "I'll go and get your roses. Now please calm down, Sasha. I'll be back with them as quickly as I can."

Sasha gave him a radiant smile through her tears as he prepared to leave the apartment. "See you later, sugar," she whispered seductively, now that she'd got her own way. "When you come back with my beautiful roses, I'll be waiting for you – and I'll be as naked as nature intended me to be!" She turned and gave him a wiggle as he waved goodbye.

Declan sighed. The last vision he had, as he left the apartment, was the sight of Sasha's gigantic arse and the promise it conveyed of glorious carnal delights on his return.

CHAPTER 19

Tom Kilmartin sat in his father's study, rummaging through piles upon piles of paper. Most of the documents made no sense to him, but then he wasn't a businessman and had never had any inclination to be one, much to his father's disappointment.

He could still remember his father's words when, during that final year at school, he had broached the subject of going on to university to study science. "Dammit, Tom," his father had said plaintively, "can't a father depend on his only son to carry on the family name? I'd hoped that you'd follow me into the business – take Business Studies at university. Instead, you'd rather play chemistry with dead frogs and beetles."

"You mean biology, Dad," Tom had said, then wished he'd simply shut up. His father was not a man you corrected. But having started, he'd felt duty-bound to explain to his father what really inspired him to study all aspects of science. "Look, Dad, I want to study as many of the sciences as I can, like chemistry, physics, zoology, astronomy – and biology too. I want to know what makes this world what it is – then maybe I can do something to right some of the wrongs that are taking place."

His father had been livid with anger and had harrumphed at what he regarded as foolhardy adolescent dreaming. Ivan Kilmartin was a man who believed passionately in the status quo and who had no time for what he called "namby-pamby do-gooders". The world was there to be pillaged by the strongest for their own benefit, and Tom had no doubt that his own father fought tooth and nail, by fair means or foul, to get the best deals for Cashen Kilmartin Construction, no matter what the cost to others.

But I'm not like that, Tom had thought. He'd been too scared to say it out loud but what he wanted most of all was to make up for what people like his father had done to the planet.

With his mother's support – and indeed, her outright opposition to Ivan Kilmartin's dictum that their son should only be allowed to take Business Studies at university – he'd got his science degree with First Class Honours. After that, he'd completed a Masters Degree in Biology, followed by a Doctorate in Environmental Science. After several years as a senior lecturer, he'd been appointed professor. Over the years, his own life and his father's had run in uneasy parallel – one of them exploiting the planet, the other trying to make restitution for the other's excesses.

After Ivan Kilmartin's death, Agnes gradually sold off all his companies. Tom had felt guilty that he hadn't wanted to take over the business empire that his father had built up, but he'd never had the slightest interest. In fact, he considered that many of his father's dealings had been downright immoral. Thankfully, his mother hadn't pressured him either. In fact, he'd got the distinct impression that she'd been quietly pleased that he wasn't interested in further developing the Kilmartin dynasty.

The sale of Cashen Kilmartin Construction created huge interest in the business world, and there had been much speculation in the media as to who would buy. The who's who of the construction industry fought tooth and nail to outbid each other for the land parcels and building contracts that went with the company, and when it was all over, Agnes Kilmartin was a millionaire many times over. How many times, Tom didn't know – and his mother never told him – but he knew that if he wanted to be idle, he need never work a single day in his life again.

But Tom loved the work that he did – he felt that in some small way he was actually contributing to the preservation of endangered species and inspiring the next generation of students with the same enthusiasm.

On the other hand, his father had stripped the planet of its raw materials – many of them non-renewable – without a thought to the needs of future generations. Nothing mattered as long as his company got bigger and his huge ego was continually massaged. For at heart, Tom concluded, his father had been a very shallow man.

I must take after my mother, he had often thought to himself. He certainly had inherited her determination. Or maybe I'm just an oddball, he concluded ruefully. So odd that Joanna Brennan wouldn't even give me a second glance.

He'd hoped that Joanna would have contacted him by now, not just because he wanted to know what was happening, but simply because he wanted to see her again. He thought of her lovely freckled face, her shoulder-length red hair, her gentle smile. And he admitted to himself, as he sat alone in his father's office, that there had never been any other woman for him but her. If he was honest with himself, he'd adored her since those long-ago days when they would sit together beside the pond at the end of his garden, and he'd explain to her how tadpoles turned into frogs, how caterpillars turned into butterflies, and he would point out the chrysalises, hanging gently from plant stalks, that would one day turn into glorious new butterflies.

And he'd explained to her about dragonflies – how they lived beneath the surface of the water for most of their lives – then they experienced only one day of glory as beautiful multicoloured flying creatures, before their brief lives were over. He'd been alarmed at how sad Joanna looked when he explained all this to her – perhaps it was at that moment, as he'd watched a tear fall from her big blue ten-year-old eyes, that his heart had been well and truly given to her forever.

He stood up and studied himself dispassionately in the small mirror above his father's desk. He wasn't really much of a catch – brown hair, brown eyes, passable looks, not as tall as he'd like to have been, and shy to boot – unless, that is, he was lecturing his students or talking about something that interested him. Like saving the whales, helping to restock endangered species or travelling to remote parts of the earth, where the world was still as nature intended. In fact, he admitted to himself, he was a boring conversationalist. He couldn't make small talk, and he was hopeless at social events.

Nevertheless, there had been plenty of women who'd shown an interest in him. And he'd gone through all the usual teenage rites of passage, like kissing and cuddling with girls in the back row of the cinema, occasional dating and brief flings throughout his undergraduate years. But he was too serious for most of the women he dated, and besides, he never met anyone to whom he was seriously attracted or who cared about the same things that he did. Perhaps that was because there was always an ideal at the back of his mind – an ideal against which all other women failed to measure up. That ideal was Joanna Brennan.

He sighed. The one time he'd tried to act suave – when he'd called in to Joanna's new office and had taken her hand in his and kissed it – she'd gone pink with embarrassment, and he'd wished that the ground could have opened up and swallowed him. What hope had he of attracting a woman like that?

Well, at least he could phone her and ask if she'd made any progress with the will. But he really longed to see her in person, to see her lovely face when it broke into a smile. The kind of smile that made his heart turn over.

CHAPTER 20

"It's very simple, Colette. Either you get rid of it, or you and I are finished. I want no children out of wedlock. I have a wife, and she will bear my children eventually."

"But Ivan – "

"Have I not made myself clear, Colette? If you want to continue living the good life at my expense, there will be no children – now or ever. I thought you understood that. However, if you persist in this notion of yours, then you can pack your bags and take yourself off this very minute."

"I – I thought you'd be pleased – "

"Well, you thought wrong, Colette. This discussion is now at an end. Make your choice – and I hope it's the right one."

"Alright, Ivan – whatever you want."

"Good – I knew you'd eventually see sense. This is the best way, believe me. Now come over here and show me how much you love me . . ."

* * *

Colette was crying softly as she buzzed Harry into her apartment block. And by the time he'd reached the first floor, the tears were streaming down her face.

"Oh God, Harry – I thought he'd be delighted that I was pregnant," she sobbed. "I mean, his wife hasn't produced anything yet, and I know that he doesn't love her, because he's told me so. So I thought that if I got pregnant, he might leave her and set up home with me."

"Oh, my poor Colette!" said Harry, hugging his young sister-in-law. "That was never going to happen, love – I thought you realised that. Men like Ivan don't leave their wives for their mistresses."

Harry had come to tell Colette that he and Maura were splitting up but he decided that in her present state she didn't need to hear such bad news – nor that he was leaving the country with the wife of the man who was presently causing her so much pain.

"So what are you going to do?" he asked.

"I love him, Harry – so I've got to get rid of the baby. Ivan has agreed to pay all my expenses."

Harry grimaced. "I thought this would have shown you the kind of man Kilmartin is – are you sure you want to stay with him? Look, Maura and I will give you all the support you need. I'm sure Maura would go with you to England for the abortion –"

"Harry," said Colette in exasperation, "it's not as simple as that! I told Ivan I was three months pregnant – but I'm actually nearly six months gone!"

Harry looked at her stomach in amazement. "Good God, Colette – I'd never have guessed! You don't look . . ."

"I know. That's why Ivan never guessed."

"Why on earth did you wait so long before telling him?"

Tears filled Colette's eyes. "I suppose deep down I was making certain that he couldn't make me abort it. I was sure he'd be happy when he got used to the idea. But now I have no choice anyway – I have to give birth to it."

"Maybe when you see your baby, you'll want to keep it," said Harry. "You'd certainly qualify for social housing of some sort – "

"No, Harry – I don't want to keep it. Maybe I can have it adopted in England. I'm going to pretend to Ivan that I've had the abortion, then while I'm in England I'll phone him and tell him that a sick friend needs me to look after her for a few weeks. Then, when I've had the baby, I'll give it up for adoption and come back to Dublin."

Harry groaned. "How long are you going to let that man dictate to you?"

"Hush, Harry – I like the good life. I couldn't survive in some council housing estate – "

"But you're only nineteen – "

"And old enough to know what I want, Harry. And I'm going to ask Maura if she'll come over to England when I'm due, and help me through the birth.".

"Of course she will. I'll tell her what's happened as soon as I get home."

"Thanks, Harry – tell her I'll phone her tomorrow."

Harry sighed. He hadn't the heart to tell her his news. He'd leave Maura to tell her sister when she felt the time was right. Maybe he was a coward not to tell her, but for now, poor Colette had more than enough to cope with.

CHAPTER 21

Declan heaved a sigh of relief as he locked his car and began walking in the direction of Orla's apartment block. He'd parked his car as far away as possible, and now he pulled up the collar of his coat to avoid being seen by anyone in the block who might know him. Thankfully, darkness was beginning to set in, the street lighting outside the apartment blocks had just come on, so all he had to do was keep his head down and turn his face away from the lights. He looked at his watch. He knew that Orla was on a late shift, so she wouldn't have left the newsroom yet. Hopefully he'd have completed his mission and left the area long before she was likely to appear.

It was Declan's plan to retrieve the bouquet of roses from the field behind Orla's apartment block and bring them back to Sasha – he certainly wasn't going to waste money on more flowers, especially when there was a perfectly good bouquet just behind the hedge. Although he'd thrown it over in a fit of temper, there was a reasonable chance that they were still in good condition. Hopefully, he could just climb over the gate, retrieve the flowers and be on his way back to Sasha before anyone spotted him.

Away from the street lighting, it was pitch black behind the apartment block, and Declan's eyes took a few seconds to adjust to the gloom. He cursed as he tripped over a stone. What a pity he hadn't thought of bringing the flashlight from the car. Still, this mission wasn't going to take him too long, he reasoned, as he crossed the boreen to the field. Even though it was very dark, he should still be quite capable of spotting a bunch of red roses in a field of green grass.

The gate was padlocked, and Declan cursed again. There didn't appear to be any of the sheep that were usually in the field, so why on earth was it locked? Declan began scaling the five-bar gate. There was a small notice attached to the gate, but in the increasing darkness, Declan couldn't quite make out what the lettering said. Anyway, he reasoned, farmers weren't exactly noted for the accuracy of their signs, and the notice was bound to be several years out of date anyway.

Climbing down into the field, Declan looked around. It was a much bigger field than he'd expected. It had looked a lot smaller from the top-storey apartment window where he and Orla had watched the lambs playing below. Well, there were no furry white blobs visible in the twilight now – but there *was* a large dark blob over in the far corner. Probably just a trick of the light.

Declan made his way in the direction of the bouquet,

cursing intermittently as he got stung by thistles or lost his balance on the uneven ground. To think he was doing all this because of bloody Sasha Miller! He must be totally out of his mind – or badly in need of a roof over his head. What an appalling mess he'd got himself into lately – he'd better start looking for a flat or a bedsit on his own, because he couldn't take much more of Sasha's tantrums. He'd never realised before what a spoiled bitch she really was – after all, shagging someone every five minutes on the floor of a Spanish hotel room hadn't provided much opportunity to explore her personality traits!

At last, Declan spotted the bouquet of roses, which caught in the lower branches of a hawthorn tree. He was relieved to see that the cellophane covering and decorative bow were still intact, so Sasha would never suspect where they'd been. If he could just avoid the nasty thorns, and the thistles on the ground, he'd soon free the roses from their perch in the tree and be back over the gate in no time at all.

Reaching up, Declan grasped the bouquet, pulling it gingerly so as not to damage the wrapping. It crackled a little, and the noise sounded terribly loud because of the silence all around him. But just as he finally rescued the bouquet, Declan heard another sound nearby – a sort of snuffling sound, accompanied by the sound of heavy feet upon the ground. A number of feet – possibly four – and they were coming in his direction. At considerable speed. And the snuffling sound had now turned into snorting. Some creature was not very happy that Declan was in its field – and Declan was suddenly most unhappy about being there!

He turned to run and found himself staring into a large black face, with flaring nostrils and two horns on top. It stared back, then bent its head and threw him skyward. All sorts of jumbled thoughts raced through his mind as he was flung through the air – was it the Devil himself, finally come to take possession of his soul? Or was it, as the logical side of his brain told him, a bull?

From the midst of the thicket where he landed, Declan had a brief chance to view his assailant before he received another headbutt, which this time pushed him further into the hawthorn tree. Yes, it was definitely a bull! By now, Declan managed to let out a piercing scream, as fear shot through him and the thorns of the tree stuck into his flesh.

At that precise moment, Orla had just arrived back from work and was closing the curtains in her dining-room after having just placed a prepacked low-calorie lasagne dinner for one in the microwave. She paused, startled for a second. Was that a scream she'd heard, coming from the field behind the apartment? She gazed out the window but could see nothing, since it was now very dark. She heard the bull snorting, but that was what bulls did, wasn't it?

Orla knew that the local farmer had recently moved his sheep from the field and brought them to another field, replacing them with his prize bull, because he'd notified the residents of each apartment block. He'd also placed a notice on the gate, so that no one could be in any doubt as to the danger of entering the field.

No, Orla reasoned, no one was stupid enough to go into a field with a bull in it. So she closed over the curtains and decided to continue with her plans for the evening, which consisted of eating her low-calorie meal, washing her hair, soaking in the bath – and hoping that she might get a phone call from Gary.

Orla couldn't understand why Gary hadn't rung – she credited herself with having a reasonable understanding of other people, and she'd felt certain that Gary had really been attracted to her. And they'd got on so well! Even when Joanna had headed off to the loo and been gone for ages, there hadn't been any awkward silences between them – they'd just chatted away non-stop! He'd told her that he was a doctor at St Brigid's – so maybe the reason he hadn't rung was because he was so busy working. Hospital doctors worked long hours, didn't they?

Orla sighed. Maybe she hadn't considered the most obvious reason – he probably had a girlfriend or wife already. Why on earth had she made the assumption that he wouldn't have? After all, he was gorgeous, personable and just because he lived with his dog didn't mean that there couldn't be a wife living there as well. Maybe she could get Joanna to find out. If she'd only thought of saying: "Gary, what does your wife think of all this trouble with the neighbours?" On the other hand, maybe not. It sounded really pathetic and obvious.

Before stepping into the bath, Orla ensured that her mobile phone was as near to the bath as possible. Now that she didn't have a fiancé any more, she'd have to keep her mobile close by at all times. Just in case some exciting man rang to ask her out!

Much later, she stepped out of the bath and dried herself, noting sourly that there hadn't been a single phone call all evening. Slipping into her dressing-gown, she went across to the window again. She could still make out the shape of the bull. He was snorting and pawing the hedge and didn't seem to have moved from where he'd been positioned earlier. Perhaps the poor creature had got himself trapped in the hedge, or maybe he was caught on barbed wire? Orla's kind heart went out to the bull. If he was in some kind of difficulty, then perhaps she should give the farmer a ring. Hopefully, that notice the old farmer had circulated round all the flats was still around somewhere . . . On the other hand, it was fairly late, and Orla knew that farming folk went to bed early, since they were up and out working at cockcrow every morning. So she decided to finish off the novel she was reading instead. There were only a few chapters to go and she was convinced that at this stage she'd correctly guessed the identity of the killer. She settled down on the couch with a packet of chocolate digestives – her favourite biscuits.

* * *

Out in the field, Declan and the bull had reached a standoff. Declan cowered among the thorns in silence, afraid to move. The bull stood staring at him, snorting indignantly and daring him to move so that he could give him another headbutt. Declan's nether regions, front and back, were feeling seriously sore, and he was hoping – but he didn't dare check – that the bull hadn't gored his genitals to ribbons. He'd already received two headbutts, one to the back and one to the front, and the bull looked as though he was just waiting for another opportunity to

126

inflict further injury. At this rate, Declan thought, I could be stuck here all night! Or until I'm dead! He decided that another yell for help was the only real option he'd got left. Because clearly the bull wasn't planning on moving.

* * *

Orla had just finished reading her book and was feeling very smug because she'd been right all along about the murderer. Suddenly she heard a blood-curdling yell and realised that there was definitely something amiss in the field below. She peered out the window. It was impossible to see, or to tell if the sound had been human or animal, and there was no way that *she* was going to investigate! After several minutes of anxious searching, she located the piece of paper with farmer Eddie Hanlon's number on it. She quickly dialled the farmer's number, suggesting that he check out his prize bull, in case it was in difficulties.

Then, feeling pleased that she had done her good deed for the day, Orla made herself a cup of tea and carried it – along with the remaining chocolate-digestive biscuits – into the bedroom. Climbing into bed, she settled down with a new novel, working her way gradually through the tea, the biscuits and the book, and hoping that Gary might ring.

CHAPTER 22

Gary's shoulders ached. It was late, he'd been on duty in the casualty department for hours and it had been a night of one emergency after another. But that, he accepted, was the lot of the hospital doctor. Soon, he'd be heading home for a nice warm bath, then to bed. Poor old Bruce would be starving by now. Gary had left him a big bowl of dry dog biscuits, but the dog would be looking forward to his evening meal of tinned dog food.

Gary's brow furrowed. That bloody woman. He didn't believe for one second that Bruce had bitten her. The dog didn't like her, that was true. But bite her? Never!

Gary rubbed the back of his neck, then started to take off his white coat. All was quiet now, so in theory all he had to do was tell the duty nurse he was at the end of his shift, sign off the duty roster and head for home. But where the hell was the intern who was supposed to take over the rest of the night shift?

In a sense, Gary was glad that he'd been busy all evening. Because it had also kept him from thinking about Orla. Ever since he'd met her at the magazine party, she'd been constantly in his thoughts. He'd wanted desperately to ask her out that night, then he'd got cold feet at the last minute and reasoned that it might be better to wait until the whole nasty business surrounding Bruce's future had been decided. After all, he now had a professional relationship with Orla's friend Joanna Brennan, and if Orla turned him down, it might cause embarrassment all round. Not that he could blame Orla if she *did* refuse to go out with him. Undoubtedly he'd bored her rigid that night, with all his worries about Bruce and the impending court case.

Gary began taking off his white coat. He'd hang it in the staff room – no point in taking it home, since he'd be back on duty again within a matter of hours. At least he'd had time off to attend the magazine's birthday party, which was where he'd met the lovely Orla. And dammit, he *was* going to ring her. He'd do it tomorrow morning, as soon as he got up. To hell with propriety. He wasn't going to risk losing her! Apart from her great joie-de-vivre, he'd also detected a deeply caring, sensitive side to her. He suspected that Orla didn't let too many people see that side of her personality, but to him, it made her all the more intriguing. And she was a woman with her own mind – he liked that. Yes, he'd definitely ring her in the morning.

Gary yawned. He was longing to get home to his bed. Suddenly, he became aware of a commotion close at hand. Suddenly, the casualty department's emergency doors opened, and amid much cursing and shouting, a man in his mid-thirties was carried in on a stretcher. He was wearing only his underpants and was clutching his torn trousers in one hand and clutching his groin with the other.

"Oh Jesus, Doctor – I think I've lost my balls!" he groaned, spotting the stethoscope around Gary's neck. "I can't feel anything down there – but it's bloody painful nonetheless!"

Gary sighed and slipped on his white coat again. If his replacement on the duty roster had turned up on time, he'd have been gone home. He'd certainly get a piece of Gary's mind when he *did* appear.

The ambulance men had by now placed the groaning patient on a gurney.

"OK – so what's the problem?" Gary asked.

The men looked at one another and then one of them drew Gary aside. "This guy's a bit of an asshole, if you ask me," he muttered under his breath. "Got himself gored by a bull. In the middle of the bloody night! Can you believe it?"

"We got an emergency call from the farmer who owns the animal," explained the other man. "This chap was in the field with the bloody bull! Maybe he was practising to be a matador!"

The three men grinned at each other.

"What sort of injuries has he got?" asked Gary, trying to stifle his grin.

"Claims the bull gored him in the bollocks," said one ambulance man. "Then it got him in the backside. We didn't really manage to get a proper look, because he keeps clutching himself all the time. But all his tackle seems to be there – I think he's more in shock than anything else."

After the ambulance men had gone off, still smirking at each other, Gary approached the patient, who was groaning softly.

"Seems like you've had a rough evening," he said. "How did you get on such close terms with a bull?"

"It's a long story," mumbled the patient, "but, Doctor, I'm in agony, back and front. Am I going to be all right? I mean, is there any chance I'm going to lose my pecker?"

Gary, assisted by the duty nurse, peeled off the patient's underpants while he mumbled on, establishing that despite a lot of blood from scratches and a cut above his genital region, the young man was in no danger of losing his manhood. Another deep cut on his backside would require several stitches and, of course, the essential anti-tetanus injection.

"I think we'll admit him for the night," Gary told the nurse, "just in case he has any kind of adverse reaction later. Give him a few strong painkillers – then I'll stitch him up. And arrange for some X-rays in the morning, Sister, will you? We'd better check in case there was concussion at any stage."

As Gary prepared to treat him, the duty nurse asked the patient for his details, so that she could fill out the casualty and admission forms.

"Your name?"

"Declan Dunne," he said, adding in the hope of impressing the doctor and the young nurse: "I'm a journalist with the *Evening Dispatch*."

"Address?"

Declan closed his eyes. This was a tricky one, since he wasn't sure where he was living at present. But he decided that he'd give the address of Orla's apartment. He had decided that all was not really lost with Orla – after all, hadn't the farmer who rescued him explained that Orla was the one who'd relayed details of his plight? That must mean she still loved him – and anyway, she'd never returned his engagement ring. Wasn't that proof that she was still probably wearing it?

"Number 27, Riverdale Apartments."

As the nurse wrote it down, Gary looked up in surprise. Was that one of the apartment blocks where Orla had told him she lived? It was an omen. He really would ring her tomorrow.

"Well, Declan," said Gary aloud, as he cleaned up the two wounds, "you've had a lucky escape this evening. What on earth were you doing, late at night, in a field with a bull?"

Now that he was assured of a continuing sex life, Declan was quite willing to co-operate and to endure the pain and indignity of being stitched and injected. In fact, he was enjoying being in the limelight. And he decided that he could embellish tonight's drama and turn himself into something of a hero.

"Well, I was actually doing an undercover story on suspect farming practices," he said, lowering his voice for effect, "but I'm afraid I can't reveal any of the details at this stage." Being a city person, Declan hadn't a clue about farming practices himself. And he sincerely hoped that neither the doctor nor the nurse did either.

"Being a journalist must be a very interesting job," said Gary, as much to distract the patient as anything else. For he knew that if he could get an egotist like this guy talking about himself, it would make the job of stitching him up a lot easier.

"Oh yes," said Declan, "no two days are ever the same. It means that I'm always at the centre of the action – where the news is being made. One day, it could be a political or sex scandal, the next day an accident or a fire." He smirked. "But it's all in a day's work for us members of the Fourth Estate."

What an asshole, Gary thought to himself as he stitched – the ambulance guys were certainly right about this one!

Declan droned on regardless, now warming to his theme and seeing himself in the role of Ireland's top journalist. "I also get to travel quite a lot," he added. Well, he'd been on one press trip to Spain – but look what problems *that* had caused in his life.

"Do you by any chance know Orla Rogan?" Gary asked casually.

"Orla?" said Declan in surprise. "Of course I do – she's my fiancée. *Ow!*"

The "ow" resulted from the fact that Gary, in shock, accidentally stuck the needle in too far.

Declan, recovering from the accidental jab, let wishful thinking take over and droned on about the fact that he and Orla would probably get married the following year, unaware that he had just dashed Gary's dreams.

In fact, Gary was wishing he could stitch up Declan's bloody mouth. "You're finished now," said Gary abruptly, cutting the vicryl on the last stitch. "Sister, will you take the patient upstairs and have him committed?" Hopefully to a mental institution for life, Gary wished unkindly.

"Thank you, Doctor," said Declan, pulling on his torn trousers. "We journalists have to take all these inconveniences in our stride!"

How the hell could Orla be engaged to an idiot like that? Gary asked himself. Anyway, he thought crossly, the question was now academic. Orla was clearly out of bounds.

He sighed with a mixture of relief and anger as he saw his replacement intern arriving.

"Where the hell have you been?" he muttered.

"Sorry I'm late, Gary," apologised the young man, rushing up in a flurry of white coat and swinging stethoscope. "My wife is pregnant again and feeling very sick, and I couldn't get our toddler to go to sleep!"

Gary said nothing. Instead he signed off the duty register and abruptly walked out. Some people have all the bloody luck, he thought angrily. They *have* a home life. Soon, I mightn't even have my *dog* any more.

CHAPTER 23

After being discharged from hospital, Declan decided that he'd make his way back back to Sasha Miller's apartment. The night before, the intense pain had caused him to hallucinate – especially while that young doctor was stitching him up – and he'd considered briefly that Orla might still love him. But now, in the cold light of day, he realised that his chances of success were likely to be better with Sasha Miller. No doubt Sasha would be hugely sympathetic about him landing up in hospital, but how would he explain what had happened? A few well-chosen lies should do the trick, Declan thought. I'll tell her that after collecting her flowers from John's house, I was knocked down by a hit-and-run driver. Then he'd ring the Newsroom and tell them the same story. After that, no one would expect him to appear in work for several days. So he could take it easy in Sasha's pad, and if she was willing, they could retire to bed and he could test his manhood – just to be absolutely sure that everything was still in full working order.

Arriving back at Sasha's apartment, Declan knocked gingerly on the door. He anticipated being given the cold shoulder to begin with, but once he'd had a chance to explain about the hit-and-run, she'd welcome him with open arms – and hopefully she'd open other limbs as well . . .

"Where the fuck have you been?" screeched Sasha, as the door suddenly opened and she appeared wearing only a flimsy nightdress that left nothing to the imagination.

"Hold on – please give me a chance to explain!" Declan begged. "I've been in hospital, Sasha." He felt smug as he watched her expression turn to one of surprise. "Yes," he continued, doing his best to look contrite, "after I collected your flowers from John Boyle's house, I was just stepping off the pavement, when a car bowled me over – and your beautiful flowers were thrown up in the air!"

What Declan didn't realise was that he'd just told one lie too many. He might have got away with the hit-and-run story, but Sasha knew more than he realised.

"Get out – you bastard!" she screamed. "There never were any flowers, were there? You lied to me!"'

"No, Sasha – it's perfectly true – I *did* have roses for you – "

At that precise moment, a sleepy male head and naked torso appeared around Sasha's door. Declan stared in disbelief. It was John Boyle!

"Well," said Sasha, "I found John Boyle's phone number in your little phone book, so I rang him myself! You didn't leave *any* roses at John's house. You lied to me!"

"Hi, Declan," said John sheepishly.

It was perfectly obvious to Declan that his former friend had spent the night consoling Sasha over her missing roses.

Now, the only thing that Declan felt he could do was retreat with some vestiges of his dignity still intact. He would swagger out of Sasha Miller's life as though he didn't have a care in the world. She needn't think that he felt gutted or short-changed by her callous behaviour. He would show her . . .

He was about to turn on his heel and march off into the sunset like his cowboy heroes of old, when he suddenly remembered that his books, clothes, football boots and precious autograph book were still in Sasha's apartment. Suddenly, he changed his "I don't care" routine to something a lot more conciliatory.

"Well, if that's the way you want it, Sasha, then I won't stand in your way. So I might as well collect my belongings and get out of your life," he said with a sigh of resignation, accompanied by a tight-lipped but dignifed half-smile. By acquiescing without a fight, he felt that he might defuse the tension in the air and leave with his property – whatever about his dignity – intact. Because right now, Declan's property was far more important to him than anything else.

Yet even as he spoke, he realised that the conciliatory approach might just be the wrong one. After all, Sasha positively *enjoyed* having men fight over her. Maybe she'd prefer him to grovel – to beg her to take him back instead. Or maybe she wanted him to become her knight in shining armour and forcibly evict John Boyle by the seat of the pants – on the other hand, John Boyle wasn't wearing any pants, was he? But now it was too late, and Declan came to the painful conclusion that he'd just made a major tactical error.

"So that's all you have to say – is it, you slimy bastard?" yelled Sasha. "Well, *I'll* show you what I think of liars and spineless toads!"

With that, she slammed the door in Declan's face. Then Declan heard the sound of a window inside being opened – from memory, he concluded that it was the bedroom window that looked out over the flowerbeds – then he heard curses, accompanied by ripping sounds, and John Boyle crying: "Aah no, Sasha, he doesn't deserve that!"

Suddenly, Declan realised what was happening inside. And he felt that he might be in danger of having a coronary. This couldn't be happening to him . . . He began banging on the door. "Sasha, don't – *please* – "

Suddenly the door opened, and a ruffled but triumphant Sasha stood before him.

"Now, you weak-kneed little shit, you can collect your belongings – they've left by express delivery out the window!"

Declan didn't even wait to remonstrate. Suddenly, he was running down the stairs, muttering to himself. "Please God! I know I haven't bothered about you for years, but I'm begging you, please don't let my precious autograph book be ruined – I swear I'll start going to church again, if you'll just do this one little favour for me –"

But clearly, Declan's God wasn't in the humour to bargain with a loser. When Declan arrived panic-stricken at the flowerbed, he found that his clothes had been ripped, his CD cases broken – but worst of all, his precious autograph book and its photographs lay in flitters among the shrubs and plants, fanned out like confetti after a wedding.

Declan Dunne, who hadn't cried since he fell out of an apple-tree at six years of age, sat down amid the wreckage of his life and wept.

CHAPTER 24

The following morning, Joanna arrived early at the trade union's headquarters in Liberty Hall, on Eden Quay. She took the lift to the sixth floor and found that branch secretary George Mullan was already at his desk and ready to see her.

"You said you wanted information on Harry Sweeney – well, I dug out his employment record, so I can give you his address at the time of his – eh – imprisonment."

"Thanks," said Joanna, taking the seat offered. "Does it mention what his wife's name was?"

"Hmm, let's see. Here it is – it was Maura."

"Anything about their child – or children?"

George Mullan scanned the card again. "There's no mention of any children here. And unfortunately I wouldn't know anything about him personally." He smiled apologetically. "He was long dead before I came to work here." Seeing Joanna's crestfallen face, he went on hurriedly, "But there's someone here who used to be a good friend of Harry Sweeney's. Would you like to speak to him?"

Joanna's eyes lit up. "Oh yes, that would be marvellous!"

Joanna took the cup of tea offered to her and sat drinking it while George Mullan telephoned his colleague, who was working on another floor of the building.

He put the phone down and smiled at her. "He'll be with you in a minute, so I'll leave the two of you to talk alone." Gathering up some papers, he left the office.

Before long, a portly, elderly man appeared and grasped Joanna's hand firmly. "Colman Donnelly," he said. "I'm glad Harry hasn't been forgotten. I presume you're going to open the case and hopefully clear his name this time?"

"Well, that's not exactly why I'm here."

"I thought George said you were a solicitor?"

Joanna quickly explained her mission, telling him about the strange bequest to the offspring of Harry Sweeney.

"But Harry didn't have any children," said Colman, looking puzzled. "He'd always wanted children – I know that because he used to say how much he envied Rose and me our three boys. He told me they weren't able to have any of their own."

"Maybe they adopted after that?"

Colman looked sceptical. "No, they didn't. Harry and I worked together, right up until his arrest, so I would have known something like that. And he would have told me if his wife had become pregnant – because he would have been over the moon about it."

Joanna looked closely at him. "So you don't think Harry murdered Colette Devane?"

Colman gave her a withering look. "Harry Sweeney wouldn't hurt a fly. Besides, he was very fond of his sister-in-law. I've always believed that he was set up."

"Colman," said Joanna earnestly, " I know very little about Harry Sweeney. I was hoping you could fill me in."

"Well, there's not much more I can tell you. Except that he was a fine trade unionist and a man of principle. Harry Sweeney was no murderer."

"Did you ever hear anything about – another woman?"

Colman looked surprised. "I've never heard of anything like that. If Harry had anyone else, he kept it very quiet. Why do you ask?"

Joanna blushed. "I don't really know. I suppose I'm trying to find out if there could have been a child by anyone else."

Colman shook his head. "Harry and I worked together for about fifteen years – since he joined the union straight from university. I never heard of any other woman in his life except his wife Maura." He smiled. "But if you ever *do* come in contact with Maura during your search, you can tell her there's a sum of money waiting for her in mortality benefit. We tried to contact her after Harry's death, but we were told she'd gone to England not long before he was charged."

Suddenly, Joanna wondered if Maura might have been pregnant when she'd left for England. Maybe even Harry hadn't known.

"None of us believed that Harry was guilty of murder," Colman added. "Many of our members attended the funeral – myself included – but there was no sign of his wife at either the church or the graveside."

142

Joanna frowned. "If he was set up for the murder of Colette Devane, who do you think might have done that?"

Once again, Colman Donnelly shook his head. "I don't know, but there were plenty of people who didn't like Harry. He didn't let anyone walk over our members – if there was a whiff of trouble on a building site, he was in there, demanding action or he'd pull all the workers off the site. As branch secretary, he was responsible for the scaffolders, crane-operators, hod-carriers and general ops. And he cared for those guys like they were his own family."

Joanna inclined her head, willing him to go on.

"Back in the late sixties," he went on, "there were lots of dodgy builders trying to get rich quick. At the time, it was said that every third house went to the builder in profit. And none of those builders gave a damn about safety on the site or paying proper wages. Many of them operated the lump system, which meant that workers were paid in cash, and the employer paid no tax or insurance – which meant there was no compensation if anyone was injured, since technically they didn't exist. But Harry kept up the pressure to get the workers protected. He was like a dog with a bone – he just wouldn't let go."

"So Harry would have made enemies."

"Lots of them. There wasn't a builder in the country who didn't loathe him. But Harry didn't care – he was offered many a bribe to turn a blind eye to certain things, but he wasn't having any of it. He used to say that he wouldn't be able to sleep at night if he took the traitor's shilling."

"By the sound of it, Harry stepped on plenty of toes," said Joanna.

Just as she was about to leave, George returned to the office. Thanking the two officials for their help, she shook hands with them both.

"Do you think there'll ever be justice for poor Harry?" asked Colman as she walked towards the door.

"I hope so," said Joanna, "I sincerely hope so."

Leaving the union offices, Joanna took the lift to the ground floor and headed back along the quays towards her own office. She was pleased that other people thought highly of Harry, but perplexed that there didn't appear to be any child. Unless Maura had been pregnant at the time of Harry's arrest? But Colman Donnelly had said that Harry and Maura "weren't able" to have children. She needed to visit Harry's last address – maybe his neighbours would know more about the Sweeney family. Well, one thing is certain, she thought to herself, the more I dig into this business, the more I realise I definitely need the services of a private detective to tackle this part of the puzzle.

Back in the office, she rang Tom. "I've got the name of Harry's wife from his trade union – it was Maura. By all accounts, he was a really nice guy."

Tom laughed. "I'm relieved to hear that Harry has some redeeming features – especially since my mother's chosen to be buried with him! But have you found out anything else about him?" He was filled with excitement and dread at the same time. "You know – any more about the link with my mother?" Part of him wanted to solve the mystery, yet the other part of him was afraid of what dark family secrets might be uncovered.

"No, I'm afraid not. Except that there are no children of his mentioned in the trade union records, and an official who knew Harry well says Harry and Maura were unable to have any."

Tom was silent for a moment while he digested this new information. At last, he said, "It's all very weird, isn't it, Jo? How could my mother leave an inheritance to someone who doesn't seem to exist?"

"Don't worry, Tom – we'll find out eventually. But it may take a little time."

"But you shouldn't have to do all this legwork yourself, Jo. Employ people to do it for you – there's no shortage of money. I realise that you have to get your own practice up and running – "

"Tom, this is personal," she interrupted. "Your family and mine have been linked together for as long as I can remember. And I'm grateful to your mother for entrusting me with such a responsibility. This is important to me."

"Thanks, Jo, I really appreciate that."

"You're welcome, Tom. But, speaking of legwork, I was in fact thinking of employing a private detective – I think it's our only option."

"That's fine by me, Jo. And if there's anything I can do – I mean, do you want *me* to contact anyone?"

"Not at all, Tom," she replied hastily. "I don't think you should have to worry about such details. I feel guilty that I haven't made the progress I'd like to have made by now. But I'll let you know as soon as I make any further headway."

Tom sighed softly. It looked like Joanna was giving him the brush-off. He was anxious about the will, of course, but he had also had the hope that if he got involved in helping Joanna, he'd get a chance to see her more often. And who knows, maybe she'd get used to having him around . . .

At the other end of the phone, Joanna was sighing softly too. She felt guilty that she hadn't more to tell him – maybe she shouldn't have taken on the lease and conveyancing cases as well. She didn't want him to think that she was so incompetent at administering his mother's will that he needed to do the actual work himself! But she feared that in her embarrassment it mightn't have sounded quite the way she meant it. If only she wasn't so attracted to him, it would be a lot easier to deal with him.

"OK, Joanna, I'll keep on searching through the study." Tom took a deep breath and plunged in. "The only problem is – since I'm not a legal person, I'm not even certain what I'm looking for." Did that sound lame? After all, he didn't need legal expertise to spot the name Harry Sweeney in a document. He plunged on. "Is there any chance you might come over here yourself – and take a look? I promise that in return for your help with the search, I'll either cook you a nice meal, or we can go out for dinner afterwards. Whichever you prefer."

There was a momentary silence at the other end of the line as Joanna waited for her heartbeat to slow down enough for her to speak.

Oh God, thought Tom, I've blown it. She's trying to think up an excuse for not coming round. I should never have said anything –

"Oh, Tom, that would be lovely," said Joanna breathlessly. "I remember what a great cook you were years ago, so I presume you still are – " Why do I sound so stupid when I want to sound interesting, she asked herself as she babbled on. "I remember how sometimes you used to cook dinner for our mothers, my dad and me – "

"When are you free?" He was hoping against hope that she wouldn't make him wait days before he could see her. Already he could imagine her in the Ballsbridge house, working at the desk in the study, making coffee in the kitchen, playing with the children – *their* children – or just snuggled up beside him on a couch by the fireside . . . Sweat broke out on his forehead. He must be mad to entertain these thoughts! She wasn't likely to think of him that way. And if he said anything, he might risk damaging a lifelong friendship . . .

Joanna thought frantically. She wanted to say: Now! Immediately! But she was also aware that Mary had made several evening appointments with clients who couldn't get to her office any earlier in the day. Up to now, it hadn't mattered, but at this instant, she wanted to cancel every other appointment in the world! And she'd need time to get her hair done as well . . .

"Can I call you after I've checked the diary?" she said miserably.

"OK," said Tom, again feeling that he was being given the brush-off. "Ring me when you've got some free time."

Then he hung up, and Joanna sat there close to tears, feeling that somehow, something had suddenly gone terribly wrong.

CHAPTER 25

Agnes dialled Catherine's number. She was in a state of excitement as she spoke. "Cat – Harry's booked the tickets! We've got our visas organised too, and we're leaving next week!"

"That's wonderful, Agnes – I'm thrilled for you both! But I'll miss you terribly."

"I know, Cat – and I'll miss you. But I'm so excited!"

"Bill and I will take you to the airport – and you must let me know if there's anything else we can do for you. We've a few hundred pounds saved – you're welcome to that. And we have some old suitcases that might be useful."

"Thanks, Cat – I'll take up your offer of the suitcases, but keep the money to buy your own tickets when you come out to visit us."

"Nonsense – I insist you take it. Bill said you must!"

Agnes laughed joyfully. "Oh, all right, Cat – thank you, I'll take it. I can hardly believe it's actually happening! We're finally on our way to Australia!"

"Have you told Harry about the baby yet?"

"Yes, and he's thrilled."

"Well, don't wear yourself out, Agnes – you should be taking it easy, you know."

"Don't worry, Cat – this time next week, I'll be lying on an Australian beach, and I promise you that from then on, I'll do nothing but take it easy!"

Catherine couldn't help being caught up in Agnes's enthusiasm. She was also relieved that at last Agnes and Harry had a definite date for their departure. Catherine had feared that the longer they waited, the more likelihood there was that Ivan would discover their plans. And she disliked that shifty-looking character Paddy Byrne, Ivan's lackey and right-hand man, who always seemed to be snooping around the Ballsbridge house supposedly doing odd jobs, because she feared that he might overhear something and report it back to Ivan. Now, however, it looked as though the future was assured for Agnes and Harry.

* * *

But the day before Agnes and Harry's departure to Australia, Catherine received an urgent phone call from Agnes.

"Cat, Dad's just had a heart attack. I'm driving over to the hospital right away – can you contact Harry and tell him? I'll try to phone him later."

"Of course, Agnes. How serious is it?"

"I don't know. I'll phone you later, Cat."

Immediately after Agnes rang off, Catherine phoned Harry and told him what had happened.

"Oh God, no! Why does it have to happen now?" Harry exclaimed. "Trust the old devil to pull a stunt like this! I hope this doesn't mean we have to postpone leaving for Australia!"

"I don't know, Harry," said Catherine sadly. She'd been so worried in case something stopped their planned departure. Now, it looked as though it might.

* * *

"Cat, what can I do? Dad is really ill – I'd never forgive myself if I left him like this. I mean, he has no one else to be there for him."

"Well, it was he himself who drove poor Joseph away," said Catherine reasonably.

"I know, but I feel guilty, Cat. After all, Dad intended the best for Joseph and me, even if it wasn't what we wanted."

"You're too much of a softy, Agnes, when it comes to your father," said Catherine. "I'm just worried in case you miss your flight tomorrow."

"Well, I've actually asked Harry to cancel the flight, Cat, and put back our departure date by a week. By then Dad will either have pulled through, or . . ."

Catherine sighed. "I understand, Agnes. What else could you do? He is your father, after all."

But even after she'd put the phone down, Catherine couldn't shake off a terrible sense of foreboding. So near and yet so far, she thought. She was inexplicably angry at Agnes's father. It almost seemed as though he'd planned his heart attack to mess up his daughter's plans. Then Catherine felt guilty for thinking ill of an old man who was frail and probably in fear for his own life. Maybe it was all for the best. If the heart attack had happened after Agnes had left for Australia, she'd probably have believed that her own departure brought it on and been filled with guilt. On the other hand, if Phelim Cashen died, Agnes and Harry would have real money in their pockets when they left for Australia. Catherine sighed. She just wished that whatever was going to happen would happen soon. Either way, she couldn't help being worried. There was now another whole week's wait before Agnes and Harry could board that plane and get safely away. Another week during which anything could go wrong . . .

CHAPTER 26

Joanna sat at her desk, thumbing through the notes she'd made about Agnes Kilmartin's will. She bit her lip. She hadn't really achieved very much. But it had been a hectic week so far – twice she'd had to attend court, over issues she felt could well have been resolved with just a little give and take by the clients on both sides. But then, she mused, if people were prepared to deal reasonably with each other, she'd be out of a job very quickly!

It was late afternoon and she was just considering whether to pack up and head home, or ring Orla and hopefully meet up for a drink on the way, when the phone on her desk rang. Joanna's heart jumped. For one wild and wonderful moment, she thought that it might be Tom.

"Hello?"

"Joanna," said Mary, "I'm putting through a call from one of Mrs Kilmartin's nurses."

Joanna perked up instantly. Why would one of Agnes's nurses be being ringing *her*?

"Is that Joanna Brennan?" the voice at the other end of

the line asked. "Hi – my name is Lisa Noonan. I met you when you called to see Mrs Kilmartin, the day before she died – "

"Hi, Lisa! How can I help you?"

"Well, I've been meaning to phone you, but after Mrs Kilmartin died, I was transferred to night duty, which meant that I was sleeping during the day, and it was too late to contact you when I got up – "

Get on with it, thought Joanna uncharitably.

"I hope you won't be annoyed with me for taking so long to get in touch, but to be honest I think she was just hallucinating – I hope you won't think I'm just wasting your time – I know how busy –"

"Lisa," Joanna interrupted, "what is it you want to tell me?"

"Well, Mrs Kilmartin told me to be sure to contact you but –"

"About what, Lisa?" Joanna asked, her curiosity now well and truly whetted.

"Well, later that evening, after you'd gone, she got very upset. I think she realised that she wouldn't last until the next day. So she grabbed my arm when I came over to the bed and said that I was to phone you, and tell you that the cat'll have the documents."

"The cat'll have the documents! Are you sure that's what she said?"

"Yes, I think so," said Lisa apologetically. "I thought she was just rambling – old folk are liable to do that. If you worked with as many as I do, you'd know how –"

"Lisa," Joanna cut in, "tell me word for word exactly what she said – it could be very important.'

"I'm afraid that's all she said. She grabbed my arm and whispered to me: 'Tell Joanna that the cat'll have the documents – it's very important.' I think that if she'd been a bit more lucid, she might have explained what she meant. Then she took a fit of coughing, so she wasn't able to talk any more." Lisa sighed. "But I promised her that I'd tell you that. It probably doesn't make sense to you, does it? Maybe she was just hallucinating after all? The medication can have strange effects."

"I don't really know," Joanna replied, "but thanks for telling me anyway, Lisa. And if you think of anything else – no matter how insignificant – please let me know, won't you?"

Lisa assured her that she would, and Joanna took down her home phone number just in case she needed to contact her again. After Lisa had rung off, Joanna sat staring at the doodles of a cat that she'd made while speaking to her. What on earth could Agnes Kilmartin have meant? There was Devil, her own cat, but Agnes Kilmartin wouldn't have known about her, because Joanna hadn't seen the old woman since she'd acquired the kitten. Could she have been referring to a china ornament of a cat? Joanna frowned as she racked her brains. Maybe Tom would know something about it.

Cat? Could she have meant Cat – Catherine? If so, that was bad news – how on earth could Catherine reveal anything? Nothing her mother said made sense any more.

CHAPTER 27

Garda Detective Sergeant Mick McHale (retired) was feeling pleased with himself. He'd been feeling quite bored when Orla Rogan from the *Evening Dispatch* had phoned him. She needed some information, and he was more than happy to oblige.

Since he'd had to retire early, Mick McHale was glad of any project that he could get his teeth into. Although he acted as a consultant on security matters for a number of companies, that was pretty routine stuff. He sorely missed his job with the Special Branch, where every day presented a different challenge. But his last job – the big heist that ended with him being shot in both legs – had effectively ended his career with the Irish police force. He'd been left with a serious limp – "a gammy leg" as he called it – which rendered him useless in undercover operations, where speed was essential for successful missions.

He could have taken a desk job but he would have

hated it. So he'd retired at forty-one, with citations for bravery and a big send-off from the lads, held at the Garda Club in Harrington Street. He'd been presented with a large-screen television and video recorder, a parting gift from his colleagues, and he'd wondered cynically if they thought that was all he was fit for in the future – watching television and seeing other people carrying out the action, instead of being part of it himself.

But Mick McHale was a man with a pragmatic approach to life, and a deep vein of humour ran through his soul. So he made light of the abrupt ending of his career – "a career break" he called it instead – and he applied himself to a number of other projects, such as the charities that he admired, for which he became an avid voluntary collector. He also gave talks on the law to the poorly funded and cash-strapped animal welfare groups around the country, occasionally intervening when they were having trouble with repeat "offenders". He could never fathom how people could be cruel to their fellow creatures. Did they have no feelings for the poor horse or donkey that pulled their cart, or the dog that rounded up their sheep? Fortunately, a few words from an ex-Garda could work wonders when someone was found abusing an animal.

Jim reached for a notepad and starting writing a reminder for himself. Orla wanted him to check a few things for her, and he was more than glad to help.

Jim liked Orla Rogan. She was a level-headed young woman with a sense of humour not unlike his own, so they got on extremely well. Their first contact had taken place years before, through the Garda Press Office, when a query from Orla regarding a particular operation being undertaken by Special Branch was referred directly to him. It had been a sensitive issue, and he'd had to confide to her – strictly off the record – a little more information than he'd have preferred. Afterwards, he'd waited fearfully in case she was one of those journalists who was more interested in gaining a one-off "scoop" than in building up confidential sources. But Orla had honoured his confidences, and over the years they'd built up such a rapport that now she often rang him directly at his home. She'd even visited him when he was in hospital having his gunshot wounds treated, and he'd made sure that she was invited to his retirement party in the Garda Club.

Orla had also met, and liked, his late wife Sheila. Poor Sheila, his childhood sweetheart whom he'd married just after he'd finished his training at Templemore Garda College, had died of a brain tumour two years before. When they'd married, he'd only been twenty and she nineteen. They'd produced three fine daughters – all now in stable relationships themselves – the eldest of whom would soon be making him a grandfather. God Almighty, he thought grinning to himself, I'm going to be a grandfather, and I'm only forty-five!

I'm getting old, he thought, yet he wasn't displeased at the thought. He'd already led a full and productive life, so maybe it was time to slow down. Yet something inside him rebelled. He was halfway through his allotted lifespan, and there was still an awful lot of living to do! Who knew what sort of challenges lay around the next corner? He chuckled to himself at his own fancifulness.

But he'd never find another woman like his beloved

Sheila. So he'd ruled out any future relationships, instead filling his time with being a good father to his daughters, and he intended to be a good grandfather to his grandkids. That was one advantage about marrying so young – it meant that he would still be young enough himself to make a real contribution to his grandchildren's lives. None of his daughters had chosen the Gardaí as a career, but maybe one of his grandchildren would, Jim mused. However, he'd definitely be ancient before *that* happened!

What was it Orla had said? Ah yes, she wanted the information for a friend of hers – a solicitor branching out on her own. This friend of hers needed the name of a good, reliable private detective, to trace some beneficiary of a will. Well, he knew just the man for the job. He'd been very impressed by Ronan O'Farrell's work – the man always got results.

Orla had also confided in him that her friend was working on a dog-bite case, on behalf of the owner of the dog – whom Orla herself fancied. Poor Orla – she hadn't had much luck with men, Jim conceded. He was relieved that she'd got rid of that Declan idiot – maybe something might work out for her with this dog owner.

Instinctively, Jim was on the side of the dog. His work as a Garda on the beat, then as a sergeant, and later still in the Special Branch, had given him a rather jaundiced view of human nature. For every decent person out there, he conceded, there was another one who was a scoundrel.

Mick McHale sighed. Well, he wished Orla's friend good luck in her new career. But she was entering a profession where she too would soon discover all that is worst in human nature. Solicitors took up the job after people like him had prepared the initial cases. And he knew how pissed off the Gardaí were when solicitors and judges seemed to conspire to get hardened criminals off on some technicality. But that was the way justice worked – and should work – even though it could be maddening at times. Mick McHale picked up the telephone and began dialling.

CHAPTER 28

"I do miss, him, Cat. I know Dad was a hard taskmaster, but at times he could be very generous."

Catherine nodded as she slipped her arm in Agnes's, while Ivan gripped his wife's other arm proprietorially. Ahead of them, the hearse carrying Agnes's father's coffin drove slowly down the narrow cemetery road towards the open grave. Behind the hearse, the trio followed, and behind them walked hundreds of mourners who had come to pay their respects.

Bill walked along behind his beloved Catherine, pondering on the old man's timing. But although Phelim Cashen's illness and death had seemed like an inconvenience at first, now it meant Agnes and Harry would be able to leave for Australia without worrying about money. Agnes would now be due a large inheritance. Bill found himself grinning with pleasure at the thought of it all. This would mean that Harry wouldn't have to worry about finding work straight away. The couple could take their time settling in, or maybe they'd even travel around Australia, experiencing the length and breadth of their *new homeland first! By all accounts, Australia was a stunning country, and since the Cashen wealth was so great, Harry could even choose never to work again!*

Bill looked at the sombre faces around him and tried his best to look mournful. Yet he couldn't stop smiling. He was so pleased for Agnes – at last she was breaking free from that bully of a husband. Catherine would miss her friend desperately, but now that Agnes and Harry would no longer need the few hundred pounds they'd promised them, maybe he and Catherine could afford the fare out to visit them in Australia. Maybe they'd go this time next year – when Harry and Agnes were properly settled in . . .

* * *

"It can't be true – I don't believe you!"

"I'm sorry, Mrs Kilmartin, but that is what your father designated in his will."

"But to leave me nothing – how could he do that to me?"

In the solicitor's office, Ivan sat grinning beside his wife. Because he had just become the sole beneficiary of Phelim Cashen's will. As Phelim's surrogate son, not only had he inherited Cashen Kilmartin Construction Ltd, but he'd also been given all the Cashen millions as well.

The solicitor smiled unctuously at Agnes. "Well, Mrs Cashen, it's not entirely true to say that your father left you nothing. Since he's left it all to your husband, you will, of course, benefit indirectly. No doubt your father intended that your husband continues to maintain you in your – ahem – comfortable lifestyle."

"But it's so unfair – are you absolutely sure there's no way around it? Surely I can contest it?"

The solicitor smiled again, and Agnes longed to hit him. "I

regret to inform you, Mrs Kilmartin, your father's will is perfectly clear. Your husband is the sole beneficiary."

Outside the solicitor's office, the smug smile left Ivan's face. And his voice was menacing when he spoke to his wife.

"From now on, bitch, you'll do exactly as I say. And don't think I don't know about Harry Sweeney – if I find out that you're still seeing him, I'll evict you without a penny."

Agnes blinked away her tears of anger and frustration. How had Ivan found out about Harry? Things were going from bad to worse, but she was determined not to let Ivan see how distressed she was. How could her father have done this to her? Had he decided that since she was "only" a woman, she wouldn't be capable of looking after herself? The chauvinist! And while she could see the logic of keeping the company in the hands of the person currently running it, why couldn't her father have left her a sum of money for her own use? There was so much money in the Cashen estate – if only he'd left her a token few thousand! Having a little money would have made such a difference to her and Harry.

Agnes turned to Ivan, trying to hide the loathing she felt. "Yes, Ivan," she said meekly.

After all, in a few days' time, she and Harry would finally be on their way to Australia! She could put up with Ivan's insults until then.

CHAPTER 29

At first the line was engaged, but finally Joanna got through to Tom's office at the university, where he was getting things organised for the start of the forthcoming new term.

"Tom – I hope I'm not interrupting anything –" Joanna's heart was beating uncomfortably.

"Not at all, Jo, delighted to hear from you."

Tom's voice *did* sound quite happy – but was it because he was talking to *her* or just because he was in good humour?

"I wonder, Tom – this will sound strange – but do you know anything about a cat? Did your mother collect china cat ornaments, for instance?"

Tom laughed. "No, I don't think so. Why on earth are you asking me about that?"

Quickly, she explained about the phone call from Lisa Noonan. Tom was astonished.

"You don't have another cat now, do you, Tom? I

know your mum didn't want another one after Binkie died – "

"No, we never replaced Binkie," he confirmed. "Honestly, Jo, I haven't a clue what Mum could have meant. Is there any chance that she was just hallucinating? Maybe her medication was making her say strange things?"

"Well, that's what the nurse seemed to think – I think that was partly why she took so long to contact me – she didn't really think it made any sense. I don't know. I guess it's going to remain a mystery for the present."

"Yes – another one," he sighed. There was a pause. "But Jo, have you decided when you can call around to the house to go through the documents?"

Joanna's heart soared. "Eh, yes – any day next week would be fine."

"Great. How about Monday evening? I'll cook a roast, if you like. You certainly *used* to like my cooking – but are you too sophisticated for such humble fare nowadays?"

Joanna could detect the humour in his voice, so she relaxed. "That sounds terrific. And, Tom – do you think you could make one of your fantastic banoffee pies? No one makes them quite like you!"

He chuckled. "OK, Jo – you're on! I'll see you on Monday evening. Is seven o'clock OK?"

"Perfect," she said, but food was the last thing on her mind.

After the call ended, Joanna sat dreamily staring into space. Only a few days to go. She would have to get her hair done, of course. And maybe she'd leave the office a bit earlier that evening and wear the lime-green dress she'd bought in the Ilac Shopping Centre. It hadn't exactly been cheap, she knew that she'd feel a million dollars in it, and on Monday evening, she'd desperately need to feel that she was looking her absolute best.

Rising to her feet, Joanna stretched languidly. Oh how she longed to wrap her arms around Tom Kilmartin's neck and kiss his adorable lips . . .

Still dreaming of Tom, she opened the door and stepped out into the reception area to bring Mary up to date. And to suggest that they have that cup of tea and one of their precious Mikado biscuits. Suddenly, she realised that Mary was hunched over her computer, sniffling.

"What's wrong, Mary?" she asked in alarm.

Mary raised a tearful face. "Oh, Jo – it's that son of mine again. Do you know what he's gone and done? He's deliberately scraped the side of a neighbour's new car – he thought it was a great joke!" She blew her nose, making it even redder. She looked a sight. "Now the neighbour's gone to the guards, and the local sergeant just rang to say that Paul is going to end up in a juvenile detention centre if I can't control him!"

There was nothing Joanna could do to comfort her friend, except put her arms around her and give her a hug.

"Let's have a cup of tea while we think about what can be done," she said firmly, trying to sound as though she had everything under control. "Don't worry, Mary – we'll sort things out in no time at all. I'm sure Paul was only doing it out of high spirits – not for any malicious reason. Give me the sergeant's phone number, and I'll have a word with him."

"Oh, Jo – thank you so much. I wasn't very intelligible on the phone, I'm afraid. I got such a shock!"

Having put the kettle on, Joanna took down the sergeant's number and headed into her office to phone. Hopefully, this would be one occasion where her status as a solicitor would be of some help.

"Sergeant O'Reilly? Good afternoon. My name is Joanna Brennan. I'm a solicitor and employer of Mary O'Dowd, to whom you've just been speaking. Yes, that's right – about her son Paul." Then, putting on her most officious voice, she asked the sergeant exactly how serious the situation was.

"Well, Ms Brennan, the situation is this," the sergeant said. "That young fellow is going to find himself in deep trouble if someone doesn't keep a close watch on him. His neighbour is up in arms, and rightly so – the boy dragged some sharp object along the side of the man's new car. I've seen it myself – and there's a big scratch that's the length of the driver's door. Needless to say, the man isn't too happy about that – and deliberately causing damage is a criminal offence."

"I know, Sergeant, I know," Joanna said. "Unfortunately, his mother is a single parent who needs to work full-time, and I don't think his dad takes any interest. Is the neighbour likely to press charges?"

The sergeant cleared his throat. "Well, as a matter of fact, I've got him to agree to drop the charges this time – as long as the damage is paid for. Seeing as the young lad hasn't offended before . . . "

"Oh, thank you, Sergeant!" Joanna said with relief.

"But I'm perfectly serious when I say that lad's going

to end up in trouble," warned the sergeant. "That's how it starts, you know. Then they get in with a gang of older boys, and their activities get more serious. Someone needs to give him a talking-to. Otherwise, he'll end up breaking his poor mother's heart."

After Joanna came off the phone, she put Mary out of her misery by assuring her that no charges were being pressed. Not this time, anyway, as long as the damages were paid for.

Mary was relieved but still worried about Paul's future. "Oh, Joanna," she said, looking up through a fresh bout of tears, "what am I going to do about that boy? He's only thirteen, but he's been a handful ever since Leo and I split up. Emma, his sister, is no trouble at all – why oh why can't he behave himself?"

Joanna patted Mary's shoulder and encouraged her to drink her cup of tea. She didn't know much about rearing children herself, but she could imagine what a traumatic experience this was for poor Mary, since she was bound to feel a failure as a parent.

"Look, why don't we all – you, me and your two kids – go out for the day, maybe on Saturday?" said Joanna. "We could go to the cinema, then maybe go somewhere for something to eat. That would give the kids a bit of fun, and you a bit of breathing space. And it would be *my* treat."

Mary smiled gratefully at Joanna as she dried her tears. "That's really thoughtful of you, Joanna – I'm sure the kids would love it. It would also be a chance for you to meet them both – and I'll kill Paul if he's not on his best behaviour!"

Joanna smiled. "Go on home now, Mary – you've done enough work for today. There's only the post to be done, and I can finish that off myself."

"Oh, Jo – you're the best employer in the whole world!" said Mary, giving her a fierce hug.

"I hope I'm also your friend – not just your employer," said Joanna, feeling a lump in her throat. "We're in this together, Mary – and I certainly regard you as *my* friend!"

After Mary had left the office, issuing dire threats as to what she was going to do to Paul when she got home, Joanna started sticking stamps on the letters to be posted. She wished that there was more that she could do to help Mary – it must be so difficult rearing two youngsters all by herself. At least she could give the kids a nice day out on Saturday. Mary probably couldn't afford to give them many treats, since Joanna knew exactly what her salary was. And Mary now had the additional expense of repairing her neighbour's car door. Joanna sighed. Hopefully, when the business established itself, she could give Mary an increase. And she resolved to try and find discreet ways of helping her, but it wouldn't be easy, since her friend was fiercely proud and would be unwilling to accept anything that she felt smacked of "charity".

Bundling up the post, Joanna locked the office, went down the stairs and let herself out of the building. A quick mail-drop in the post-office box at the corner, and then she would head home.

CHAPTER 30

Jackie Byrne drove the car onto the ferry at Dun Laoghaire. It was a beauty – a dark green Jensen – and he felt powerful and important as he saw the ferry terminal officials looking respectfully at him as he drove past them. The car screamed money and privilege, and the smell of the leather seats was intoxicating. Pity the car wasn't his, but in a day or two, when he drove it from Holyhead to London, it would net him a tidy sum. It had been stolen to order, and soon it would disappear into a lock-up in East London, to re-emerge later with a new English number plate and log book. And Jackie would return to Dublin by train and ferry, having changed his sterling to euro, with a big wad of cash in his pocket.

Jackie Byrne was what Detective Sergeant Mick McHale would have described as a "low-life". He was a sour, bitter individual, who'd grown up in one of Dublin's tower blocks in Ballymun, a disastrous highrise social housing project. As a child, he'd watched his mother commit suicide from the top of one of the towers.

Jackie's life improved when his father went to work for Ivan Kilmartin. Over a period of years on building sites, Paddy Byrne proved his worth to the millionaire businessman, gradually assuming the position of lackey and right-hand man. When Ivan needed a job done, Paddy got it sorted. There was plenty of money by then, and Paddy and his son moved into a very comfortable house in the south city suburbs, so that Paddy would be near when Ivan needed him. Paddy used his influence with Ivan to get work for Jackie too. But Jackie didn't have quite as strong a stomach as his old man . . .

Jackie was relieved when his father died, and now, several years later, he could look back on events with equanimity. Over the years, his father had involved him in too many hair-raising stunts for his liking. He'd had to drive the getaway car for a robbery at seventeen, and his father had him dealing in drugs by the time he was eighteen. And once, when he'd only been in his late teens, his father had made him agree to be a witness in a murder trial. Of course, the guy hadn't done it, but Jackie had been primed to say that he'd seen him at the murder scene. Jackie had been worried in case his own criminal record emerged, but fortunately he'd never actually had to testify – his dad had ensured that the case never got to court. Jackie was very relieved, because he'd been afraid he might lose his cool under cross-examination.

While Jackie was far from being a philosophical man, there were times when he liked to think back on how bad things had once been and how much better off he was now. As he surveyed the interior of the car, now parked up for the sea crossing, he felt invincible. If only he wasn't tied to that useless cow, Ellen. Back then, he'd really fancied her, and his father had urged him to marry her with the promise of his own house, paid for in full by Ivan Kilmartin.

At least he'd taught her who was boss – in the early years he'd taken too much lip from her, but he'd learned to shut her up with a well-aimed blow to the side of the head or a kick to her barren stomach. Jackie still felt angry and cheated after all these years. His father had conned him into marrying her, then he'd discovered she couldn't even give him a child. The dirty bitch had been infected by a john long before he'd come on the scene.

He made a face as he stepped out of the car. Now, there was this messy business of a court case. He'd been too decent in letting his wife go to the doctor after he'd bitten her. The bitch deserved it, after all – she'd been whining at him as usual, and a man needed to keep his woman in check. The trouble was – she'd started bleeding badly from the bite, and he'd been frightened.

He'd got her to tell the doctor that the next-door dog had done it, then he'd tried to shake a few euro out of the guy who owned the dog. But the miserable toe-rag had refused to cough up. So he'd sent Ellen to the police to teach him a lesson, but now the whole episode had got out of hand. Jackie sighed. In his anger, he hadn't realised that it was the state itself who would take a case against the offender – and he might be roped in as a witness. One thing Jackie didn't need was close scrutiny from the police.

Having locked the car, he joined the throng of passengers climbing the stairs to the ship's various lounges. At one point, he aimed a sly kick at an old man ahead of

LINDA KAVANAGH

him, just for fun. The old man stumbled, and Jackie grinned
with satisfaction. The old geezer wouldn't dare complain –
anyway, who'd dare to challenge a guy driving a top-of-
the-range Jensen? In one of the bars, Jackie elbowed his
way to the counter and shouted his order over the heads of
others who were still waiting to be served. Then, taking his
beer – and ignoring the dagger looks he got from
passengers who should have been served before him – he
found himself a quiet corner seat and surveyed the scene.
Too many bloody kids running all over the place – if he had
his way, they'd all be dumped overboard.

As he sat sipping his pint, Jackie watched the Irish
coastline recede and the seagulls gather overhead, as the
ship dipped and rose though the waves. This is the life,
he thought to himself – it certainly beats a regular job.

In fact, Jackie had never had a regular job. He'd started
his career as a petty criminal, robbing elderly women's
handbags, before he'd even finished his schooling, which
had ended at primary level, anyway. The bane of his
teachers' lives, they'd been overjoyed whenever he
played truant – so much so that they never reported his
absences to the authorities. A classroom without his
disruptive influence was far preferable to one where
pupils and staff had to endure his glowering discontent
and barely suppressed anger.

Over the years, Jackie graduated from handbags to
housebreaking – and of course the riskier pursuits that
his father shoved him into – and had served a one-year
sentence in Mountjoy Jail by the time Paddy went to
work for Ivan Kilmartin. But his one and only stay in
prison provided Jackie with the education he was

previously lacking. But it wasn't the type that resulted in exam qualifications. Rather, he graduated to a different type of crime, having learnt all about auto-theft from another prisoner with whom he used to share cigarettes during recreation hours.

Since then, Jackie had beavered away in his new line of business, stealing, on average, two or three cars a month and taking them by boat to England. The tools of his trade were a lock-up garage in the suburbs, a set of Irish number plates, a set of English number plates and a set of skeleton keys. Additional outlay was minimal – no more than the price of a return ticket on the car ferry (he always bought a return ticket to allay suspicion, but he never used the return half). Yet the rewards were considerable, especially when he stole to order. And in tandem with his burgeoning criminal career, he also signed on for unemployment benefit, so that if he was ever questioned, he would be seen to have some legitimate income.

Jackie smiled to himself as the boat docked at the port in Holyhead. Heading down to the car deck to reclaim the Jensen, he began whistling as he approached the car. It would be a pleasant drive down to London on the motorways in such a classy car. Then maybe he'd visit a nightclub before making the return journey the following day. Hopefully, he'd also manage to pick up some accommodating bird in London, who'd satisfy his sexual needs. And hopefully, she'd take him back to her place, so he'd get free overnight accommodation as well. Jackie smiled at the thought of a free night of passion. He considered himself a thrifty man. Anyone else would have called him a cheapskate.

CHAPTER 31

Night was descending on the Phoenix Park, the largest city park in Europe, where countless Dubliners walked their dogs, played sports, rode horses or visited the zoo. But now, at eight o'clock, all the commuter traffic using the Park's main thoroughfare to reach Castleknock and environs had long since abated. Silence had replaced the earlier hum of traffic, and the only sounds to be heard now were the occasional walkers and their dogs, kids still using the playing fields as twilight descended and an occasional rustle of a plant being nibbled by the herd of sika deer that roamed the acres of green parkland.

The Phoenix Park was also an ideal location for lovers, and many couples availed of the privacy it offered. It was an ideal meeting place for Harry and Agnes, since they couldn't risk being seen together in public. Agnes had parked her new car in Parkgate Street, at the main entrance to the Park, and slid into Harry's car as soon as he arrived. Then they drove to one of the many secluded areas, where they could be together without fear of being interrupted.

Harry turned off the ignition and slipped his arms around Agnes. "God, I love you so much! I never knew what love was until I met you!"

"I love you too, Harry."

Time passed with no need for further words.

At last, as they sat quietly together, blissfully contemplating the future, Agnes said, "I can't wait to get out of this country, Harry, so that we can be together openly – not hiding all the time. I just wish my father had left me some money – I still can't believe he left everything to Ivan."

"I'm sorry too, love, because I'm sure you must feel hurt by what your father did. But I don't think he did it vindictively." Harry grinned as he lit up a cigarette. "After all, he didn't know that you'd need the money to run away with me! He obviously thought that you'd be living happily with Ivan for ever and ever."

"No one could ever live happily with Ivan," said Agnes, shuddering.

"Well, in just a few more days, you won't have to, either, my love," said Harry. "And don't worry about the money – we'll get by."

Agnes sighed. "I'm just furious that Ivan's getting it all, and neither Joseph nor I are getting a penny."

They sat on in silence, arms around each other. Then, outside the car, they suddenly heard a rustling sound.

"What was that?" said Agnes anxiously.

"Probably a squirrel," Harry replied, then he grinned. "Soon, my love, we'll be seeing kangaroos outside our window!"

Agnes smiled. "I've done a deal on the new car Dad bought me, Harry. I went to a little out-of-town garage today – Cat came with me – but the guy would only offer me half what it's worth! I was livid, but at least he's agreed to pay me cash upfront as soon as I can hand it over. So it'll give us some money towards our new life."

"That's great, love – but I wish you didn't have to do it."

Agnes looked at him tartly. "So you think I should leave Ivan yet another car? He's got four of his own already!"

"You know what I mean – I'm worried that I won't be able to give you the standard of living that you're used to."

"Harry," said Agnes, "nothing matters to me except being with you. Well, you and our baby."

Pulling her into his arms, he smothered her face with kisses. "It's wonderful, isn't it? I can still hardly believe it! I've always longed to be a father!"

Agnes laughed. "And you'd better give up the cigarettes when the baby arrives – I'm not having you blowing smoke all over it!"

"Say no more – I'll give them up immediately!" he said, lowering the window and throwing out the butt of the cigarette he had just finished smoking.

Smiling at his joy, Agnes luxuriated in the warmth of his embrace, but then she pulled away from him. "So, Harry, we really do have to leave now – before Ivan notices my bump, because it's going to start showing soon."

Harry nodded. "Don't worry, love – this day next week we'll be on the plane for Australia – look!"

Eagerly, he produced the updated tickets from the glove compartment. Then, as she examined them, he pulled her close to him again. "God, Agnes, I'm the happiest man in the world!"

Agnes smiled back at him. "You've sorted things out financially for Maura, haven't you?"

"Yes, of course. Poor Maura – it's the least I can do for her.

I've already signed the house and the insurance policies over to her, so she'll be OK."

"Good. I really liked her when I met her – but I can't imagine what she must think of me, since I'm stealing her husband!"

"Don't feel bad, love – I know how you feel – I feel guilty myself about our happiness when it means she'll be left alone. I'm just hoping, now that she's free of me, she may find someone who will make her as happy as we are. But, Agnes, she doesn't hate or resent you – like me, she accepts that the spark went out of our relationship long ago."

Agnes shivered. "I hope that never happens to us."

Harry took her face in his hands and kissed her fiercely. "Agnes – my love – my dearest love – you're more important to me than life itself. We'll be together forever, believe me. And our child will grow up strong and healthy in the Australian sun. And maybe there'll be brothers and sisters later – "

Outside, another car glided slowly by, stopped a little further up the side street and turned off its lights.

"Who do you think that is?" said Agnes anxiously.

"Dunno," said Harry. "Probably just another couple looking for somewhere quiet! They're probably pissed off because we got the most secluded spot!"

"I'm scared," said Agnes suddenly. "I wouldn't be surprised if Ivan had someone following me. He's ordered me not to see you any more."

"Jesus, Agnes – I didn't realise he knew that much about us!"

"I didn't want to worry you even more. But Ivan misses very little. He's told me to stay away from you, and I suspect his horrible lackey Paddy Byrne has been keeping an eye on me.

It's not for love of me, of course — Ivan's only worried about his own reputation. He'd hate anyone to know he was being cuckolded. He likes to be regarded as a great stud, and I know he has mistresses — well, at least one at the moment, anyway."

Harry nodded and sighed. "I suppose it's time I told you that I know who it is."

"My God — who?"

Harry took a deep breath. "She's my sister-in-law Colette, actually. Look, I know I should have told you before now, love. But I was afraid you'd be upset and that it might somehow affect your feelings for me —"

"Oh, Harry! How could it?"

He squeezed her hand. "I couldn't expect you to like your husband's mistress, but she's actually a decent kid. She's only nineteen, and she ran away from a very strict, religious family and was on the streets for a while before she met Ivan. The sad thing is — she thinks Ivan is wonderful. She's bowled over by his wealth, and she told me she's been asking him to leave his wife."

Agnes laughed. "Well, as the wife in question, you can tell her she's welcome to him! And the wealth she's so impressed with should rightly be mine! But Ivan wouldn't take kindly to being pestered — maybe you should warn her, Harry, for her own sake, to cool it a bit." Then she gave him a big smile. "Anyway, none of this will matter soon — because we'll be on our way to Australia!"

But Harry still looked sad. "I'm not likely to see her again before we leave, because I think she's still in England. You see," *he hesitated, "she's pregnant, and Maura's gone over to join her, to help her with the birth. In fact, she may well have had the baby by now."*

Agnes raised her eyebrows. "Is this Ivan's child she's having?"

Harry nodded. "But Ivan doesn't know – he thinks she's having an abortion. But I believe she's having it adopted before she comes back to Dublin."

"I see."

Harry looked anxiously at her face. "Are you all right about this news, love?"

Agnes nodded. "I think I'd have found it a bit hurtful, Harry, despite my hatred for Ivan, if it weren't for the fact I'm pregnant myself." She looked at him and smiled. "But now that I'm carrying your baby – it couldn't matter less!"

Harry heaved a sigh of relief as he hugged her. "Thank God for that! Nevertheless, I'm worried about her. I hope she'll be OK – Maura will support her through the birth, but poor Colette is so naïve."

Agnes kissed him. "That's just you, Harry. You're such a caring person – always worrying about someone else! The workers on building sites have been lucky to have you on their side. That's one of the reasons why I love you so much – you find good in everybody."

Harry grinned. "Nevertheless, I'll make an exception of your husband!" Then he looked serious again. "But I hate leaving the union without telling them, although I don't think I have any other choice. We daren't let anyone know about our plans."

"I know, Harry – but it will all be worth it in the end."

Agnes smiled. Soon, Ivan would be just a distant memory. "Will Maura be back before we leave?"

Harry wrinkled his brow. "I don't know – I'd hate to leave without saying goodbye to her. But she didn't say when she'd be back – anyway, I don't have any right to know what she's doing any more, do I?"

LINDA KAVANAGH

"No, you forfeited that right when you became involved with me."

Harry grinned. "And I don't regret a second of it!"

Agnes shivered as she looked out the car window. "Harry – I'm worried about that car parked across the road – why is it still there?"

"Stop worrying!" said Harry, scooping her into his arms. "It's just another courting couple, for heaven's sake – the Park is full of them!"

"Then why don't they want to go somewhere more private than here so close to us?"

Harry shrugged and looked at his watch. It was just eleven o'clock. "C'mon, I'd better get you back to your car," he said softly. "I didn't realise it was so late, and you'd better get home before Ivan."

Agnes nodded, reluctant to end this magical time together but knowing that Harry was right. He started the engine and drove back towards the lights of the city.

Finally, in Parkgate Street, he held her tightly before allowing her to step out of his car. "Chin up, my love," he whispered. "In only a few more days we'll be off!" Grinning, he attempted to imitate the sound of a didgeridoo, and Agnes ended up laughing at his pathetic attempts.

"That's better!" said Harry, with a satisfied smile.

As Agnes climbed into her own car, she and Harry blew silent kisses to each other. Maybe I'm just being paranoid, Agnes thought. Harry's right – our new life is just around the corner. Nothing can possibly stop us now.

CHAPTER 32

It was chaos at Mary's house when Joanna arrived mid-morning on Saturday. A feral cat had decided to give birth to several kittens in the shed, and both children were in a state of high excitement. Mary was having a difficult time getting them to leave the poor cat in peace. They kept bringing out food and trying to tempt the cat to eat, whereas she merely wanted to be left alone. So Mary was roaring at the top of her voice when Joanna arrived.

"Paul, Emma – get your bloody beds made – this is the tenth time I've told you! Nobody's leaving this house until your rooms are tidy!"

Joanna sat among the debris of the breakfast dishes, then decided that maybe she could help out by doing the washing-up while she was waiting. Mary emerged from the children's rooms, where she had been laying down the law about their responsibilities, and collapsed into a chair.

"Look, there's no need for you to do those, Joanna –

it's supposed to be Paul's turn to do the dishes this week, but he tries to avoid it every chance he gets."

"You look like you could do with a cup of tea," said Joanna, putting the kettle on. "Now, what are we going to do today? There's a good choice of movies on at the Odeon – hopefully, we can all agree on one of them. But first, I suggest we try out that new restaurant near the cinema. I've heard good reports about the food there. They do everything from burgers to pheasant and caviar, so hopefully we'll all find something on their menu that we'll like."

"That sounds great," said Mary. "I just hope the kids behave themselves."

"Of course they will," said Joanna, sounding more confident than she really felt. Being totally inexperienced with children – and teenagers to boot – she was simply hoping that the novelty of the day out would be sufficient to keep them from being bored and looking for mischief.

While Joanna and Mary were drinking their tea, both teenagers appeared, grinning conspiratorially, and declared that their rooms were spotless. As she was formally introduced to them, Joanna was surprised at how handsome and healthy both of them were. She could immediately see that Paul was the demon of the piece – he was clearly hyperactive and couldn't stand still for more than a few moments. That young lad needs a firm male hand, she thought – what a pity his father no longer takes any interest in him. Nor did he support the family financially – which probably accounted for Mary always seeming so tired and unable to handle the kids. Joanna sighed. No doubt the children were also aware of their father's lack of interest in them. It wouldn't take a child psychologist to figure out that any child's sense of self-confidence would be badly affected by that fact.

Looking surreptitiously at Mary, Joanna also realised what an attractive woman she really was – but her continually harassed expression made her look older and more severe. Wouldn't it be nice if Mary could meet a caring, loving man? Someone who could give her emotional support, share the financial burdens and give her the necessary back-up in dealing with the children. Probably all Paul needed was a firm hand. But Joanna didn't know of any suitable men – after all, she hadn't even found one for herself yet – and she felt sure that Mary wouldn't be pleased at anyone interfering in her life anyway.

"So – are we ready to go?" she asked, and two smiling teenagers nodded excitedly, their faces shining, their hair freshly washed and not yet quite dry. They both look quite angelic, Joanna thought, then quickly changed her mind as she saw Paul kick his sister on the shins, to which Emma responded by pinching his backside, and Paul then let out a piercing holler.

Nevertheless, they all set out eventually, piling into Joanna's trusty old Mercedes, the kids tunelessly singing the latest chart hits as they travelled along. Joanna opened the window and let her hair blow in the breeze. She enjoyed driving – in fact it was quite a novelty, since she used public transport to get to the office during the week. And Mary seemed happy too – she was actually smiling, and Joanna thought once again how young she looked when she was happy.

Joanna was happy too – especially when she thought about her forthcoming visit to Tom's house for dinner on Monday evening. Only two days away! She felt sick with apprehension and wild with joy at the same time. Would the occasion be some sort of turning point, or was she just imagining that she'd detected a degree of interest on his side? Well, she intended doing her utmost to make herself totally irresistible. She'd already made an appointment with Karen, her hairstylist, to have a trim and a blow-dry on Monday afternoon. Then she intended to go home, feed her cat, then cover her hair with a shower-cap and soak in a luxurious bath that would leave her skin smelling fragrant and soft to the touch. Hopefully, Tom's touch . . .

"I see you're smiling, Jo," said Mary, cutting into her thoughts. "Seems like you're thinking of something – or someone – very special."

Joanna shook her head, grinning back. She knew that Mary had detected her liking for Tom Kilmartin, but she wasn't going to tell her – not yet anyway – where she was going on Monday evening. Joanna felt that she would be too nervous if too many people knew. Just for now, it would be her own little secret.

Of course, Orla knew about Monday's "Big Date". But then, there weren't many secrets the two close friends didn't share. Joanna's thoughts drifted to the friendship between her mother and Agnes Kilmartin. Talk about chalk and cheese! Yet those two women had been inseparable for as long as she could remember. She'd once asked her mother how they'd become friends, and Catherine had reluctantly explained that she'd once done a favour for Agnes.

"It was nothing, really," Catherine had said.

"But Agnes is so – so *different* from you, Mam," Joanna had persisted.

"Friends don't have to be like peas in a pod, you know," Catherine had told her daughter, smiling. "The most important ingredient in a friendship is trust – and being there for each other through thick and thin."

Joanna smiled. Her mother's definition had sounded rather fanciful for a middle-aged housewife.

"But what do you and Agnes talk about?" she persisted.

"Don't worry – we've always had plenty to discuss," Catherine said dryly. "Agnes has been one of the best friends anyone could ever have had. We've helped each other through the good and bad times."

"Bad times?" Joanna had quickly asked.

Catherine had smiled whimsically. "We all have our ups and down, Jo – all you can hope for is that there are more 'ups' than 'downs'. And God knows, poor Agnes has had more than her fair share of trouble."

"What do you mean?" Joanna had asked, intrigued that her mother's staid and unbending friend might have had another dimension to her life. Surely there were few problems that Agnes's wealth couldn't have sorted out?

But Catherine refused to be drawn any further. "Forget I said that, love. There's nothing more to be said."

And Joanna had been left to her own bemused speculation.

"Joanna – we're almost there!"

Mary's voice cut in on Joanna's thoughts, and she realised that she'd been lost in her own memories and rudely ignoring poor Mary and the kids, despite her intention of creating a special day for them.

"Sorry, Mary – I was thinking of my mother," she said apologetically.

Mary patted Joanna's hand. "It must be awful – having your mother in a nursing home, and her so lost and confused."

Joanna grimaced. "Sometimes she'd in great form, and we can have a reasonable chat – but on the bad days, she doesn't even remember who she is. And you never know if it's going to be a good day or a bad day. That's hard to cope with – and it's only going to get worse."

Mary squeezed her friend's arm and Joanna suddenly realised that she was being too self-indulgent. This was Mary's day out, so she'd better stop wallowing in self-pity. However, it *was* good to be able to occasionally unburden oneself.

She smiled and tried to look cheerful. "Now, let's keep our eyes peeled for a parking space."

As they drove through the city centre, Joanna suddenly spotted a parking space quite close to the restaurant and cinema. Someone was just conveniently vacating it, so with no time to lose she quickly slid the car into the space. That was one problem out of the way!

In the restaurant, a table near the door became vacant as they arrived.

"This is our lucky day!" said Mary happily, and Joanna was touched to see such delight on her friend's face.

Having just managed to place their orders before the lunch-time hordes descended, they were quickly served, and everyone munched happily. Looking surreptitiously at her three companions, Joanna fervently hoped that life would soon become more financially secure for them all, and she hoped that the practice would enable her to increase Mary's salary before long.

Outside the cinema, the four of them held a lengthy discussion regarding the merits of the various movies on offer. Despite their differing choices, Joanna was relieved that neither of the teenagers looked like sulking if the other one's choice was decided on. Glancing at Mary, Joanna realised that Mary genuinely didn't care what movie they went to see – for her it would simply be an opportunity to relax – and maybe even doze – while the children were absorbed and didn't need her constant supervision.

At last one of the movies was selected, and having bought the teenagers gigantic boxes of popcorn and ice creams, Joanna led her three guests inside.

The movie that had been selected was an action thriller – not Joanna's favourite type – but she watched with amusement and pleasure as the two teenagers stared rapturously at the screen, never taking their eyes off the action for a moment, even when they were stuffing their mouths with popcorn. Within minutes, Mary had fallen asleep and was snoring gently. Joanna smiled to herself in the dark. This was certainly a different way of spending a Saturday afternoon!

Joanna found it hard to get into the plot of the movie, and before long, her mind was wandering again. Back to Tom Kilmartin, then to Harry Sweeney and his mysterious link to Agnes Kilmartin, and Agnes's dying remarks about the cat. Then her thoughts turned to Orla and her friend's humiliation at Declan Dunne's hands. What a pity, she thought, that Gary never asked Orla out. Especially since the two of them seemed to be getting along so well together. Which reminded her that the date for Gary's court appearance was fast approaching . . .

Suddenly, Joanna jerked awake, and she grinned to herself as she realised that Mary wasn't the only one who had fallen asleep! Mary was still snoring gently, and glancing down at her watch, Joanna was pleased to discover that the movie must nearly be over. The kids' eyes were still glued to the screen, so she doubted that they had even noticed her little lapse. But something else was niggling at her brain, some piece of information which was tantalisingly evading her, hovering on the edges of her consciousness, just out of reach.

What on earth could it be? And why wouldn't it make itself known? Suddenly, she remembered. Just as she was dozing off, one of the characters on the screen had said: *"When things don't seem to make sense, look at them from another angle. We interpret things the way we believe they should be – not as they really are."*

That was it! Maybe that was the solution to her own dilemma! Maybe Lisa Noonan had interpreted Agnes's last words in a way that made sense to *her*. She would ring her as soon as she could. This could be the breakthrough she'd been hoping for.

CHAPTER 33

Monday morning dawned fine and bright, and as Joanna jumped out of bed and headed for the shower, she hoped that maybe the good weather augured well for her evening date with Tom. Of course, it wasn't really a date, she had to admit to herself. It was just a meeting of old friends, who would share a homemade meal and a bottle of wine, search for the missing documents and probably chat about their mothers. That was probably all that it meant to Tom. A chance to get nearer to solving the riddle of his mother's will.

But at least, I'm going to go in there with all guns blazing, she thought determinedly. I'm going to do my best to look casually stunning – an oxymoron if ever there was one – and I'll try not to lose my nerve and look away if he catches my eye. Instead, I'll hold his gaze seductively, the way women brazenly do in the movies . . .

Joanna made a face at herself in the bathroom mirror. I really am pathetic, she thought. I'd never have the nerve to hold his gaze, even if he *did* look at me "that" way. I know I'd turn the colour of beetroot.

God, she sounded just like an insecure teenager! She was supposed to be a woman of the world, a professional. A few weeks ago, Tom had been no more than a warm and happy memory from the past. But being catapulted into Agnes's life had brought him back into her life as well, and suddenly she was seeing him in a whole new light.

He had matured well. He'd become stockier, and there were muscles where once there'd just been the body of a skinny, albeit attractive, young man. Was it her imagination, or had his voice deepened too? Or had she just never realised how seductive his voice was? Oh God, she really was going mad!

But first – before she made a total fool of herself – she'd have to find out if there was any other woman in his life. Because she was playing for keeps here. She would gradually broach the subject over dinner, and if she discovered even a whiff of another female around him, she would take herself and her sexy knickers, bra and new dress home as quickly as possible. At least if she knew that there *was* another woman in his life, she could stop this silly day-dreaming and get on with her life. She'd go out with Orla to all those receptions and launches, and surely she'd eventually meet someone else.

Joanna managed to put Tom out of her mind for the rest of the day, and get on with her workload with single-minded devotion. There was a lot to be got through – Mary had certainly been right on that score – and she was quite exhausted when she looked at her watch and discovered that it was almost five o'clock!

"God – I'd no idea it was so late," she told Mary. "I meant to leave a bit earlier than this. Can you hold the fort until closing time?"

"Of course," said Mary, giving her the once-over. "That's a very nice cut and blow-dry you had done during lunch hour – are you going somewhere special this evening?"

"N-no – not really," said Joanna, blushing under Mary's scrutiny. She was a hopeless liar, and she felt certain that Mary could see right through her. "I'm just meeting an old friend for an hour or two. Nothing special."

"So why the special hairdo?"

"Hairdo?" said Joanna, acting surprised. "Oh that – I just felt too lazy to wash it myself when I get home."

Thankfully, Mary didn't ask any further questions.

But I *will* tell Mary about it tomorrow, Joanna decided. No matter how the evening turns out.

She lifted the phone and dialled Lisa Noonan's mobile phone, hoping that Lisa had somehow got the sense of Agnes's last words wrong, or inserted a word to make it seem like sense to her. Joanna knew she was clutching at straws, but Agnes had obviously expected her to understand.

"Oh hi, Lisa – it's Joanna Brennan here."

"Hi, Joanna."

"I was just wondering if you'd thought any more about Agnes Kilmartin's last words, or if you've remembered anything else?"

"Sorry, Joanna, no. That's all I can remember."

"You're still sure she said: 'Tell Joanna the cat'll have the documents'?"

191

Lisa sighed at the other end of the phone. "I think so, Joanna. She was so weak, I had to lean across her to hear what she was saying – so maybe I didn't catch every word."

"Do you think she could have said: 'Tell Joanna Cat'll have the documents'?"

"Eh – isn't that what I told you she'd said?"

"No, you said '*the* cat'll have the documents' – you put the word 'the' before 'cat' when you told me the first time. I'm just trying to figure out if she could have meant my mother, Catherine, who Agnes always called 'Cat'."

"I think you're right," said Lisa suddenly. "Maybe I put in an extra word to make sense of it. Yes, I think she actually said, 'Tell Joanna Cat'll have the documents. She could hardly speak, she was so weak, and she had to stop between words."

Success, thought Joanna. But after she'd rung off she sighed. Even if Lisa was right, what use could Catherine possibly be?

As soon as she could, she would visit her mother and see if she could get any sense out of her about Agnes's wishes. This made her feel guilty as she was overdue a visit to the nursing home. Well, she thought sadly, I don't think poor old Mam will even notice that I haven't turned up.

The thought of living beyond this forthcoming evening and its possible outcome was something that Joanna now considered. *If* all went well with Tom, she might be visiting her mother in a state of great excitement tomorrow. If *not* – well, she preferred not to think about that.

CHAPTER 34

"Hi, Jo – c'mon in."

Tom opened the door of his Ballsbridge home wearing a butcher's-print apron.

Joanna, carrying two bottles of wine, could immediately smell the delightful aromas that were wafting their way up from the basement kitchen.

"Hi, Tom – you're certainly looking the part!"

He grinned, and Joanna's heart flipped over. "Well, we aim to please. Will m'lady step this way?"

With an exaggerated bow, he ushered her in, and soon she was heading down the back stairs to the homely room she'd always loved so much. Placing the bottles of wine on the table, she looked around the old-style kitchen that hadn't been modernised in at least thirty years. A microwave cooker, a hob and an oven had been added, but these were the only concessions to modernity. Nevertheless, it was perfect. The large dresser was still there, with all the assorted china that Agnes had collected over the years. And the pantry, with its original chicken-wire door panels, would now be considered the height of fashion again. Joanna gave a sigh of pleasure. She'd always loved being in this kitchen. It was truly the heart of the Ballsbridge home.

"Jo, I hope you don't mind – but I decided to try out a new recipe," said Tom, looking slightly worried.

"No problem, Tom – you know that I'll eat virtually anything," she said, grinning ruefully. "In fact, that's the problem – I need to shift at least a stone!"

Tom gave her another of those appraising looks that made her insides do somersaults. "Don't be ridiculous, Jo – you're just perfect the way you are."

Blushing, Joanna busied herself opening the first bottle of wine and wished desperately that she knew how to accept a compliment graciously. That had been just the sort of opportunity that was needed to take the conversation onto a more personal level and as usual she'd blown it. Still, the night was young . . .

"I've done a lamb roast, with garlic and orange sauce, with roast potatoes and vegetables," Tom explained. "Is that OK?"

"That sounds wonderful!" said Joanna warmly, thinking to herself that if he'd gone to so much trouble, she must still be in there with a chance.

"And, of course, I've done the banoffee pie for dessert, just like you asked."

"Oh, that's great! I have to admit that I'm starving!" Starving for the touch of your lips and the feel of your arms around me, she added in her own mind. How on earth was she going to steer the conversation around to his love life, so that she could find out if there was

194

another woman in his life? Better wait a while – hopefully the opportunity would present itself naturally.

She busied herself pouring out two glasses of red wine and handed one of them to Tom.

"Thanks, Jo – cheers!"

"We have to drink a toast to something," she said impishly.

"Well, how about . . . to life – and love?"

"You're on. Here's to life – and love!"

The two of them clinked glasses, and each took a sip of wine, locking eyes as they did so.

However, Tom was the first to break the gaze, nervously filling the silence between them with, "How's the business going, Jo?"

"Fine – I'm getting quite a few clients at this stage. But as regards Harry Sweeney, I'm still not much farther on."

He looked chastened. "I didn't ask you for that reason, Jo – I realise that this business of my mother's will is going to take ages."

Joanna blushed. "Well, hopefully, it won't take too long. As soon as we get some information on who exactly Harry Sweeney's wife was, that may reveal his connection to your mother." Impulsively, she reached out and touched his arm. "Tom – how are you coping? I mean, it's only two weeks since your mother died . . ."

Tom smiled gently. "At times, I miss her terribly. But life goes on, and I have my work to occupy me. I'm arranging a field trip for thirty students and myself to the Antarctic in December, to study penguins, so the plans for that are keeping me busy just at the moment." His eyes twinkled. "And, of course, there's still a full lecture term before then. I really love getting the students involved in the conservation projects too – there's a great sense of achievement in seeing their enthusiasm when they first come to college after the rote learning of the school curriculum. It's like a whole new world of possibilities suddenly opens up for them."

It's now or never, thought Joanna. "But what about your personal life, Tom? Surely you need to take time out to enjoy yourself, be with friends?"

And lovers, if there are any, she wanted to add.

"My work *is* my personal life," he said seriously. "I love it, Jo. Maybe I sound like a dickhead to you, but I get such a kick out of working on these issues. And encouraging the adults of tomorrow to develop a passion for these issues." He grimaced. "I feel that if even half a dozen of those taking zoology and biology are willing to work towards saving the planet's endangered species, I've achieved something." Suddenly, he grinned guiltily. "Sorry for going on about it – you're probably thinking that I take it all far too seriously. But a personal life, as you call it, has taken a back seat." He smiled directly at her. "Until now, anyway."

Oh my God, thought Joanna, her heart pounding furiously, maybe something wonderful is about to happen – or did he simply mean that he'd recently met someone else? God, she was going to crack up if something didn't happen soon, one way or the other!

Abruptly, he turned away and went to check the contents of the oven.

"Where would you like to eat?" he said. "We can go up to the dining-room if you like – I put on the radiators, just in case. Alternatively, we could just eat here."

"Oh yes – let's eat here in the kitchen," said Joanna. "It's so cosy and I have so many happy memories of us eating here when we were kids."

He took the roast out of the oven, inspected it and decided that it was perfectly cooked. The roast potatoes, done in the juices of the roast, topped up with fresh orange juice, were also ready. He drained the broccoli and cauliflower, then got the plates out of the warming drawer and began to carve.

"Do you still like the crispy outside bits?" he asked her, and Joanna was inwardly thrilled that he had remembered.

"Oh yes, please!" she said fervently, wishing and hoping that there would be further moments of intimacy before the evening was over. She felt confident now that there was a real chance of something starting between them. Emboldened by this possibility, she felt her mood become more upbeat and, as they ate, she found that her conversation became more sparkling and witty, and soon she had him relaxed and laughing, as she told him about Sasha and the *Celebrity* birthday cake.

"You always were a brat," he said affectionately. "I remember the time when you were only six – of course I thought I was really grown-up at seven – but you found my coloured pencils and started scribbling all over the homework I'd just finished!"

Joanna laughed, but still blushed, as she remembered. "That's right – and my mother got all fussed and wanted to take me home immediately, but your mother said that it would teach you not to leave your exercise copies where a younger child could get at them – "

"And I got into terrible trouble in school the next day!" said Tom, grinning at her.

Their eyes locked again, and Joanna felt a desperate urge to tear off all her clothes – including her new bra and knickers – and throw herself at him. Her hormones were hopping all over the place, so to distract herself she concentrated on her dinner, attacking the broccoli and cauliflower with gusto and enthusiastically spearing the succulent roast potatoes. She was tempted to knock back some more wine to help her relax, but she was also aware that she shouldn't drink more than two glasses, since she was driving home afterwards. On the other hand, if all went well tonight, she *mightn't* be going home at all . . .

"This is wonderful," she said, eating while she talked, to cover up the quiver of longing in her voice.

"Glad you're enjoying it," he replied, looking pleased. "Y'know, I really enjoy cooking, especially for somone as appreciative as you." He grinned at her almost empty plate, and momentarily she wondered if she was eating too enthusiastically – was he secretly thinking that she was a glutton? But he *did* look happy.

Suddenly, as she popped the last forkful of food in her mouth, Joanna had a dreadful thought. Why hadn't he asked *her* if there was anyone special in her life? Did this mean that he simply wasn't interested – that he only saw her as an old friend?

Almost on cue, he said, as he cleared away their dinner plates: "And what about yourself, Jo – is there anyone special in your life?"

God, could he actually read her mind? In shock, she

took a gulp of wine, it went down the wrong way and she ended up almost choking.

Hurriedly, Tom abandoned the dinner plates and rushed to thump her on the back. "Are you OK, Jo?" he asked anxiously, his proximity as he touched her making her feel almost weak.

Finally, she managed to clear her throat. God, she must seem a total idiot! "Thanks," she said at last. "I don't know what happened – "

"I'd just asked you if you had someone special in your life," he said gently, retiring once again to his own side of the table, "but that was hardly the kind of reaction I was expecting!"

Joanna smiled wanly at him. "No, Tom – there's no one special – in fact, no one at all. Like you, I suppose I've just been concentrating on getting my career up and running." Well, at least now he knows, she thought, annoyed with herself over what had happened. Tom had been standing up close and personal, yet all she could do was splutter and cough. Another opportunity missed!

Suddenly, he got up, went to the fridge and took out a gorgeous banoffee pie and began to cut it into segments. "Cream?"

"Yes, please – that looks gorgeous!" said Joanna, then wondered guiltily if he'd think that she was just downright gluttonous. First, she'd completely cleared her dinner plate; now it looked like she was going to commit hara-kiri on the dessert.

But Tom looked happy at her comments, and he served her a gigantic portion, topped with whipped cream. He then dished out his own portion, and joined her at the table. Suddenly, their eyes locked again, and Joanna felt the now familiar shiver of excitement down her spine. So she rushed to speak, to fill the embarrassing void.

"Have you had any luck with your mother's documents, Tom – has anything useful turned up?"

"Afraid not – at least, not in the ones I've looked at so far." He pushed the banoffee around on his plate. "But we can start going through the ones in the library after we've finished our meal. If that's OK with you?"

"Of course."

"But I did make an interesting discovery." He gazed at her. "D'you know, Jo, my mother kept detailed accounts of every penny she ever spent! I've found notebooks for each year, listing all the household expenses, going back years – even including the cost of my school copybooks and uniforms! And I could even tell you how much our weekly grocery bill came to, on any given date from the sixties up until she died!" He frowned. "But in each of the accounts books, there were a series of unspecified payments – it looked as though my mother wanted to keep her accounts in order but that there were payments she clearly didn't want anyone to know about – no doubt, especially my father. Although there was never a shortage of money, my father could be very tight-fisted at times."

"Could they have been for magazine subscriptions?"

"Good lord, no – the sums were far more substantial than that. My mother also sent a postal order to someone unspecified every month, over the last thirty years."

"My goodness! That is interesting! Could she have been sending money to her brother Joseph?"

"No, I don't think so – because the payments continued

200

long after his date of death. But that's not all. There were also bank drafts paid around September each year up until 1992, but my mother kept no record of who they were paid to. Naturally, I'm wondering if they're in some way connected to Harry Sweeney's offspring." He sighed. "There's so much about my mother that I never knew.

"What an amazing woman she was," said Joanna softly. "So tough on the outside, but really so kind at heart. I know my mother regarded her as her dearest friend – but what an odd couple they made!"

Tom nodded. "We'll probably never know what drew them together. But friends are so important, aren't they?"

Joanna nodded.

"By the way, how *is* Catherine?"

"As well as can be expected," said Joanna sadly. "Some days, she's alert and can understand what I'm saying. Then other days, she gets quite paranoid, and thinks that the people in the nursing home are trying to wheedle information out of her."

"It's a horrible way to end your life, isn't it?" he said sadly. "And it must be awful for you – watching her go downhill and not being able to do anything about it." He grimaced. "In some ways, I think my mother's death was easier – for her and for me. At least it was quicker, and more dignified than the gradual disintegration of Alzheimer's."

Both of them were silent for a few moments, their minds filled with thoughts of their mothers and of their extraordinary friendship.

Tom finally broke the silence. "As you know, I used to go to Catherine's nursing home with Mum sometimes. And even though Catherine didn't always know what was going on, the bond between them was still there. My mother would always come away from that nursing home broken-hearted."

Joanna felt near to tears as she thought of her once happy, cheerful mother, now reduced to a mere shell of the person she once was.

Suddenly, she remembered that *she* had something interesting to tell *him*. And she'd almost forgotten about it, since all her thoughts and efforts had been focused on getting him to declare his interest in her. How unprofessional, she thought disgustedly. I'm turning into a brain-dead bimbo!

She gave him a big smile. "Tom – I almost forgot to tell you – I *may* have discovered something that will help us!"

Tom was all agog. "C'mon – what?"

"Remember what your mother's nurse Lisa Noonan told me? About the message Agnes asked her to give me?"

"The cat'll have the documents?"

"Yes. Well, I got in contact with Lisa again. It had dawned on me that she herself must have added the word 'the' because it made more sense to *her*! But if you listen to the sentence without the 'the' in it – 'Cat'll have the documents' – it means I'm to get the information from 'Cat'. And who is Cat? My mother! Your mother always called my mother 'Cat' – it was a special name that no one else ever called her."

"So what did the nurse say to that?"

"She agreed that she probably got it wrong. So it now seems your mother's last words were: 'Tell Joanna Cat'll have the documents.'"

Tom's brow furrowed. "Yes, I see what you're getting

202

at, but poor Catherine can hardly be of any help to us now – she's not likely to remember anything about my mother's affairs, is she?"

"Well, it's worth a try, isn't it? So maybe you should come with me when I visit her next time. Maybe having you present will jog her memory."

"Well, I'll be glad to go with you, Jo – just let me know when."

Joanna shovelled the last dollop of cream into her mouth and noted balefully that she hadn't even left a polite amount uneaten.

"Jo?"

"Yes?"

"Would you like some more banoffee?"

"Oh – no, thanks, I'm full. But it was gorgeous!"

They both leapt up and proceeded to take their empty dessert bowls over to the draining-board. Tom placed his in the sink and was turning just as Joanna arrived with hers. Suddenly, they were facing each other.

"Jo – "

Tom looked down at her tenderly, and Joanna steeled herself not to lose her nerve. This could be the moment . . .

"Yes, Tom?" she whispered, her lips slightly apart. He was so close to her that she could feel his breath. Time stood still as they gazed in wonder at each other, and Joanna just knew that something wonderful was about to happen. He touched her arm and leaned towards her, and she knew with certainty that he was about to kiss her . . .

Suddenly, they both froze. Joanna's mobile phone was ringing! They gazed at each other in dismay, the moment ruined.

"Your phone, Jo," said Tom unnecessarily, turning towards the worktop and plugging in the kettle.

"I suppose I'd better answer it," she said, miserably. Damn, damn, damn! She could cheerfully strangle whoever was ringing her! On the other hand, it could be someone from the nursing home – maybe something was wrong with her mother . . .

"Hello?"

"Oh, Joanna – I don't know what to do! I'm sorry for bothering you, but there's no one else I can turn to!" It was Mary, and she was crying hysterically. "It's Paul again – you won't believe what he's done this time! He's broken into a neighbour's house and taken the old man's radio. Now the old man's discovered the house has been broken into and called the Gardaí!"

"Look, calm down, Mary – I'll come over as quickly as I can."

"Oh, would you, Jo? That would be marvellous! Maybe you can figure out what to do!"

Joanna ended the call and turned sadly towards Tom. "I'm afraid I'm going to have to go," she said glumly.

"Is your mother OK?" he asked, concerned.

"Yes, the call wasn't about her – it was from Mary, who works with me."

"Oh yes, I remember meeting her in your office. Nice woman."

"Well, she's having serious problems with her teenage son, and he's done something really bad this time – broken into someone's house and taken a radio. She's really in an awful state and wants me to come over."

"Then of course you must go. Is there anything I can do to help?"

Just kiss me, Joanna longed to shout. But out loud she said: "Thanks, Tom, but there's no need to bother you. I'm just sorry that the evening's ended like this – "

He smiled gently, but the intimacy that had been there was definitely now gone, and Joanna could have cried with rage and frustration.

"And we haven't even managed to search for the documents!" she said.

"Don't worry. We'll just have to do that some other time."

"OK," said Joanna dully. *Some other time!* What on earth did that mean? In a month's time, next year, maybe never?

"I'll phone you if I find anything useful among Mum's stuff," he said as she left.

"Thanks, Tom – and I'll be in touch as soon as I've any news from this end."

What a lousy end to such a promising evening, Joanna thought in disgust as she drove towards Mary's house. It's my own fault – if I'd told Mary where I was going this evening, she'd never have rung. At least I haven't drunk enough wine to prevent me driving . . . on the other hand, if I had drunk too much, she thought angrily, I could have explained to Mary that I wasn't fit to drive. If only I'd thought of turning off the damned mobile phone!

Then Joanna was overcome by guilt. Poor Mary needed her help – that was what friendship was all about, right? Wasn't that what she and Tom had just been talking about? Just before the damned phone rang . . .

CHAPTER 35

It hadn't been a great evening. Colette was tired and fractious, having just arrived back in Dublin, within days of giving birth. She hadn't expected to feel so despondent at having abandoned her baby so soon. But a baby didn't fit into her present lifestyle and would be better off with someone who could love it wholeheartedly. She was also dreading the likelihood that Ivan would want sex after their three-month-long separation. She hoped that if she kept fighting with him, he'd become so exasperated that he'd leave her alone. She was still sore after the birth and wanted nothing more than a good night's sleep.

Ivan, unaware that she'd given birth, expected her to be thrilled to see him again. Instead, she was argumentative all evening and livid about being confined to the private dining-room of their regular expensive restaurant.

"You treat me like you were ashamed of me!" she said crossly, as Paddy Byrne picked them up outside the restaurant in Ivan's limousine. "After all the sacrifices I've made to be with you!"

"As far as I can see, it's I have made the sacrifices!" Ivan

retorted. "I've told you before, Colette – I can't be seen dining out with an attractive young woman when I've got a wife at home! There were too many people that I know booked to dine there tonight. Thank God I can always rely on the owner of Luigi's to tip me off."

Colette pouted. "But what's the point of me getting all dressed up if no one sees me?"

"I see you," Ivan said angrily, "and that's all that should matter to you!"

Ivan glanced at Paddy, but his driver and lackey was staring straight ahead, idling the car as he waited for the traffic to clear, and seemingly unaware of the argument taking place in the back of the car. Ivan relaxed. He could always rely on Paddy Byrne to do the right thing. It cost him, but Paddy was worth every penny he earned.

"Well, Harry always thinks I look nice!" said Colette, casting an impudent look at Ivan.

"Harry? Harry who?"

"Harry Sweeney – the Worker's Champion!"

Ivan turned puce in the dark of the limousine, but Colette was unaware of the impact her words had just had. "You know Harry Sweeney?" he asked.

"Yes," said Colette, delighted that she'd discommoded him. "He's my brother-in-law. And he thinks I'm crazy to be wasting my time with you!"

"Jesus Christ, Colette!" Ivan exploded. "You never told me! You fucking bitch! Do you think I'd have set you up in an apartment if I'd known you were related to that bastard?"

At last, Colette realised the error she'd made in attempting to make him jealous.

"Look, Ivan, I hardly ever see him. I mean, he just happens to be married to my sister, and you know I don't see my family any more. Harry just calls by sometimes, to see if I'm OK – "

"Christ almighty – you mean he's been in the apartment?" Ivan was working himself into a rage. "And you've probably been passing information to him about my business! You little traitor – you wormed your way into my life so that you could feed information to that bastard – you conniving bitch!"

"W-what? No, of course I didn't!"

In a fury, Ivan grabbed Colette by the hair and, as she screamed, he slapped her across the face. Paddy heard the commotion in the back, but he had learned to turn a blind eye to Ivan's rough tactics with women.

"Ivan – please – stop hurting me!"

Ivan grabbed Colette by the throat. "I can't believe you'd do this to me – after all I've given you! You know how I hate that bastard! Maybe you've been screwing him too!"

"I'd never – do that! Stop, Ivan – you're really hurting me!"

"You don't deserve all the things I've given you, all the things I've done for you. If it wasn't for me, you'd still be on the street!"

Ivan's fingers closed around Colette's windpipe, and her eyes began to bulge. No sound came out – only a faint gurgle at the back of her throat.

As he forcibly shook her, there was a sudden snap, and Colette's head lolled over to one side. "Answer me, bitch! Why did you . . ." As his voice trailed away, and he became aware of what he'd just done, he released his grip on Colette, and her body crumpled onto the floor of the car.

"Oh Jesus, oh my God, Paddy!"

Paddy Byrne looked in the rear-view mirror, gradually easing the limousine out into the traffic lane. "What is it, boss?"

"She's – Jesus, I think I've killed her!" His voice rose to a howl. "What the fuck am I going to do?"

"Take it easy, boss – we'll think of something. First check and see if she's actually dead."

"She's dead, Paddy. I was never surer. Oh Christ, Paddy!"

"Look, I'm going to keep driving around while we think. We've gotta stay calm while we figure out what to do."

"Jesus, Paddy – how can I stay calm when there's a dead body beside me?"

"Listen, boss – try to calm down. Is there anything in her flat that might connect the two of you?"

"No – I don't think so."

"No documents, aftershave, monogrammed pyjamas?"

A brief sneer flitted across Ivan's face. "I never wear pyjamas. But maybe I've left some aftershave – Jesus, I can't be sure." The sneer was quickly replaced by a scowl.

"Look, boss, I'm going to drive to the flat anyway – it's only down the street. You have your set of keys?"

"Yes."

"Right. I'll take a quick look inside, just in case. We don't want you leaving anything there that might link you to Colette. And, boss, prop her up on the seat and support her so it either looks like she's drunk or like the two of you are love-birds. Just in case someone looks into the car and sees her on the floor."

As Ivan, shuddering, proceeded with his grisly task, Paddy drove the short distance to the block of flats where Colette had lived.

"Aw, shit – who the fuck is that?" Paddy muttered, as he noticed a young woman standing outside the street door to the flats, her finger on what looked like Colette's bell.

Ivan peered out. "That's Colette's friend – I've forgotten her name – just our bloody luck that she'd decided to call now!"

"I'll drive around the block – she'll probably be gone by the time we get back."

Sure enough, the street was clear when they returned for the second time.

Paddy parked the limousine down a side street opposite the block of flats, then withdrew a pair of latex gloves from the car's front storage compartment and slid them on. Ivan handed him the keys for the flat and the street door. Paddy then pointed to Colette's limp body. "Pretend she's drunk if anyone comes near the car. I'll be as quick as I can."

With a speed that belied his bulk, Paddy climbed the stairs and let himself into Colette's first-floor flat. He began searching the rooms with an eagle eye. In the bathroom, he slipped the aftershave and razor into his pocket, dampened a clean handkerchief in the sink, then swiftly proceeded to wipe down every surface in the flat.

Time passed as he worked methodically, not allowing himself to dwell on the huge risk he had taken by parking the limo, dead body and all, in the sidestreet across the road. He noticed a file of papers that had Harry Sweeney's name on them. Assuming he left them there, maybe they could somehow implicate that Sweeney bastard . . .

Eventually it was done. He did another quick tour of the flat, then decided that it was clean. Within a day or two, the cops would be crawling all over the place, but they'd no longer find anything to connect Ivan with Colette. Satisfied, he unlocked the door and pulled it open – to find himself confronted with the same young woman who had been ringing Colette's bell earlier.

Damn! Someone must have opened the street door for her.

"Who the fuck are you?" he barked.

"I could ask you the same thing," she said cheekily. "Is Colette in?" Then she noticed his gloves and asked in alarm. "What are you doing here?"

Paddy gave a harsh laugh. "I'm, eh – from security. Colette has gone out for the evening."

"I know – I saw her in Ivan Kilmartin's limousine earlier. Oh, I recognise you now – you're his driver, aren't you? So why would you be doing a security check here? "

He was shocked and had to think quickly. Just getting rid of her wouldn't be good enough. He stepped back inside, gesturing to her to follow. She warily followed him in.

"It'a a spot check," he said. "I also work for the company that carries out these checks. They wouldn't be of much use if everyone knew about them, would they?" He gave her a menacing glare. "Now, what do you want? You're trespassing, you know."

The young woman looked crestfallen. "Colette said she'd lend me some money – I'm in a bit of difficulty right now."

"You doing tricks, like Colette was?" Paddy suddenly realised that he'd spoken of Colette in the past tense, and hoped that the girl hadn't noticed.

The young woman coloured. "No – well, just occasionally, to pay the rent. Until I get back on my feet again . . ."

"So you've a cash-flow problem." Paddy fished a wad of notes from his pocket, peeled several off and handed them to her.

"Oh, thank you!"

"There might be more of that if you know how to keep your mouth shut. Where do you live? Write it down for me."

The young woman took a small notebook and a pen from her bag, wrote down her name and the address of her bedsit nearby and handed it to him.

"OK – now clear off – and don't mention being here, if you know what's good for you." He patted her shoulder. *"I'll see what can be done to get you sorted out. A nice place to live and regular money coming in, without doing any more tricks – how does that sound?"*

The young woman's eyes looked wistful. "Sounds great."

"I'll be in touch. By the way – are you clean?"

"I-I beg your pardon?"

"No VD?"

The young woman blushed. "God, no –" She hoped he didn't notice her blush – she was currently being treated for something the doctor had called chlamydia.

Paddy nodded. "Good. Now remember what I said: if you open your mouth about being here – or seeing me, or seeing Colette with Ivan Kilmartin – no dosh, no help."

She was suddenly shaking with fear. Because she now realised the implications of his request. "I won't say anything – I promise."

After she left, Paddy wiped the outside lock and handle of the door and the area around them, then locked the door and ran down the flight of stairs.

Now, he thought, we've got to dump the body somewhere. He grinned as an idea suddenly came to him. Maybe, if he discreetly informed his tabloid press contacts about Colette's former life as a runaway, the cops would assume she'd been on the game and killed by a customer.

Back at the car, Paddy found that Ivan's earlier ranting had now deserted him, and he was reduced to a gibbering wreck. "Oh Jesus, Paddy – I thought you'd gone and left me here. What the fuck kept you so long?"

"A minor complication, boss. That young lady came back."

"I know, she walked past the car a few minutes ago and I was terrified she'd come over and try to speak to Colette."

"Don't worry, boss, I think I've sorted her out. It's going to cost some money, but . . ."

"Whatever it takes, Paddy – as long as you get me out of this mess."

Ivan shuddered as he glanced over at Colette's body. "Get us out of here quick, will you? I think rigor mortis is setting in already – if we don't get rid of her soon, it'll be impossible to get her out through the car door."

Paddy began driving slowly through the city streets, keeping within the speed limit so as not to attract the wrong kind of attention. "Don't worry, boss," he said again. "Rigor mortis won't set in for a while yet." Paddy Byrne had more experience of dead bodies than most.

Ivan put his head in his hands and began to weep. "Oh Jesus, Paddy – what are we going to do?"

"We could dump her in some alley, I suppose. I'm just trying to figure out where . . ." Suddenly, Paddy had an idea. He reached for the car phone and dialled his own home phone number. After several minutes, a sleepy voice answered.

"Hello?"

Paddy switched the phone to Transmit mode. "Son – how did you get on tonight?" Then he switched the phone to Receive mode to hear his son's answer.

"OK, Da – they went to the Phoenix Park in his car at around eight, and they sat talking in the car all evening. It was eleven o'clock when he drove her back to her own car that she'd left in Parkgate Street."

"Son, I need to know the exact spot where they were parked. Meet me at the main gate of the Park in fifteen minutes."

"Aah Jesus, Da – I'm already in bed!"

"Well, get out of it, and get dressed – now. This is an emergency." Putting the phone down, Paddy Byrne turned to Ivan. "Look, boss – I have a plan that just might work. And if it does, you'll get your pound of flesh as well. Harry Sweeney won't be giving you hassle any more."

CHAPTER 36

The following morning, Joanna made an effort to smile gratefully as Mary placed a cup of tea and a Mikado biscuit on her desk. She was tired – tired of trying to get somewhere with Tom Kilmartin, tired of the antics of Mary's son Paul and thoroughly fed up with life in general.

When she'd called to Mary's house the previous night, chaos had reigned, with Mary in a high state of distress, Paul truculent and unwilling to admit that he'd done anything wrong, and Emma in tears over the disgrace that her brother was bringing to the family. After doing her best to calm everyone down, Joanna contacted the local Garda station, where the complaint against Paul had been registered.

Once again, she pleaded with the local sergeant to overlook Paul's stupid behaviour, especially since he'd returned the radio at Mary's insistence and apologised to the elderly neighbour who'd forgotten to close his downstairs window before retiring for the night.

Of course, Joanna was well aware that entering and stealing from another person's property was a criminal offence, yet she hoped that once again she could persuade the local sergeant to be lenient with Paul, based on his emotional distress at the break-up of his parents' marriage.

The sergeant had finally, but reluctantly, agreed. "Maybe that lad would benefit from attending a meeting with the Garda Juvenile Diversion Programme," he warned. This was a caring scheme, operated by the Gardaí, and aimed at discouraging young people from a life of crime at a stage when they might still benefit from a serious talking-to. At such meetings, they were given a clear picture of where their actions would take them if they continued on the same downward path.

"I'm sure you're right, Sergeant," said Joanna, "but hopefully, there won't be any further incidents like this."

Just as Joanna replaced the phone after speaking to the sergeant, it rang again. "Hello?"

"Good morning, my dear friend," said Orla chirpily. "How did your evening with darling Tom go? Did he rip your knickers off?"

Joanna groaned. "For your information – nothing happened."

"What? Are you losing your touch, Brennan?"

Joanna sighed and glanced up to ensure that the door between her and Mary was tightly closed. "You won't believe what happened –"

"Go on!" said Orla eagerly.

"We were getting on brilliantly, and I really believed that something was about to happen – then Mary rang, and I had to go round to her house, because her son Paul was in trouble again."

"Shit!" said Orla vehemently. "That kid is becoming a right pain in the arse. In fact, what he needs is a good *kick* in the arse!"

"I know – but the poor lad is devastated because his parents have broken up. He's just not good at handling the situation."

"Well, his sister is managing OK," Orla replied acerbically. "Does he realise how much stress this is causing his poor mother?"

"I don't know, Orla, and I don't know where to go from here. The sergeant suggested sending him to the Garda Juvenile Diversion Programme – maybe that would knock some sense into him. What do you think?"

"Hmmm. Maybe I should have a discreet word with Mick McHale. Is that OK with you?"

"*Any* help or advice would be welcome," said Joanna gratefully, "otherwise I think poor Mary will implode. And there's only so many scrapes that I can get Paul out of."

"OK," said Orla, "I'll give Jim a ring and see what he has to say. By the way, he's given me the name of a private detective for you."

"Thanks, Orla – what is it?"

Joanna wrote down the name and phone number. "Great – once this guy can find Maura Sweeney, *née* Devane, I can hopefully get Agnes's will sorted out. At this stage, it's beginning to do my head in."

"You poor old thing! Look, I'm really sorry that things didn't work out with Tom – but I presume you're seeing him again?"

"Well, not really," said Joanna forlornly. "He just said, as I was leaving, that we'd have to get together again soon. But he didn't say *when*."

Orla let out an exasperated sigh. "You went to his house to go through Agnes's documents, right? And there wasn't time because Mary phoned, right? Well, you'll just have to go back again! After all, regardless of your personal feelings, you still have to administer his mother's will."

Joanna sighed. Her friend was a lot more confident than she was in conducting matters of the heart. Yet on the other hand, poor old Orla hadn't succeeded with Gary, the guy she'd really wanted to attract.

"Yeah, yeah," she replied, "I suppose you're right. But wanting to do it and being *able* to do it are two different things."

"Want to meet up for a jar tonight?" Orla asked.

"OK," said Joanna, laughing, "as long as I don't have to sit watching you chat up every guy within a mile's radius!"

"I can't help it if they're all smitten by my charms," said Orla, chuckling. "Remember that guy I was chatting to in the pub the other night? Well, he rang me, and we've arranged to meet next week, when he gets back from some business trip."

"Do you like him?"

Orla shrugged. "He seems OK. I suppose it was his persistence that got to me in the end – sometimes that's what a bruised ego needs more than anything."

"You're not still pining over Gary, are you?"

"No," said Orla firmly. Perhaps a little *too* firmly. "But sometimes I think it's easier to date someone you *don't* care about. Talking of which – that scumbag Declan Dunne rang me yesterday. He wants to meet me, but he wouldn't say why."

"And you agreed?"

"Why not? I feel nothing for the bastard any more, so it doesn't matter to me. Maybe he wants to apologise for the way he treated me – which would be nice, but I doubt it. Or maybe he's going to return my three Tom Petty CDs, which he borrowed before he went to Spain." There was a moment's silence before Orla laughed. "I don't think he did too much listening to CDs on that trip!" Abruptly, she changed the subject. "Anyway, I'll ring Mick McHale straight away, while I have a few minutes free. And I'll see you this evening at about eight – say, in the Morrison Hotel?"

"Great," said Joanna. "Now I'd better get on with some work myself. And make arrangements to meet this detective. Mary was right when she said that we'd soon be inundated with cases!"

CHAPTER 37

The following morning, Mary popped her head around the door, looking all excited. "There's a man outside. His name is Ronan O'Farrell, and he's gorgeous!"

Joanna smiled. "Oh yes, that'll be the private investigator that Orla's friend, Mick McHale, recommended. Send him in, Mary – and put the kettle on, will you?"

But nothing prepared Joanna for what happened next. The door opened – and in walked the most incredibly gorgeous man she'd ever seen. His smile lit up the room, and his blue eyes twinkled directly at her. Joanna's heart began to pound, and she fervently hoped that she wasn't blushing. As he leaned forward to shake hands, his unruly curly brown hair fell forward over one eye and Joanna had to restrain herself from reaching across to brush it out of the way.

"Hello!" he said, eagerly grasping her hand.

As she returned his handshake and mumbled a greeting, she wondered if this was what love at first sight felt like. Whatever it was, she was no longer functioning as a human being, but as an automaton on auto-pilot, her senses totally absorbed in the vision of male magnificence before her.

"Mick McHale said you were trying to trace someone," Ronan said, looking boyishly eager to please. "Well, that's my speciality – finding people."

Joanna eventually found her voice. "I need to trace a woman who went to England around 1970," she told him.

"No problem. I work a lot in the Irish community in England – I'm often employed to find heirs to farms back in Ireland. I've lots of contacts there, so hopefully your job should be a doddle." He sat down, spread his long legs out in front of him and grinned disarmingly. "Will we get started? Are you happy for me to do the job?"

"Oh lord, yes," said Joanna, finding her voice at last. "I have the details right here in front of me." Quickly, she filled him in on the limited information she'd already gathered through Harry's trade union and gave him a set of the newspaper photocopies that Orla had given her. "I was planning to visit the road where Harry and Maura used to live – and maybe make contact with some of their old neighbours if they're still there. But I just haven't had time yet."

"Well, technically, that should be my job, so why don't we go there together?" said Ronan smiling. "Don't worry," he added, noting her surprise, "the meter won't be running as long as you come with me."

Joanna laughed. "That's certainly an unorthodox way of doing business, but yes – why not? I've a personal interest in this case – my mother was Agnes Kilmartin's closest friend." She didn't add that only a day before, she'd been trying to seduce Agnes's son!

Ronan O'Farrell unfurled his long legs, and Joanna couldn't help wondering how they'd look naked. She was certain they'd be hairy and athletic, and the muscles would ripple when he was making love. Then she went hot with embarassment, and she could feel her neck and face turning puce. Hopefully, she hadn't broken out in a rash.

"What do you think, Joanna?"

"Oh God, I'm sorry – what did you say?"

"I think you need a break from the office," Ronan said, grinning. "I think the heat is affecting your concentration. I asked if now would suit – for visiting the Sweeney's place?"

"W-what?"

"Well, why not? You need some fresh air, there's no time like the present and I'm ready for action!"

I'll bet you are, Joanna thought, and I wish the action was with me. But aloud, she said: "I'm not sure that I can manage the time – "

"Why not? Have you another appointment?"

"Eh, no actually – "

"Well, then . . ." said Ronan, grinning cheerfully, "let's get out of here."

Just at that moment, Mary appeared with a tea tray, and began pouring tea and making small-talk.

As Mary chatted to Ronan, Joanna got a chance to surreptitiously check him out. My God, she thought, he really is stunning. Yet he didn't seem to be conceited, unlike so many men, who thought they were God's gift to women, even without half his good looks. As she noted his strong, tanned hands, she shivered with excitement at the thought of them touching her bare skin . . . Suddenly, she realised that Ronan had turned to look at her, and she felt herself blush, worried that he'd seen her staring at him. But he grinned complicitly and gestured towards the door.

Joanna laughed, abandoned her tea and stood up. "Ronan and I are going to Ranelagh together, Mary – to check out Harry and Maura's neighbours."

"W-what?" Mary looked shocked. The work was piling up, yet Joanna was running off for the afternoon with a stunning man she'd only just met! Looking from one to the other, Mary shrugged, deciding that Joanna had lost her marbles altogether.

As Ronan drove out towards Ranelagh, he whistled happily.

"Why did you ask me to come with you?" asked Joanna, using the occasion to gaze at his handsome profile.

"I thought it was a good opportunity for us to get to know each other," he replied, smiling.

Joanna felt ridiculously pleased, although she said nothing. Businesswise, there was no need for a private detective to get to know the solicitor he was working for. Did that mean that he had another agenda? And if so, was she part of that agenda? She shivered with excitement, all thoughts of Tom Kilmartin banished from her mind.

For the entire journey, they chatted animatedly to each other. Ronan kept up a light-hearted banter, and Joanna found herself enjoying the trip immensely. She felt like an irresponsible teenager, mitching from school and going on a jaunt with the handsomest boy in the school. There was something about Ronan that made her feel carefree and irresponsible. To hell with Tom Kilmartin, she thought suddenly. He'd had his chance and he hadn't availed of it. It obviously wasn't meant to be.

In Ranelagh, Ronan parked on the quiet road where Harry and Maura Sweeney used to live. Joanna felt a sense of awe as she got out of the car. It was almost as though she was stepping into someone else's history. It was here that Harry and Maura had lived out their married life, and from here that Harry Sweeney had been arrested and taken to Mountjoy Prison.

"Are you OK?" said Ronan softly, taking her arm protectively.

"It's sad, isn't it?" Joanna replied, "to think that a man went to prison, then to his death, from here. Before that, he was just living an ordinary life." Well, maybe not so ordinary, she thought to herself. He'd been a thorn in someone's side and needed to be eliminated. He'd also been important enough for Agnes Kilmartin to want to be buried beside him. I wonder, thought Joanna, what does Maura Sweeney – wherever she is – think about another woman now being buried alongside her husband?

In companionable silence, Joanna and Ronan walked along the road until they reached the house where Harry and Maura had lived until 1970. Outside, there were rows of flowerpots providing a colourful display of plants. The place looked cheerful, and there were several discarded dolls and teddies in the porch. At last, thought Joanna, the Sweeneys' house has children in it.

Ronan arched an eyebrow at her, and she nodded in assent. It was time to knock at the door. While they waited for someone to answer, Joanna smiled to herself. Already, she'd learnt, and was responding to, one of Ronan's quirky mannerisms!

The young woman who opened the door was unable to help them, having only moved in some months before. But she directed them to an old man who lived across the road, who she felt had probably lived there for many years. Yes, she told them, shivering, she and her husband had only heard about the murderer after they'd moved in. But that was estate agents for you, wasn't it? They didn't tell you anything. If she and her husband had known in advance, they'd have bought a house somewhere else. But they'd got the house cheap, probably because the murderer had reduced house values in the area.

"Look, we think he was innocent –" Joanna began, but Ronan pulled her away gently.

"You'll never change her mind," he whispered softly. "People like that just love drama. She'll probably spend her life making capital out of the Sweeneys' misfortune."

"Hopefully, not for long," said Joanna firmly, as they crossed the road. "Some day, I'm going to come back here and tell her that Harry's name has been cleared!"

Joanna's hand was still tingling pleasantly from where Ronan had held it.

At the house the woman had recommended, the door was opened by a very elderly man, who looked surprised and slightly intimidated at finding two strangers on his doorstep. Clearly, he wasn't used to many visitors, but when he learned of their mission, they were invited into his kitchen, where he offered them tea but, noting the cracked grubby mugs on the dresser, they declined. But they were anxious to bombard him with questions. And he, in turn, was delighted to be the centre of attention.

"It was a nine-day wonder in the area," the old man explained. "No one could believe that Harry Sweeney was a murderer. I mean, Harry was such a nice, decent fella, who worked hard for the union – there wasn't an ounce of harm in him. But he was being held for that young girl's murder, so what were we supposed to think?"

"But what about his wife – Maura?"

The old man scratched his head. "Harry's wife disappeared a few weeks before he was arrested. She just disappeared – no one knew where she'd gone. I began to wonder if she'd been Harry's victim too, but another neighbour says she saw her leaving the house with a packed suitcase one morning. Then, after Harry died in prison, the house was sold – but an estate agent handled the sale. Maura Sweeney never appeared back here again."

"Did they have any children?"

"Not to my knowledge. But don't take my word for it – I could be wrong, you know," said the old man hastily. "Unfortunately, my wife died last year – nothing much happened in the neighbourhood that she didn't know about. But why don't you call on the woman who saw Maura the morning she left?"

Thanking the old man, Joanna and Ronan crossed the road again, to the house that he had indicated. And soon they were sitting in a warmer, cleaner kitchen, where they risked accepting an offer of tea, from cups that weren't quite as dingy as the ones they had seen on the old man's dresser.

"Did the Sweeneys have any children?" Joanna asked.

The old woman shook her head. "Maura and Harry Sweeney never had any children. I suppose you'd have called me a friend of Maura's in that I kept a key of their house for emergencies, and they kept one of ours. And we'd sometimes have a sherry together in O'Brien's pub down the road. My Gerry was alive back then."

"You're absolutely sure that Maura had no child?" asked Joanna softly.

"Yes, I'm quite sure," said the old woman. "Maura often said to me that she'd love to have children of her own, but nothing ever happened in that department." The old woman sighed. "I used to feel so sorry for her, because I had my own two children, both grown up now and long left the nest, of course."

"Do you know where Maura Sweeney went?"

"She went to England. In fact, I met her the morning she was leaving. Let me think now – it was just before her husband was charged with that young girl's murder. I was at the corner shop, buying the morning paper, when she happened to walk past, with a suitcase in her hand. 'Where are you off to, Maura?' I said, and she told me she was going to London, to visit someone who was ill. She said she'd be back in a few weeks, but then her husband was charged and she never came back again. I'm sorry if this sounds harsh – but I can't understand why a woman wouldn't come back to give her own husband some moral support."

227

"Does that mean you don't believe Harry Sweeney was guilty?" Ronan asked.

The old woman looked at him disdainfully. "No, I don't. And no one else on this road did either at the time."

She went on to talk about what a good neighbour Harry was and what a kind, decent man he was.

Then, at last, as she let them out the front door, she said, "Oh, I've just remembered – there was one other thing – but I don't suppose it's important –"

"Go on," said Ronan eagerly.

"Well, just as she was walking towards the bus stop, Maura turned round and started walking quickly back to her house. 'Have you forgotten something, Maura?' I said. 'Yes,' she said and hurried on. I thought it was odd the way she answered me so shortly and, well, I'm ashamed to admit it now, but it made me curious." She paused, and seemed to be embarrassed by what she was about to say. "So I watched until she came out of her house again – she was only inside a minute – and when she came out she had a folded paper in her hand."

"Do you mean a newspaper?" asked Ronan.

"No, no, like a certificate of some sort – it reminded me of a birth certificate. It was that greyish colour like the old birth certificates."

"OK – thanks for telling us that," said Ronan. "It could prove very useful."

As they walked back to his car, Joanna said, "So Maura probably took her birth cert with her? What did you mean when you said that might be 'useful'?"

"At the moment, I haven't a clue, but it was obviously important enough for Maura to go back to collect it. Now why would anyone need a birth cert? Perhaps she intended staying in England permanently, and she needed it for identification purposes. That seems the most likely reason, doesn't it?"

"But if that's the case, why was Maura leaving Harry? She couldn't have known in advance that Harry would be arrested for her sister's murder, could she?"

"I wonder if she knew something – say, that Harry and Colette were having an affair – and she'd decided to ditch Harry?"

Joanna sighed. That seemed unlikely, given all that she'd been told about Harry so far. His colleagues at the trade union and his neighbours in Ranelagh had all spoken highly of him, so he was hardly the sort of man who'd have an affair with his own sister-in-law. She gave a deep sigh. There were so many twists and turns and so many blind alleys. Would they ever solve the mystery of Agnes's will?

"Nobody seems to think Harry was guilty," Ronan said, as he zapped the car doors open. "What do you think, Joanna?"

"I don't believe he was guilty either," she replied, "and Agnes Kilmartin was clearly confident enough of his innocence to be buried beside him."

Ronan grinned at her. "Well, he's pretty harmless there anyway, isn't he?"

Joanna laughed. She was enjoying being in this man's company. His sense of humour asserted itself at every opportunity, and she found herself longing to spend more time with him. Now that she'd got over the shock of his stunning good looks, she was finding other things about him that she liked very much. She'd seen how kind and thoughtful he was with the people they'd been talking to.

And he kept looking at her in that way that all women understand. He was clearly attracted to her, and all she had to do was indicate her reciprocal interest. Joanna blushed at the very thought of being so forward. She'd die rather than make the first move. Maybe he was married anyway. Or if she came on to him, he might turn her down with some amusing riposte. Besides, they were now colleagues – in fact, he was working for *her* – so it would be totally inappropriate to have a relationship with him . . . wouldn't it?

"Joanna, has the heat attacked your brain yet again? This is the second time I've asked you if you'd like to go for a drink before I drop you back to your office?"

For a moment, Joanna was tempted. In fact, she desperately wanted to get drunk, then use it as an excuse for throwing herself at him and begging him to make love to her! "Eh sorry, Ronan – I can't this evening. I'd love to, but I'm meeting my friend Orla this evening. Maybe another time?"

"Of course. Anyway, I'll see you next week when I'm back from London. Hopefully, I'll have news of Maura Sweeney *née* Devane."

He smiled at her, and Joanna was relieved to see that he hadn't misunderstood what she meant, the way Tom Kilmartin had when she'd been unable to accept his invitation to dinner. She was also pleased that she'd managed to make herself clear to Ronan. She'd said exactly what she'd meant – she was meeting a *woman* friend – and hopefully they could go for a drink another evening. Besides, she felt that she needed space to evaluate how she felt about this man. And to find out if he was married. Because with this man, there would be no turning back if she fell in love with him.

In fact, she thought, maybe I already am . . .

CHAPTER 38

Today was a good day for Ellen. Jackie was away in England, so there would be no violence for the next two days. She was working this afternoon, at the café where she was employed as a waitress. She really enjoyed the craic and the cameraderie of the café, even more so when it was busy. The fare was simple: bacon, egg and chips or omelette, peas and chips – in fact, it was chips with everything. But the customers were decent, working-class folk, Trudy, the other waitress, was great fun and Vince, the chef, always had a selection of great jokes. So her shift always passed quickly and happily.

Ellen didn't like the idea of Jackie stealing cars. Nevertheless, she was his co-conspirator, if only because she felt she'd no other choice. She dutifully purchased Jackie's tickets for the car ferry, made up his sandwiches for the journey and sighed with relief when he headed off to England to deliver yet another stolen vehicle. Because this meant there would be several days during which he couldn't hit her.

Amazingly, it never crossed her mind – or his – that she had the option to leave him. But seeing women being hit was all she'd ever known – she'd seen it happen to her own mother, and both her sister and aunt were married to violent men. During her brief time on the streets with Colette, Ellen had found that many men weren't averse to a bit of rough action either. Even Colette had told her that Ivan would sometimes hit her when his business dealings weren't going well. To Ellen, violence was part and parcel of man-woman relationships.

Since their marriage back in 1970, Ellen had become the punch bag for all the pent- up anger and resentment that Jackie Byrne had accumulated. And, as is the way of people who are continually put down by others, Ellen accepted that perhaps she *did* deserve this violent treatment that Jackie meted out to her on a regular basis. Perhaps she *was* guilty for the fact that he'd had a miserable childhood and that he'd never made it to the top of the criminal fraternity. Ellen knew that Jackie longed to be a serious criminal – the big guy who made all the profit, a fixer like his dad, a man who was revered by his peers. But he also knew in his heart that he was, and always would be, a small-time operator. And he blamed Ellen for that too, and took out his rages on her, simply because she was there. A good day for Ellen was one when Jackie didn't hit her.

Ellen sighed. Sometimes, when he was in a particularly foul mood, Jackie would shout that he'd been forced to marry her, that she was an ugly cow and that he'd never have given her a second glance if his dad hadn't pushed him into it. Ellen was always surprised at these outbursts, since she hadn't been in the family way when they'd married. A woman being pregnant was the only reason Ellen could think of for a man being forced into marriage. In fact, she'd never been able to have a child – in her teens, an untreated dose of chlamydia had left her barren.

Ellen longed to know why Jackie said the nasty things he did, but when he was hitting her, it never seemed the right time to ask. She shivered as she thought of Jackie's father – a revolting old man, now dead, thank God – who used to sit grinning at her, as though he possessed some secret information to which only he was privy.

As she opened the front door and left the house, Ellen cast a surreptitious glance over the hedge that ran between her garden and the young doctor's next door. She felt terribly guilty about his dog – especially since the poor animal hadn't done anything to her.

She'd certainly needed medical treatment, but that was because Jackie himself had bitten her viciously during a row, and he'd been scared that the doctor would report him to the police if he knew what really happened. So he'd made her tell the doctor that the dog next door had caused her injuries.

But it had all gone horribly wrong. Jackie had tried to make capital out of the situation by asking the young man next door to pay him not to go to the police. When he'd refused to pay, Jackie had lost his temper and made her go to the local police station. Ellen sighed. No wonder Jackie was such a small-time criminal. He hadn't the brains to figure out that he was only making things worse for himself.

From then on, the incident had gathered a momentum

of its own. Given the severity of her injuries, the Gardaí had decided to take a case against the owner of the dog, so it was no longer possible to let the matter drop. Of course, Jackie had backed off and left Ellen to continue with the charade. Sometimes Jackie could be incredibly stupid, and through losing that hot temper of his, he often found himself out of his depth. But of course, she'd never dare tell him so. Because she knew what would happen to her if she did.

Quickly, Ellen hurried out the gate and down the road, wanting to put as much distance as possible between herself and the young doctor next door. She knew, of course, that if they happened to meet – over the garden hedge or on the street – he would always be pleasant and polite, despite the trouble she and Jackie had caused him. And that made Ellen feel even worse. She found it easier to cope with men who were surly and violent.

She sighed and headed down the road towards the café. Maybe Trudy would have a few new jokes today – she was always good for a laugh – that at least would help her to forget her reluctant involvement in this nasty business over the dog. Because no matter what the outcome was, Ellen knew that Jackie would blame her for it anyway.

Hopefully Matt, the owner of the café, wouldn't spot her black eye, which she'd taken great pains to cover with heavy make-up. It had been a parting gift from Jackie, who'd been in a temper because she'd made him egg sandwiches instead of corned beef. Ellen found Matt's eagle eye disconcerting. She didn't like it when he peered too closely at her heavy make-up or asked her point blank if Jackie had been hitting her. The bruises could be covered up reasonably well with make-up, but it wasn't quite so easy to explain away a half-closed eye or a gash that the make-up wouldn't adhere to. Then she'd tell Matt or Trudy or Vince that she'd fallen accidentally or walked into an open door. And all the while telling them how good Jackie was to her.

Ellen Byrne shuddered as she anticipated her husband Jackie's return from England the following day. She loved the days when Jackie was safely out of the country, but her all too brief hours of pleasure made his return all the harder to bear.

CHAPTER 39

Relieved, Agnes slipped into the darkened house. Thankfully, Ivan wasn't back yet, so she'd have time to take a shower, get to bed and pretend to be asleep before he arrived. Hopefully, he wouldn't bother her tonight. Presumably his floosie would have taken care of his sexual needs.

The grandfather clock in the hall chimed midnight, and Agnes yawned. She was tired but exhilarated, and her lips still tingled from Harry's kisses in the Park. Everything was on course for their journey to Australia, and nothing could go wrong now. She only needed to endure another few days of Ivan's barbs and nasty remarks. She was still livid that her father had left everything to Ivan, since it meant she'd be leaving the country empty-handed. As she climbed the magnificent stairway to the next floor, Agnes eyed the many antiques that she'd bought over the years. Regrettably, Ivan would now have the benefit of them too. If only she'd been able to sell some of them to get funding for their trip – but she simply couldn't risk Ivan noticing anything amiss.

She had just crawled into bed and was on the verge of sleep when she heard the slamming of the front door. For an instant, she wondered if she'd closed it properly when she came in, but then she heard Ivan's heavy footsteps as he climbed the stairs.

Agnes and Ivan had always kept separate bedrooms, and fortunately, in recent years, Ivan didn't come to her room very often. The only times he bothered her was when he was drunk or had no other outlet for his lechery.

Now, as she heard the door of her bedroom open, Agnes held her breath and pretended to be asleep. Hopefully, if Ivan was fooled, he would wander back to his own room and leave her alone. Her heart was thudding painfully in her chest, and it sounded so loud that she was sure he must be able to hear it.

"Agnes – wake up!"

Agnes continued to lie quietly, maintaining her pretence of being asleep.

"Agnes – do you hear me? Wake up!" This time, he came over to the bed and shook her roughly.

Agnes feared the worst. Presumably he wanted sex, and would force himself on her, whether she was willing or not. Slowly, she opened her eyes, pretending she'd just awoken. She was shocked at her husband's appearance. His clothes were all dishevelled, and his eyes were bloodshot. He looked terrible, and for a moment she almost pitied him.

"What's the matter, Ivan?" she asked, sitting up in her bed. Being conciliatory for another few days wouldn't hurt. And it would smooth her exit from his life forever.

"Listen here," he muttered, his voice slurring as he spoke, "if anyone asks where I've been this evening, you must tell them I was here with you."

"Of course," Agnes nodded. That suited her own purposes

perfectly. Luckily, she'd just got back to the house before Ivan, so there was no way he could have known that she'd been out earlier herself. She was also relieved that he didn't seem interested in making any sexual demands.

Ivan shambled out of her room, and Agnes listened as he made his way noisily along the corridor to his own room. Eventually, when no further sounds were heard, Agnes sighed with relief. He'd obviously gone to sleep, so finally she could go to sleep herself. She yawned, then settled down to wonderful dreams of Harry . . .

* * *

In his own room, Ivan was smiling to himself as he got undressed. What had started out as a disastrous evening had actually ended very satisfactorily. When he'd accidentally killed that stupid bitch, he'd been terrified of what would happen to him. But good old Paddy had come up with the perfect solution. Now, he was going to use the evening's events to his own benefit and destroy that Sweeney bastard at the same time. How dare that man think he could charm Agnes away from him! Not only was he trying to turn Ivan's own workers against him, he was also a sly, cheating wife-stealer as well! As for Agnes, he couldn't wait to see her reaction when Harry Sweeney was accused of murder! That would teach her to betray him.

Ivan snuggled down in his bed. He'd been getting fed up with Colette anyway. She'd been making too many demands lately – and she'd even gone off to England and left him on his own for three whole months! What was he supposed to do? Well, as it happened, her absence hadn't been a problem. There were plenty of other women available, and now he would start looking for a replacement. Maybe this time, he'd even have two, since money was no object. He now had the Cashen fortune as well as his own.

He'd been clever, of course, by ensuring that the lease on Colette's flat was in her own name, and paid for in cash, so there wouldn't be any links to him when Colette's murder became public knowledge.

He yawned and pulled the bedclothes up around him. Anyway, Colette had deserved what she got. He'd never have taken up with her if he'd known that she was Harry Sweeney's sister-in-law. That was why she hadn't told him in the first place – she didn't want to lose the expensive lifestyle in which he'd maintained her. No doubt she'd been Harry Sweeney's ally and had been feeding information back to him . . . Ivan's outrage grew stronger by the second. How dare she try to make a fool of him! Anyway, he'd shown her. She'd never cause him any trouble again.

When they'd reached the Phoenix Park, Jackie Byrne had shown them the exact spot where Agnes had been canoodling with Harry Sweeney earlier in the evening. They'd been pleased to spot a fresh cigarette butt on the ground, near the tyre marks from Harry's car. If it had Harry's fingerprints on it, they'd be home and dry.

Colette's body had been laid on the ground beside some bushes, just a few feet away from the cigarette butt. She was already beginning to stiffen by the time they got there, so they'd had to move fast.

Before they'd driven to the Phoenix Park, Paddy had insisted that Colette's body be laid out along the back seat. It had something to do with the sinking of the blood to the lower level, Paddy said. Ivan had hated touching Colette's cold flesh, but he'd done as Paddy asked. After all, Paddy was an expert at this kind of thing. And they needed to fool the authorities into thinking that Colette had been murdered in the Park, and at an earlier time than it had actually happened.

In the Park, Ivan had stayed in the car while Paddy and Jackie recreated the crime scene. Paddy had been worried about the restaurant where Ivan and Colette had dined earlier. But Ivan wasn't worried. He knew that the man who owned Luigi's would keep quiet. Because he himself had saved him from bankruptcy and given him a soft loan to tide him over. If the man opened his mouth, he'd be cutting his own throat.

Ivan smiled contentedly. He was dying to tackle his wife about her carry-on with Harry Sweeney, but he liked the idea of biding his time even more. Instead, he would savour the thought of her expression when her lover-boy was charged with murder. The bitch thought she'd fooled him tonight, but he'd have the last laugh. It would be almost as amusing as when her father's will was read out and she discovered she'd been left nothing. Chuckling to himself, Ivan rolled over and fell into a deep sleep.

CHAPTER 40

"Orla, there must be something seriously the matter with me," Joanna told her friend as they sat in the bar of the Morrison later that evening. "I mean, only a few days ago, I fancied Tom Kilmartin like crazy. Now I've met another man – this gorgeous private detective – who has me wanting to tear off my clothes and leap into bed with him on the spot!" She gave an exasperated sigh.

"Well, the answer to your query is simply that you're a slut," said Orla with a grin. "A trollop, a hussy – call it what you like. And with this Ronan guy, you're also attracted to the element of the unknown. This is what happens when you lead such a sheltered life, my dear friend. I mean, it's pathetic – when were you last in the sack having a good shag?"

Joanna grinned back. "OK – point taken. But there's something about this guy. He's handsome in a rugged sort of way, yet he's boyish and funny."

"You're definitely in need of a good seeing-to," said

Orla, wrinkling up her nose. "Anyway, you'll probably discover that he already has a wife and ten kids. Or that the wife has died in mysterious circumstances and is probably buried beneath the floorboards."

Joanna couldn't help but laugh. "I guess you're right – about the wife and kids bit anyway. Someone that gorgeous wouldn't be still single."

Then she thought of Tom – *he* was still single. God, Orla was right – she *was* a trollop. Fancying two different men within the space of two minutes!

"So when are you seeing this Ronan fellow again?" Orla asked.

"Next week. He's heading off to London, to search for Harry's wife. When he comes back, I'll also have to arrange for him to meet with Tom, since he's the one who's paying Ronan's bill."

Orla grinned mischievously. "That'll be quite a meeting – how are you going to control those hormones, Jo? Two fanciable men, both in your office at the same time! Some people have all the luck! Maybe you could arrange to have a threesome on your office floor?"

Joanna made a good-natured swipe at her friend. "Talking of men – any word from Gary?"

Orla immediately looked sad and shook her head. "The only man who wants to see me right now is that scumbag Declan. When I meet him tomorrow, I hope he's going to grovel. Then I can tell him where he can shove his apology!" She sighed. "But I guess Gary wasn't as interested as I was. Although I could have sworn he was keen at the time. It just goes to show how we can pick up the wrong signals." She looked eagerly at her friend. "I presume he hasn't asked for me when he's been in your office?"

"Sorry, no," said Joanna. "Maybe when he gets this court case over his dog sorted out, he'll be in a more sociable frame of mind. Perhaps he's just too preoccupied."

Orla snorted. "Look, the court case isn't for a while yet, is it? If he was interested, he'd have contacted me by now."

Joanna nodded. She had to agree that if a man was genuinely interested in a woman, he'd have made the necessary moves by now. Of course, in these days of equality, a woman could also make the first move . . . "Why don't you phone Gary yourself?" she suggested to her friend.

"No way!" said Orla. "I think I could be forward with a guy if I just wanted a one-night stand with him, because I wouldn't really care what he thought. But with Gary – well, I wanted more, I guess." She looked earnestly at her friend. "I really did fancy him, Jo – there was something really special about him . . . " She shrugged.

Joanna said nothing, because there wasn't anything she could really say.

"Anyway, I don't intend to sit around moping over someone who doesn't want me," Orla said determinedly. "What do you think of that guy sitting at the end of the bar – he's cute, isn't he? He keeps looking over here, and just a minute ago, he winked when I caught his eye."

Joanna laughed. "Orla, you're incorrigible! And you dare to call *me* a slut! Talk of the pot calling the kettle black – "

"OK, OK – why shouldn't a woman go after several

men at the same time?" said Orla, grinning. "*I* think the world would be perfect if it was socially acceptable for women to have several husbands or partners each – after all, one man alone can't possibly satisfy all a woman's needs."

Joanna smiled. "That would be fine if it worked only in women's favour – I wouldn't want *men* being able to do the same!"

Orla snorted. "I thought they did that already! Most of the ones I've met let their dicks control their lives, yet when a woman behaves the same way, they label her a slapper."

"Well, the guy sitting at the end of bar is certainly eager to satisfy *your* libido! He hasn't stopped staring at you since we arrived!"

Just then, one of the barmen arrived at their table with a round of drinks. "These are courtesy of the gentleman sitting at the bar," he told them, as Orla grinned wickedly at her companion.

"What did I tell you, Jo? It's my charm and personality – it gets them every time!"

"Well, we'd better invite him to join us," said Joanna, gesturing their thanks to the man at the bar and indicating for him to join them. "Maybe he'll have a friend arriving later."

"That's the spirit!" said Orla, grinning. "I'm certainly in the mood for a bit of mischief tonight. And next week too, if the other guy decides to ring. Even if Gary Culhane doesn't want me, I'm not going to sit around moping!"

CHAPTER 41

Mick McHale parked his car and made his way towards the address that Orla had given him. He couldn't move too fast – his gammy leg saw to that – but he'd got a parking space reasonably near to where he was going. Besides, he needed the exercise anyway. The doctors had told him to keep the leg mobile, or it might seize up on him.

Jim found himself walking through a pleasant housing estate, where there were plenty of trees and mature hedges. Grass verges were neatly trimmed, and all the lawns were beautifully manicured. Except for the one at the end. Which was the number that Jim was looking for. The house and front garden had a slightly decayed look about them as though someone had struggled valiantly against the elements and the weeds, but had lost the battle and finally surrendered. This place needs a firm hand, he thought. A new coat of paint and some new guttering would work wonders, and the grass simply needed a good mowing.

He rang the doorbell. Inside, he could hear the sounds of children running downstairs, doors banging and muffled voices as someone's footsteps came down the hallway. He smiled to himself. All the familiar domestic sounds that he hadn't realised he missed until now.

Suddenly, the door opened, and he found himself staring at a pretty but harassed woman, who looked as though she was about to collapse from exhaustion.

"I'm Mick McHale," he said, smiling and extending his hand.

The woman took it and smiled back at him, the impact of her smile having a powerful effect on him.

"I'm Mary O'Dowd," she said. "Come on in. I really appreciate you calling round."

"It's no trouble at all," he assured her. "Maybe I'll be able to help."

"I've got the kettle on," said Mary, smiling shyly at him, and Mick McHale suddenly felt about a foot taller.

If there was anything he could do to help this poor woman, he'd move heaven and earth to do it. She was clearly in difficult circumstances – that much he'd gathered from his conversation with Orla – but he'd already detected an inherent sense of pride in her that he admired. He didn't like people who moaned about their lot. Usually they were the sort who had more than enough, anyway. Wanting more was a state of mind – he preferred people who just got on with things and didn't feel that other people owed them anything.

Mary led Jim straight into the kitchen, and he was pleased at the informality of this gesture, even though the reason for their meeting was serious enough. He'd have been less pleased if she'd installed him in the parlour and treated him with formality, as many people did where agents of the law were concerned.

"It's very good of you to agree to talk with Paul," said Mary quietly. "I really don't know what to do about him, Jim. I don't seem to be able to make him understand that he'll destroy his own life if he keeps on misbehaving like this."

Jim smiled at her. He liked the way she'd immediately called him by his first name. "Don't worry, Mary," he said gently. "Go and make the tea, then we can sit down and you can explain the whole story to me."

Sitting at the table while Mary filled two mugs and brought them to the table, Jim felt a sudden tremendous longing for the warmth and comfort of domestic life. It was a feeling that, since Sheila's death, he had kept under tight control. *His* days of domestic bliss were over.

He smiled quickly at Mary to cover up any sadness that might have appeared fleetingly on his face. He was here to help this woman, not to become maudlin about his own situation.

Mary smiled shyly back and produced some buttered slices of brack and a selection of small cakes. Jim took a slice of brack gratefully. This was one of his favourite snacks, but he also hoped that Mary hadn't been spending her hard-earned cash on a spread in order to thank him. He knew from talking to Orla that, as well as her difficulties with her son, Mary wasn't in the best of financial circumstances.

"Now, tell me about Paul," Jim said gently.

So Mary told him everything – the departure of her

husband to live with a younger woman, her present financial difficulties, her unsuccessful attempts to keep young Paul under control. And in turn, Jim found himself telling Mary about his late wife Sheila, his retirement from the force, the loneliness that he often felt now that his own family were grown up and no longer seemed to need him so much. Yet his revelations weren't told in any kind of self-pitying way – he just found that Mary was a marvellous and empathic listener. And before long, he felt as though he had known her for ages.

Suddenly, Jim looked at his watch and realised guiltily that he'd been chatting to Mary for over an hour!

"Isn't it time I met Paul?"

Mary smiled wistfully. "He's sulking upstairs in his room – he's not too happy about me asking you to talk to him."

"Well," said Jim, "I promise I'll keep the lecture to a minimum. Let's get started anyway. Can you ask him to come downstairs, Mary? And then maybe you'd leave Paul and me alone for a few minutes?"

Mary nodded, left the kitchen and called up to Paul from the bottom of the stairs. There followed the sound of a door banging, the clump of reluctant feet on the stairs, then a sullen Paul appeared and stood looking bored at the kitchen door.

"Hello, Paul," said Jim warmly, rising up and extending his hand.

Paul looked a little surprised as he shook the hand that was offered. He'd expected an instant tirade like the one he'd received from his mother, which had been followed by another tirade from the local sergeant. He was sick of being chastised. But this guy seemed kind of OK.

Mary disappeared, closing the kitchen door behind her. Paul sighed. Now the tirade would probably begin. Yet surprisingly, it didn't.

"Your mother tells me that you're a Gaelic football fan," Jim said, pouring himself another mug of tea and gesturing to Paul in case he wanted a cup.

Paul shook his head, taking a piece of brack instead. He loved brack, but they didn't get to eat it very often nowadays. Too expensive, his mam said. So there was *some* benefit to be gained from having this guy paying a visit.

"Yeah," said Paul, speaking with his mouth full, precisely because his mother had always told him *not* to do it. But this Jim guy didn't seem to notice – or care.

Jim smiled. The conversation – if he could call it that – was as difficult as climbing Mount Everest without an oxygen mask. But he would persevere until he'd gained the young lad's interest. "I believe you play for the school team?"

Another "yeah" was reluctantly forthcoming. But Paul was slightly more interested now. Was this guy still leading up to a telling-off? Or was he mistaken, and this *wasn't* the ex-cop who was going to give him a lecture on being a model citizen?

"And you're a follower of the Dublin team too?"

Paul looked really surprised now. How did the old geezer know that? It was gratifying to discover that he wasn't just labelled as a bad kid in need of a good kick up the arse.

"Yeah," he said for the third time, but this time it was followed by a whole sentence. "I go to their matches when I can afford it. It's brilliant that they've reached the finals of the All Ireland."

"Will you be going to the match?" Jim asked idly.

Paul's face darkened, and his lip curled disdainfully as he answered. "Are you joking?" he said bitterly. "Those tickets cost a fortune – and anyway, they've been sold out for months."

Jim smiled. "It just so happens that I have two tickets myself. I'm a great Dublin fan too – would you fancy coming along to the match with me?"

Paul's face lit up. "Cool!" was all he could say, but his expression of sheer delight said it all.

"That's settled then," said Jim. "I'll collect you about one o'clock on Sunday fortnight. Now – how about having another slice of brack before we tell your mother that it's safe for her to come back into the kitchen?"

Paul grinned and helped himself to another slice. "But – aren't you supposed to be giving me a talk – about behaving myself?"

Jim laughed. "Do you want me to?"

Paul coloured. "No."

"Neither do I," said Jim, patting Paul on the shoulder as the two of them stood up. "Now go and tell your mam that we've finished talking. And I'll see you, as arranged."

With a grateful smile, Paul disappeared and Mary quickly reappeared in the kitchen, looking surprised that Jim and Paul had spent such a short time together.

"D-did the two of you get things sorted?" she asked anxiously.

"Oh yes," said Jim, smiling. "He's a nice lad – I think he and I are going to get on like a house on fire. I don't

251

think you need have any more worries about him, Mary. Now how about putting that kettle on again and making me another cup of tea?"

* * *

Alone in his room, Paul heaved a sigh of relief. He'd been expecting a heavy lecture, and maybe even veiled physical threats. But the guy downstairs was pretty cool, actually. Paul couldn't fathom why this Jim fellow hadn't come on all heavy over the way he'd behaved. He knew that he'd upset his mam – and he never really meant to – it was just that life seemed so unfair. Since his dad left, there'd been no money for anything. His dad didn't seem to care about him, his sister or his mam any more – he now preferred to lavish all his dosh on that stupid bimbo he'd shacked up with.

It also pissed Paul off big-time that since money was now so tight, he couldn't always afford to go with his mates to football matches any more. Nor could he afford to buy the supporters' gear that all his school friends had. As a result, his mates had started giving him a hard time.

Paul knew that those guys didn't know what it was like to be poor and, of course, he didn't want them to know. So he pretended not to care, but deep inside he really did care. Desperately.

Paul suddenly grinned. Anyway, now his pals would be mad jealous because he was going to the All Ireland Final – none of *them* were going, because tickets were as rare as hen's teeth. Yippee!

Suddenly, he was overwhelmed by doubt. Maybe the guy downstairs wouldn't come up trumps in the end.

After all, Paul had been let down by his own dad so many times. How often had his dad said that they'd do something together, then simply never turned up? At first, Paul had supposed that the bimbo had put her foot down, objecting to his dad spending time with his own kids. That idea was more comforting than accepting that his dad simply couldn't be bothered any more. But as time went by, and Paul saw his mother becoming more and more harassed, and their financial situation becoming more and more precarious, he sadly admitted to himself that his dad *didn't* care about them any more.

That was when his anger and disappointment had bubbled over into stupid acts of defiance. Since being good didn't work, he'd make people – especially his dad – aware of him by fair means or foul. The only problem was – he'd hurt his mother too. He knew that it wasn't fair, but somehow he found it impossible to stop doing stupid things.

Anyway, he'd better be on his best behaviour now, just in case this Jim guy really *did* intend taking him to the All Ireland Final. Despite his cynicism, Paul couldn't help but feel a thrill deep in the pit of his stomach. It would be really cool to get to the Final – especially since none of his friends were lucky enough to be going. And if Dublin won . . .

Paul took out his schoolbooks and settled down at his makeshift desk. He's better get those outstanding school projects completed, so that nothing could get in the way of him enjoying the match when the time came. *If* this Jim fellow really intended to keep his word . . .

CHAPTER 42

Joanna sat dreaming at her desk. Her thoughts were filled with visions of Ronan O'Farrell. This very minute, Ronan was in London, searching for Maura Sweeney, *née* Devane. He'd been gone for several days, and she missed him so much already! It would be wonderful if he came back with some good news too. Maybe he'd discover that Maura did have a child after all, and so he'd manage to find out the name of Harry Sweeney's child and where he or she was living. Then, hopefully, administering Agnes's will would be plain sailing.

While she and Ronan hadn't managed to go for that drink yet, at least she'd discovered that he wasn't married or living with anyone. Mick McHale had rung to talk to Mary about Paul, and she'd collared him about Ronan's background – purely for professional reasons, of course. She was longing to see Ronan once again, and this time, she'd definitely go for that drink with him . . .

"Hello, Joanna!" Suddenly, Ronan O'Farrell stuck his

head around the door of her office, and Joanna was catapulted from dreams into reality.

What a wonderful reality, she thought. She felt weak at the knees. He was every bit as gorgeous as she'd remembered! Somehow, she managed to find her voice. "Hi, Ronan – I didn't expect to see you back so soon! Does this mean you've got good news?"

Throwing himself into the seat opposite her desk, Ronan sprawled out in front of her. "I'm afraid not – but I did find something. I tried lots of my contacts in the Irish community in London, but I couldn't track down anyone answering to either Maura Devane or Maura Sweeney. Most of the people living there now wouldn't have any recollection of somebody who was there in 1970 anyway – but I scouted around and found a GP who used to have his practice in that area. He checked his old files for someone called Devane, and hey presto! He found a card for Maura Devane."

"Fantastic!"

Ronan smiled. "Then he remembered that she'd been heavily pregnant and had come to him for a check-up in 1970, and a referral to a midwife. He referred her to the local community midwife who was also Irish, and that was the last he ever saw of her."

"My God – so Maura Devane really was pregnant! Can we assume it was Harry's baby?"

"Who knows? But whether, biologically, it was his or not, it would be his *legal* offspring – since he and Maura were not divorced at the time. And therefore that child would fulfil the requirements of the will."

"And my job would be done!"

"Yes, but . . . the old doctor also gave me the address Maura had given him, and it turns out that it was a made-up address – no such place exists, nor did it exist back then."

"Well, the address won't matter if you can track down the midwife."

Ronan smiled. "I'll go back to London again next week and continue the search. In the meantime, I have a few other cases pending that I need to work on. But are you free to have something to eat later? We can talk through the whole scenario, and I'll explain in detail what I've done so far." His eyes twinkled. "I'd hate to bill you for work that you didn't know I'd done!"

"That sounds great," said Joanna, unsure of whether she meant the food or the update. "Where do you suggest we meet?"

"How about the Haven on George's Street? At seven o'clock?"

"Great. See you there."

After Ronan had left to pursue his other investigations, Joanna found herself smiling for the rest of the afternoon. It had all been so simple. Ronan wanted to see her, and he'd made his interest clear. And she had indicated *her* interest, without any game-playing either. It was all going to be so straightforward – she was falling in love with Ronan O'Farrell, and she liked the way it felt. There was none of the uncertainty that had characterised her attempts to have a relationship with Tom Kilmartin. Well, Tom was now history – at least as a romantic possibility. Maybe now, since she no longer fancied him, it would be easier to sort out the mess his mother's will had created.

When Joanna arrived at the Haven, Ronan was already there, and she was pleased to note that he wasn't the sort of man who played games by turning up late. He was keen, and he didn't mind her knowing it. They ordered quickly, then he began to tell her about the kind of work he did, detailing some of the strange scenarios he'd got himself into in the pursuit of missing persons. Soon they were both laughing and trading stories about their careers

Joanna couldn't believe how easy it was to talk to Ronan now. Perhaps the bottle of wine he'd ordered had something to do with it. Wouldn't Orla be astonished when she told her about this gorgeous new man in her life!

"How about a nightcap in Daly's?"

Joanna looked at her watch in astonishment. Had they really been chatting for several hours? "My God – I'd no idea it was so late!"

But why shouldn't she go for a drink in the pub next door? There was nothing to go home for, except her cat. She felt sure Devil wouldn't mind if she stayed out a bit later. She'd make it up to her by buying her some gourmet cat food . . .

"Of course – I'd love to, Ronan."

In the pub, Joanna switched to vodka and wondered briefly if this was a stupid thing to do. She'd have another hangover in the morning, but thankfully she didn't have any court appearances lined up for tomorrow. She could recover in the office, and hopefully, it would be an easy day . . .

It was nearly midnight when she and Ronan stepped

out of the pub. He slipped his arm around her as they walked along, and it seemed the most natural thing in the world. He hailed a taxi, then the two of them settled back comfortably in the plush seats, his arm still around her.

"Where are we going?" she asked, although she didn't really care.

"We're going to your place, first. Then when I leave you off, the taxi will take me on to my place."

She felt a stab of disappointment. He wasn't intending to stay with her!

At last, the taxi drew up outside her house in Blackrock and they got out.

"Are you OK, Joanna?" he asked.

"No," she said truthfully. "I can't find my key."

He helped her to find it in the depths of her handbag. "Here – let me open the door for you," he said kindly. "At this rate, you could be left outside all night!"

She couldn't restrain herself. "Ronan – will you stay with me tonight?" she whispered urgently. "Tell the taxi-driver to go."

So Ronan paid the taxi-driver and followed her into the house. For a moment they stood staring at each other.

"Is this really what you want?" he asked softly.

"Yes, there's nothing I want more."

As he ran his finger along the hall table, Joanna shivered with excitement at his seemingly casual gesture, which seemed laden with raw sex appeal to her. Suddenly, he was at her side, and that same finger now touched her lips gently, then ran down her neck and lightly touched her breasts. She was rooted to the spot with a mixture of shock, fear and excitement as his lips met hers. Suddenly, her arms were around his neck and they were kissing passionately.

"Oh my God, Joanna – I've wanted to do this since I first laid eyes on you!" he groaned. He began opening the buttons of her blouse and lowering the straps of her bra so that he could reach her nipples.

Now she was groaning with desire as she slipped her fingers beneath his jacket, pulling his shirt loose and feeling the hairiness of his belly and chest.

"Let's go upstairs," he whispered. "I presume there's somewhere convenient."

In a daze, Joanna led him upstairs. She was still holding his hand as she opened her bedroom door. There in front of them was her large double bed, and when he pulled back the bedspread, underneath were crisp, clean sheets. Briefly, she was grateful that she'd changed the sheets only that morning before she'd left for work.

Turning back to Joanna, Ronan saw that there was assent in her eyes, and slowly they proceeded to undress each other.

Momentarily, she worried about her grey-white, much-washed underwear and wished that she'd worn her new sexy satin bra and panties. But then, she'd never expected this to happen, had she? Besides, she thought, Ronan was so excited that he was unlikely to notice what she was wearing, since it was all ending up on the floor anyway . . .

Then they were both naked and on the bed, with him kissing her body all over. In ecstacy, she ran her fingers through the hair on his chest and downwards until she found his gigantic manhood and gasped with pleasure.

Suddenly, he opened her thighs and began tasting her as she writhed in pleasure. Then he was in her, and they were both bucking back and forth as though possessed.

"Is this good for you, Joanna?" he whispered.

"It's wonderful!" she whispered back, her passion rising even more because of his show of concern. No man before had ever showed such consideration in love-making, and it heightened her pleaure until she could hold off no longer, and shuddering she reached her crescendo of pleasure.

Then Ronan reached his peak, and together they lay exhausted.

CHAPTER 43

Suddenly, Catherine heard impatient rapping at the front door. Opening it, she was surprised when a distraught Agnes brushed past her and hurried into the kitchen.

"Cat, you're not going to believe this, but Harry's been arrested – for murder!"

"W-what?" Catherine embraced her friend as the tears started to fall. "What on earth are you talking about?"

Agnes gulped. "Did you hear about that young woman who was killed a few nights ago? In the Phoenix Park?"

Catherine nodded.

"Well, she was Harry's sister-in-law and they're saying Harry did it!" Agnes began crying again. "But he didn't, Cat – he was with me that night! We spent the whole evening in his car in the Phoenix Park planning our future!"

"Well then, can't you clear his name easily?"

"No, Cat, I can't – if I give Harry an alibi, it will be a public disgrace for Ivan and his rage will be uncontrollable! He'll do anything to prevent me from seeing Harry, and we'll *never manage to get away to Australia – and, Cat, what about the baby? Oh God, I've got to speak to Harry!"*

"Where is he now?"

"I don't know – I think he's been taken to the Bridewell police station to be charged. Then he'll be kept on remand in Mountjoy prison until the trial."

"Look, calm down, Agnes – we've got to think this through," said Catherine, sounding more confident than she felt. *"You can't be seen contacting Harry at this stage – let me go and talk to him. Since he's innocent until proved guilty, they can't stop him writing to you. I'll go and visit him, bring back a letter from him, then you'll know what he wants you to do."*

"Oh would you, Cat? You're a friend in a million!" Agnes started to cry again. *"Ivan's having me watched all the time – if I went to see Harry, it would confirm what he only suspects at the moment. And he might do something to me and the baby. And there's more to it than that, Cat,"* Agnes sobbed. *"Ivan's insisting that I give him an alibi for that evening, if anyone comes checking on him."*

"Why on earth would Ivan need an alibi?"

"I don't know – but I'm beginning to wonder if he had something to do with the murder of that poor girl."

"Oh my God!" said Catherine, unsure of whether she was praying or swearing. *"What makes you think that?"*

"Well, he came home looking frightened and tetchy, and his clothes were all dishevelled. And this woman who's been killed – not only was she Harry's sister-in-law, she was Ivan's mistress as well!"

Catherine looked aghast. *"Oh God, I see what you mean. Do you think Ivan might have had her killed to put the blame on Harry?"*

"I don't know! But isn't Harry a very convenient scapegoat, Cat?"

"Surely Ivan wouldn't commit murder."

"My husband is not a man you cross," Agnes said bitterly. "I've seen him annihilate other businesspeople who challenged him. He's a ruthless bastard, Cat. I doubt if that poor girl is the first person he's had eliminated. And even if he hasn't actually committed other murders himself, he's instructed his lackey, Paddy Byrne, to do it. When the stakes are high, people like Ivan see human life as very cheap."

"Why was Harry arrested? What sort of evidence has been trumped up?"

"Apparently some young chap is claiming that he saw Harry kill her. But I know that's untrue. Oh Cat, will you go and see Harry as soon as possible?"

"Of course. I'll go first thing tomorrow morning."

As the two women sat in silence, it gradually dawned on Catherine that she must urge Agnes to do something that would be anathema to her. The room was now almost in darkness, but neither woman made any move to turn on a light. It was as though the darkness mirrored their mood.

At last Catherine spoke. "I know you're not going to like what I have to say —"

"You're right — I won't."

"But you've no other option, Agnes. You'll have to seduce Ivan — and quickly," said Catherine, speaking briskly to lessen the unpleasantness of what she was saying. "If your pregnancy starts showing before Harry is released, you may need Ivan to believe that the child is his — at least until you can leave for Australia."

Agnes started to cry again. "Oh God — do you really think Harry will be in prison that long? OK, OK, I'll do it — but the

263

mere thought of it makes me sick. Ivan and I haven't slept together in ages – ever since I met Harry, I couldn't bear to have Ivan touch me. I've managed to find excuses – you know, painful periods, a headache. The thought of being intimate with that lying, cheating bastard disgusts me. I can't bear him to touch me any more –"

"You have no choice, Agnes. You have to do it – for the baby's sake."

As the silence lengthened between them, Catherine had an idea.

"A few drinks might help," she said softly. "There's a bottle of gin in the cocktail cabinet."

"I hate gin," said Agnes stubbornly.

"Well, we've nothing else in the house – although maybe there's a small drop of sherry left over since last Christmas."

"The gin will do," said Agnes resignedly, "as long as you've got some tonic to go with it. Now let's get started before I change my mind."

Catherine got out the bottle and two glasses from the cocktail cabinet. "I'll keep you company," she told Agnes solemnly, "but you'll have to leave your car here and take a taxi home."

"Maybe I won't bother going home at all."

"Well, there wouldn't be any point in getting drunk then, would there?"

"No, I suppose not. So let's get started."

The two women filled their glasses.

"Here's to Harry's quick release!" toasted Catherine, as their glasses clinked.

CHAPTER 44

Declan Dunne was sitting at a table in the large city-centre café. He looked up as Orla arrived and slid into the seat in front of him. Declan gave her the benefit of what he regarded as his killer smile – the one that he used to great effect in pubs and nightclubs, where the women just loved it. Or so he thought anyway. It appeared to have no effect on Orla, so he leaned forward and placed a kiss on her cheek. She looked slightly startled – which, he reckoned, was a good sign. He'd seen that kissing stunt done to great effect in some movie he'd recently reviewed, and he'd instantly decided to add it to his repetoire.

Although he and Orla had broken up, they still saw each other regularly at work when their shifts overlapped. Of course, she ignored him in front of other people. But he knew that secretly she was longing to speak to him, but her pride wouldn't allow her to give in. So he'd selected a more private location for the speech he was about to make. And while a restaurant wasn't exactly private – after all, it was a busy centre-city café – it offered a non-threatening environment in which to make another attempt at getting back with her. And if that didn't work – well, he had another strategy up his sleeve, and the public location he had chosen would also ensure that Orla couldn't overreact.

"Hi, Orla. You're looking gorgeous – as always."

"Cut the crap, Declan – what do you want?"

Uh oh. So she was going to act tough. Well, he would gently disarm her with his caring, empathic New-Man routine. Before long, he'd have her laughing at his jokes, preening at his compliments and throwing herself at his feet once more. And by tomorrow night, hopefully he'd have moved back into the apartment with her.

"I got you a coffee, Orla," he said, ignoring her question and pushing a cup across to her. "It's a cappucino – which I know you like – and a blueberry Danish. Remember when we used to buy Danish pastries by the dozen and stuff ourselves back at the apartment?" Declan smirked. Memories. That was how to get them. They made all women feel sentimental, he reasoned. Maybe Orla would remember the good times they'd once shared, and the memories would make her long to repeat them.

"I don't eat Danish pastries any more," said Orla, pushing the plate back towards Declan. "I stopped eating them after we split up. For some reason, they turn my stomach nowadays."

OK, so the reminiscences weren't working. It was time to try something else. "How have you been keeping,

Orla?" he asked, in his most caring voice. "I know we see each other at work sometimes, but I really wanted to have a *personal* chat with you."

"What about?" Orla asked abruptly, looking at her watch. "I haven't got all day, Declan – I've an interview to do this afternoon and notes from yesterday to write up for tomorrow's issue. So get on with it, will you?"

Declan decided that it was time to get to the point, since Orla might decide to up sticks and depart at any time. This certainly wasn't going the way he'd planned – but no one could say he wasn't a trier.

"Orla, I miss you terribly," he said, reaching across the table to grasp her hand, but Orla deftly moved it from the table before he could reach it. "I still love you, you know. I've been such a fool – Sasha meant nothing to me. I made a terrible mistake – can you please forgive me, and let's start again?"

Orla laughed harshly. "Are you out of your mind, Declan? I wouldn't be caught dead with you – even if you were the last man on earth! You did me a big favour, you know – by running off with that trollop. It made me realise what a sleazebag you really are."

Declan took a mouthful of coffee and burned his tongue. This was all going horribly wrong.

"So – you're absolutely certain that you don't want to continue with our engagement?"

Orla snorted. "Engagement? We're not engaged any more, you asshole – that ended when you started shagging Ms Big-Arse. What do you take me for?"

"Then – isn't it time you gave me back the ring?"

There. He'd said it. And even if Orla wanted to throw

something at him, she'd hardly do it here, would she? After all, she had her reputation to think of. It wouldn't do to be seen behaving violently in a public place.

Anyway, surely he was entitled to have the ring back? After all, he was still paying up for it. If he could at least sell it, that would help to ease the pain of his loss. Maybe he could dangle the prospect of an all-expenses-paid holiday in front of Sasha – that would surely make her drop John Boyle pretty quickly! God, how that beautiful arse of hers still turned him on! And to think that John Boyle was now deriving pleasure from those magnificent twin orbs! Declan held his breath and waited.

Orla's voice, when it came, was menacingly low. "You absolute scumbag," she said softly. "I already knew that you were nothing but a toe-rag, but this is the absolute pits! If we're going to go down *that* road, then what about all the gifts I gave *you*? Like the designer jacket that cost me a month's salary, the money I gave you to service your car last autumn, the holiday in Tunisia that I paid for and the Rolex watch that cost a lot more than the bloody ring you gave *me*?"

Declan swallowed. This wasn't going well. Trust that bitch to have a memory like an elephant. And he'd lied when he'd said she looked great. Maybe he should tell her that she really looked like the back of a bus, just to get his own back. "OK, OK, " he said, sighing and raising his hands in supplication. "But don't you think you're being a trifle petty about all this?"

"Petty?" snarled Orla, enraged. "You bastard! You're quite happy to keep all my gifts to *you* – yet you want back the only lousy present you ever gave *me*! And

speaking of petty – where are my Tom Petty CDs that you
'borrowed' when you left for Spain?"

"Look, all those gifts were different," said Declan in
desperation. "They were given freely! But an engagement
ring signifies the sealing of a contract – "

"Oh, so now we're reduced to contractual obligations!"
Orla retorted. "Get out of here, Declan, while you're still
ahead. Because if you persist in this – this stupid carry-on
about a contract, you'll soon be receiving a letter from my
solicitor, demanding the return of all the gifts that I gave
you!"

"OK – keep the damned ring!" said Declan, standing
up. He couldn't wait to escape Orla's wrath. Yet he still
couldn't resist one last try before he left. "But are you
absolutely sure we couldn't get back together again?"

Orla ignored his question. "Goodbye, Declan," was all
she said.

* * *

Gary Culhane had spotted Orla as she arrived at the café
and had seen her greet that dork she was engaged to, who
was sitting over on the other side of the café. Miserably, he
kept an eye on them while attempting to keep his sister
Breda's two young children from climbing all over the
table. Breda had gone to the self-service counter to get them
two more coffees. He wished she would hurry up – already
it seemed like she'd been gone for aeons, and he'd already
had enough of her unruly offspring. Give him a busy
hospital ward any day! How did she and Aidan manage to
have any kind of love life, he wondered, with these two
monsters demanding attention all the time?

Now, Colm, aged three, was attempting to wrestle an almond bun from his five-year-old sister, Aoife. Why was it, Gary wondered, as he grabbed Colm's jacket and hauled him back, that whatever another kid had was always deemed more desirable? He sighed and directed the child to his own, identical, almond bun. But Colm wasn't having any of it and decided that bawling his head off might be a more effective method of getting his own way.

Breda returned with the coffees, made a swipe at Colm – who miraculously decided to behave now that his mother was back – and sat down.

"You're looking pretty miserable," said Breda.

"I am," said Gary truthfully.

"Tell me," said Breda, reaching across and patting his hand affectionately, "is everything alright at the hospital?"

"The hospital's fine," said Gary. "It's my personal life that's in tatters." He didn't like to moan, but it was such a relief to be able to unburden himself to his sister. So he told her about his dog Bruce, the upcoming court case that he was dreading and about Orla, who was engaged to someone else.

"You poor love," said Breda affectionately, leaning over and planting a kiss on his cheek. "I wish I could help. I know how much Bruce means to you. What will the court case do?"

"Well, according to Joanna, my solicitor, the court will rely on the testimony of the plaintiff. Assuming that the judge believes the dog is dangerous, he or she could either fine me – I've no problem with that – or insist that the dog be always restrained on a lead – which I've no problem with either – or," his voice trembled, "or the court can order the dog to be destroyed." Gary looked earnestly at his sister. "Breda, *you* know how docile Bruce is and how well he gets on with the kids. But this bloody woman next door swears that he bit her. I can't believe it's true – in fact I *don't* believe it's true. I think her husband's put her up to it – he treats her like shit, and I'm sure she's only doing it because she's afraid of him."

"Can't you talk to her – get her to change her mind?"

"Not a chance. She's too scared of her husband."

Breda sighed. "And this woman you like – the one who's engaged to someone else – is there any hope that she'll finish with the other guy?"

Gary shook his head vehemently. "Not a chance – in fact, the two of them were sitting in here until a minute ago – I've just seen them leave, and they looked pretty chummy to me. I even saw him kissing her cheek."

Breda sighed. Poor old Gary – he was such a sweetie. She wished that he could find happiness, the way she had with Aidan. She also knew how deeply her brother loved that dog of his – it had become a surrogate friend for him during all the years of studying for his medical exams. She smiled sympathetically at her brother. "Want to come back with us – for some real home cooking?" she asked him as she buttoned up the children's coats. "Aidan is doing the cooking tonight, so you can be sure it will be good." Breda's husband Aidan was a chef at one of the city's top restaurants. And even on his nights off, he *still* loved to cook.

Gary shook his head. "Thanks, Breda – I'd love to, but I'm on duty tonight. Besides, being busy helps to keep me from brooding."

As they prepared to leave the restaurant, Gary hoisted his nephew onto his shoulder and took his niece by the hand. Now that their mother was back, they were both behaving angelically. He smiled to himself. Maybe it would be nice to have kids – they didn't seem to be quite the same hassle when you knew what you were doing. He sighed. When he'd entertained hopes of wooing Orla, he'd pictured them having two little girls, both looking just like her. He sighed. Now, any kids she'd be having would be with that asshole from the *Evening Dispatch*.

CHAPTER 45

Gary gave Bruce a final hug before he left the house. He'd left out extra dog food and a special chewy treat before leaving, much to Bruce's surprise and delight. But it was the dog's innocence that made Gary feel even worse that morning. Poor Bruce had no idea how bad the day could yet become. All he knew was that his master was upset, and he'd licked Gary's face vigorously in an attempt to convey his concern. There were tears in Gary's eyes as he locked the front door and walked down the path – after today's court decision, he mightn't have Bruce any more.

He wondered if Ellen Byrne next door had already left for court, or if she was waiting until he was out of the way before leaving? Gary wished that he could hate her, but he suspected that it was her nasty husband who was behind this court case. If only he'd paid up when Jackie Byrne had first suggested a cash settlement! Because if things went against him in court today, it would be his own fault that Bruce had to be destroyed.

Joanna was waiting for him outside the District Court. She squeezed his arm. "Are you OK?" she asked gently.

Gary nodded. "I've been better," he replied tersely. "How long have we to wait before we actually get into court?"

"It shouldn't be too long," said Joanna. "We're listed for an early appearance. And once we get inside, the whole hearing shouldn't take more than fifteen minutes."

Fifteen minutes. In that space of time, poor Bruce's fate would be decided. Gary looked around him at the other people milling around, most of whom were also making court appearances. He expected to see a gloating Ellen and Jackie Byrne watching him from the crowd, but as yet there was no sign of them.

At last, Gary heard his name being called, and with Joanna protectively taking his arm – as though he was a small child – they proceeded into the court chamber. At another time, he might have been amused by her protective gesture, but right now, he was far too nervous to be other than grateful for her support.

Both Gary's and Joanna's hearts were filled with dismay when they realised that the case was about to be heard by the judge they dreaded most – the one renowned for his dislike of dogs.

"Oh shit!" said Joanna under her breath. This wasn't looking good. She was feeling just as tense as Gary was, because she knew how important the outcome of this case was to him. She tried to smile as she wished him luck. But right now, she doubted that luck would have anything to do with the outcome of the case.

There was still no sign of Ellen Byrne when the judge

began proceedings. "Is the prosecution ready to proceed?" the judge barked at the prosecution's solicitor, who was apologetically grovelling to the now enraged creature on the bench. "This court's time is valuable," the judge declared, his jowls wobbling indignantly, "and your witness could find herself in contempt of court if she doesn't appear soon, or have a very good excuse!"

After what seemed like an eternity – but which was only minutes in reality – the judge banged his gavel furiously and declared that the case would be re-entered for hearing the following week. The prosecution's solicitor was then given a severe tongue-lashing by the judge, over the tardiness of his witness and the wasting of the court's valuable time.

Gary was both relieved and furious. "I've had to take time off work to come here! Does this mean that we've got to go through all that again next week?" he asked Joanna in disbelief.

Joanna nodded. "I wonder why Ellen Byrne hasn't put in an appearance?" she mused. "I'd better have a word with the prosecution's solicitor. I presume he's made it clear to her that she can't simply bow out of this case, even if she's had second thoughts – she'll be held in contempt of court if she doesn't appear, and she could end up going to prison herself."

Leaving Gary briefly, Joanna spoke to other solicitor, then returned with a puzzled look on her face. "He has no idea what's happened either. He's terribly embarassed and angry himself – it doesn't look good for any solicitor to have a witness who doesn't turn up." She turned to Gary and smiled. "C'mon – let's get out of here. Let's have a cup of coffee in the café down the road, then I'll have to head back to the office."

As they drank their coffee, each of them tucking into a cream doughnut, they were both careful not to mention Orla's name. Gary longed to ask how she was, but what was the point? And Joanna longed to ask Gary why he hadn't asked her friend out, but loyalty to Orla prevented her from doing so. Instead, they chose neutral subjects, finally coming back to the court case that was still hanging in the balance.

Gary became even more despondent when he realised that the case would still be heard by same judge. "So there's not much hope for poor old Bruce," he said sadly, staring into his empty coffee cup. "At least I'm not on duty at the hospital until tomorrow night – so I'll head home now and take Bruce out for a long hike in the mountains. He loves the open spaces – it'll probably be the last decent run he'll ever have." Quickly he changed the subject. "Sorry – I'm being a bore. I've been so wrapped up in my own problems that I forgot to ask you how you're enjoying being your own boss – I mean, since you set up your own practice."

Joanna smiled. "At first, I was worried that I'd never get any clients – now I'm inundated. In fact, my very first client has left me with quite a mystery to solve."

Gary looked interested.

"Sorry, but I can't really discuss the details with you," said Joanna, "but it involves a trade union official called Harry Sweeney, now dead, who was on remand for the murder of a young girl named Colette Devane back in 1970."

Gary smiled wanly. "Wow, nothing like starting your solo career with interesting stuff – murderers and dog-bite cases!" He sighed. "I hope your mystery case isn't going to drag on like poor Bruce's."

Joanne grimaced. Two cases, and neither with a neat solution in sight.

CHAPTER 46

"Son – I want you to deliver this envelope." Paddy Byrne handed his son a bulky package which Jackie quickly identified as legal tender.

"What's this, Da – a bribe?"

"No, son." Then he grinned. "Well, maybe it is a sort of bribe. In fact, it's really a thank you for someone who's kept their mouth shut."

"Why do I have to deliver it?"

Paddy Byrne smiled. "I thought you might be interested. The person in question is a very attractive young lady."

* * *

"Hello. I was asked to give you this."

The young woman looked suspiciously at the fellow standing at the front door of the house where she had a bed-sit. She eyed the package in his hand – could it be one of those incendiary devices? Since she'd read about Colette's murder in the newspapers, she'd been in fear for her own life. The more she recalled that weird guy

Paddy Byrne who'd been nosing around in Colette's apartment on the night of her murder, the more worried she became. And she'd stupidly given him the address of her bed-sit too!

"I don't want it, whatever it is," she told the young man, as he offered it to her.

"It's money," he said scornfully. "What the hell else did you think it was?" Jackie Byrne had never met anyone who would turn down an envelope full of cash.

"M-money?"

"Yeah, my dad said he'd promised it to you. For some favour you did him."

"Oh." The young woman eyed the envelope full of bank notes. So maybe it was all right, then. Maybe they weren't going to kill her for what she'd seen that night.

"Well, if you don't want the money –"

"No, hold on – I'll take it. I'm behind with my rent, so it'll come in useful."

Jackie eyed her from head to toe and decided that he liked what he saw. His dad had asked him to be particularly nice to her and, fortunately, that wasn't going to cause him any hardship. His dad had also said that there could be serious rewards from the Kilmartin coffers if he could see his way to asking her out. Jackie grinned to himself. That wouldn't be too painful either. Just as he was handing her the envelope, he ostentatiously extracted two banknotes from it, and stuffed them into his own pocket.

"And that, my darling, will be our spending money for tonight. Fancy going to the cinema, or would you rather come for a drive in my car?"

Even at such a young age, Jackie Byrne was already a skinflint.

CHAPTER 47

Around 10 a.m. on Saturday morning, Mary's doorbell rang. Who could be calling at this hour, she wondered anxiously? At best, it might be someone collecting for charity; at worst it could be another complaint or a summons for some dreadful deed that young Paul had committed. With trepidation, Mary came down the stairs in her tatty old dressing-gown. She could see the outline of a man through the frosted glass panel in the door, but it wasn't a silhouette she recognised. Taking a deep breath, she opened the door and prepared for the worst.

"Mary – I was just passing by and thought I'd drop in." Mick McHale stood on the doorstep.

At first, Mary was relieved and delighted, then she realised that she was wearing a shabby dressing-gown and no make-up. "Come in, Jim come in," she said, trying to hide her embarrassment at being caught in such unflattering attire. "Go into the kitchen and stick on the kettle, will you? I'll be down in a minute."

Then she charged upstairs, pulling savagely at the clothes in the hot press until she found clean jeans and a fluffy pretty sweater. She pulled them on, then quickly applied some lipstick and eye-shadow, combed her hair and tied it into a pony-tail. Critically surveying her appearance, she decided that she would have to do. If only she'd had a few minutes' warning that he might drop in!

Downstairs, Jim cursed himself for calling too early. But in his enthusiasm to see Mary again, he hadn't given a thought to the fact that many people liked a lie-in on Saturday mornings, after having had to get up early for work during the week. Anyway, he was here now, so he would make the most of it. And since the weather was fine, he would start by cutting the grass. Then he would see what other jobs Mary would like him to do.

Mary suddenly appeared in the kitchen and they both stood still, momentarily delighted and embarrassed to see each other. Neither of them was quite sure if they should let their delight show, so they both masked it with brisk, businesslike conversation.

"I thought that since I've some spare time, I'd come and cut the grass for you," said Jim tentatively. "Is that OK? I mean, you're not offended, are you?"

"Good lord, no," said Mary, smiling. "That's really nice of you, Jim. As you can see, neither the kids nor I are great gardeners. But here – have your cup of tea first."

So Mary and Jim sat talking once again, and Jim marvelled at how swiftly the time flew by and how much he was enjoying this woman's company. Eventually, he rose reluctantly to his feet and headed for the garden.

"No more tea until I do some work," he said jovially. "Now where do you keep the lawnmower?"

When the children arrived back from swimming around lunchtime, they were amazed to discover that the gardens back and front had been mowed, the sad-looking flowerbeds had been tidied up and their mother was looking pretty and alive in a way they hadn't seen her look for ages.

"Hello, Paul, hello, Emma," Jim said warmly when they appeared. "Fancy coming out for a pizza? I don't know about you two, but I'm starving after all my exertions."

The children looked at their mother for approval, and seeing her happy expression, they too nodded happily.

"You've done a – great job," said Paul, suddenly flushing because he wasn't used to paying compliments.

"Yes – it's brilliant," said Emma in awe. "The place hasn't looked this good since – since – " What she meant to say was that the place hadn't looked so cared-for since her father had left. But as she floundered around, Jim came to the rescue.

"Glad you approve," he said smiling. "Now, who's ready to head out for some grub?"

At the café, Mary sat back and relaxed happily. For the first time in ages, she felt as though she was part of a normal family who was enjoying a normal Saturday lunch-time outing. She also felt an inner sense of joy for the first time since Leo had left. Being dumped for a much younger woman hadn't exactly helped her ego. But Jim hadn't made any attempt to disguise his admiration – or was she reading everything wrong? Probably, he just felt sorry for her. Well, she was grateful to him anyway, even if that was all there was to his visit. And he'd achieved wonders with Paul – even in the space of one week, Paul was much better behaved. Mary still lived in fear of every knock on the door, but gradually her blood pressure was returning to normal.

"Penny for them?" asked Jim, smiling gently.

Mary blushed. "I was just thinking – " She looked over to ensure that Paul was engrossed in his pizza and out of hearing range. "I was thinking that you've had an amazing effect on Paul. I don't know what you did, but it seems to have worked wonders. He's even started doing his homework without me having to nag him about it!"

"He's a nice lad," said Jim, looking over at Paul affectionately. "You've got two lovely kids, Mary. You should be very proud of them both."

"I am, now – thanks to you," said Mary shyly.

When they returned to the house, Jim insisted on spending the afternoon repairing the gutter. That necessitated buying some new fittings, and Jim was surprised when both youngsters volunteered to come to the builders provider's store with him. And throughout the afternoon, Paul worked alongside him, asking questions and appearing anxious to acquire new skills as he went along. At seven, Mary called a halt to their activities, pronouncing that dinner was ready. She'd prepared a big stew, with tons of mashed potatoes, carrots, onions and herbs, followed by an apple-pie which she'd just freshly baked. All four of them tucked in, and the sounds of banter, gentle teasing and laughter soon filled the kitchen.

Later, as Jim prepared to leave, Mary touched his arm shyly.

"I can't thank you enough, Jim," she said earnestly. "You've been so good to us."

"And thank *you*, Mary," said Jim, smiling back at her. "It hasn't all been one-way, you know. You've given me a lot today, too. You've let me be part of your family, and I've had a great time." Impulsively, he kissed her on the cheek. "I'll see you next week, when I take Paul to the All Ireland game. Then if it's okay with you, I'd like to give the outside of the house a coat of paint during the week – if you wouldn't mind, that is – "

"I'd love that, Jim. I mean, I'd love you to call, but not because of the painting – I mean – " She blushed, and was furious with herself for being as tongue-tied as a teenager. After all, she was a woman in her early forties!

"I *do* know what you mean," Jim said, smiling. Then he headed down the garden path, turning to wave before he reached the corner.

Then he was gone, leaving Mary standing there like an insecure teenager, already longing for his next visit. Pull yourself together, she told herself crossly. Why would a man like that ever look at *you*? He's just being kind. But somehow, the bubbly feeling just wouldn't go away.

CHAPTER 48

Gary turned the key in his front door, opened it and let himself and Bruce into the house. He was absolutely knackered – he and Bruce had just completed a ten-mile hike over the Sally Gap in the Wicklow mountains, and he was ready to drop from exhaustion. His feet were killing him, and all he wanted to do was to flop into an armchair and fall asleep. But Bruce had enjoyed himself immensely – the mad mutt was still wagging his tail – and Gary felt that at least he had done something to give Bruce a treat before . . . Gary refused to think of what might happen next week.

But before he could relax, poor old Bruce had to be fed and watered. So he opened two tins of dog food and poured out a bowl of fresh water. Now he could think about making a large mug of tea for himself, and maybe later he'd send out for a takeaway. Right now, he was just too exhausted to even think about food.

Sitting down in front of the flame-effect gas fire with his tea, Gary began to unwind a little. He felt himself beginning to doze off, which was fine by him, except that

Bruce had suddenly started whimpering. When Gary reluctantly got out of the chair to see what was wrong, the dog was pawing frantically at the back door.

Gary sighed. "Surely you can't want to pee again so soon?" he asked his dog, rubbing him affectionately behind his ears. But Bruce didn't seem interested in being stroked – he just wanted to get out into the back garden. Urgently.

Maybe his bladder was starting to cause problems, Gary thought. After all, he was getting on in years. Better look into that, in case he's developing a problem. But then Gary remembered that in a week's time poor old Bruce could be facing a death sentence anyway . . .

Gary opened the back door and Bruce bounded out. Gary eased himself back into the chair and was about to doze off again when Bruce came bounding in, but this time he clearly wanted Gary to come out into the garden with him.

"Sorry, old chap," said Gary, "you've had your walk for today. I'm not throwing any more balls or sticks!"

But Bruce continued to push his snout under Gary's hand, and Gary responded by patting him. That wasn't enough for Bruce, however, and the dog now began tugging gently at Gary's trouser leg, making it impossible to ignore him.

"This had better be worth it!" said Gary darkly, rising reluctantly from his comfortable chair and following the dog outside, his muscles now seriously aching since he'd begun to relax in the chair.

It was pitch black outside, and Gary was anxious to get back inside to the warmth of the house as quickly as possible. So he stood by the door and waited. Maybe

Bruce just wanted company while he urinated, Gary reasoned. The dog was absolutely spoiled, he had to admit, but what the heck. There are times when none of us wants to be alone.

"Have you finished yet?" he called from the doorway, directing his query into the darkness beyond, since he could no longer see Bruce anywhere. Then he heard Bruce barking – a high-pitched worried bark – so he hurried out to where the sound was coming from. Had something happened to the dog?

Suddenly, he heard a faint groan, and the hairs rose on the back of his neck. Someone – or something – was in trouble, and Bruce had found them. Urgently now, he followed the sound of Bruce's barking and found himself looking over the hedge into the next garden. There on the ground lay Ellen Byrne, although at first glance she was barely recognisable. One leg was twisted unnaturally beneath her, and her face was completely swollen – so swollen that she could barely speak. Blood trickled from her mouth, and for one awful moment, Gary feared that he might have arrived too late. Then she made another gurgling sound, and Gary quickly jumped over the hedge to help her.

After soothing Ellen and assuring her that help was on its way, he dialled the emergency services on his mobile phone, requested an ambulance and gave details of her condition.

"Bruce – get a blanket!" Gary urged his dog, and Bruce trotted into the house.

Gary began to examine Ellen, quickly establishing that she had sustained a broken arm as well as a compound fracture of the thigh-bone. Bruce returned with his own blanket from his basket. "Good boy, Brucie!" said Gary, taking the blanket and wrapping it gently around Ellen, in order to keep her warm and prevent her from going further into shock. Feeling gently, he concluded that some of her ribs might possibly be broken as well, so he eased her into a more comfortable position in order to prevent the likelihood of a lung puncture, talking softly to her all the time so that she wouldn't be frightened.

Then he hurried into Ellen's house, just in time to admit the ambulance crew. Before long, Ellen was placed on a stretcher and driven to the casualty department of the local hospital, with Gary beside her in the ambulance, holding her hand. Bruce had reluctantly accepted that he had to stay behind. But he wagged his tail happily as Gary praised him for his help, before locking him in the house until his return.

In the light of the ambulance, Gary and the team were better able to assess her injuries, and Gary knew immediately what had happened.

"It was Jackie, wasn't it?" he said softly, while the look on Ellen's face confirmed what he already knew.

"I-I'm sorry about y-your dog!" Ellen blurted out, her words barely comprehensible through swollen lips. "If it wasn't for B-Bruce . . ." she left the rest of the sentence unsaid because it was too much effort, but Gary patted her hand because now he fully understood.

Jackie had also been the driving force behind the court case – and the cause of Ellen's present multiple injuries. Gary took a deep breath. He'd make sure that the bastard paid for what he had done – not just to him and Bruce, but also to poor Ellen.

CHAPTER 49

Catherine intently studied the tablet that she held in one hand and the glass of water in the other. A nurse was distributing medication to inmates of the nursing home, and Catherine wondered momentarily who he was and what he was doing. Thinking once again that she was in her own home, she surmised that he might be the plumber – or the man from the gas company. But what were all those other people doing in her sitting-room? And why was the man from the gas company giving out sweets to everyone? It really was most confusing . . .

Increasingly, Catherine found it difficult to tell reality from her imagination. Sometimes, the world around her faded totally, and the world of the past replaced it. Then she was young again, and her body and mind weren't weighted down by all the intervening years. At other times, she realised that those days were now in the past, and she accepted the reality of her situation. But then the past would suddenly subsume her yet again . . . In fact, it was rather like being in a science fiction movie, when the characters could move from one dimension to another. Sometimes Catherine felt that she was living in a movie herself.

Yet even though her thought processes were gradually disintegrating, Catherine still felt protective and concerned about Agnes, although why this was, she no longer knew. But right at this moment, she felt certain that Agnes was close by. Her friend was asking her something, calling to her – asking for her help. Naturally, she would give her life for her dear friend – but what was it that Agnes wanted her to do? Catherine shook her head in agitation. If only she could talk to Agnes! Where was her friend? When would the time be right to reveal the truth? Oh, she was so confused! She couldn't even remember where things were hidden any more . . .

Catherine had been able to cope with secrets when she'd felt in control of the situation. But lately, with all these other people around her, she'd become increasingly confused. And where was her dear friend Agnes when she needed her most? More than anything, she longed for Agnes's assurances that she hadn't inadvertently given away any secrets. Increasingly, Catherine felt that she was losing her grip on the situation – people were trying to trick her into saying things that she didn't want to say. If only Agnes would come! She sighed. Ivan was probably still keeping Agnes a prisoner in that big house in Ballsbridge.

Catherine looked around her. Where had Agnes gone? She'd been just about to ask her something . . . what on earth was it? Her memory wasn't as clear as it used to be, and sometimes she forgot things . . . important things . . .

Suddenly, she remembered. Joanna had been badgering her about the secrets – the ones that only she and Agnes knew about. The ones they'd sworn never to speak of, until the time was right. They'd vowed that some day those children would be told the truth. "Oh Agnes," she whispered, "where are you? How will I know when the time is right? Please, Agnes, tell me what I should do . . ."

CHAPTER 50

As the taxi drove off, Agnes unsteadily weaved her way up the garden path. She'd finished off the gin bottle at Cat's house, even though she knew that it wasn't wise to drink too much during pregnancy. But the only way she could approach Ivan was through a haze of alcohol. Oh Harry, she whispered to herself, I wish we were safe in Australia . . .

Having tried unsuccessfully to fit her front door key into the lock, she was eventually forced to ring the doorbell.

"I see you've been drinking," Ivan said with a sneer, as he opened the door. "No doubt you were with that little flibbertigibbet friend of yours. And where the hell is your car?"

"Outside Cat's house," said Agnes, trying to speak without slurring. "I took a taxi home."

"That woman's a bad influence on you, Agnes. I don't want you seeing her any more."

Before Agnes could answer, Ivan pulled her inside and slammed the front door. "And I absolutely forbid you to have anything more to do with that murdering bastard, Harry

Sweeney, who's now thankfully behind bars. I've had reports about your behaviour, Agnes — you've been seen in that man's company too often for my liking. I won't be made a laughing stock — least of all by you. You're my wife, dammit, and it's totally inappropriate for you to be friendly with another man — and especially one whose sole aim in life has been to destroy my business!"

The alcohol had loosened Agnes's tongue, and she was ready to defend the man she loved. "Harry's only trying to ensure that your employees get proper wages. If you treated them fairly, then he wouldn't need to protect their interests!" Agnes was amazed that she could speak so lucidly after consuming so much drink.

Ivan's face turned beetroot with rage. "How dare you speak to me like that!" he roared. "I will not tolerate this treatment from my own wife. If you persist with this attitude, you'll be sorry! And just in case you were thinking of visiting that bastard in prison, I'm cutting off your allowance and grounding your car!"

"You can't do that!" Agnes retorted angrily. "Besides, my father gave me that car — not you! And if it wasn't for my father's money, you wouldn't be where you are today!"

"Yes, and your father had the good sense to leave everything to me," said Ivan triumphantly. "He knew that it was pointless leaving it to you, or that half-baked brother of yours, who ran away when the going got tough!"

"Joseph stood up to my father — and he had the guts to leave when he knew that they'd never see eye to eye!"

Ivan's eyes narrowed. "I meant what I said, Agnes — "

"So did I! How dare you even think of stopping my allowance or touching my car! I'll bet that my allowance is nothing compared to what you spend on all those floosies of yours!"

Even as she spoke she knew she was sabotaging the plan she and Cat had taken such pains to accomplish.

Ivan scowled. "If you'd been a proper wife, I wouldn't have needed them, you frigid cow! No doubt you've been giving Harry Sweeney what you've been denying me!"

Her anger overcoming any desire to seduce her husband, Agnes turned to walk unsteadily out of the room, but Ivan grabbed her arm.

"Don't you dare walk away when I'm talking to you, bitch!" he roared. "Who do you think you are? You need someone to take you down a peg or two, you high and mighty trollop! Get upstairs to the bedroom – I want some of what you've been giving Harry Sweeney!"

"Is that all sex is to you, Ivan – a weapon to use against women?"

"You're my wife, Agnes – a lousy wife, but my wife nonetheless. So I'll have my conjugal rights whenever I want! And I want them now!"

Meekly but unsteadily, Agnes climbed the stairs to the bedroom, Ivan directly behind her. *At least,* she thought wryly, *I haven't had to lower myself to actually seducing him. And I'm so tipsy that hopefully I'll fall asleep while he's doing it. A small consolation perhaps, but at that moment even a small consolation was better than none.*

CHAPTER 51

Orla tried to pretend that she was in good form, but by late afternoon she finally admitted it to herself – she was miserable. Her meeting with Declan had been ego-boosting – she couldn't believe that the creep still thought that she might take him back. The nerve of him! And asking for the engagement ring back – well, that was typical of the opportunistic asshole. How had she ever seriously thought of marrying him? How could she have been conned to that extent?

But despite the dubious satisfaction of being able to give Declan the bum's rush – what a pity it couldn't have taken place in front of all those spineless geeks in the Newsroom – her mood was far from upbeat. All she felt was misery, having seen Gary in the same café, with a woman and kids who were obviously his family. Why hadn't he said that he was married? She sighed. Stupidly, she'd believed that their chat was leading towards a date, whereas *he* had simply been enjoying a night out and would, no doubt, have chatted happily with anyone to whom he'd been introduced.

Quickly, Orla grabbed the phone and dialled Joanna's number. Soon, she was pouring out her misery to her friend, who was one of the few people in the world to whom she was willing to unburden herself. Having told her about Declan's attempts to get back with her, and then to get the engagement ring when she turned him down, the two friends had a good chuckle together at Declan's pathetic behaviour. But Orla's mood quickly changed again as she told her friend that she had also spotted Gary in the café.

"Oh, Jo!" she wailed. "I can't believe that he's married! But there he was, with two small kids crawling all over him, and a young woman with short blond hair who was all over him too!"

Joanna wished she could ease Orla's pain – in fact, she couldn't remember when her friend was last so smitten by a man. Normally, Orla was a "love 'em and leave 'em" type who wouldn't take crap from any man, and typically, she'd blown out Declan when he humiliated her with his nasty little fling behind her back. Orla was a strong confident woman, but clearly Gary Culhane had touched something deep within her friend's psyche, and Joanna felt guilty because she was the one who had introduced them.

Obviously, they'd both been wrong about Gary's intentions at the *Celebrity* magazine party. Therefore, the only thing to do in a situation like that was to put that someone firmly out of your mind. She blushed when she thought of how she keen she'd been about Tom Kilmartin only a week ago – before Ronan O'Farrell came into her life! Now, she was dying to tell Orla what had happened with Ronan, but her poor friend felt so downhearted, it would be like rubbing salt in a wound. No, she would look forward to telling Orla later, when she'd got over Gary Culhane

"Anyway," said Orla, "there's always that guy that I met in the Morrison the other night. If *he* rings, I'll go out with him and see what happens. You know what they say – 'use it or lose it'."

Joanna laughed. "Well, I'm glad to see that you're not letting the grass grow under your feet, to quote yet another metaphor!"

CHAPTER 52

Carrying a large bouquet of flowers, Gary headed to the Intensive Care Unit, where Ellen Byrne had been taken on arrival at St Brigid's Hospital. It was early morning. He had just finished his own shift in the Casualty Department and had nipped outside to the local flower shop before heading upstairs.

To his surpise and delight, he discovered that Ellen had been moved out of Intensive Care, which meant that she was already on the road to recovery. Yet when he'd been directed to her new ward, he hadn't spotted her immediately. Her injuries were so bad that her face was still barely recognisable.

"Hi, Ellen," said Gary, placing a light kiss on her swollen cheek, as she turned to see who was visiting her. There had been a momentary flicker of fear in her eyes, and Gary knew why.

"Don't worry about Jackie – he won't be allowed near you," Gary assured her. "The police on both sides of the

Irish Sea are searching for him – he's not going to get away with this."

Ellen relaxed slightly and clutched the flowers. "Th-thank you so much, Gary," she whispered slowly. "It's very decent of you not to be angry with me for all the trouble I've caused you. I don't deserve such kindness."

"Don't be ridiculous," said Gary, smiling. "Isn't that what neighbours are for? To help each other?"

"I've never d-done anything to help y-you," Ellen whispered. "Nor has Jackie. Except cause you hassle. B-Bruce never bit me – it was Jackie who did it. Then he got scared and told me that I had to blame your dog."

"I guessed that." Gary patted Ellen's arm, which was heavily encased in plaster. "But don't worry about anything right now – except getting better."

But Ellen was still agitated. "B-but Bruce – the court case – what will happen now?"

"I don't honestly know," Gary told her, "but I'm going to ring my solicitor shortly and ask her. I presume it was your injuries that prevented you from getting into court yesterday?"

Ellen nodded and started to cry, her tears running sideways into her ears. "I was getting ready to go to court – J-Jackie said I had to. He was leaving for England himself yesterday morning – he does that regularly – then he got a phone call. S-some deal of his had fallen through, and he was furious. So he took it out on me. L-like he always does. I blacked out after that. I don't know how long I lay on the floor, but when I woke up, I managed to crawl out into the back garden."

"Well, he won't be doing that any more," Gary assured

her. "I think Jackie's going to find himself behind bars for quite some time, after this attack."

Ellen looked surprised and shocked. It seemed incomprehensible to her that a man might be sent to prison for beating his wife. She'd always believed that violence was a given in all men-women relationships, and she was gratified and emotional that the Gardaí – those people in uniform whom she'd always despised up until now – were going to ensure that Jackie couldn't harm her any more. Two officers had already visited her in the hospital, and they had treated her with compassion and respect. The tears started again.

"I d-don't deserve all this kindness!" Ellen sobbed.

"Of course you do!" Gary said, squeezing her hand supportively. "Your problem, Ellen, is that you've been treated so badly for so long that you've just accepted it as normal. It's *not* normal. You've just as much right to be treated fairly as anyone else."

"I-I was once on the game – just for a while, though. Did you know that?"

"No – I didn't," said Gary lightly. "But what has that got to do with anything? You're still entitled to the full protection of the law. And your dignity as a human being."

"Jackie's always hated me because I picked up a venereal disease when I was on the streets all those years ago, and I couldn't give him any children," Ellen said, speaking slowly through her bruised and swollen lips. "He often told me that his dad made him marry me. I don't know why Jackie would do something like that just because his dad told him – he didn't like his dad much.

Nor did I – he was a horrible man. And why would his dad make him marry me? It doesn't make sense. Anyway, I think that's why Jackie was always hitting me."

"Whatever Jackie's reasoning was, he had absolutely no right to do what he did," Gary told her, doing his best to suppress the anger that he felt towards Jackie Byrne. "You know you've got to leave him, don't you, Ellen?"

Ellen nodded. "Poor Jackie," she whispered.

And Gary marvelled at the type of battered woman who could still feel some level of compassion for the man who had caused her so much grief and pain.

"He was never a really clever criminal," Ellen whispered sadly, almost to herself. But she wasn't sure if she was sad because of Jackie's failures, or because it was the end of one life for her and the beginning of something new and equally frightening.

CHAPTER 53

Joanna had just arrived into the office when the phone rang, and Mary put the call through to her private office.

"Joanna –"

She immediately recognised Gary's voice, and her expression changed to relief as he told her about the events of the previous evening, Ellen's injuries and how she had confessed that Bruce had never bitten her at all.

"That's great news – for Bruce anyway," she said, smiling. "But your poor neighbour – I presume she's not going to stay with the guy who's made a punchbag out of her?"

"Thankfully, she's agreed to leave him," Gary said. "I'd like to think that there's a new and happier life ahead of her now."

"I'm thrilled! I'll get on to the court straight away, explain what's transpired and see if I can get the case struck out. Ellen Byrne will need to get a letter from the hospital to explain her absence from court and may need

302

to sign an undertaking regarding her lies over Bruce's behaviour, but in the light of her injuries it should hopefully be just a formality. Unless, of course, you want to put in a claim for aggravated damages against her – "

"Lord, no," said Gary. "I'm just relieved that it's all over. And maybe it will actually have achieved something, if I can get Ellen to make a new life for herself. The poor woman has no confidence – she'll need a lot of support and counselling."

"Well, she's lucky to have your support right now. Bye, Gary," said Joanna, ringing off and thinking that it would be nice if Orla could have had his support and affection too.

* * *

After she'd finished speaking to Gary, Joanna lifted the phone and dialled Tom Kilmartin's mobile phone.

"Hi – Tom?"

"Oh hi, Jo – how are you? Sorry I haven't got back to you sooner, but I've been so busy planning the student curriculum for the new term that'll be starting soon – so I haven't had a chance to search for any more documents yet."

A few days earlier, Joanna would have been distraught if she hadn't heard from Tom, and she'd have jumped to the conclusion that his time was being taken up by another woman. But now that she had Ronan, she didn't care what he did with his time. Although she did hope he was free that evening.

"Well, you do need to go through the stuff in the library as soon as possible," she said, "but that's not why

I'm ringing. I was wondering if could I ask you a favour? I'm going to visit Mam in the nursing home this evening – are you free to come with me? I thought that maybe between us, we could try to question her on the basis of Lisa Noonan's comments – 'Cat'll have the documents'?"

"Good idea, Jo. Do you want me to collect you or meet you there?"

"I'll meet you there – that's probably the easiest. I'll go straight there after work."

They arranged to meet at the nursing home at seven o'clock.

It was funny, she mused, how easy it was to deal with him when she had another man on her mind! Maybe Orla's right, she mused – maybe I really am a slut!

Later that evening, she and Tom arrived at the nursing home almost simultaneously. He was parking his car in the manicured grounds as she drove up in her old Mercedes, and he waited until she'd parked, then they entered the nursing home together.

"Do you think that Catherine will be able to tell us anything?" asked Tom. "I mean, how do you think we should broach the topic?"

"I honestly don't know," said Joanna sadly. "It all depends on whether she's having one of her good or bad days. But thanks for coming along – it's probably a pain for you, but I thought that we might get more out of her by both being present. Seeing you might jog her memory."

"Do you think she'll still recognise me?"

"I don't know, Tom – but if anyone could get her talking about Agnes, it's you. Just having you around might get her thinking about your mother and their shared past. It's only a hope at this stage, but it's all we've got right now."

"But we're not going to tell her that Agnes is dead, are we?"

Joanna pulled a face. "I don't know – let's just play it by ear. Besides, I think we're more likely to glean some information if she's happy rather than upset." Joanna bit her lip. "But, then again, I don't really know, do I? This Alzheimer's business is a mystery to me. I'm sure that some day in the future, they'll discover that it was caused by something terribly simple. Maybe lack of a particular vitamin, hormone or enzyme. Or something in the environment. But for now, it's causing misery to millions of families."

Tom said nothing, but he patted Joanna on the back as they walked along the corridor to the patients' room.

Catherine was sitting in an armchair, looking vacantly out the window, and Joanna's heart constricted with love and pity for her mother. What a cruel trick of fate life played on some people, she thought. For she knew that if her mother had been in a position to make a choice, she'd never have opted for such a long-drawn-out goodbye. Alzheimer's was a living death, and Joanna knew that she might yet have to face the day when her mother would no longer even recognise her own daughter.

But this was not yet that day, and Catherine's face lit up when Joanna leaned over and kissed her cheek. "Joanna," she whispered with delight, "how are you? And how is your father?"

Joanna smiled, but could feel the tears pricking at her

eyelids. She ignored her mother's query and drew Tom forward. "Mam – you remember Tom, don't you?"

Catherine looked puzzled.

"Agnes's son?" said Joanna hopefully.

Catherine smiled and clapped her hands. "Agnes – of course! How are you, Tom? And how is your dear mother?"

He took her hand in his. "Hello, Catherine," he said, ignoring her query about Agnes and hoping that she wouldn't ask him about his mother again.

"Mam – I've brought you some magazines," said Joanna, leaving a pile of them on the nearby coffee table. Joanna knew that her mother didn't really read any more – she seemed to lack the concentration required, or maybe it was because she could no longer understand the content. Nevertheless, the bright and colourful illustrations might prove a distraction. It was almost like dealing with a baby.

"Thank you, dear," said Catherine. "Would you both like some tea?"

Joanna shook her head. Catherine had no tea-making facilities – indeed, the nursing home made a point of ensuring that no patients in Catherine's condition could cause harm to themselves or others by accidental scalding or electrocution. Tea was available, but it was provided by the nursing or catering staff.

"No, thanks, Mam – we're fine."

"Well, do you think that I could have a cup?"

Joanna smiled, her heart inwardly breaking. "I'll see what I can do."

In the corridor, Joanna found a nurse who arranged

for the kitchen staff to bring tea and biscuits for them and her mother.

So she returned to Catherine's room, where her mother appeared to be deep in conversation with Tom.

"Tea is on its way," she said, smiling at her mother. She sat down and looked at Tom. "Have you asked Mam anything about . . . yet?"

He shook his head, so Joanna leaned forward, took her mother's hand in hers and addressed her directly.

"Mam – did you know Harry Sweeney?"

Catherine's eyes lit up with affection, then they turned sad. "Aah – poor Harry!" she whispered. "He was a lovely man. The salt of the earth."

"Did you know that he was on remand – for murder?"

Catherine looked indignant. "Well, of course I knew." She suddenly began studying her feet. "But I'm saying no more. Secrets are meant to be kept. I promised Agnes."

Joanna and Tom exchanged a glance, but already Catherine's concentration was gone, and with it any thoughts of Harry Sweeney.

"Do you like my new shoes?" she asked sweetly. "I got them yesterday in town. I went shopping, you know."

Joanna and Tom exchanged another anguished glance.

Joanna tried again. "Mum – do you know what the connection was between Agnes and Harry Sweeney?"

"Ask Agnes yourself. Maybe she'll tell you," Catherine snorted, "if she wants you to know. But I'll never tell anyone. Never!"

As if on cue, a member of the kitchen staff arrived with a tray of tea and biscuits.

"Hurray!" said Catherine, clapping her hands at the

sight of the chocolate biscuits. Deftly, the young girl deflected Catherine's hand away from the teapot, before Catherine could reach for it and possibly scald herself. The girl began to pour the tea.

Joanna looked at Tom. "We're going to have to tell her, aren't we?" she said miserably. "About your mother – otherwise, we're going to get nowhere."

He nodded. "But take it easy, Jo – it's bound to be a big shock to her. I mean, her best friend and all that."

After the young kitchen worker had left, and they were all drinking their tea, Joanna attempted to broach the subject again.

"Mam – was Harry Sweeney a friend of Agnes's?"

Catherine said nothing.

"Mam – Agnes hasn't been well for a while." Joanna gulped. "In fact, she's dead."

Catherine looked up, as though staring through a fog. And her old eyes filled with tears. "Agnes is d-dead? Never! They'd never do to Agnes what they did to Harry Sweeney!"

"What did they do to Harry Sweeney, Mum?"

"They had him murdered, didn't they?"

"No, Mam – you're getting mixed up. Harry Sweeney is the one who was on remand for murdering a girl called Colette Devane."

Catherine snorted again. "Harry never killed anyone. But they murdered him anyway."

"Did Agnes love Harry Sweeney?" Joanna said suddenly, then instantly regretted it.

But Catherine's reply left her in a state of shock. "Of course – Agnes always loved Harry. And he loved her.

She would have left Ivan for him, but there was no point. Harry begged her to stay with Ivan – for Tom's sake." Catherine looked at the stricken face in front of her. "Now stop trying to make me tell tales on Agnes!" she said angrily. "Go and ask her yourself."

"Mam – I've told you – Agnes is dead. But before she died, she asked me to talk to you," said Joanna, bending the truth slightly.

But Catherine wouldn't be coaxed any more. "Go away, please," she said wearily. "I'm tired, and you're trying to confuse me. Tell Agnes to come and see me. *She* can tell me what she wants me to do with the letters and documents."

"Letters and documents?"

Joanna felt like a parrot, but what her mother was saying could open up a new door into the past – the past that Catherine had shared with Agnes, Harry, Ivan and all the other ghostly figures who had once been vibrant people with lives to lead, decisions to make – and secrets to keep.

"Of course. Agnes kept Harry's letters from prison. And we stored the other ones there too."

"Mam – these letters and documents – where are they?"

"I hid them."

Joanna could feel the excitement rising in her chest. In fact, she thought for an instant that she was about to suffocate. "Where did you hide them, Mam?"

Catherine looked distressed. "Why are you trying to catch me out?" she said plaintively. "We knew this would happen – but I promised Agnes I'd never tell anyone. We've always kept each other's secrets."

"Have you got secrets too, Mam?"

Catherine gazed at her daughter and her eyes filled with tears. "It wasn't my fault," she whispered. "Ivan Kilmartin is to blame for all our troubles." She suddenly looked puzzled. "Besides, Agnes can't be dead – she has to tell Tom her big secret first."

"What secret, Mam?"

"I forget the words," said Catherine huffily. "They won't come to me any more. But I can remember 'Away in a Manger'."

Then she began to sing in her sweet high-pitched voice:

"The cattle are lowing,
The baby awakes – "

"Hush, Mam – that's a Christmas carol – it's months to Christmas yet." Joanna looked at her mother in despair. Catherine's period of lucidity seemed to be over for the present.

Catherine gave a childlike smile, and Joanna felt tears pricking her eyelids once again. How strange it was that old people always remembered their own childhoods vividly, yet often they couldn't remember what had happened to them the day before. To stop herself from communicating her stress to her mother, she busied herself by tidying up the cups and saucers and stacking them on the tray.

She kissed and hugged her mother, promising her to visit again as soon as possible. Luckily, Catherine appeared to believe that she was in her own home, so the parting was not too painful. She left her sitting happily in her armchair, gazing vacantly once again over the manicured lawn outside her window.

As they walked out to their cars, Tom slipped his arm

around Joanna's shoulder, and gratefully, she leaned against him. It was so comforting to feel his quiet strength. How strange to think that only a few weeks ago, she'd been trying to seduce him! Now, it was easier to get on with him, since she simply regarded him as a friend. Besides, Ronan was now taking up her time in bed! That man was a human dynamo, and she'd been happily sated when they'd finished making love . . .

Tom kissed her on the cheek as she opened the door of her car. "Jo – I think it might be worth looking in Catherine's cupboards and in your attic – just in case she might have stored my mother's stuff there. It must be well hidden – they wouldn't have wanted my father to find any letters from Harry, would they?"

Joanna nodded. Then she suddenly realised that the comments Catherine made would have had a very devastating effect on Tom. After all, it wasn't every day that a son discovered that his mother had been having an extra-marital relationship!

Affectionately, she touched his hand. "Are you OK, Tom? I mean, all that must have been a bit of a shock to you. Assuming we can believe anything my mother told us."

"I'm fine, Jo. I suppose I guessed, after hearing about my mother's strange request to be buried with Harry Sweeney, that there was bound to be a lot more to be uncovered." He smiled at her. "At least we now know that Harry and my mother loved each other. And I'm not upset by it. I just hope they found happiness during their brief time together. It couldn't have been easy for them."

"But, don't you feel angry – on your father's behalf? My mother wasn't very complimentary about him!"

Tom shrugged his shoulders. "To be honest, I don't. You see, Jo, I never really got on with my father, and there was always tension in our house, between my parents. I doubt if anyone else was aware of it, but *I* was. It didn't make for a very happy childhood, although my mother did her best to make up for my father's lack of interest. Anyway, my father was rarely at home – and I doubt if my mother was the only woman in his life. So if she had some happiness with Harry, then I'm glad for her."

Joanna felt tense. Because she'd just done her sums. Agnes was involved with Harry shortly before Tom was born . . . She looked at him and wondered if she should mention this. But if he hadn't figured it out for himself yet, maybe she should leave well enough alone. "So you believe my mother? That Harry Sweeney didn't murder Colette Devane?"

Tom looked pensive. "I'm sure Catherine knows the story better than anyone else. If only she could tell us."

Joanna nodded. "It's difficult to think of our parents as having such troubled and traumatic lives." She sighed. "I mean, you think of your parents as just being there – to feed you, clothe you and love you – you never think of them as having secret lives of their own."

Tom nodded. "I think that the friendship between my mother and yours had depths we can only speculate about." He paused. "By the way – while you were getting the tea organised, your mother mentioned Maura."

"In what way?"

"She just said that Maura had told her it was time they all told the truth."

"So she knew Maura?"

"It would seem so. But then I asked her when Maura had told her that, and she said last week."

"She's obviously rambling again. Mam never has any visitors except me, and previously you and your mother. I suppose all this talk of Agnes and Harry has brought the past back into her mind. Oh Tom, I hate to see her this way!"

He kissed Joanna's cheek before she climbed into the driving seat. "I know it's awful for you, Jo. But I'm here if you think I can help in any way."

"Thanks, Tom," said Joanna as she turned on the ignition.

She drove slowly out of the nursing home grounds. A week earlier, she would have been thrilled at Tom's remarks, interpreting them as confirmation of his interest in her. Thankfully, she could now simply take them at face value – he was just an old family friend, anxious to help another old friend. And she was filled with a terrible sadness for him too. She fervently hoped that there wouldn't be too many strange revelations before his mother's will was finally resolved.

CHAPTER 54

It was the first time she'd ever visited a prison, and Catherine fervently hoped that it would also be the last. The buildings were dark and oppressive, the facilities archaic, the wardens surly and uncommunicative. The sooner poor Harry was out of this environment, the better.

"Oh, Harry!" was all Catherine could say, when he was finally led into the visitors' room.

"Is Agnes OK?" Harry asked anxiously.

"She's fine. Well, as fine as she can be, given the present situation. I just hope all the worry won't affect the baby." Catherine delved into her handbag. "She's given me a letter for you – can you write something for me to bring back to her? She won't take my word that you're OK – you'll have to tell her yourself."

Eagerly, Harry read the letter from Agnes, then penned a quick reply to her on some spare paper that Catherine had brought with her.

As Harry handed Catherine the letter he'd written, he grimaced. "This charade can't go on much longer, Cat. The witness is obviously mistaken, so as soon as his testimony gets sorted out, I'm bound to be released."

"Agnes wants to clear your name immediately. She wants to tell them that she was with you that night, Harry."

"God, no – don't let her do that, Cat. If she went public about our relationship, it would humiliate Ivan, then there'd be hell to pay for poor Agnes. And who knows what he or his lackey might do to her? At the very least, Ivan would kick her out without a penny. And right now, I'm not there to protect her." He smiled. "Look, Cat, it's all just a horrible mistake, and it's bound to get sorted out soon. So there's no need for Agnes to risk her reputation yet. There'll be scandal enough when we leave for Australia."

"I hope you're right, Harry. But Agnes is convinced that Ivan is behind all this. And that he either killed Colette or had her killed, then arranged to have Colette's body dumped in the Park, near where your car had been parked when you and Agnes were there. Obviously, you were both under surveillance that night."

Harry frowned. "You may be right, Cat – Agnes had a feeling we were being watched, and there was a car parked suspiciously close to us."

"So you mightn't be out of jail as quickly as you think. Maybe you should let Agnes go to the police."

"No, Cat – please. It would make life hell for her. Ivan might hurt her, or the baby."

"But the fact that you knew Colette makes the evidence seem so convincing," said Catherine. "After all, she was your sister-in-law! To the public, that makes your guilt all the more believable."

Harry covered his face with his hands.

"They've also found a cigarette butt at the murder scene, which they're claiming is yours. And they've discovered a folder of notes belonging to you in Colette's apartment."

For the first time, there was real fear in Harry's eyes. "My God, Cat, now I remember – I threw a cigarette butt out of the car while Agnes and I were in the Phoenix Park! As for the folder – I left it in Colette's place when I went to see her before she left for England. But by then, it was too late to collect it – "

"Well, that file is now being touted as proof that you were somehow involved with Colette."

"Poor Colette! How could anyone think I'd kill her? Poor girl! She was only a kid, you know. When Maura and I got married, she was still at school. The next thing we heard was that she'd run away from home after a row and was hanging around certain hotels."

"So what did you do about it?"

"When we found out where she was living, we both called round to see if we could help her out with a few bob, and sometimes, I went there on my own. We tried to persuade her to train for some sort of career – Maura and I would have helped her financially – but she said she'd found a rich fancy-man and didn't need any help."

Catherine groaned. "Oh God, Harry – by admitting that you called around there alone, people will assume that you were having an affair with her! And Ivan could put that story into circulation to protect himself."

Harry looked ill. "I'm the perfect scapegoat, aren't I, Cat? By pinning the murder on me, Ivan gets himself off the hook and disposes of his wife's lover at the same time." His hand shook. "This isn't just a simple case of mistaken identity, is it? If Ivan murdered Colette, then he'll do his best to make sure that I never get out of here." He let out a heartrending groan. "That's all the more reason, Cat, why Agnes mustn't speak out. She must protect herself – and our baby."

CHAPTER 55

Sasha Miller sat at her desk in the *Trident* and chewed her pen viciously as she looked down her list of assignments for the week. Boring! And she was bored with John Boyle as well. What had started as an amusing fling had gained a momentum all its own, and she didn't like it one bit. John Boyle had now virtually become her slave, and while Sasha liked her men to be interested, John's behaviour was totally over the top.

She'd never expected to get involved with someone like him. She'd simply phoned him to see if Declan had collected her flowers – which he hadn't because he'd been lying about them all along. Then she and John got talking, and he'd offered to drop round to her apartment to console her.

And console her he had! Initially, she'd enjoyed their rough, puppy-dog grappling on the floor, then in the bedroom. John was an enthusiastic, though not very skilled, lover – and there was the added fillip of getting her own

LINDA KAVANAGH

back on Declan for lying to her. But by now, John's lack of technique and his endless sexual demands were pissing her off. It was time to drop him and get back to men who were more her type.

I mean, she thought angrily, he's a bloody freelance journalist – he doesn't even have a full-time job! And because he didn't have enough work to keep him busy, there was too little cash available for lavishing on *her* and too much spare time for cavorting around the floor! She didn't mind giving a guy a good time, but she wasn't prepared to give it away for nothing in return!

Without doubt, John Boyle would have to be given the heave-ho. What a pity that she'd fallen on top of that bloody cake at the *Celebrity* magazine birthday party! Up until that moment, she'd been getting along brilliantly with Seamus McGrath, the managing editor. In fact, she'd been hoping that if things had worked out with Seamus, Declan Dunne would have been turfed out of her apartment the following day, and there would never have been any fling with John Boyle.

Sasha wanted to be the one to snap up the newly divorced Seamus McGrath. While the incident with the cake had put things temporarily on hold, Sasha intended to snare Seamus as soon as possible. Perhaps she could turn around her humiliation by pretending that she was glad his magazine had gained such great publicity at her expense. She would phone him to congratulate him, then ask him out for a drink and before long . . . Sasha grinned. No doubt his boring wife had been useless in bed, so Seamus would be ripe for some top-class rumpy-pumpy. Then she would make him chase her – until she let him catch her.

Seamus McGrath had everything that Sasha wanted –
prestige, power and a big bank balance. With Seamus it
would have to be marriage – she was tired playing for
much lower stakes. And apart from the fact that she was
getting on – my God, she was almost thirty – it would be
nice to lord it over her colleagues for a change. If she was
the wife of the managing editor, they'd have to treat her
with respect. She'd get the best assignments for a change
– on the other hand, maybe she wouldn't work at all!
She'd just swan into the office occasionally, dressed to the
nines, and let them see how successful she'd become.
And she'd get her revenge on several of the colleagues
who now treated her shabbily – she'd either get Seamus
to sack them, or she'd leave them quaking in their boots,
living with the fear that at any time she might click her
fingers and they'd be gone!

Sasha looked at her list of assignments again, and
sighed. Why on earth had she been selected to interview
some boring guy who was travelling to the Antarctic this
December? Who on earth gave a damn? *She* certainly
didn't. And she doubted that their readers did. And even if
they did, why wasn't this job given to someone who was
interested in it? God, how she hated nerdy do-gooders! She
was furious that the little bitch Julie-Anne Jones was being
sent from the *Evening Dispatch* to cover some big fashion
show in Paris , yet her own paper was too mean to send *her*.
"Budget constraints" they called it. But I've got fantastic
fashion sense! Sasha thought angrily. Instead, she'd have
to listen to the boastings of that Jones bitch, who would
corral her in Mulligan's pub and humiliate her with jibes
about not being sent there herself.

On the other hand, being the true professional, Sasha decided that she would do a bit of research on this boring guy and his penguins, since male interviewees were always worth checking out as potential husband material. This guy was probably about ninety, bald and with ill-fitting dentures that clicked annoyingly when he spoke. But a *rich* ninety-year-old widower was a different kettle of fish altogether . . .

CHAPTER 56

Joanna sat at her desk, thinking dreamily of Ronan O'Farrell. He was absolutely gorgeous! And she couldn't believe that he wanted her too. She could hardly wait till he got back from London – just thinking about him made her all hot and bothered!

Was this the start of a long-term relationship? Or did Ronan hit on all the women he met through his job? His work was undoubtedly varied and interesting – did it include interesting women too? Suddenly, Joanna had visions of gorgeous women lurking round every corner, just waiting to drag Ronan into bed at the first opportunity . . .

From being elated, Joanna suddenly found herself plunged into despair. Maybe she shouldn't have succumbed to his charms so quickly. Maybe she should have maintained an air of mystery for a bit longer, or waited until his search for Harry's wife had been finished – it wasn't really professional to sleep with someone who –

"Look, you'll have to stop this daydreaming," said Mary brusquely, dumping a pile of letters in front of her. "There's a backlog of work piling up, and that woman with the crazy tenant has phoned three times. I'm tired of telling her that you're either with a client or in court. And Freddy O'Rourke rang – ostensibly to see how you'd got on with the dog-bite case."

"Maybe we need to take on another solicitor," said Joanna.

"We wouldn't need one, if the present one would just do her job," said Mary dryly.

Joanna laughed. "You don't pull any punches, Mary – but I love you nevertheless! Just keep everyone at bay for another few hours. If necessary, I'll work late or come in early tomorrow."

"Oh, by the way," said Mary, not looking at Joanna as she sifted through the post, "that man Mick McHale – Orla's friend who's retired from the Special Branch – he called round to the house and had a chat with Paul."

"Oh, good," said Joanna. "Do you think it will have any effect?"

"It has already," said Mary, now looking up and smiling.

"Well, that's great news!" Joanna replied. "What did he do – frighten the life out of Paul with dire predictions of a future in prison?"

"No – that's the strange thing," said Mary, her face now wreathed in smiles. "Whatever he did, it's created a great bond between them, and Jim is taking Paul to the All Ireland Final in Croke Park next week."

"Wow – those tickets are like gold dust!"

"Thanks, Joanna," said Mary, impulsively hugging her. "I really think that we may have turned the corner with Paul!"

"Who's 'we'?" said Joanna impishly. "That smile of yours looks a tad too bright to be just for this guy's help with Paul!"

"Oh Joanna, he's gorgeous!" Mary whispered, then she coloured. "I mean, he's very nice, and kind – he mowed the lawn last week – "

"So you fancy him. Does he fancy you?"

"I doubt it," said Mary, looking downcast. "I mean, he's good-looking, charming, kind – there must be hundreds of women who'd fancy him."

"So what? Why shouldn't it be *you* that he likes?"

"But, Jo – why would he look at me? He could have any woman – "

"You need a bit more confidence, Mary, that's all," said Joanna firmly. "You're a good-looking woman too, you know – it's just that your ego's taken a bashing over Leo's departure. By the way – when's your birthday?"

"Next month – why?"

"Because I'm going to buy your birthday present in advance. You are going shopping – for a stunning outfit that will have the eyes popping out of his head!"

Mary laughed. "How am I going to fit in time for shopping – with this backlog of work?"

Joanna grinned. "Maybe we could offload a case or two onto Freddy O'Rourke!"

CHAPTER 57

"It's good to see you home again, Ellen," said Gary, hugging his neighbour as he helped her out of his car. On picking her up from the hospital, he was pleased to see that there was no longer any visible trace of her injuries – apart from the scars that undoubtedly lurked within. But time, and professional counselling, would hopefully take care of that. At least, thought Gary happily, she's determined to finally leave Jackie and his cruelty behind and make a fresh start. Jackie had been picked up by British police and was presently awaiting extradition back to Ireland, where he would face charges of causing grievous bodily harm to his wife. He had also been found in possession of a stolen car, so the future wasn't looking too bright for Jackie Byrne. If Ellen gave evidence against him in both cases, he would be unlikely to get out of prison for many years.

Ellen had become a minor celebrity in the hospital, especially since it became known to the staff that she was a friend of Gary's. Trudy, her waitress colleague, Vince, the chef, and Matt, the owner of the café where she worked, had all been in regularly to visit her. And they were delighted to learn that she was finally going to ditch Jackie. There were many offers of support, both financial and emotional. Ellen felt overwhelmed by it all, and especially grateful to Gary, who hadn't turned his back on her, when in all fairness he might well have done.

And Bruce. Ellen had always been afraid of dogs, but now she was determined to overcome her fear and make friends with the animal who had been, in a roundabout way, the catalyst for all the good things that had since happened to her.

"Gary – can I come in and see Bruce?" Ellen asked Gary shyly. "I know he won't understand, but I'd like to thank him – "

Gary grinned. "He'll understand perfectly well, Ellen – and I know he'd like to be friends with you. And I was going to ask you in for a cup of tea anyway!"

Ellen shuddered briefly as she looked at her own house next door – the place that had been the scene of so much violence and so much unhappiness over the years. Even though Jackie was unlikely to be back for a long time, the house held too many bad memories for her to want to live there permanently any more. She would ask Gary's advice about what she should do. She smiled happily, thinking about how dramatically her life had changed already. Almost overnight, she had gone from thinking she had no friends to being surrounded by people who wanted to help her. And they'd always been there – she just hadn't realised it. She'd also learned a valuable lesson – if you didn't let people know that you wanted their help, how could you expect them to know? They couldn't mind-read a situation. She'd never let that happen to her again.

Gary had explained to her that many battered women were too broken in spirit to be able to ask others for help. Maybe, if she herself could help other battered women to see the light, then she'd be glad to do so. After all, who better to help them than one who'd been there herself? Gary had told her that there were a number of refuge houses dotted around the country, where women and their children could seek shelter from violent partners while they awaited court rulings against them. These facilities were seriously underresourced, yet they did Trojan work in protecting the lives of these tragic victims of violence. If Jackie had continued to be a problem, Gary had explained, she could have been housed in one of the refuges. But luckily for her, Jackie was already out of the picture. And hopefully would remain that way.

In Gary's kitchen, Ellen set about getting the mugs ready while Gary filled the kettle. It's so nice, Ellen thought, having neighbours that you can be friends with. Jackie had never wanted them having anything to do with the people who lived on either side of them. I suppose, she thought, that was because he was afraid people might look too closely into our lives and might have seen what was going on. She'd also realised that you have to give something back when you develop friendships, and Jackie wasn't capable of that.

Bruce lay on the floor, sleeping peacefully. But when Ellen arrived, he'd come and snuffled at her ankles and let her pat his head, but he hadn't forced himself on her, instinctively knowing that she had to come to terms with a long-time fear of dogs.

"Gary – I don't think I want to go on living next door, because of the memories and all that," Ellen said, "but I'll stay there until I can find out what my legal rights are."

"Of course," said Gary. "I can understand why you wouldn't want to stay there. But in the meantime, are you able to survive financially? Maybe you'll be eligible for some kind of state allowance when Jackie goes to prison." He grinned. "Or are you a wealthy woman?"

Ellen laughed dryly. "I wish! If Jackie had any money, I certainly never saw it. And even if he had, I'm sure it would be considered ill-gotten gains and impounded by Revenue. No, I'll get by with my part-time job at the café. Matt has already offered me extra shifts if I want them."

"I think you need to see a solicitor about your rights," said Gary. "I could ask Joanna, my solicitor, to check things out for you if you'd like?"

"Thanks, Gary, that would be marvellous," said Ellen gratefully, "but I'd be embarassed to meet her after all the trouble I've already caused you and her."

Gary smiled and patted her arm. " Joanna won't mind in the slightest – she's a lovely person. Anyway, let's forget about the past, Ellen. It's only the future that matters now."

As they drank their tea, Ellen was struck by the peacefulness of it all. No more tension, no more waiting for the blow that would come if she accidentally said something that Jackie didn't like. And the rest of her life could be like this! Ellen was overwhelmed by the idea of a stress-free life and all the peace that lay ahead of her.

Suddenly, Gary interrupted her reverie. "Ellen – why on earth did you marry Jackie? Did he seem like a nice guy when you met him?"

Ellen's lip curled disdainfully. "Jackie was never a nice guy, Gary. But I'd been on the game for a while, I was tired of it and one of my friends had just been murdered. So when Jackie came along and offered to marry me shortly after that, I said yes. I thought I was getting away from a life of drudgery to something better." She laughed harshly. "Instead, I walked into a nightmare. We were no sooner married than he started hitting me." She sighed. "I suppose I didn't think I deserved any better. Like I told you, we weren't long married when he started telling me that he'd only married me because his dad had made him – that he had paid him to do it."

Gary looked surprised. "Paid him? Why on earth would his father do something like that?"

"I don't know – but, like I told you, his father was a horrible old man. I hated him. He worked for Ivan Kilmartin – you know, the millionaire property developer – as his right-hand man, and I know that Kilmartin was responsible for the murder of my friend Colette Devane – the girl who was strangled."

Gary looked startled. "You mean, the woman that Harry Sweeney, the trade union guy, is supposed to have murdered?"

Ellen nodded. "I can assure you – she wasn't killed by Harry Sweeney."

"My God!" said Gary, all excited. "What a coincidence! Joanna, my solicitor, mentioned that she's trying to find out certain facts about that case – I think it relates to some other case she's dealing with. Would you mind talking to her about it?"

Ellen shrugged. "Of course not – if I can be of any help, that is. But why would something that happened more than thirty-five years ago be of any interest now?"

"I don't know," Gary replied, "but we can soon find out."

CHAPTER 58

"I don't care what you say, Cat – I'm going to the police. I don't care about my reputation, or Ivan's prestige – all I want is to clear Harry's name. And I'm the only one who can do it."

Catherine gripped the phone tightly. "Agnes – if you do that, you'll be going against Harry's wishes! He wants to keep you and the baby safe – he's worried about what Ivan might do if you let it be publicly known that you're involved with another man. Worse still, imagine if he found out you were expecting Harry's child!"

"I don't care, Cat – what good is it if I keep silence and Harry is tried and found guilty? No, I must get them to release him. We can head off to Australia straight away – I won't come back here, not even to pack. Maybe you'd take my car to that dealer we went to and collect the money for me, Cat. Because Harry and I will need every penny we can get – "

"Agnes – please! Slow down! You mustn't do anything rash. With a bit of luck, Harry will be released soon, so there's no need to publicise your relationship at this stage. Because if

330

you do, you'll make it even harder to get away to Australia, as Ivan will try to stop you!"

Agnes sighed. *"This is something I have to do, Cat. And nothing you can say will stop me. How could Harry love a woman who thought only about her own safety while he's fighting for his freedom?"*

"But the baby, Agnes! What about its safety?"

"Cat, I can't stand by any longer." Agnes picked up her car keys, which lay on the phone table beside her. *"Look – I've got to go – "*

"Do you want me to come with you?"

"No, thanks – I don't want to waste any more time. I'm driving down to the Garda station in Donnybrook this very minute. I promise I'll ring you later to let you know what happened – hopefully, I'll be telling you that Harry's been released."

"Agnes, I wish you'd reconsider –"

"Bye, Cat." Agnes replaced the phone, and headed outside to her car.

* * *

"Boss, we've got a little problem – and it needs urgent action."

Ivan clutched the phone in his site office. *"Go on, Paddy."*

"I'm here at your house in Ballsbridge, and at this very minute, your wife is leaving your house to drive to the police station. I've been keeping an eye on her like you asked, and I happened to hear the tail-end of a conversation she's just had with her friend Mrs Brennan on the phone. Your wife is going to tell the guards that she was with Harry Sweeney on the night Colette Devane died."

"Jesus Christ – we've got to stop her, Paddy! Oh fuck –

331

what can we do? An accident – or a mugging – anything! She's got to be stopped!"

"Leave it with me, boss – I think I can arrange something like that."

Paddy Byrne finished the call, then rang his son, whom he rightly guessed would still be in bed at home.

"I need a little job done now – this very minute."

"What's wrong?"

"Is your car at the house?"

"Yeah – why?"

"I want you to cause a little accident – you need to get yourself to Ballsbridge this very minute and stop Agnes Kilmartin from reaching the police station in Donnybrook. Just graze her car, then puncture one of her tyres if you have to. Just do what's necessary to stop her getting to the cops."

"Aah, Jesus, Da – I've only just got my car resprayed!"

"Look, I'll get Ivan Kilmartin to buy you a new car – just get around there now!"

"OK, Da, but –"

"Now!"

* * *

Agnes wasn't quite sure what had happened. One minute, she was driving along the road, then as she reached the intersection with the main thoroughfare, a car came flying around the corner and seemed to drive straight into the side of her own car. The impact left her dizzy, and she wasn't too sure what happened next. A young man seemed to be apologising profusely for what happened, then Ivan had arrived – someone must have notified him, but Agnes had no idea who – and now he was arranging to have her brought back to the house to rest.

"No!" Agnes tried to get out of the car but found she couldn't. Her hands cradled her stomach protectively. Oh God, was the baby all right? Where had she been going? Then she remembered. She'd been on her way to the police station, to save Harry!

"Look, I've got to go," she mumbled. "I'm fine, honestly –"

"You're going nowhere," said Ivan abruptly. "You've had a nasty shock, so when we get home, I'm phoning one of the nursing agencies and getting them to send someone to the house to look after you."

"I don't need anyone –"

"Don't be silly, Agnes – you've had a terrible shock. You need to rest."

Suddenly, Agnes felt lightheaded. So she sat back in the car, closed her eyes and listened idly to the conversation taking place outside the car. Suddenly, she realised that something very strange was going on. The young man whose car had hit hers was talking to Ivan. And Ivan was promising him a brand new car! Agnes felt weary. What was going on – surely she hadn't been the one in the wrong? She was certain that the accident had been caused by the young man, so why was her husband being so generous? That wasn't like Ivan at all.

Having driven her back to the house, Ivan ordered Agnes to bed and rang for an agency nurse to come to the house immediately.

"You need something to help you sleep," he told Agnes. "When she arrives, I'll ask the nurse to give you a sedative."

"No – I don't want to sleep –"

"You'll do as you're told, Agnes. Where on earth were you going today, anyway?"

"Just out."

There was a noise on the stairs, then the agency nurse arrived into the bedroom where Agnes lay.

Ivan turned on his charm. "Ah, there you are, nurse – I think my wife could do with a sedative to help her sleep."

"No, I don't want to be put asleep!"

The nurse smiled. "There, there, Mrs Kilmartin, you've had quite a shock. Just take this sleeping tablet for me, like a good girl."

Agnes was furious. Everyone seemed to be treating her like a baby! Oh my God – she suddenly remembered her own baby! She mustn't take the tablet.

She took the tablet from the nurse and held it in her hand. What could she do? Pretend to take it? But that would be impossible with both Ivan and the nurse watching her every move.

"Good girl," said the nurse. "I'll get you some water."

"I'll get some – there's a carafe in my bedroom," said Ivan, leaving the room.

Agnes thought frantically. She knew this might be her only chance. Could she risk telling the nurse? She hesitated for a few more fatal moments, then whispered urgently. "I can't risk taking any medication – I don't want my husband to know yet, but I'm pregnant – "

"What's that, Agnes – did I hear you say you were pregnant?" Ivan came striding back through the doorway with the carafe.

Agnes's heart sank. He must have paused to listen outside the door when he realised she was whispering to the nurse.

"That's wonderful!" said Ivan, smiling at the nurse. "I'm going to be a father!"

"Congratulations to both of you!" said the nurse. "In that

event, maybe we'll just give Mrs Kilmartin a nice sugary cup of tea. We mustn't do anything that might harm the baby, must we?"

Ivan and the nurse left the room, Ivan flirting outrageously with her. Agnes lay back in the bed and closed her eyes. How dare Ivan consider himself the father! She would go to the police station the following morning, just as soon as she could get rid of Ivan and this wretched nurse. She wondered if the nurse had been engaged by Ivan to keep her from leaving the house. And that revolting lackey of his, Paddy Byrne, was also hanging round a lot lately. Everywhere she looked, Paddy Byrne seemed to be there. Yet he always had a plausible excuse for whatever he was doing – he claimed that Ivan had either asked him to check the central heating, the plumbing or the wiring. But Agnes suspected that Ivan had asked him to keep an eye on her instead.

Well, if that was the case, she'd still outwit them all. She'd leave the house just as soon as Ivan left for work. Before the nurse arrived and before Paddy Byrne could offer yet another excuse for being there. Agnes took a deep breath. The sooner she could get to the guards, the sooner dear Harry would be released, and they could be on their way to their new life together . . .

* * *

Ivan was closeted in his office with Paddy Byrne.

"Jesus, Paddy – we have get rid of that Sweeney bastard quickly! We've managed to stop my wife going to the police station this time, but as soon as she's OK, she'll be off to the Garda station again. Even if I could confine her to the house, that bloody friend of hers will come nosing around here before long! Can you do something?"

"OK, boss — I'll have a word with some people who can help. But it'll cost a few thousand."

"That's the least of my worries, Paddy — just get it sorted! I can't risk having Agnes going to the guards again."

Paddy Byrne smiled to himself. Arranging a killing was no problem to him. He had contacts — and people who owed him — in lots of places. There were one or two prison wardens who'd be more than happy to do a little job for him, and a few others who'd be willing to turn a blind eye to what was going on. At a price, of course.

Just as well, Paddy thought. It was a safer option than worrying that his son Jackie might lose his cool in the witness box. As the prosecution's main witness, Jackie was already getting cold feet — even though Ivan had promised him a big pay-off for lying about seeing Harry with Colette that night in the Phoenix Park. But even though Paddy had been coaching him, Jackie wasn't sure he could carry it off, and Paddy had to admit to himself that his son would never amount to much. Now, Paddy thought with relief, his son wouldn't be put to the test and found wanting.

CHAPTER 59

Mick McHale was doing a lot of soul-searching. In fact, he'd spent the past week pacing the floor, wondering if he was going out of his mind. He'd planned a calm, ordered life that did not include a relationship with another woman – he'd said goodbye to all that when his beloved Sheila had died. He'd made up his mind to concentrate on his grandchildren, his security work, his charity work – and that was it.

Yet suddenly, he'd found himself deeply attracted to another woman. And not just a casual attraction either, in the way one might eye up a pretty woman walking by, or chat up someone in a pub to pass away a few pleasant hours. No, this was a deep, gut-wrenching attraction, and he needed to be sure what he was doing before anyone got hurt.

It was exciting as well as distrubing, he had to admit. Here he was, a man in his mid-forties, contemplating asking a woman out on a date. A *date*, at his age! What on earth would his own daughters think? Did they think he was just an old fogey, with one foot already in the grave and no energy for anything, other than filling in his time before the end?

And would they feel that he was betraying their mother – whom he would always love dearly, anyway – by becoming involved with another woman? Kids could be funny about things like that – although they felt entitled to do what they wanted with their own lives, they didn't always want their parents stepping out of line. A friend of his was now estranged from his own kids because they hadn't liked him starting a relationship with another woman so soon after his wife's death. Mind you, Jim thought, smiling wryly, his friend's wife was hardly cold in the grave before he'd taken up with a woman half his age . . .

Why was he questioning things anyway? He was already deeply involved, dammit; he couldn't think of anything else except her lovely face and the overwhelming tenderness he felt towards her. He wanted to protect her, to smooth away those harassed lines around her eyes, to see her laugh with sheer delight.

And he even liked her kids. Paul was a good lad at heart, and he knew that they could become good mates. But did Mary want him for the man he was or as a handyman and substitute father for her children? He certainly hadn't got that impression, but maybe it was too early to know.

He sighed. It must certainly be easier if you picked someone up in a pub or a nightclub. Then, if it didn't work out, you didn't ever have to see each other again.

But with Mary, he already felt a strong sense of commitment. And she seemed to like him a lot too. He especially liked the way she blushed and looked embarrassed when he paid her a compliment. It made him want to keep paying her compliments and telling her how lovely she was.

But maybe the time wasn't ready yet. After all, he knew nothing about her beliefs and ideals, her political views, her attitude to all sorts of things. Maybe it was too early to go for the heavy stuff. Maybe he should just try to stay friends with her for a while and gradually suss out whether she was equally attracted to him. Yet his heart told him that she was and that all the other obstacles that he'd been trying to throw up were unimportant anyway. He was a great believer in instinct – in listening to one's gut feelings. And he knew that what he felt for Mary wasn't a flash-in-the-pan feeling. It was something real and vibrant, and he was scared rigid at the thought of how his ordered life might suddenly be about to change.

Oh, Sheila! He spoke silently to his dead wife – what do you think I should do? Wherever you are – if you're anywhere at all – maybe you'll think kindly of me, still tied as I am by earthly concerns, and help me make the right decision. Would you mind if I grew to love someone else?

Yet even as he spoke, Mick McHale knew that it was too late to seek advice from anyone – even Sheila. Or to take it either. He was already in love with Mary. And experiencing a mixture of fear, excitement and heady recklessness, accompanied by a bubbly feeling that another stage of his life was just about to begin.

Jim lifted the phone and dialled Mary's house, to confirm if Paul was still available to accompany him to the match. He knew that the youngster would need reassurance that he wasn't going to be let down again, like the lad's own father had done on many occasions.

Paul himself answered the phone, and Jim felt a little stab of disappointment. He'd hoped to have a chat with Mary. But Paul was all excited about going to Sunday's match, and Jim couldn't help but be caught up in the young lad's enthusiasm.

"So I'll collect you on Sunday at around noon, OK?" said Jim, smiling. "Then we'll go and get some lunch and tog ourselves out in supporters' gear. I need some new stuff – how about you, Paul?"

"Well – yeah, great. I – eh – I don't have much stuff, just a blue and navy shirt. But it's a bit tight on me now –"

"Well then, let's see if we can get you a better-fitting one. See you Sunday, then?"

"Yeah – great."

Jim rang off, pleased with the way his relationship was developing with Paul. He'd been able to sense the uncertainty in the boy's voice when he'd first answered the phone, no doubt afraid that Jim was ringing to cancel their arrangement. Then Jim had detected the sheer joy in his voice when he confirmed their plans for Sunday, and his heart was equally saddened for the boy who had lost so much when his father left the family home. The boy had lost a role model too, although Leo O'Dowd didn't sound as though he'd ever been an ideal dad.

Next, Jim dialled Orla's number. She'd been looking for some inside information on Harry Sweeney, a man who'd been on remand for murder thirty-five years ago. He smiled to himself. The things that young woman got involved in! Still, he'd managed to get some information from a colleague who'd actually worked on the case. And by a stroke of luck, that colleague's brother had been a prison warden during the brief time that Harry Sweeney was inside. He'd said that if Harry Sweeney was guilty, he had been the most likeable murderer he'd ever met.

His colleague had also indicated that he'd never been happy about Harry Sweeney's remand himself. However, the powers-that-be had pushed ahead relentlessly with the case since there hadn't been any other suspect, and poor Harry didn't have an alibi for his whereabouts at the time that young Colette Devane was killed.

It seemed that Sweeney had been constantly at loggerheads with a number of builders, most notably millionaire property developer Ivan Kilmartin. The company Kilmartin owned employed hundreds of workers, and Sweeney had become a thorn in the company's side through his demands for higher wages and better working conditions for his union's members. When one of the workers died in an accident on a building site, Sweeney had ensured that Kilmartin's company was fined for its poor safety record – which didn't endear him to the company's management.

Hopefully, Jim thought, this information would be of some use to Orla. It certainly sounded as though this Harry Sweeney guy had got a raw deal. His colleague's brother also suggested that Harry Sweeney might not have hanged himself either – there had been rumours at the time that someone in the prison had been paid to kill him. There had been an internal enquiry about the death, but nothing further came of it, and a verdict of suicide had been registered, bringing Harry Sweeney's life to a tidy and convenient end. After all, it wasn't as though anyone cared. Harry's wife had apparently left the country before he was remanded in custody. And dead was dead, anyway.

"Newsroom? Hi, Orla – it's Mick McHale. Yes, I've got some information for you . . . " Mick McHale settled back in his chair, poured himself another cup of coffee from the large cafétière on the table and proceeded to tell his friend Orla what he'd learnt about Harry Sweeney.

CHAPTER 60

"I've a confession to make, Orla," said Joanna.

"I'm all ears."

"I can't keep it from you any longer."

"Sounds ominous. Have I bad breath or something?"

"Don't be daft! But you're not going to believe what's happened," said Joanna, her face flushing as the memories flooded back.

She and Orla were sitting in the bar of the Morrison Hotel in the city centre. The two friends had arranged to meet for a quick drink on their way home from work, and Joanna was finding it impossible to keep the news of her new relationship from her friend, especially when they were sitting face to face. Even though Orla was still pining for Gary Culhane, Joanna felt duty-bound to tell her about Ronan.

"Go on," said Orla, "surprise me. You're going to tell me that you had mad passionate sex with a client. On the floor of your office. Watched by Mary and several other clients."

"You're not far wrong," said Joanna, looking as

343

though she was about to burst into tears. "Oh Orla!" she wailed. "I've had sex – with Ronan O'Farrell!"

"W-what?" Orla sat up with a jolt. "I don't believe you! The private detective? But you've only just met him. *And* he's employed by you!" She looked aghast, then she started to grin. "So how does a private dick do it? I guess his dick's not so private any more!"

"Orla, it's not funny," said Joanna, although she had to smile herself. Orla had a most bizarre sense of humour at times.

"You're just winding me up, aren't you?" asked Orla. "I didn't really hear you correctly, did I? I *thought* you said that you'd slept with Ronan O'Farrell, but you always said that you'd never sleep with a client or employee – "

"We didn't sleep – that's the problem!" said Joanna, breaking into peals of almost hysterical laughter. "We did everything *but* sleep! Oh, Orla, he's the most amazing lover!"

"And when did all this happen?" asked Orla, eager for every detail. "When I spoke to you yesterday afternoon, you said nothing about it."

"It actually happened long before then," Joanna said, "but you were so depressed about Gary, I didn't want to make you feel worse. But Orla, can you believe it? I made love to Ronan O'Farrell, in my own bed! First, we went for something to eat, then to the pub, so we could discuss the Kilmartin will – "

"My God, you work fast!" said Orla. Then she grinned. "So I was right – you *are* a slut!"

Joanna buried her face in her hands, whether from

embarrassment or laughter she wasn't quite sure. Her emotions were all over the place!

"I can't believe what I did," she whispered. "Oh Orla, I feel as though I've behaved totally unprofessionally! Although, strictly speaking, Ronan isn't an employee, I still think that professionally I did the wrong thing – "

"Wow – you've certainly got an interesting scenario on your hands," said Orla, matter of factly. "Was it the start of a grand passion or just a typical night of solicitor lust? Either way – some people have all the luck!"

"I don't know – we just got carried away – "

"Whoa – slow down!" said Orla. "I'm lost already – why don't you start this story right at the beginning? I don't want to miss even the tiniest detail! I know you had the hots for him from Day One, but how did you get it together so quickly?"

Joanna grinned and proceeded to tell her friend exactly how it all happened.

"So – what's next on the agenda?" asked Orla. "Are you and Ronan an item now? Or is this just a fling? And is Tom out of favour?"

Joanna wrung her hands in despair. "Oh God, I don't know, Orla – about anything! I don't know how I feel, I don't know what I want! Ronan is absolutely gorgeous – you'll have to meet him soon. He said he'd phone me when he gets back from England – but he has to see me again over the Kilmartin will, anyway. Quite honestly, think I'll feel embarrassed at seeing him again!"

Orla grinned. "To think that only a few weeks ago, I was doing my best to drag you away from work and get you to socialise more!"

"Oh, Orla – what am I going to do?" Joanna wailed.

Orla grinned. "Enjoy it!" she said. "It seems to me that you're having a more interesting life than anyone else I know – including me!"

"Oh, Orla!" said Joanna, grasping her friend's hand sympathetically. "I wish you and Gary could have got it together too!"

"So do I," said Orla regretfully, "but it obviously wasn't meant to be. Don't worry about me, Jo – I'm not going to pine away because of him. I'm supposed to be meeting Peter next week – remember the guy who bought us drinks in the Burlington?" Orla gestured to the barman and ordered another round of drinks. "By the way," she said, "I have a bit more information on Harry – Mick McHale came up with some interesting stuff through a cop whose brother worked in Mountjoy." Quickly, she explained what Jim had told her, and Joanna was able to forget her own immediate dilemma for a few minutes.

"Well, what you've told me seems to confirm that my own mother was actually telling me the truth," said Joanna thoughtfully. "The other night, I took Tom along to visit her, and she told us that Agnes and Harry had been in love."

Orla nodded. "So poor old Harry would have had more than a few enemies, wouldn't he? I mean, since he was continually sticking his neck out for his colleagues, there must have been some powerful people – Tom's father included – who wouldn't have been very fond of him. I wonder if Ivan Kilmartin knew that his wife was bedding Harry?"

"If my mother's to be believed – and already she's been right on one of the things she told me – then Harry didn't commit any murder. And now your friend Mick McHale has cast further doubts on his guilt."

"But if he didn't do it – then who *did*? Is there anyone out there who knows what really happened? "

"Maybe I'll talk to my mother again," said Joanna thoughtfully, "but it's a problem sorting out the gobbledegook from what may actually be real information. Just when I thought I was getting some information from her the other day, she started singing a Christmas carol. But she's also come up with some interesting bits – so who knows?"

"How did Tom react to the information – that his mother and Harry were in love?"

"He seemed OK about it – and, you know, I found it much easier to talk to him, now that it's Ronan I fancy, and not him – " Suddenly, she looked up. "Oh my God!"

Quickly, Orla looked in the direction that Joanna was staring, and saw Sasha Miller sashaying into the bar – with Tom Kilmartin in tow! It was obvious that neither of them had spotted the two friends, and Joanna shrank lower in her seat so that she wouldn't be seen.

"Can you see what's happening?" she hissed at Orla, who was craning her neck to see over the crowds gathered around the bar.

"He's buying her a drink – and she's giving him the works – you know, she's in full flirtation mode. Tom's looking a bit embarrassed, but I think he's enjoying it!" Orla looked at her friend. "But you've got Ronan now – so why should you care?"

"You're right," said Joanna, trying to sound indifferent. "If Tom wants to shag that tart, why should I care?"

"Especially since you're shagging Ronan O'Farrell."

Joanna knocked back her drink, which she always did when she felt under pressure. The truth was that she *did* care who Tom Kilmartin shagged. What she felt was irrational, illogical – but she wanted to have her cake and eat it too! She wanted to keep Tom virgin-like in the background, waiting in the wings until she made up her mind as to whether Ronan and she were going to take their budding relationship any further. But now Tom was with that disgusting little tart Sasha Miller, and it was obvious from her low tops and skin-tight skirts that Sasha never took no for an answer . . . Besides, what single man would see anything wrong with availing of what was so blatantly on offer?

Joanna shivered. She felt quite sick. All the effervescent feeling she had experienced earlier had evaporated. Why oh why did it have to be Sasha Miller, of all people? It certainly didn't say much for Tom's taste in women, did it? So maybe she'd had a lucky escape. If that was the kind of woman that turned him on, then he clearly wasn't the sort who was interested in a *real* woman. Slappers were obviously more his cup of tea, she thought viciously.

"They're looking for a table now, I think they might be coming this way – "

"Oh God, no!"

"It's OK, relax!" Orla suddenly pronounced. "They've found a table over by the wall."

"What do you think he's doing with that cow?" Joanna asked her friend.

Orla laughed. "The same as all the other guys do, I guess – I mean, what else is there to Sasha Miller except that arse and those floppy tits of hers?"

"Oh, Orla – I really thought that Tom would be a bit more discerning in his choice of women!"

"By picking a woman like you, Jo?" her friend grinned back. "I think you may have blown it there – but surely it doesn't matter now, if you're involved with Ronan?"

"*If*," said Joanna looking doubtful. "I really don't know where I'm going with Ronan. I suppose it all happened so quickly that I didn't have a chance to think about us as a couple with a future together. I don't know if *he's* thought of us that way either. Maybe he'll be as embarrassed as me when he has to see me again."

"Well, you'll find out soon, won't you?" said Orla reasonably.

"I wish it was that easy," said Joanna miserably. "He *has* to see me again, since he's searching for Maura Sweeney in England and will have to report back. So I'm not sure how I should behave when I see him. I mean, maybe he isn't interested in taking things any further."

"What do you *want* to happen?" Orla asked her. "You're obviously madly attracted to him – you said he's amazing!"

"Oh – he's – yes, he *is* – he's gorgeous – about six feet tall, with masses of brown curly hair just reaching his shoulders – "

"Hmmm – sounds dishy, as well as arty. *And* he's good in the sack. What more could any woman ask for?"

Joanna didn't answer, since her eyes were riveted on Tom Kilmartin, who had just stood up from the corner table and was helping Sasha Miller to put on her coat. And she – the *bitch*! – was rubbing up against him and making it plain that she fancied him. And *he* was smiling and laughing back at her. Joanna felt sick.

Orla followed Joanna's line of vision. "Uh oh – Ms No-Knickers is taking Tom away for an evening of lustful pursuits. She certainly doesn't waste any time, does she?"

"Maybe it's not the first time," said Joanna dolefully. "For all we know, they've been at it for ages. After all, it's several weeks since Declan and Sasha broke up, isn't it?"

Orla snorted. "Oh, Sasha doesn't waste any time – there's been another guy in between Declan and Tom, if you'll excuse the pun!" said Orla. Then seeing her friend's sad face, she added: "Look, one thing about Sasha Miller is that she never keeps a man for long – although I don't know if she dumps *them* or they dump *her*. All she has is those physical attributes – I doubt if a guy could have an intelligent conversation with her."

Joanna laughed harshly. "What guy would *want* an intelligent conversation, when he's fondling that big fat arse of hers?"

Orla laughed, but she could see that Joanna was far from happy as she watched Tom and Sasha leave the bar. "Look," she said. "You've been shagged by a handsome, sexy man. That's more than happened to *me*."

Joanna smiled back. "You're right – I suppose I just feel edgy because a lot of things are changing too quickly for my liking."

"It's old age, m'dear. Will I order another drink for my much loved, but elderly, friend?"

Joanna nodded. "Why not? I'm in no hurry."

But a tiny voice inside urged her to rush home to her little cat and lock her doors so that she would feel secure from the big bad frightening world outside. Right now, she was scared of so many things – of losing her mother as she sank further and further in dementia, of losing Tom's friendship – maybe even his love – and of beginning something new with Ronan. If the choice of a relationship with Ronan was hers to make. Oh God, I am pathetic, she thought. Maybe I'll just stay here with Orla and get pissed, until I can feel no pain any more . . .

CHAPTER 61

The following morning, Agnes jumped out of bed, determined that she was going to the police station. Thankfully, Ivan was currently working on a big housing project and started work very early, so he'd already left the house. Agnes savoured the peacefulness. The nurse was due shortly, but Agnes had no intention of being there when she arrived. Quickly, she showered and dressed, then went down to the kichen where she snatched a quick breakfast. Almost gagging as she tried to swallow her toast, Agnes wondered if her morning sickness would ever end. It seemed to go on forever! She was grateful that her cleaning lady wasn't due that morning either. The less people to snare her, the better.

In the car, Agnes turned on the ignition and began to head down the driveway. She felt exhilarated at the thought that her beloved Harry would soon be free, his name cleared and a new life ahead of them. There wasn't anything Ivan could do to stop them now, since the evidence of his innocence would soon be clear to everyone. She wouldn't go back to the house at all –

she'd go and stay with Cat and Bill until Harry was released.

She switched on the car radio as she reached the road, looking left and right before she turned out onto the road. The news bulletin was just coming on, so Agnes turned it up and listened as she drove along. She was happy because she felt she wasn't hiding behind Ivan any more – she was about to make a public statement about her love for Harry, and she didn't care who knew about it. In fact, she hoped that the whole world would know about it before long.

The news bulletin droned on, with Agnes only half-listening. She was too full of joy, too excited, to fully concentrate on what the newscaster was saying. Suddenly she heard a mention of Mountjoy prison. Something about a statement from the governor. What was it the newscaster had said – that someone had died there? While it wasn't anything to do with her, she always felt sad when someone's life ended so tragically . . .

Suddenly, her heart almost stopped. Had someone just mentioned the name Harry Sweeney? No, it couldn't be. She was imagining it, simply because Harry was in her thoughts, in her whole being. But something made her turn the radio up louder, just in time to hear the newscaster say: "Prison authorities believe that the prisoner committed suicide by using the sheet off his bed. Harry Sweeney was on remand in Mountjoy pending his trial for the murder of . . ."

But Agnes heard no more. Her mind refused to operate, and her body went into spasm. She was no longer in control of the car, and it veered off the roadway, up onto the verge and crashed through someone's garden hedge. Stunned, Agnes lay slumped over the wheel, her heart pounding, her throat dry. A small, strangled cry escaped her lips, a sound more akin to an animal in pain. She tried to breathe, but the air wouldn't enter her *lungs. Let me die now, she thought, please let me die, because this pain is too much to bear.*

* * *

Later that morning, Catherine phoned to find out how Agnes had got on at the police station. She was informed by the agency nurse that her friend was ill and was under sedation in her bedroom. Immediately, Catherine knew that something was very wrong, so she climbed into her old banger and hurried to Agnes's house. She didn't care if it meant another row with Ivan – she wasn't going to leave the big Ballsbridge house until she'd seen her friend.

Filled with foreboding, Catherine rang the doorbell of Agnes's house and waited. Hopefully, Ivan was out at one of his building sites, because if he was there, he'd probably refuse to let her in. But she intended to stay there – all night if necessary – because it was clear that Agnes was in some kind of trouble.

Inside the house, Ivan and Paddy Byrne stood talking in the large hall as the doorbell rang.

"That'll probably be Catherine," said Ivan. "Open the door for her, will you, Paddy?"

Paddy Byrne looked in surprise at Ivan. "I thought you didn't want that trouble-maker around your wife, boss?"

"Let her in this time," said Ivan, smirking. "I want to see her face when she hears the news."

CHAPTER 62

Mary stood in front of the bathroom mirror and studied her face anxiously. God, she was looking awfully old and tired. She sighed. But what could she expect? She was already in her early forties. How she wished she could look young and pretty again! Especially since Mick McHale was calling by in half an hour to collect Paul and take him to the All Ireland Football Final.

She smiled happily. Thank goodness Jim was going to keep his promise to Paul – she hadn't doubted his word, but she'd been terribly worried in case something more important might genuinely crop up, and Paul would be let down again.

Her son was so excited to be going to the match, and his enthusiasm had spread right through the family! Even Emma, who wasn't remotely interested in sport, had been reading up on the subject of Gaelic football and teasing her brother unmercifully about his choice of team. Just because *he* was supporting the Dublin team, Emma had decided that she would support the other side in the finals! But it was all good-natured banter, and it filled Mary's heart with joy to see her kids getting on so well with each other.

She looked in the mirror again and brushed her hair into a different style. Did that make her look a little younger? Maybe if she tied her hair up, she could manage to look casual, yet well-groomed. She really must go to the hairdresser's to get a decent cut and a conditioning treatment. Even if she couldn't do anything about the lines on her face, she could at least ensure that her hair looked good.

Now for a little lipstick. Was that colour too obvious? Too young? She looked at the new shiny pink lipstick she had bought. So what? If it drew attention to her lips, Jim might notice them, and if she pouted them a little, it might make him think about kissing her . . .

She laughed at her silly fantasies. Why would a man like Mick McHale want to kiss the likes of her? Firstly, since he was so attractive, he could have the pick of much younger women, and secondly, hadn't he said, on his first visit to the house, that his late wife Sheila had been the love of his life? A man like that didn't go round kissing a woman just because she'd put shiny lipstick on!

Nevertheless, Mary boldly applied the shiny pink lipstick. It's not for Jim, she assured herself, it's to make *me* feel good. Which amounted to the same thing anyway. Because she knew that if she could feel positive about herself, it would be easier to deal with Mick McHale.

Suddenly, Emma was banging on the bathroom door. "Mum – you're not still in there? God almighty! You've been in there for *ages*!"

Mary had to admit to herself that she'd been hogging the bathroom for the last half-hour. "Coming!" she called, opening the door to a sour-faced teenager, who pushed past her, growling.

"Look, Mum, I'm meeting Claire and Emily in fifteen minutes – and I need to wash my hair!" Suddenly, the teenager looked at her mother. "What on earth are *you* getting yourself all done up for?" Then suddenly she laughed. "It's because of this Jim bloke, isn't it?" And she grinned with delight as she received confirmation through her mother's blushes. "Mum – you're going all red! And what's with the shiny pink lipstick? At your age?"

"Thanks for the vote of confidence," Mary said dryly.

Emma was immediately contrite. "You look great, Mum – honestly. For a woman of your age, that is."

Mary laughed. Maybe she was being silly in attempting to attract such a gorgeous man. But regardless of the outcome of her friendship with Mick McHale, he made her feel excited and alive, and he had given the kids a new sense of their own importance – which Leo had taken from them when he'd left. So whatever happened – or didn't – she would always be grateful to Mick McHale for what he'd given freely to her family. If only he could love her too, then everything would be just perfect . . .

Paul was sitting in the kitchen when she went downstairs, and Mary could almost see the excitement rippling through his body. This would be one of the most important days in his young life and would restore his status within his peer group at school. Which had been badly dented by the family's financial difficulties after

Leo's departure. Now Paul's school-friends were envious of his trip to the All Ireland, and while Mary didn't want either of her children lording it over others, she was pleased that Paul was being accepted in his peer group once again. Kids could be so cruel to each other – or did they just mirror what most adults did, albeit less obviously?

Suddenly, the doorbell rang, and Mary hurried to answer it, but Paul had beaten her to it, and he was already welcoming Mick McHale as she reached the hall.

"Hi, Mr McHale!" said Paul, grinning.

"Hi, Paul – and please call me Jim – being called 'Mister' makes me feel ancient!"

"Hi, Jim!" said Mary, smiling. "How about some lunch before you two head off?"

"No, thanks, Mary," said Jim, looking conspiratorily at Paul. "We men have important things to do – like getting ourselves properly kitted out! We'll get something to eat on our way."

"Well, you'll eat with us this evening, Jim," said Mary firmly. "Unless, of course, you've got other plans – "

"No, I've got no other plans," Jim replied. "Thanks for the invite, Mary – I'd be delighted." He raised an eyebrow. "Then afterwards, maybe you and I could go down to the local pub for a nightcap? I used to drink in O'Malley's years ago – does it still have a good atmosphere?"

Inwardly, Mary was thrilled at the prospect of being alone with Jim, but her reply was as relaxed and cool as his invitation. "Yes, Jim – O'Malley's is still the best pub within miles. And a nightcap sounds great."

After Paul and Jim had left for the match, Mary rushed upstairs to search her wardrobe for something to wear to the pub and nearly collided with Emma, who was on her way out to meet her school-friends. Emma gave her mother a sly look and Mary giggled to herself. There were far too many teenagers living on the premises – even if she herself was a recycled version!

Rustling through her wardrobe, Mary concluded that she had absolutely nothing decent to wear. She used to have nice clothes when Leo was around, because he expected her to look good for the many business dinners they used to attend. But all that stuff in her wardrobe was now terribly dated. She cringed as she examined some of the dresses that had once made her feel so elegant. She'd be a laughing stock if she appeared in any of these! It was time to fill up a sack for the local charity shop or get out the sewing machine and start making alterations!

Of course, she still had that very generous bank draft that Joanna had given her as an advance birthday present. She hadn't got around to spending it yet. In truth, she was terrified of spending it – it seemed so indulgent to lavish so much money on herself. But Joanna had insisted that it wasn't to be used for groceries, and she'd demanded that Mary show her what she'd eventually bought. Maybe some day soon, she'd buy an outfit that would have Mick McHale's eyes popping out of his head!

But in the meantime, should she go to the pub wearing something totally casual, like jeans and a sweater? Or would Jim expect her to make an effort and maybe wear a black, sexy dress? If only she had a great social life, then she'd know what to wear. But she hadn't been to a pub in ages, and she hadn't dated anyone since she and Leo broke up.

Briefly, she thought of phoning Joanna. But no, why bother her on her day off? That wouldn't be fair. Anyway, Mary thought, I'm an adult woman – even if I'm behaving like an insecure teenager! Surely, I'm capable of picking *something* by myself. She grinned to herself. This uncertainty was one of the disadvantages of being back in the dating game!

Mary frowned. But then, it wasn't really a date, was it? Jim was probably just being kind, knowing that she was a single mother. He was just asking her to the pub out of sympathy. He would be the sort of guy who would instinctively know that it still wasn't easy for a single woman – even a liberated one – to go into a pub on her own. So he was just giving her a chance to socialise. Well, she still intended to look as good as she could. She didn't want anyone in the pub wondering why such a good-looking man was in the company of such a badly dressed woman!

Finally, she selected a pair of tight black trousers and a black sweater, which looked casual but nevertheless elegant. Then she selected some gold costume jewellery to go with it. Hopefully, this outfit would strike the right balance. She didn't want to look too eager and overdressed, yet she still wanted Jim to know that she'd made an effort and could still look reasonably good.

Suddenly, she looked at her left hand and realised that she was still wearing her wedding ring. Quickly, she slid it off and placed it in the back of the drawer. Her finger looked odd without the gold band after so many years, but she experienced such a heady, bubbly feeling inside when she removed it! It was as though she had just completed some rite of passage that would lead her on to another stage of her life.

Stop being so fanciful, she scolded herself as she left her bedroom and headed downstairs to the kitchen. It was time to stop the wishful thinking and get on with preparations for the dinner. There would be four of them for grub that evening, so she'd better start getting organised!

CHAPTER 63

Joanna looked around her kitchen in anguish. Where on earth could her mother have hidden those letters and documents? *If*, in fact, they existed. Yet in her present condition, it was unlikely that Catherine was capable of telling a downright lie. If the documents did exist, they could be the key to everything.

Joanna sighed, made herself a cup of tea and stroked Devil, who had climbed onto her knee. Nibbling a biscuit absentmindedly, she decided to start with the attic and work her way down through the house. I wonder, she mused, if this counts as overtime? Is this part of my brief as a solicitor? Then she admitted to herself that she was as much engaging in the search because she herself badly wanted to know the outcome. Already, since Agnes's death, her own life had become inextricably tied up with Agnes's beneficiaries – whoever they were. And somehow, her own mother was involved as well. So now it had become a family mystery as well as a professional one.

Wearily, Joanna removed Devil from her knee, put her into her cat basket and climbed the stairs to the top floor of the house. She was pulling down the attic ladder when the phone rang. For a moment her heart stood still, then she rushed into the bedroom to take the call. Could it be Ronan?

"H-hello?"

"Hi, Jo!"

"Oh, hi, Orla."

"Are you OK? You sound lousy."

"Oh, I suppose I *am* a bit down. I'm about to start searching the house for documents and letters that my mother claims she was minding for Agnes."

"So there's been no word from Lover Boy?"

"No – and I feel absolutely lousy. I thought I'd have heard from him before the weekend. He's obviously not interested in me personally, or he would have been in touch, wouldn't he? I feel like an absolute slut – just like you said."

"Jo – that was only a joke," said Orla, sensing her friend's distress. "He's probably still in England – after all, it was you who sent him there!" She paused. "Anyway, I'm ringing because I have the answer to all your problems – how do you fancy coming out on the town tonight? A few drinks, a bit of dancing and maybe a bit of you-never-know-what! You'll probably meet some gorgeous hunk – "

"I'd rather not, Orla – "

"So you'd rather sit at home with your cat, brooding and feeling sorry for yourself?"

"No, it's not that – "

"Then I'm not taking no for an answer," said Orla firmly. "We both need a bit of craic to lift our depression. I'll call for you at eight o'clock. OK?"

"OK," said Joanna, smiling. Maybe another evening out with Orla would help her to forget. And no doubt, it would also help Orla to forget Gary for a little while. Although Orla didn't talk about him very often, Joanna knew that her friend was still hurting. She had never known any man to have such an effect on her friend.

After Orla rang off, Joanna climbed into the attic and began her search for the secret documents. It was a tedious yet emotional task, as she waded through boxes of old photographs, recipes, postcards, newspaper cuttings and letters, yet nowhere did she find any documents or diaries relating to Agnes's life. Eventually, after several hours of digging, she sat down on an old threadbare chair in the attic to take a break.

Suddenly, the doorbell rang. Dammit! Joanna thought crossly. Probably, by the time she got downstairs to the door, the caller would have gone. She was tempted not to bother but, sighing, she left the attic and climbed down the ladder, brushing off the dust as she opened the front door.

Ronan O'Farrell was standing outside.

"Hello, Joanna – I've just got back from London," he said, smiling. "I've had no luck finding Maura Sweeney *née* Devane yet – she's proving to be a very elusive creature! But I'll find her eventually – I promise. Now, how about a kiss?"

Joanna tried to look nonchalant, but her heart was pounding. She'd forgotten how absolutely gorgeous he was! She ignored his request for a kiss. "I'm searching through the attic," she told him. "My mother told me that she'd hidden documents and diaries belonging to Agnes Kilmartin, but she wouldn't tell me where. So I'm taking the house apart, room by room."

"Let me help you," said Ronan, taking off his coat and hanging it on the coatstand in the hall. Then he grabbed her round the waist and kissed her longingly.

Joanna found herself responding, and suddenly, they were once again tearing each other's clothes off.

"Oh God, I've missed you, Joanna!" Ronan whispered in between kisses. "I want to make love to you all night!"

Taking his hand, Joanna guided him upstairs to her room, and within seconds, they were coupling frantically.

Wrapped around each other, they were dozing happily in a post-coital slumber, when Joanna suddenly jumped up. "Oh my God – I forgot! Orla is calling for me in half an hour. I'll have to take a shower and get dressed!"

"Where are you off to?" Ronan asked drowsily, peering at her from the big double bed. "It's getting cold in here already."

"We're going drinking and nightclubbing," Joanna explained. "I wish I didn't have to go, but I did make the arrangement prior to your unexpected arrival!"

"Of course I understand. A prior arrangement must be honoured. Do you want me to wait here in your bed, ready and willing to ravish you again, when you get back?"

"Sounds great!" said Joanna, grinning. "I'll be thinking of you every moment that I'm away."

"If you like, I could continue with the search while you're gone," Ronan offered. "But if you'd rather I didn't, just say so. After all, I'm still something of a stranger in your life – "

Joanna chuckled. "After all the intimacy, I don't think I'd exactly call you a stranger, Ronan!"

Ronan sat up in the bed. "Well then – can I help with your search? After all, it's as much in my interests as anyone's."

"Of course – that would be great," said Joanna, dashing into the shower and turning on the water. "I've finished searching the attic, so you could start on the desk in the downstairs drawing-room. Or anywhere else that looks promising. You'll find some food in the freezer if you're hungry."

"I've just had my hunger satisfied, Joanna," said Ronan, grinning lasciviously at her.

While Joanna showered, Ronan got up and dressed and went downstairs to begin searching. When Joanna was dressed and ready to go, she found him checking through papers in the desk that had served as an office for her mother's jewellery business.

"Nothing much here," he remarked. "Anyway, I think it would be a bit too obvious, assuming the stuff needed to be hidden from prying eyes."

Ronan's eyes appraised the room, and Joanna felt acutely aware of the shabbiness of the entire house. Now that it was technically hers, she must get the paintwork freshened up soon – just as soon as Agnes Kilmartin's will was sorted out.

"Someone has excellent taste," said Ronan, examining one of several bronze sculptures that adorned the mantelpiece and sideboard.

"Oh yes – they were Mam's," said Joanna, as he lifted up a large sculpture. "She's been collecting them all her life. In fact, Agnes gave her the one you're holding, and that other one over there – " Suddenly, Joanna was overcome with sadness at the thought that her mother could no longer enjoy the things that had once given her so much pleasure.

Ronan saw her sadness and pulled her into his arms. "Look, you're under a lot of pressure right now – with your mother and the Kilmartin will. Just go out and enjoy yourself tonight," he said, kissing the top of her head. "We'll have lots of nights ahead of us."

Joanna was secretly thrilled to hear Ronan's words. So they weren't just having a fling – as far as he was concerned, this was just the start of a long-term relationship. Joanna could hardly stop smiling as she heard the doorbell ring. Tom Kilmartin could shag that tart as often as he liked. She didn't care any more – she now had a man who really wanted her.

Orla was surprised to see her friend in such good humour when she stepped out the front door and closed it quickly after her. "Well, you seem to be in better form than when I spoke to you earlier," her friend said suspiciously. "What's put you in such good humour?"

"Oh – nothing," said Joanna, knowing that Orla wouldn't recognise Ronan's car parked outside her house. After all, her friend had never met him! She'd keep her secret to herself for a while longer, since she didn't want to spoil Orla's night out. It would lessen Orla's enjoyment if she knew that she was just dying to get away and go back home to her new lover! She smiled to herself. She would tell Orla the following day. But for now, she'd ensure that her dear friend had a great night out!

After a few drinks in McDaid's, followed by a visit to the Morrison Hotel Bar, the two friends ambled along to the Leeson Street strip and went into Saucy Sue's nightclub. By now, Joanna was tired and just longing to get back to Ronan. But as she sat sipping her wine, she was pleased to see that Orla was having a good time. In fact, her friend had been dancing with the same guy for ages now. Maybe, if Orla was going to spend the rest of the evening with this guy, she could slip away soon and leave them to it.

She slipped outside and rang Ronan on her mobile to tell him there was a good chance she might be home soon. She didn't want him to fall asleep on her! He was watching TV, having given up on his document-search with no result.

Almost on cue, as Joanna reached her seat again, Orla indicated, with much gesturing, that she wanted to meet her in the women's toilets.

"What's the story?" Joanna asked, as Orla rushed into the washbasin area and grabbed her friend's arm in delight. "This guy – Kieran is his name – I really fancy him, Jo. And he's keen to come back to my place."

"Isn't it a bit risky taking him home after just meeting him?" asked Joanna anxiously, concerned for her friend's safety. "He could be a rapist or a murderer."

"Oh, don't worry," said Orla firmly, "I'm no fool. I've checked him out – I know the company he works for, and we know several of the same people. Besides, I'll kick him in the balls if he steps out of line."

Joanna grinned with relief. "Oh well, I suppose he's OK. So you won't mind if I go home now?"

Orla looked contrite. "Oh, haven't you met anyone tonight, Jo? Look, I hope I'm not spoiling your night – "

"Not at all! You go on back to what's-his-name, and enjoy yourself. I'll talk to you tomorrow."

Before Orla could protest any further, Joanna gave her friend a hug and slipped out the side door of the nightclub, hailing an empty taxi that was just passing by.

"Blackrock," she told the driver, sitting back in her seat and grinning secretively to herself. There was something *very* exciting about going home to Ronan O'Farrell.

CHAPTER 64

After Harry died in prison, Agnes seemed to lose the will to live. She functioned like an automaton, and Catherine was deeply concerned about the state of her friend's health and mind. Both women were in no doubt that Ivan was somehow instrumental in Harry's death, because they knew Harry would never commit suicide, as had been claimed by the prison authorities. Because Harry had everything to live for.

In the days that followed, the newspapers and the public seemed convinced of Harry's guilt and of the veracity of the witness's statement. Now, his alleged suicide was being seen as confirmation of his guilt in their eyes. There was also the fact that Harry's car had genuinely been at the place the witness alleged – and Harry had never denied it, since he'd been there with Agnes – and the tyre marks matched his car, and the cigarette butt, found on the ground near Colette's body, carried his fingerprints. There was also the fact that he'd left some documents in Colette's flat. The case seemed proven, even before it had got to court.

"I'm still going to the police," Agnes said to Catherine. "Even though he's dead, I want to see Harry's name cleared, and I'm the only one who can do it."

"You mustn't do that, Agnes," said Catherine forcefully. "First of all, he was never actually convicted of Colette's murder. Secondly, there's too much at stake for you and the baby. If you go to the guards, you'll create a major scandal, Ivan will throw you out without a penny and he might even succeed in getting custody of the baby when it's born. Even if you managed to keep it, you'd be depriving your child of a life full of opportunities."

Agnes looked shocked. "What? It never crossed my mind that Ivan might take the child. Could that really happen, Cat?"

"Well, under the present marriage legislation, any child born during a marriage is deemed to be the husband's. So he's as likely to get custody as you are."

"Oh God – it's just the kind of thing Ivan would do to spite me if I left!"

"Look, I'm only trying to make you see sense," said Catherine. "This baby you're carrying is Harry's and your future, so you must eat well and keep up your strength – for both their sakes. Just ask yourself – what would Harry want you to do? He'd want you to do what's best for his child. And that means staying with Ivan."

Eventually Agnes saw the wisdom of Catherine's words, and in due course, a healthy baby boy was born – for which Ivan claimed full credit and was awarded much publicity and congratulations for in the media and business worlds.

"All I've got left of Harry is a few letters," said Agnes bitterly, as she sat in her maternity hospital bed, "and I can't even keep them in my own home, for fear that Ivan will find *them and destroy them. He's still spying on me, you know – oh how I hate the bastard!"*

"Don't worry – I'll keep the letters safe for you," said Catherine loyally. "And all the other documents too. I guarantee you that no one will ever find them – I've found the perfect place to hide them. But Agnes, that's not all you have of Harry – he lives on in Tom. Your job now is to honour Harry's memory by raising his son to be as fine a man as his father was."

Agnes nodded, kissing the rosy cheeks of the baby in her arms. "The only pleasure I have left is knowing that Ivan can never be sure if the child is his or not."

Catherine grinned. "It's nice having the upper hand for a change, isn't it? Luckily, there's no test to prove paternity."

"I'm sure they'll devise one some day soon," said Agnes, smiling, "but right now, I'm the one in control."

Catherine nodded, leaning across to stroke the baby's downy head.

Agnes gave a deep sigh. "I wish Tom could know who his real father is. Maybe I'll tell him when he grows up. Or do you think he'll despise me for what I did?"

"Don't be ridiculous!" said Catherine loyally. "Some day soon, all these stupid laws and religious hypocrisy won't exist any more. Divorce will be available, and the courts will ensure that assets are fairly divided. Then people won't be forced to stay in empty marriages. By the time Tom grows up, all that will matter to him is that he was conceived in love." Catherine smiled, reaching for her friend's hand. "Then you can show him all the letters that you and Harry exchanged – what better way for him to see how much his parents loved each other?"

Agnes grimaced, determined to be negative. "What a sad

way to find out about your father – by reading his letters from prison."

"Try to think of how lucky you are," Catherine said gently. "At least you have a child by the man you loved – Bill and I haven't been so lucky."

"Oh God, sorry, Cat," said Agnes contritely. "I'd forgotten about that. But you've only been married a few years – I'm sure it will eventually happen for you both."

"No, Agnes, it won't ever happen, because Bill and I have already been for tests."

"My God, you never told me. What did the results say?"

"Basically, we can forget about ever having a family."

"Oh, dear. Are you sure nothing can be done?"

"No. And please, Agnes, I'd rather not talk about it."

"Oh – sorry, Cat."

The two women sat in silence, until Catherine spoke. "Isn't it odd how polarised – yet strangely similar – our situations are?" she said softly, almost to herself. "You have a baby but no man who loves you any more, while I have a man who loves me, but no baby – now or ever."

Agnes nodded in agreement. "How I wish I could leave Ivan!" she said angrily, "Outwardly, it's looks as though I have everything I need – and in one sense that's true, Cat. Ivan's even engaged a nanny for the baby and, if only for the sake of appearances, he has to maintain me in a reasonable standard of living." She looked fierce. "If only my father hadn't left his entire business and all the family money to Ivan!"

"It's not that bad – you could be penniless," said Catherine, trying to cheer her friend up. "At least Ivan gives you a decent monthly allowance, so you can pamper yourself, have a massage, get your hair and nails done regularly – "

Agnes laughed bitterly. "And make myself more attractive to that bastard? I'll see him in hell first! Because there'll be no more children, Cat. Ivan can have his floosies – but he'll never be allowed near me again!"

"Maybe he'll die soon," said Catherine helpfully.

"No such luck – that lying, murdering bastard will live forever! But if there's any justice, at least Tom will have a good life. In the meantime, I'll just have to play the meek and dutiful wife, run the house efficiently and hold wonderful dinner parties. And dream of what might have been." Agnes's eyes filled with tears. "But some day, Cat, I want to see Harry's name respected and revered again. And I want to be buried beside him when my time comes. That way, at least, we'll be together for all eternity. The way it was meant to be."

CHAPTER 65

Gary Culhane was catching up on hospital paperwork. It was quiet in the Casualty Department, but Gary knew that this was just the lull before the storm, especially at the weekend when people were out in the pubs and clubs, having a good time. A surfeit of alcohol, combined with human nature, was often an explosive combination which filled hospital casualty departments all over the country, as the results of fights and accidents were carried in. Gary looked at his watch. It was 1 a.m. – time to put away the paperwork and get ready for the onslaught. In fact, he was sure he'd just heard an ambulance draw up outside . . .

Almost on cue, the automatic double doors from the outside courtyard opened, and an ambulance man came in with a young woman leaning heavily on his arm.

"I'm perfectly OK ," she said loudly. "I'm not a bloody invalid, you know!"

Gary started. It was Orla Rogan!

His heart started thumping painfully, but he did his best to look calm and in control. Anyway, it was unlikely that Orla would notice his discomfiture – she was well and truly pissed.

"Orla!" said Gary, taking the opportunity of putting his arm around her. It felt good, and he wished that he could leave it there indefinitely, but the ambulance man needed to have a few words with him.

"Stroppy cow," the ambulanceman muttered darkly, as he surrendered his patient to Gary's care. "She fell coming out of Saucy Sue's nightclub, but she's been insisting that she's fine and she just wanted us to drive her home. Luckily the nightclub staff phoned us, because I think she may have done serious damage to her left ankle."

"Thanks, Stephen, I'll take over now," Gary assured the ambulance man. "No doubt we both have a busy night ahead of us!"

Grinning, the ambulance man left to join his driver and colleagues for another trip into the city.

"Hi, Gary," said Orla, grimacing at the pain, but still determined to show Gary Culhane that she didn't care about him. "It's amazing what the cat drags in – what on earth are *you* doing here?"

Gary grinned. "This is a hospital, Orla, and I'm a doctor who happens to work here. Does that answer your question? Besides, it was *you* who, literally, was dragged in here!"

"This is a *hospital*?" said Orla, hiccuping. "But I asked those ambulance guys to just take me home!"

"They operate an ambulance service – not a taxi

service," said Gary grinning. Orla had clearly consumed a skinful tonight. She'd probably feel mortified in the morning!

Orla sat quietly in the treatment room while Gary touched her leg gently, probing for painful areas that might indicate a breakage. The tip of the tibia seemed particularly tender, and Orla squealed when he touched her ankle-bone.

"And where is himself this evening? Isn't he with you?" asked Gary dryly, not really wanting an answer but unable to resist the urge to probe Orla's relationship with her fiancé.

"My God – I'd forgotten all about him!" said Orla, suddenly realising that Kieran had scarpered as soon as the ambulance arrived, no doubt unwilling to get involved once the situation became more complicated. He was probably married anyway, Orla thought suddenly. So naturally, he wouldn't want to be seen hanging round a nightclub – and certainly not a hospital – when things got messy.

"The scumbag! But that's men for you, isn't it?" she said, smiling venomously at Gary. "They always disappear at the first sign of problems, right?"

Gary felt troubled. What kind of man would desert his future wife when she was in need of help? Orla deserved better than that asshole. But he said nothing, realising that since Orla had consumed a fair amount of alcohol, any comment from him would only inflame the situation further.

"Come on, Orla – let's get that leg sorted out. I want to get X-rays of that ankle and possibly your knee as well."

"Ouch! Can't you be a bit more gentle?" she croaked. "That's bloody sore!"

"Well, if you weren't out tripping the light fantastic, you wouldn't be in this position," Gary muttered, then remembering that Orla was a patient and entitled, like every other patient, to his non-judgemental help, he grinned apologetically. "Sorry – I suppose I'm just envious."

"Of what?" asked Orla, picking up on something unsaid.

"Oh, nothing," said Gary abruptly. "Now, what's your guy's name? Perhaps I should telephone him and let him know what's happening. We'll have to notify a locum radiographer, so it could be a while before you get back home."

Gary couldn't remember Orla's fiancé's name – in fact he didn't *want* to remember it, but he knew that it began with the letter D. Perhaps it was Dominic, Dennis or something like that. As far as Gary was concerned, the D stood for Dork!

"Kieran," said Orla. "But don't bother calling him, because he won't want to know. I only picked him up at the nightclub tonight, anyway."

Gary looked aghast. Was Orla for real? She had a fiancé at home, yet she was out cavorting around in a nightclub and blatantly scoring with another man! Maybe he'd had a lucky escape himself. Nevertheless, he could still feel the tug at his heart-strings as he looked at her dishevelled appearance. In fact, he wanted to take her into his arms and kiss away all her problems – of which she undoubtedly had many. Especially if her fiancé found out that she'd had another man in tow earlier in the night!

Nevertheless, Gary decided that, given Orla's inebriated state, it was better not to give vent to *any* of his feelings, especially the anger he felt about her cheating on her fiancé. Anyway, it was none of his business. On the other hand, it gave him a delightful sense of revenge to think that she was doing the dirty on that prat.

Nevertheless, Orla detected his disapproving glance, and she reacted angrily. "So you don't think I've any right to be out enjoying myself, eh, Gary? Well, I've got news for you – I'll do whatever I want – and it's none of your goddamned business anyway!" Orla stubbed the big toe of her other foot and yelped furiously. "There – look what you've made me do! Anyway," she looked at him closely, "talk about the pot calling the kettle black! *You* don't mind leading people on in your spare time, do you? So who are you to tell me what I can – and can't – do?"

Gary looked askance at Orla. What on earth was she rambling on about? Still, it was always best to ignore inflammatory remarks from people under the influence. Was she referring back to the night they'd met? The night when he'd thought she was free and single, and he'd hesitated to ask her out because of his business relationship with her friend Joanna? Well, in view of what he'd found out later, it seemed that he'd had a lucky escape. He hadn't known at the time that she was engaged to that prat Dominic, or Desmond or David – whatever his name was. But obviously Orla didn't see an engagement as a barrier to a bit of fun on the side. Gary sighed. But he wasn't like that. He would have wanted Orla all to himself. *Still* did, if he was truthful.

"Come on," he said abruptly. "Let's get you to the X-ray department." He gestured to one of the nurses. "Would you mind taking this patient up to X-ray?" He squeezed Orla's hand. "I'll see you later – you'll be coming back here for treatment when we find out how serious the problem is."

Orla was silent as she was wheeled into the lift and taken upstairs. She had been deeply affected by Gary's gentle squeeze of her hand. And even though she knew there was a wife and a string of kids in the background, she couldn't help but wish that things might have been different. If only *I'd* met him first, she thought sadly. Because I know that there's some special kind of feeling between us. She sighed. On the other hand, maybe she was just feeling maudlin because of the drink. She was now sober enough to know that she'd consumed several bottles of wine. And her ankle was hurting like hell.

CHAPTER 66

"I'm really enjoying the evening, Jim," said Mary, as Mick McHale returned to their table in the pub with another round of drinks, "and I can't thank you enough for what you did for Paul today – it's been a long time since I saw him looking so happy."

Jim smiled as he placed her vodka and Coke on the table in front of her. "Mary – *I* enjoyed myself at the match today, just as much as Paul did. So you don't have to keep thanking me. If you keep up the thanks, then I'll have to start thanking *you* for coming out for a drink with me – because you're making *my* evening very enjoyable."

Mary laughed as she poured the Coke into the vodka and took a sip. "Sorry, Jim – you're right. It's just that I'm so relieved about Paul. His problems had almost taken me over – now I feel that I can relax and starting living again."

Jim stared nervously into his pint as he spoke. "Mary, do you think we could go out for a meal together some evening – just you and me? I mean, I'm very fond of your kids and I love helping out around the place, but –" He looked up and saw that Mary's eyes were shining.

"Go on, Jim," she whispered softly.

"Well, it's just that – I really *like* you, Mary – and I want us to –" He squirmed with embarassment. "What I mean is – I'd like us to go out on a *date*."

Mary reached across and touched his hand. "I'd love that, Jim. I really like you too, and already I regard you as a very dear friend."

Jim sat upright, reached out and gripped her outstretched hand. "Mary, I don't want to be just your friend – I want something more. Oh God, this isn't sounding the way I want it to, is it?"

"Oh, Jim," said Mary, stroking his hand. "I know exactly what you mean. I feel the same way – I don't just like you, Jim – I *fancy* you!" She looked down at her drink. "There – I've got it out at last. But maybe that's not what you meant. Maybe I've just got courage because of the few vodkas I've had. And if you don't feel the same, then we'll just forget about what I said."

"No, I feel the same, Mary. But I'm scared – I never expected to become fond of another woman after Sheila."

Mary's eyes were shining. "I know, Jim. After Leo left, I vowed that I'd never have anything to do with a man again. My plan was that I'd rear the kids as best I could, then maybe some day I'd be a grandmother. Then I'd spoil my grandchildren, put my snow-white hair up in a neat bun and wear a string of pearls around my neck!"

Jim laughed. "I can't imagine you ever looking like that!" he said. "You're much too glamorous!"

Mary was delighted at his compliment. It was a long

time since anyone had ever told her that she was attractive. Looking down at her glass, she realised that she'd somehow drunk all her vodka and Coke. So much for nerves – she always drank too fast when she was anxious or excited. And right now, she felt very excited. The future was taking on a whole new dimension.

"I'll get another round," she said, jumping up. Although she could ill afford it, she didn't want Jim to think that she wouldn't buy her round. Then she experienced a very sobering thought. If she was going to see Jim on a regular basis, how was she was going to cope with the expense? Not only would she need to dress better, she'd also need money for treating him when it was her turn to pay for the meal and buying her round – or rounds – in the pub. It just wasn't possible on her salary, and it wouldn't be fair to indulge in her own pleasures at the expense of the kid's needs. After all, Paul needed new shoes, and Emma wanted to take drama classes after school. Then there was the cost of their daily lunches – no kid nowadays wanted to be shamed by having to eat home-made sandwiches in front of their classmates. And she wasn't going to let her children be bullied by anyone if she could help it.

When she returned to the table with Jim's pint and her own vodka and Coke, Mary had already made up her mind.

Jim was smiling as Mary placed the drinks on the table and sat down. "Thanks, Mary. Now when can we go for this meal? What kind of food do you like to eat?"

"Oh, anything – I'm not fussy about food."

"Well, if you like Indian, I was thinking of Paradise in Westmoreland Street – it's got a great reputation for curries. What do you think?"

Mary took a deep breath. "Look, Jim – there's something I've got to make clear if we're going to start seeing each other on a regular basis."

"Sounds ominous."

"Look, I enjoy your company, and I'd love to go out with you, but . . ."

Jim felt a stab of disappointment. "Mary, I hope I haven't offended you by anything I've said. If you don't want to go out with me, I'll understand."

If Mary wanted to take things really slowly, well, he'd do whatever she wanted. Then he wondered if he'd come on too strong. But no, unless he'd read the signs all wrong, Mary had seemed as keen as he was. Suddenly, he was reminded of those awful feelings of insecurity that had plagued his teenage years, when you didn't know if the other person was interested or simply playing games with your heart.

"No, no – that's not it," said Mary, looking embarrassed. "It's just that – well, I simply can't afford to go out on dates, Jim. I have two children to rear, and I can barely manage as it is. It wouldn't be fair –"

Jim grinned and clasped her hands in his. "God, Mary – for one minute I thought you were giving me the bum's rush! Look, money's no problem for me – so I'm happy to pay for any meals we have, theatre tickets and the like. I never intended to let you shoulder any of those costs anyway!"

"But a liberated woman should be able to pay her own way," said Mary in exasperation. "I want to be able to take you for a meal too!"

"Well, you can invite me for a meal at your house

sometimes, if you like," said Jim, leaning over and planting a kiss on her head. "So is that settled? We'll take this as slowly as you like, Mary. Look, it's a big step for me too. So let's not rush into anything, right? Let's just enjoy each other's company for the immediate future, OK?"

Mary nodded, relieved that she'd been straightforward with him about her financial situation.

At the end of the evening, as they set out to walk back to Mary's house, Jim slipped his arm around her. Mary was apprehensive about what would happen next. Did people kiss on a first date? Was she expected to ask him in for coffee? And if she did, would he get the wrong idea? In fact, what *was* the wrong idea? Part of her longed for Jim to sweep her into his arms and profess undying devotion, whereas the other part wanted to have time to come to terms with the magical thing that was happening between them.

In any event, she needn't have worried. Jim simply kissed her gently on the cheek and was gone. "I'll phone you during the week," he called as he walked to his car.

Feeling vaguely disappointed that he hadn't kissed her passionately, Mary waited at the door until he'd started his car and waved as he drove away.

Letting herself into the house, Mary touched her cheek where Jim's lips had brushed it. She felt excited and apprehensive all rolled into one. Her life was suddenly taking an unexpected turn. She'd met a man she really fancied, and he seemed to fancy her too. He was kind and generous, and the future was suddenly starting to look good . . .

CHAPTER 67

"Orla, I'm afraid the news isn't great – you've broken your ankle," Gary told his patient, as she was wheeled back into the casualty ward. "There's a bad break just here." He pointed to one of the X-rays that were pinned onto the light-box on the wall.

Orla slumped in her chair. What rotten luck – what on earth was she going to do now?

"We'll have to put it in plaster," Gary explained, "but you'll be able to hobble about on the crutches that the hospital will lend you. It's not the end of the world – if you take it easy, you should be back to normal in about six to eight weeks."

"Six to eight weeks?" Orla whispered. "But I have a job to go to!"

"Yes, I know," said Gary cynically, "and nightclubs to attend, and men to pick up. Well, Orla, I have news for you – if you don't take it easy for the few weeks, you'll end up with far worse problems. That break needs time to heal. So cut the crap – I'm just doing my best for you."

Orla was silent as the impact of her short-term disability registered in her brain. And why was Gary being so horrible to her? He had no right to be so sarcastic. But she decided to hold her counsel since she still needed his skills to get her back on her feet.

"How am I going to get around?" she asked Gary humbly. "I mean, I won't be able to drive a car, will I?"

"No, you won't – but I'm sure that some of the men in your life will look after you," Gary said cynically. He was angry with himself for his pettiness, but this woman had messed with his emotions big-time. And she didn't seem to care either.

Orla tried to look bored. But inside she felt deeply troubled. Why was Gary going on about "the men in her life"? There weren't any, worse luck. And who was he, with his cosy domestic situation, to criticise what she did with her life, anyway? The cheek of some people! Gary Culhane was really stepping way beyond his authority. Maybe she'd write a feature on sarcastic doctors sometime. If she ever got back to work, that was.

"Nurse!" Gary called to one of his colleagues. "Are you free to get this patient attended to? She needs plaster of Paris around her left ankle, up as far as the knee."

The nurse nodded, and Gary turned briefly to Orla and smiled sarcastically. "I'll see you before you go – but now, I must go and attend to some other patients. On Friday nights, we get more than our fair share of drinkers and clubbers!"

"My apologies for detaining you," Orla said haughtily. "If I'd known you were on duty here, I'd have gone to any other hospital in the city, to save you the trouble."

"It's no trouble at all, Orla," Gary said tightly, aware that he was letting too many of his personal feelings show. "That's what we're here for."

"Yes – to attend to drunkards like me!" she retorted.

In the treatment room, the nurse deftly wrapped up Orla's foot and leg, making pleasant but inane conversation while she worked. Orla made perfunctory replies, but all the time her mind was on Gary Culhane. Oh, how she hated him! He had no right to be so sarcastic about her lifestyle. She was perfectly entitled to go nightclubbing if she wanted to. She couldn't fathom Gary – he'd been so nice to her the first time they'd met. She sniffed. Of course, that first meeting had been her downfall. It was then that she'd fallen for . . .

Orla pulled herself up straight and the nurse sternly told her to stop moving while the plaster set. Fallen? Why had she used that word? Was it a Freudian slip – was she finally admitting to herself that she'd fallen for Gary in a big way? Yes, yes – she answered herself impatiently. She really *did* care for that nasty doctor. But she'd never have anything to do with a married man. Her sense of survival was too strong for that kind of carry-on. OK, so her heart was bruised. But she'd get over it. After all, there were lots of good-looking single men out there, all just dying to become her Mister Right.

Yeah, sure, she thought sarcastically. Like that plonker Kieran that she'd met earlier that evening. My God, was that only a few hours ago? It felt like a hundred years ago since she'd so eagerly sought his beer-laden kisses, as they'd groped their way around the dance floor. Yuck, she thought, the things we do under the influence of a few drinks – well, quite a few drinks actually. Probably that scumbag was now tucked up in bed beside his unsuspecting wife, to whom he'd probably told a pack of lies about being at a business meeting.

How on earth was she going to get home? Orla bit her lip. This was Saturday night, when the entire nation went out on the razzle, so there was always a shortage of taxis. Under normal circumstance, she wouldn't mind the wait, but right now she wanted to get away from Gary Culhane at the earliest possible opportunity. In fact, there would be a childish satisfaction in not being there when he came to check on the new plaster cast. Well, she'd show him. She'd ask the nurse if it was OK to turn on her mobile phone, then she'd book a taxi and get to hell out of the hospital. Even if she had to prop herself up against the courtyard wall while she waited for the cab to arrive.

But Orla wasn't to have that dubious satisfaction, because Gary appeared at precisely the same moment that the nurse declared her handiwork completed. "Now then, I'll go and find you a set of crutches, and then we'll see about getting you home," the nurse said, smiling. "Is there someone collecting you, or will you get a taxi?"

"I'll call a taxi," said Orla quietly, wishing that the ground would swallow Gary up. "Is it OK for me to use my mobile phone in here?"

"There's no need," said Gary, cutting across the nurse before she could reply. "I'll drop Orla home. I'm just about to go off duty."

"Take a running jump, Gary!" said Orla ungraciously, as the nurse left the cubicle. "I'm perfectly capable of getting home by myself. After all, if I can get myself to

389

nightclubs to pick up men, then I must be capable of getting myself home again, right?"

Gary laughed. "You really are an impudent cow," he said, "but I can't help liking you, Orla. And you're right – it's none of my business what you do. So I promise not to make a single comment on the journey to your place."

"Well, alright," said Orla grumpily, "but I don't want to take you out of your way. I mean, I live near the M50 turn-off for the North-West. That's quite a distance from where you live, isn't it?"

"It doesn't matter," said Gary. "In fact, I quite enjoy driving in the early hours, just before dawn. I often drive for miles after I finish a nightshift. The roads are traffic-free, the air is wonderfully fresh and the birds are just beginning to launch into the dawn chorus – "

"I thought *I* was the wordsmith," said Orla sarcastically.

"Well, I do have some other talents apart from being a brilliant doctor," said Gary, enjoying the banter and looking forward to spending an hour or two on the road with Orla by his side. It would allow him – albeit briefly – to believe that she was his woman. I'm a sad, pathetic fool, he told himself, but he still couldn't dispel the bubbling joy that filled his heart.

"Well, one of your undoubted talents is insulting people," Orla retorted, just as the nurse arrived with a set of crutches.

After showing Orla how to use them, Gary helped her out to the staff car park and opened the passenger door to help her in. Their hands touched briefly, and Gary found himself gazing longingly into Orla's eyes.

"Oh, Orla," he said miserably, "I wish that you and I

didn't always seem to rub each other up the wrong way. I've no quarrel with you – I suppose I just don't like the way you live your life. I mean, all those guys. Isn't the one guy enough for you? What are you trying to prove?"

"How dare you speak to me like that, you great oaf!" said Orla furiously. "You've got a nerve – and how dare you chat me up at the *Celebrity* party when you'd no right to!"

"Well, how was I to know that you were engaged – it was *you* who had no right!"

"Oh – so your wife and kids aren't a barrier to a bit on the side, then?" Orla retorted. "Anyway, I'm not engaged – and I wouldn't be caught dead with a married man either!"

Gary held up his hands to ward off any further verbal attacks. Something wonderful was happening, and a big grin was spreading all over his face.

"What's so funny?" shouted Orla. "You accuse me of –"

"Whoa! If you're not engaged – "

"W-what?"

Gary gripped Orla's shoulders tightly. "Is it really true – that you're not engaged?"

"No, of course I'm not – I *was* engaged to Declan Dunne, but it's over for ages – "

"But what about this Kieran?"

"Just some guy I was dancing with tonight – but he disappeared as soon as I hurt my ankle. Bastard."

"And I'm not married."

"You're not?" Orla's expression was a mixture of incredulity and dawning happiness. Then she frowned.

"But hold on – I saw you with a woman and two children in that café – "

"My sister Breda and her kids," said Gary, kissing the top of her head. "Oh, Orla, my wonderful Orla – please tell me that tonight could be the beginning of something special between us!"

"It might be, if you stop leaning against my broken ankle," said Orla, raising her lips for Gary's kiss.

"Oh God, I'm sorry," said Gary, side-stepping her plastered foot, "but I'm just trying to get close to you, Orla! I just adore you – I've been crazy about you since the night we met!"

"Then why didn't you ask me out?" said Orla, planting kisses all over his face."I fancied you too, but you never contacted me again."

"What a mess I made of everything," Gary said, kissing her lips again. "I'd fully intended to phone you as soon as the court case was over – but with Joanna acting as my solicitor, if you turned me down it would've proved embarrassing for all of us. I wasn't sure if it was ethically correct to ask you out, either."

"Well, aren't there ethics about doctors and their patients, too?" said Orla mischievously, as an ambulance pulled up, disgorging paramedics and several new patients, all of whom looked curiously at her and Gary, since they were standing in a clinch, their arms tightly round each other. "Surely you're not supposed to kiss your patients?"

Gary grinned. "This minute, I couldn't care less! Orla – I just can't believe my luck. You and me – together at last! You've no idea how often I've dreamed of this moment."

"Me too," said Orla shyly. "But Gary, why did you think I was engaged? I'd broken up with Declan before you and I met – "

As Gary gently helped her into his car and drove out the hospital gate, he explained his late-night encounter with her former fiancé.

"Bloody Declan!" said Orla in disgust. "Trust him to mess up my life, even when he's no longer part of it! If it wasn't for that lunatic, we might have got together weeks ago."

"My sentiments entirely," said Gary. "But now," he reached over and clasped her hand, "you're mine, and you're not going to escape ever again."

Suddenly, Orla laughed. "So Declan was gored by a bull – serve him right! I wonder – but no, it couldn't have been – "

Orla was remembering the night she'd reported hearing someone in the lower field with Eddie Hanlon's bull. But Declan wouldn't have been near the apartment after they'd broken up, would he?

Orla sat back in her seat and sighed happily, still holding Gary's left hand tightly as they drove along. Who would have believed that one's entire universe could change in the space of a single night? Joanna would be astonished to hear what had transpired – her friend wasn't the only one to whom weird and wonderful things happened!

CHAPTER 68

The door of the Ballsbridge mansion was flung open by Ivan Kilmartin. He glowered at Catherine, who was filled with a strange sense of forboding.

"Hello, Ivan. Is Agnes in?" she asked.

"It's none of your damn business," Ivan roared. "I've sent her and the child away for a break – I don't want her anywhere near the likes of you, you scheming bitch!"

Catherine said nothing. While she knew Ivan didn't like her, she'd never seen him quite so furious. Only a few months earlier, he'd been gloating at the news of Harry's death and, in his triumph, his attitude towards her had mellowed somewhat. But now, it was clear that something had got him all riled up.

"Some friend you are," Ivan ranted on, "encouraging her to break her marriage vows! I know you encouraged her to deceive me and helped her to arrange trysts with that fellow behind my back!"

"Of course you've never broken your marriage vows, have you, Ivan?" Catherine asked sweetly.

Ivan Kilmartin turned puce with fury. "You impudent bitch! I should have stopped Agnes seeing you years ago – you were always a troublemaker and a bad influence on my wife!"

"I think Agnes is quite capable of choosing her own friends," said Catherine.

"Well, not for much longer!" he screamed. "You're barred from this house, you evil trollop! I can't believe the depths of deceit you've sunk to! I've just found out that even when that murderer Harry Sweeney was in prison, you were visiting him on behalf of my wife!"

Catherine was momentarily surprised. But she was not going to let Ivan see that she was nonplussed. "So your spies have been busy – have they, Ivan?" she said, smiling brightly, determined not to let him know how frightened she was beginning to feel. "I hope you pay them better than you pay your employees."

"You – you – " Ivan was momentarily lost for words. But what he lacked in vocabulary, he made up for in strength, gripping Catherine by the arm and dragging her inside the house, slamming the door behind them.

Frightened now, Catherine nevertheless stood her ground. "Take your hands off me, Ivan," she said quietly, hoping that she sounded more in control than she actually felt.

"How dare you tell me what to do!" Ivan roared, but he stepped back and slackened his hold on her. "Nobody ever tells me what to do!"

"You may control the lives of your unfortunate employees, and your poor wife's too, but you don't control mine," said Catherine defiantly.

"Don't I?" Ivan jeered. "All I have to do is just click my fingers, and everyone jumps!"

"Well, as you can see, I'm not jumping, Ivan," said Catherine quietly.

"You cheeky bitch! You need to learn who's boss around here!" His face was puce. "You need someone to take you down a peg or two. And I'm just the man to do it!"

And grabbing her by the hair, Ivan pulled Catherine down onto the floor, and ripped at the seam up one side of her skirt exposing her legs and knickers. Momentarily, Catherine was stunned, and her mind could hardly contemplate what was happening. This was her friend's husband!

But no such taboo was constraining Ivan Kilmartin. The sound of ripping cloth seemed to act as a further catalyst to his pent-up fury, and he quickly tore open the other side of Catherine's skirt. He seemed possessed of the strength of a hundred men as he dragged her torn skirt up around her waist, pulled her knickers down, and threw himself on top of her. While she struggled to ward him off, he bit her shoulder, and she cried out in pain.

As she tried to come to terms with what was happening, Ivan undid his trousers, pulled her legs apart and roughly forced himself into her. "That'll teach you, bitch!" he roared, spraying spittle everywhere.

After what seemed a lifetime but which was in fact only minutes, Ivan climaxed with a grunt, then climbed off her and headed for the downstairs bathroom, without a backward glance. In shock, Catherine lay immobile on the floor, tears welling up in her eyes. She couldn't think straight, her heart was thumping wildly and the mental anguish of her violation was so intense that she felt as though she was about to have a heart attack.

Then, as the initial shock of what happened began to wear off, she was suddenly galvanised into action. She needed to get out of there fast, in case Ivan decided that he wanted to repeat his performance. Staggering to her feet, she rushed to the front door, opened it and ran down the driveway, her torn skirt flapping around her bruised legs. Thankfully, her car keys were still in her jacket pocket, and Catherine shuddered to think of what else might have happened if she'd lost her keys during the tussle.

Seated in her car, Catherine was in such a state of shock that she could barely fit the key into the ignition. Her hands shook violently, and she was overwhelmed by an urge to vomit. Even her fingernails were broken, where she'd tried to fend off Ivan's advances. She felt like a small, frightened child, and she longed for the security of her own home. Only when she reached it, and closed the door behind her, would she begin to feel safe again. Praying that the car would start, Catherine turned on the ignition, sighed with relief as it purred into life, then drove quickly home to Blackrock.

When she finally reached her front door and let herself in, her shoulder was aching painfully, and she noticed that the blood from the bite on her shoulder had dried into her blouse, and it was now stuck firmly to her skin. Peeling the blouse away started the wound bleeding again. Thank God Bill is away, Catherine thought. I couldn't bear to tell him what happened. Quickly, she went to the bathroom, turned on the shower and moved the dial to its highest setting. She knew that the hot water would burn her already torn and bruised skin. But what she wanted most of all was to wash all evidence of Ivan away and eventually feel clean again.

CHAPTER 69

Joanna was sitting in her office, wading through a pile of conveyancing documents, when Mary called through to tell her that Orla was on the phone.

Orla was bubbling with excitement. "Jo – have I got great news for you! You're not going to believe it – "

"Orla, what on earth's happened? I presume that Kieran fellow has something to do with your good humour?"

"Well, maybe indirectly – but you're going to have to meet me if you want to find out what it is."

Joanna sighed. "I'm up to my neck right now – couldn't you just tell me now?"

"No way – this is just too special to share over the phone!"

"OK, OK – I'll meet you briefly at lunchtime. This had better be worth it, because I'm going to have to juggle my afternoon appointments – "

"It *is* worth it – well, to me anyway. See you at one thirty in McDaid's?"

"OK." Joanna smiled to herself. She was glad that Orla seemed so happy. Maybe her friend was finally managing to forget about Gary Culhane.

* * *

Orla sat in the newsroom, wishing that it was time to go to lunch. She couldn't concentrate on the piece she was writing, but it was needed by the chief subeditor within the next half-hour. Dammit! She was too excited to work – Gary Culhane had seen to that. She was so happy that she could barely sit still.

She'd insisted on taking a taxi into work, although Gary had tried to make her take at least a few days off, to give her ankle a headstart at healing. "I'll write you out a sick note from the hospital," he'd begged her, but she'd been determined to go into the newsroom. Besides, she had two assignments to finish, and it wasn't fair to expect another journalist to take over a half-completed story. Unless, of course, the journalist's name was Declan Dunne.

Suddenly, the phone on her desk rang, and she almost leapt into the air with the shock of being catapulted back to reality.

"Hello – Newsroom."

"Hi, Orla, it's Mick McHale."

"Hi, Jim – how are you?"

"Never better. Just thought I'd bring you up to date on something the prison warden just told me – about a regular visitor that Harry Sweeney had. He phoned me when he remembered, but I'm not sure if it has any relevance."

Jim told her what he'd heard.

LINDA KAVANAGH

"Thanks, Jim. I'll tell Joanna when I meet her for lunch – maybe it will mean something to her."

* * *

At lunchtime, Orla hobbled down to McDaid's on her crutches, eager to see the look of consternation on Joanna's face.

"My God, Orla – what happened?" Joanna asked anxiously, pulling out a chair and trying unsuccessfully to help her friend to sit down comfortably. "I thought you said you'd *good* news to tell me!"

"Oh, don't mind this – it's just a broken ankle," Orla said dismissively. "And you're right, I *have* good news for you. It's Gary – we're an item at last!"

"Hold on, Orla," said a bemused Joanna. "I left you with another guy in the early hours of this morning! What on earth could have happened since then?"

"Well," Orla replied spiritedly, "only the other day, *you* were the one who had two men on the go!"

Then a grin spread over Joanna's face as she made the connection between the broken ankle and the hospital.

Sprawling in an ungainly fashion in the chair beside Joanna, Orla proceeded to give her friend a blow-by-blow account of what had happened.

"Did he stay the night?" Joanna wanted to know.

"No," said Orla. "When he brought me back to the apartment, he said that he thought we'd both had enough excitement for one night." She grinned lecherously. "But he's calling round this evening to take me out to dinner. So I'm fairly certain that we'll consummate our relationship either before or after the meal!"

"Better do it before, because he might develop brewer's droop after all the wine," Joanna advised.

"On the other hand," Orla reasoned, "afterwards means that we don't have to get up and go out again. And my hair would be all mussed up if we did it before the meal – so I'd look a right mess at the restaurant."

Suddenly, both women looked at each other and burst into laughter. "Oh God, Jo – I'm so happy!" said Orla. Then she looked slightly shamefaced. "But what about you?"

"Well, now I can tell you about *my* news," Joanna said, smiling. And she proceeded to tell her friend about Ronan turning up the night before.

Orla squeezed Joanna's hand emotionally. "Oh thanks, Jo – if it hadn't been for your unselfishness in coming out with me last night, I might never have bumped into Gary again!"

Joanna grinned. "But you could also claim that I'm responsible for your broken ankle!"

The two friends hugged each other.

"Well, it's certainly been an interesting weekend," Joanna said. "Even Mary seemed to be on a high today – and she had a hangover too. I wonder what she's been up to? I must remember to ask her this afternoon."

"By the way, that reminds me, Mick McHale rang this morning with another bit of information."

"Oh?"

"Yeah – he found out that Harry had one regular visitor when he was in prison. A small red-haired woman."

The two woman looked at each other.

"That was my mother," said Joanna at last. "I think I'd better pay her another visit soon."

* * *

Mary smiled dreamily as she sat in Joanna's outer office, cradling the phone and stroking it, as though it was Jim's head. Although they'd agreed to take things slowly, that still didn't stop her fantasising about having Jim's arms around her, his lips eagerly crushing hers . . . Suddenly, realising what she was doing, she slammed the phone down and looked around guiltily. Already this morning, Joanna had commented on her absentmindedness. And the awful hangover she had wasn't helping either.

Suddenly, Mary remembered that Gary Culhane had rung and left a message for Joanna the previous Friday afternoon. Oh God, she thought, I've forgotten to tell her – and he *did* say that it was quite important. Something about information he had about Harry Sweeney . . .

Well, she thought crossly, Joanna was out all Friday afternoon, so I couldn't have given her the message until this morning. Nevertheless, Mary was annoyed with herself – she prided herself on being ultra-efficient, yet here she was, behaving like a lovestruck teenager! She wondered if she should tell Joanna that she'd been out to the pub with Mick McHale, but concluded that there was nothing much to tell her anyway. Jim had only kissed her on the cheek, so it wasn't as though she could report a grand passion. Hopefully, their relationship would develop and become something special as time went by . . .

Anyway, Mary thought, grinning, Joanna also seems a bit spaced out herself this morning!

"Mary – would you be an angel and get me the O'Meara file?" Joanna asked, appearing at Mary's desk and almost making her jump out of her skin. Seeing her discomfiture, Joanna laughed. "Feeling a bit under the weather today, Mary? Now let me see – when I was previously in that state, you recommended a few aspirin and a hearty breakfast at the café next door. Haven't you been taking your own advice?"

Mary grinned back. "I'll have that file for you in a minute. By the way, Gary Culhane rang on Friday afternoon. Something about Harry Sweeney . . ."

"Harry Sweeney?"

Joanna was amazed. What could Gary possibly know about poor Harry? She remembered mentioning to him that there was a bit of a mystery surrounding one of her other cases – in fact, she'd been bragging, to make it sound as though her professional services were very much in demand. Well, she'd better ring him as soon as possible.

She smiled to herself. Besides, it would also be an opportunity to congratulate him on his new relationship.

CHAPTER 70

Orla was in a state of high excitement as she waited in her apartment for Gary to collect her. This was their first official "date" and she'd checked her appearance in the mirror at least twenty times.

What an absolute sweetie he was – she had offered to get a taxi into town meet him, but he wouldn't hear of it. "No, I'm going to collect you, my darling Orla," he'd said. "I wouldn't trust you to get there without another mishap!" Orla had feigned annoyance, but secretly she was enjoying the totally new experience of being cherished and cared for. Declan had never made any effort to be considerate, although he expected other people to go out of their way for *him*. To think that I might have settled for that asshole, she thought. What a lucky escape she'd had – right now, she almost felt like thanking Sasha Miller for having the fling with Declan!

She sighed happily. She was just crazy about Gary Culhane! She'd spent over an hour tidying the apartment after she'd got home from work so that Gary would hopefully think that it always looked like that. It hadn't been easy with the added encumbrance of a plastered foot, but Orla now regarded her injury as her own personal good-luck charm. After all, if she hadn't slipped on the steps while leaving the nightclub, there wouldn't be any Gary in her life! She'd also changed the bed linen, putting on a brand new duvet cover, sheets and pillowcases. She wanted the bed to look sensuous and inviting when she and Gary climbed in there together for the first time!

In fact, Orla was quite tempted to grab Gary when he called to the door and drag him into the bedroom straightaway. But she decided to let good sense prevail – instead, she would allow the sexual tension to build up between them during the meal. She was wearing her most glamorous – and daring – dress, and she would flaunt her womanly curves over the table, hopefully driving him wild with lust.

Besides, she'd suddenly realised that, apart from the night of the *Celebrity* magazine party, she and Gary had never actually had a proper conversation! So there were lots of things that they still needed to learn about each other. But she knew that this would happen gradually, as part of the wonder of a new and meaningful relationship that they both wanted. The great thing was that they'd got the most important business sorted already – their admission that they were crazy about each other.

Orla looked sourly at her crutches. It wouldn't be easy to look glamorous while using them, but she'd just have to do her best. At least, when she was sitting down at the meal, and lying close to Gary later, it wouldn't matter – well, the plaster would cramp her style quite a bit –

The doorbell rang, and Orla leapt to her feet, only to realise that she couldn't get to Gary as quickly as she'd like to! Grabbing her crutches, she headed for the door, grinning from ear to ear, unable to contain her excitement. Then suddenly, she was in his arms.

"God, I've missed you!" he whispered in her ear, planting kisses all over her face and neck. Then he grinned mischievously. "Do we really have to go out?"

"Yes!" said Orla firmly, although her own will was weakening. "Do you realise that we've never had a meal together yet? We've never even gone out on a date together! There's so much we don't know about each other – "

"And there's such a thing as gut feeling, my darling – call it what you like," Gary said, nuzzling her ear. "Oh, Orla, you're my woman – that's all I need to know for now. But you're right – let's go and chat each other up over a couple of bottles of wine."

So they went to a nearby trattoria, where they fed each other spaghetti, spilled their food because of so much laughing and wiped the sauce off each other's chins, laughing again, touching each other at every opportunity, each of them basking in the warmth and the joy of their new relationship.

"Oh God, Orla, I'm dying to make love to you!" Gary whispered, when at last they were back in her apartment. "All evening, I've been wanting to jump on you, but you made me sit through an entire meal – " he nibbled her ear, "and you even insisted on having a dessert! I don't believe that you've got a heart at all! "

"Well, since you're a doctor, maybe you'd better check it out for yourself!" said Orla, and Gary unzipped her dress, removed her bra and gently caressed her breasts while pretending to search for her heart.

"My God, Orla," he said between kisses, "I must be the luckiest man in the world. Is this really happening to me? I keep worrying in case you're suddenly going to disappear, and I'll find that it was all a dream – "

"I'm not going anywhere, Gary – except into the bedroom! Oh, come on – I can't wait any longer – "

"Maybe I should make *you* wait now," he said, now teasing her, "seeing as you didn't mind torturing me all evening – "

"Gary, if you don't make love to me soon," Orla groaned, "I'm going to kill you!"

"I wouldn't be much use to you if I was dead, would I?" he whispered, still teasingly taking his time.

She gasped as he played with her nipples. "Well, if you were dead, at least you'd have rigor mortis!"

He laughed. "Rigor mortis only lasts for a while – but if you keep me alive and treat me well, I could service you for a lifetime!"

Orla's breath was now coming in short gasps. But she still couldn't resist the urge to reply, "Well, could you please get started on the first one? If I'm satisfied with that, maybe I'd be interested in the lifetime aspect of the deal – "

"Does that mean you'll marry me, Orla?"

"For God's sake, stop talking and let's just *do* it, Gary – "

"Not until you promise to marry me."

"Shouldn't we make sure that everything's in working order first?"

Gary grabbed her hand and placed it on his erect manhood. "Does that seem in working order to you, ma'am?"

"Oh Gary, it's beautiful!"

Quickly, Gary pushed her back onto the bed, and Orla groaned in ecstasy as their bodies fused together, and they both came at the same time in a shuddering climax.

It was a few minutes before either of them spoke. But that was because no words were necessary. Instead, they cuddled each other, relaxed and happy, knowing that nothing but happiness lay ahead of them.

At last, Gary spoke. "Orla – did I pass the test? If so, will you please say that you'll marry me?"

Orla smiled, pleasantly exhausted. "Yes, Gary, I'll marry you."

Then she pushed herself up on one arm, surveying her new fiancé and grinning at him. "I can't believe I just said that – but I really do love you, Gary. And there's nothing I want more than to be your wife."

Gary pulled her down to him again. "That's settled then – oh, there is one little proviso – "

Orla giggled. "I knew there had to be a catch. Well, I'm not agreeing to either an open marriage or to living with your mother – I insist on having you all to myself!"

"I'm afraid you'll also have to live with something very big and hairy – "

Orla chuckled, deliberately misunderstanding his reference to Bruce. "Is that what you call this very interesting thing that I'm stroking?" she said, reaching for his manhood, which was already beginning to respond once again to her ministrations.

"Oh God, Orla, at this rate you'll have me worn out in no time – "

"Well, at least you'll die happy," she said, kissing his nose. Then there was no further need for words. Their bodies were once again speaking the language of love.

CHAPTER 71

"Joanna, this is Ellen Byrne," said Gary, making the introductions in Joanna's office. "Ellen, this is Joanna Brennan."

"Good morning, Ellen, Gary," said Joanna smiling, "and thanks, both of you, for coming in. I'm really interested in hearing your story, Ellen. When I was asked to administer my mother's friend's will, I never thought that it was going to become such a complicated and convoluted business!"

Gary smiled at Ellen to put her at her ease, since he knew that she had a natural distrust of anyone connected with the law. However, Gary had assured her that this was an off-the-record discussion and that no further steps would be taken without her permission.

"I've asked Mary to bring us in some tea and coffee," Joanna added, "to help to get the adrenalin going. On the other hand, I'm so excited about what Gary told me on the phone that I don't need any stimulant!"

On cue, Mary appeared with a tray laden with mugs,

pots of tea and coffee and the requisite plate of Mikado biscuits.

Joanna smiled at her secretary as she turned to leave the room. Mary was looking radiant – and had been for the last week. If they hadn't been so busy each day, Joanna would have had time to ask her what her secret was – maybe she'd discovered some amazing new vitamin pills? Whatever it was, Joanna wanted the recipe.

While they all sipped their cuppas, Joanna steered the conversation gently towards the events of the night of Colette Devane's murder, back in 1970.

"Gary tells me that you know who killed Colette Devane," she prompted, smiling encouragingly.

"I suppose he also explained that I was on the game back then?" Ellen said, holding her head up high, as though defying anyone to look down on her.

"Yes, he did – he's filled me in on most of the background information," Joanna said matter of factly. "I was very sorry to hear about your injuries – I'm sure that life will get better for you, from now on." She was pleased to be rewarded with a smile from Ellen. Hopefully she had passed whatever test Ellen had set for her, because the result would decide how much information Ellen was willing to impart to her.

"Well, I happened to be walking past the posh restaurant Ivan Kilmartin always took Colette to," Ellen began.

Joanna's heart skipped a beat. "She was with *Ivan Kilmartin*?"

"Yes," said Ellen, unaware of the impact that her words were having, "she was Ivan Kilmartin's fancy woman. He

411

was a wealthy businessman back in the sixties, but he's long dead now. Anyway, I was surprised to see Colette and Ivan being collected by Paddy Byrne – who later became my father-in-law – in Ivan's limousine, because I thought Colette was still in England. But I was relieved she was back, because I needed to borrow money from her. I stepped back into a doorway and hid there while Paddy Byrne waited a few minutes for the traffic to clear. There was no way I'd approach her while she was with Ivan Kilmartin! I saw that Ivan and Colette were arguing in the back of the car. He was shouting at her, then he slapped her and she screamed. Then I saw him put his hands around her neck and shake her." Ellen shuddered. "I didn't realise it at the time, but I must have seen Ivan murdering her, there in that car, because that was the night she was killed, and there was never a mention of her being with Ivan Kilmartin when Harry Sweeney was arrested and charged. And Paddy Byrne paid me to keep quiet about seeing him in Colette's apartment and seeing Colette and Ivan together. If everything had been innocent and above board, surely they'd have gone to the police?"

Joanna took a deep breath. "So why had Colette been in England?"

"She went there to have her baby."

Joanna opened her mouth in surprise. "Her baby? Colette was pregnant?"

Ellen nodded. "Poor Colette was so thrilled when Ivan Kilmartin set her up in an apartment. She knew he was married, but gradually she fell in love with him, and she wanted to have his baby. So she deliberately got herself pregnant, hoping that he'd leave his wife for her. But he was livid and packed her off to England for an abortion."

"Hold on," said Joanna. "You just said there was a baby?"

Ellen looked uncomfortable. "Sorry, I'm not explaining things very well. Colette left it too late to have an abortion, but she pretended to Ivan that she was going to London to have one. Then, when she got to England, she planned to make up some excuse about having to stay there to nurse a sick friend, so that she could have the baby and recover. She planned to return to Ivan after the baby was born – and he'd never know what actually happened."

Joanna took a deep breath. My God, she thought, Agnes's will says "the offspring of Ivan Kilmartin". If Tom is actually Harry's child – or possibly *one* of Harry's children, if Maura Sweeney did have a child in London as Ronan thinks – then this must be the other child mentioned in Agnes's will. But why would Agnes want to leave money to a child by her husband's mistress? It didn't make any sense.

"So what did she do with the baby?"

"I don't know, because the last time I saw her was before she left for England."

Joanna sat back in her chair, her mind reeling. "My God – this is amazing information. But, go on with your story. What happened after Paddy Byrne drove off?"

"Since I didn't realise that Colette had actually been killed until later, I walked along to her flat to see if Ivan had dropped her back yet. Given the mood he was in, I doubted that he'd be spending the night with her. I was desperate for the money Colette had promised to lend me – if I couldn't pay up, I was going to be evicted from my bed-sit the very next day! But there was no answer when I rang the outside doorbell. Then, just as I started walking back up the street, I saw Colette and Ivan Kilmartin being slowly driven along by Paddy Byrne, in Ivan's limousine." Ellen paused and blew her nose. "Later still, I called back to the flat again, because I really needed the money. The limousine wasn't there, so I hoped that Colette might be back in her apartment. Another tenant was coming out – he knew me, so he let me go in, and I went upstairs to Colette's flat. When I got there, the door of the flat opened and there was Paddy Byrne, wearing gloves. He wasn't pleased to see me and tried to tell me some yarn about him being working for a security company as well as for Ivan Kilmartin. I then realised that something must have happened to Colette. Paddy Byrne was anxious to get rid of me, so he gave me a pile of money and promised to look after me if I kept my mouth shut about seeing him, and he also said that I wasn't to say a word about seeing Ivan with Colette." Ellen paused. "When I left the building, I turned down the narrow side street opposite, and suddenly I realised the limousine was parked there. I had to walk right past it and, as I did, I peeped quickly inside. Colette looked as though she hadn't moved since I'd seen her earlier. At that moment, I just knew, instinctively, that she was dead . . . so I ran as fast as I could back to my own bed-sit. I knew it was too late to help Colette, but I was afraid that after what I'd seen, I might be the next to die."

"But the next day – you must have heard about the murder."

"Yes – it was all over the newspapers."

"So what did you do?"

"Do?" Ellen looked surprised. "I did nothing. What was I supposed to do?"

Joanna took a sip of her tea, as though she had all the time in the world to wait. But her heart was hammering loudly in her chest. "But since you knew that Harry Sweeney wasn't the man who'd murdered Colette, why didn't you go to the police when he was charged?"

Ellen looked at Joanna as though she was a total imbecile. "The police?" she said in surprise. "What attention do you think they'd pay to the word of someone like me? Anyway, I'd just been paid to keep quiet about what I'd seen. And I was terrified that if I said anything, I might end up dead myself."

Joanna said nothing. She simply took another Mikado biscuit and began chewing it as though it was the most important thing in the world to her. She'd already learnt that silence could be a powerful tool in getting information out of her clients.

Ellen laughed bitterly. "Cops and women on the game are natural enemies, you know. Maybe it's not all the cops' fault – they have to do what the law tells them. I mean, why don't they go after the kerb-crawlers if they want to clean up an area? Prostitutes wouldn't be in business if there weren't dirty old bastards out there willing to pay for it."

Gary looked uncomfortable, but Joanna gestured to the coffee-pot, and he busied himself by pouring himself and Ellen a refill.

Joanna sighed. "So poor Harry Sweeney never killed Colette Devane. Yet he couldn't – or wouldn't – produce an alibi for the night in question. I wonder why?"

Both Gary and Ellen looked blank. No one could

understand why a man wouldn't want to defend himself from a charge of murder.

"How did you and Colette meet?" asked Joanna.

"We'd both run away from home – she from very religious parents, me from an abusive father. We met at one of the Simon Community's soup kitchens and decided, in all our teenage wisdom, that the best way we could survive was by hanging around the city hotels, where we might pick up guys who'd pay us to sleep with him. We did this a few times, although we didn't like to think of ourselves as prostitutes. It wasn't long before Colette was lucky enough to meet Ivan Kilmartin – " Ellen grimaced. "Sorry, 'lucky' isn't the right word under the circumstances, is it? But at the time she was thrilled to find a wealthy man paying her lots of attention. And when he offered to set her up in her own apartment, she was over the moon." Ellen bit her lip. "But even though our situations were suddenly very different, Colette was always good to me. She always made sure I had enough food and money to survive. She said that friends should always be there for each other."

After a pause, Joanna asked softly, "This baby, Ellen – you've no idea what happened to it after Colette was killed?"

Ellen shrugged her shoulders. "I assume she left it in England."

"So you don't know if it was a boy or girl. Or what she named it?"

"No, sorry. After she left for England, I never spoke to Colette again."

Joanna's mind was in turmoil. Suddenly, she was making connections between Maura's departure to

416

England and Colette's pregnancy. What could be more likely than that one sister would help the other. If so, could Maura Sweeney – wherever she was – have kept Colette's baby?

"Ellen, did you know Colette's sister Maura?"

Ellen shook her head.

Joanna sighed. What a pity she knew nothing about Maura, but she had nevertheless supplied vital information that had taken them another step closer to solving the mystery.

"How did you come to marry Jackie Byrne, Ellen?" Joanna asked, changing the subject.

Ellen answered her in an equally direct manner. "Just after Colette's murder, Jackie called to my bed-sit with a pile of money from Paddy Byrne. Then he asked me out," she wrinkled her nose, "but he took some of *my* money to pay for the cinema tickets on our first date! He always was a cheapskate. But I was young and foolish back then, and I couldn't believe my good fortune when he asked me to marry him soon afterwards. I was scared and lonely being on my own, my friend Colette was dead and I was trying to survive by picking up dirty old men in hotels. So an offer of marriage meant escaping from all that." She sighed. "Or so I thought. I was in such a hurry to get the ring on my finger that I didn't realise what a violent man I was taking on. But Ivan Kilmartin had bought the house for us, and it looked as though I'd never have to worry about money ever again. I knew Jackie did a bit of burglary and stole cars for a living, but someone like me wasn't likely to find a clean-living knight in shining armour, was I?"

There was a few moments' silence, but neither Gary

nor Joanna said anything, not wanting to interrupt Ellen's train of thought. At last she sighed and continued.

"But the most stupid thing of all was that I never questioned why Jackie was marrying me. I should have guessed that it wasn't because he cared about me. And when he started hitting me soon after we were married, I just accepted it as the price I had to pay for the respectability of being married. But I later learned that Ivan Kilmartin, through Paddy, paid Jackie to marry me – to keep me quiet, I suppose."

Joanna smiled grimly. "And Jackie's been up to a bit of auto-theft too, has he? Well, if you're also willing to tell that to the Gardaí, Ellen, I think we can be certain that your husband won't be troubling you again for a while."

"Husband indeed!" Ellen spat the words out with contempt. "I want to get a divorce – as soon as possible."

"Well, you'll have to wait the statutory four years, I'm afraid," said Joanna, "but since Jackie will hopefully be behind bars during that time, it should be a fairly painless process."

The meeting seemed to have reached its natural conclusion, so Ellen stood up to leave, and Gary followed suit.

Ellen grasped Joanna's hand. "I'd like you to act for me, Joanna – if you'd be willing – in my divorce proceedings. For one thing, I need to know my rights regarding the house."

"Well, technically it's the family home and you should have the right to stay there – but I'll start looking into the matter straight away," said Joanna. She looked thoughtful. "So Ivan Kilmartin bought the house for Jackie – interesting!" She paused. "One other thing, Ellen. I feel honour bound to build up a case to clear Harry Sweeney's name. Since he was never actually convicted, no court case can be reopened to prove his innocence. But since it's obvious that people at the time believed he was guilty, he deserves our help now, to prove his innocence once and for all. And I believe it's what Agnes Kilmartin would have wanted." She looked directly at Ellen. "Would you be willing to speak openly about what you saw that night back in 1970?"

Ellen nodded. "I will – as long as I don't end up in prison myself for perjury or something."

"Of course you won't," said Joanna, smiling. "There is no law that compels a witness to come forward if they believe that doing so would put their *own* life in danger. But you could help to restore a dead man's good name."

"Is what I've told you of any use?" said Ellen, looking worried.

Joanna smiled at her. "Ellen, you've come up trumps on this one. I just need time to digest all that you've told me." She looked at Gary as he ushered Ellen out the door. "Take care of this woman," she said, smiling. "She's going to be a star witness in getting Harry's name cleared."

When they'd left, Joanna slumped in her chair, feeling quite exhausted. She now knew that the second beneficiary of Agnes's will was Colette's child by Ivan Kilmartin – but she had no idea where this person was today, what sex they were or how she would ever find them. And the doctor Ronan found had Maura's name on the card in his file – so was there a third child? Another child of Harry's who would also be a beneficiary? She sighed. Ronan was already back in England, doing his best to track down

Maura through the midwife – hopefully this new information would be of use. Originally, his brief had been to find Harry's wife Maura, but now it looked as though he needed to look for *two* women who were in London together just prior to April 1970. She'd better ring him on his mobile phone immediately.

* * *

"Are you OK, Joanna?" Mary asked anxiously, as she entered Joanna's office shortly after Ellen and Gary departed. Because Joanna was sprawled back in her seat, looking quite dazed.

"I've just been given the most astonishing information," Joanna said and proceeded to tell Mary all that had transpired during her meeting with Ellen Byrne.

"So Harry Sweeney wasn't guilty of that murder," mused Mary. "But what do you think happened to the child?"

"I've no idea," said Joanna. "Mary, I'd like to ask Mick McHale to do a bit of research on Ellen's husband, Jackie. Do you think you could phone Orla and get his number? Oh – " suddenly she remembered, "but maybe you have it yourself, since he was helping Paul?"

Mary blushed. "Yes, I do have it. Joanna – I've been meaning to tell you, but we've both been so busy – "

"Tell me what?"

Mary went an even darker shade of puce. "Well, it's just that," she grinned, "Jim and I have been out for a drink together and . . . it's early days yet, but – "

"Well, you sly old devil!" said Joanna, laughing. "I'm thrilled, Mary – and *I've* got news for you. Orla and Gary got together at the weekend!"

"That's great!"

"And I've another bit of news for you – Ronan and I are now seeing each other too!"

Mary looked startled. "You – and Ronan?"

"Yes – don't you approve?"

"No, it's not that – I just thought that Tom Kilmartin and you – "

"Nothing ever happened between Tom and me, Mary," said Joanna. "It might have, but it didn't. Then Ronan came on the scene . . ." She grinned, leaving the sentence unfinished.

"Well, I'm happy for you – if Ronan's the one you want," Mary said doubtfully.

"Of course he is!" said Joanna. "Now will you get me Jim's number before I forget to make that call?"

Dialling Jim's number, Joanna realised with dread that she'd better ring Tom too . . . She felt deeply sorry for him, since each new discovery seemed to change his knowledge of who he was and who his actual family were. It was one thing to be told that your mother had a love affair with a guy convicted of murder, but quite another to discover that the man you'd always regarded as your father had a mistress, and that he was probably be the one who had actually murdered her…

Well, she thought testily, at least Sasha Miller will be able to offer him plenty of comfort . . .

"Hello?"

"Jim? It's Joanna Brennan, Orla's friend –" And Mary's friend too, she mischievously wanted to add.

"Oh, hi, Joanna – how can I help?"

"There's a guy I need to get some background on –

421

Jackie Byrne is his name. He's been inside once already and he's currently being extradited from England for badly beating his wife. And his wife may be willing to testify to his long-term involvement in auto-theft between here and England."

"Hmm – sounds interesting! My colleagues in the Gardaí have been trying to discover who's behind an auto-scam that's been going on for years. I wonder if this could be the same one? If so, this might be just the break they need. So maybe we can help each other."

"And have you ever heard of a guy called Paddy Byrne, Jim? He's Jackie Byrne's father, and apparently he used to be Ivan Kilmartin's lackey –"

"Paddy Byrne? A very nasty character. But he died long ago – why do you want to know about him?"

Joanna sighed. "Ellen Byrne, Jackie's wife, claims she witnessed what may well have been Colette Devane's murder. She saw Ivan Kilmartin attack her inside his limousine on the night she was killed. It looks as though Paddy Byrne played a major role in protecting Ivan Kilmartin. He bought off Ellen and forced his son Jackie to marry her. I'm wondering if he played a part in Harry Sweeney's murder as well."

"Good God! Does this mean that Ellen Byrne will be able to help clear Harry Sweeney's name?"

"I hope so. She's agreed to tell her story to the press when we have all the information ready."

"That's great news. Maybe I can pursuade my friend's brother, the ex-prison guard, to tell his part of the story too. He was always adamant that Harry hadn't killed himself."

"Thanks, Jim. It'll be great to finally lay this tragedy to

rest." Joanna smiled to herself. "It's also great to see Ellen gradually realising that her fate is no longer linked to Jackie's. And when her soon-to-be ex-husband is behind bars, I think she'll feel even more confident about telling her story and reclaiming her life."

"I'm so pleased for her," said Jim, "and I'll see what information I can get on the Byrnes, father and son. It's good to know that at least one of them is going to pay for their crimes!"

When she finished speaking to Jim, Joanna dialled Tom Kilmartin's number.

"Tom, I have some interesting news for you . . ." And she proceeded to tell him what Ellen had told her about Ivan having a mistress and that there was a child from their liaison. However, she decided not to tell him – just yet – that Ivan was probably responsible for murdering his mistress as well . . . there was only so much information the poor man could take in.

Tom wasn't surprised that his father had kept a mistress but was astonished that his mother wished to acknowledge the offspring of this relationship in her will. "Why on earth would my mother leave money to the child of my father's mistress, Jo?"

"I don't know, Tom. In the meantime, I think you should meet the private detective who's searching for Harry's wife Maura in England. If he can find her, then hopefully we'll have found this other beneficiary."

"But we still need to find the offspring of Harry Sweeney."

"Yes," said Joanna, wondering how long she could avoid voicing her suspicions about Tom's parentage.

CHAPTER 72

Back from her imposed trip to Ivan's relatives, Agnes was looking forward to seeing her dear friend Catherine. She tried telephoning, but no one answered the phone at the Brennan house in Blackrock. After several days of trying, Agnes was puzzled. She knew that Bill was away on business, but Catherine should definitely be there. Why on earth wasn't she answering the phone? So Agnes kissed little Tom goodbye and handed him to the nanny, reached for her car keys and left the house.

As she drove out along the coast road to Blackrock, she took stock of her present situation. Since her beloved Harry died, Ivan had more or less left her alone. Thankfully, he'd never followed up on his threats to impound her car and keep her housebound. Ivan seemed to have opted for a peaceful home life, while reserving his energies for his extra-marital activities.

What a hypocrite he is, Agnes thought with contempt. The previous week, she'd organised a dinner party at their house, to which various prominent people, including a bishop, had been invited. Ivan, of course, had played the role of charming host,

slipping a cheque to the bishop afterwards ("for the missions").
Yet the following night he was out with his latest floosie!

Pulling up outside Catherine's house, Agnes surveyed its
exterior with distaste. As always, it looked shabby and
neglected. Agnes felt guilty about having so much comfort in
her own life, but Cat would never accept the money to do her
house up, no matter how often Agnes offered.

Eventually, Catherine answered the door to Agnes's
insistent knocking. One look at her friend's pale and drained
face told Agnes that there was something seriously wrong.

"Cat – my God, you look terrible!"

"Hello, Agnes."

Agnes marched past her friend and into the shabby kitchen,
filled the kettle and turned it on. Then she sat down at the
kitchen table.

"Now – tell me what's happened. Have you got the flu?"

"No."

"Has something happened to Bill?"

"No – he's fine."

"Then why haven't you been answering the phone?'

Catherine's lower lip trembled as she sat down. "The truth
is – I've been avoiding you, Agnes. Because I don't know how
to tell you what's happened."

Agnes felt her heart quicken. "Whatever it is, the sooner
you tell me, the sooner we can deal with it."

"This is very difficult, Agnes. I know you hate Ivan, but at
the end of the day, he's still your husband – "

"Cat – stop beating around the bush."

"I – he raped me, Agnes. Ivan raped me."

The colour drained from Agnes's face. "My God! When?
Where? How did it happen?"

Quietly, and as unemotionally as she could, Catherine explained what had happened the day she'd called to the Ballsbridge house, all the time holding tightly onto Agnes' hand.

"Oh God – the bastard! Oh, Cat, you poor love!"

Catherine smiled through her freshly flowing tears. "I'll get over it, Agnes. The important thing now is to put it behind me. Try to forget it ever happened and get on with my life."

"Are you going to tell Bill when he gets back?"

"God, no. Why upset him? I'll get through this on my own."

"You're not on your own – you've got me, Cat."

"I know, Agnes, I know."

Agnes stood up, made two mugs of tea and brought them back to the table. "Oh, Cat – I feel so guilty!"

"Why? It's not your fault that it happened!"

"No, but Ivan's my husband – and if you hadn't been helping me to deliver those letters to Harry behind his back, this would never have happened."

"Don't blame yourself, Agnes. What Ivan did is his responsibility, no one else's."

"The bastard – I'll scratch his eyes out when I get home!"

"Please, Agnes – don't do or say anything. I don't want him to think that he's succeeded in punishing me." Catherine smiled suddenly through her tears. "Isn't there a saying about getting revenge by living well? That's what I intend to do, Agnes. Hold my head high, and to hell with Ivan Kilmartin."

Now Agnes began to cry. "Oh, Cat, you're so brave! Are you sure there's nothing I can do to help –"

Catherine patted her friend's hand. "Just knowing that you're there for me, Agnes – that's all I need. Now, let's drink our tea before it gets cold."

CHAPTER 73

"Joanna – Ronan is here," said Mary, closing the door behind him.

Joanna looked up from the document she was studying to find Ronan lowering himself into the seat in front of her desk.

"Hi, Ronan," she said, blushing as thoughts of their previous lovemaking sessions danced through her head. "Did you manage to find the midwife this time?"

Ronan nodded, lowering himself into the chair in front of her. "She's retired now, but at one time she used to deliver hundreds of babies to Irishwomen living in that area –" he paused for effect, "and when I showed her the newspaper photograph of Colette, she remembered her immediately. Colette and her sister were staying in a flat in Cricklewood. Naturally, the midwife wanted Colette to go to hospital since it was her first baby, but the two women were adamant that she'd have it in the apartment."

"Go on!" said Joanna eagerly. "What happened then?"

"Colette gave birth to a healthy baby in the flat, assisted by the midwife and her sister. But when the midwife returned to the apartment a few days later – to check up on the baby's progress and advise them on where to register the birth – the flat was empty and the two women had disappeared."

"Was it a boy or a girl?"

"The midwife couldn't remember. First, she said it was a boy, then she said a girl. In the end, she had to admit she didn't know. Which I suppose is reasonable when you're delivering lots of babies each year."

"Oh God. And she kept no record of the sex of the baby?"

"Unfortunately not. When she retired years ago, she disposed of her files. You see, once she's notified the authorities of each birth, her responsibility is over, and her notes are purely for her own use."

Joanna sighed. "Well, we know what happened to Colette – she came back to Dublin and was strangled by Ivan Kilmartin. But what happened to Maura? And the baby?"

Ronan shook his head. "I've no idea. The midwife never saw any of them again."

Joanna slumped in her chair. "So near – and yet so far. And wasn't Maura pregnant too, according to that doctor?"

"No, I don't think she was. I have a theory. Remember that neighbour of Maura and Harry's? The one who said she'd gone back to collect something that looked like a birth certificate?"

Joanna nodded.

"Well, it probably *was* Maura's birth certificate, and she was bringing it with her to England so that she could register Colette's baby as hers after the birth. That would explain why Colette gave the doctor her sister's name when she went for the check-up – to ensure that the baby was always listed as Maura's. But since I've searched unsuccessfully for a child registered to either Maura Sweeney or Maura Devane, I can only conclude that she must have used some other name."

Joanna sighed but said nothing. Every time they took one step forward, they seemed to take two steps back.

"Oh, God. It's looking like a dead end, isn't it?"

Ronan shrugged. "Not necessarily. Whatever way you look at it, we are making progress! Now," he grinned, "isn't it time you told me how much you missed me?"

Joanna's heart gave a leap of joy, but she played it cool. "You've done well, Ronan," she said, smiling. "In fact, I might even decide to pay you! But I haven't had time to miss you – I've been far too busy."

"Well, I've missed you. Can we go for something to eat soon – and can I come home with you tonight? Or would you like to come to my place?"

Joanna shivered with delight at the prospect of another night in Ronan's arms.

Just then, Mary stuck her head around the door. "Tom Kilmartin's here – will I send him in?"

"Of course – hi, Tom." Joanna rose from her desk as Tom entered, and introduced the two men.

As the three of them sat around Joanna's desk, she had a split-second vision of the three of them grappling on the

429

floor, taking part in a threesome, as per Orla's suggestion! She couldn't help an embarrassing flush pervading her face, then she turned an even deeper colour when Ronan spotted her trying to cover up her grin.

"What's so funny, Jo?" he asked, smiling at her.

"Eh, nothing," she said hastily, trying to compose herself. She'd kill Orla later for her vivid imagination! "Now let's bring Tom up to date on where we've got to, so far."

Then Joanna, with interjections from Ronan, brought Tom up to date on the search for Colette's baby and Harry's wife.

CHAPTER 74

"Hi Mam – how are you today?"

Joanna pulled up a chair beside Catherine, who was sitting on the outdoor terrace of the nursing home, staring into the distance as usual.

"Oh, there you are, my dear," said Catherine, offering up her face for a kiss. "The doctor says I can leave hospital soon and go home again."

Joanna hid her distress well, as she played out the game that was enacted by countless families of Alzheimer's patients. "That's great news, Mam," she said, giving her mother a hug and trying to change the subject. Because she knew that no doctor had said any such thing. However, if believing that her incarceration was only temporary gave Catherine hope, who was she to interfere?

"Isn't Agnes with you?" said Catherine, looking puzzled. "I phoned Agnes yesterday, and she said that she'd call round to visit me. You see, I have something very important and very private to discuss with her."

431

"I'm just here on my own," Joanna said, picking her words carefully. "What was it you wanted to tell Agnes?"

"It's private – didn't I just tell you that?" said Catherine, exasperated. "I need to talk to her about Harry."

"That's Harry Sweeney, isn't it, Mam?" said Joanna. "Well, Agnes asked *me* to talk to you instead. About Harry."

"Well, I'm very cross with her for not being here," said Catherine, "but I suppose you'll have to do."

Anxiously, Joanna held her breath and waited for Catherine to say something, but it seemed as if her mother had drifted off into some kind of reverie. Then suddenly, she spoke, and Joanna almost fell off her seat with the shock.

"When I spoke to Agnes, I told her that it was time Tom knew the truth."

"About what, Mam?"

Catherine looked exasperated. "About Ivan not being his real father, of course."

Joanna felt that her heart was beating too fast – she could hardly breathe, but she was afraid to move or say anything, in case Catherine's train of thought was interrupted. Catherine was confirming her own suspicions.

Catherine sighed. "I've been telling her, ever since Ivan died, that it was time to be honest with her son. But she's scared of his reaction. She's afraid he might hate her, so she's written him a long letter about it, and I'm minding it for her."

Joanna took her mother's hand in hers. "Is Harry Sweeney Tom's father, Mam?"

Ignoring her, Catherine began singing.

"The cattle are lowing,
The baby awakes
But the little Lord Jesus
No crying he makes – "

In frustration, Joanna changed her line of questioning. "Mam, please – what about Harry's wife, Maura? Did she know about Agnes and Harry?"

"Of course. Maura fully understood."

"Mam – do you know where Maura is now?"

"She came to see me last week. We had a long chat about everything."

Joanna sighed in exasperation. Once again, her mother was rambling. But she would humour her, in case there were any other snippets of information that might emerge.

"So how is Maura?"

"Oh, she's very well. She thinks it's time we all told the truth to our children. But like Agnes and me, she's scared too."

"What's this truth you all need to tell us, Mam?"

Catherine looked at Joanna in annoyance. "Stop hassling me! I told you I want to see Agnes myself before doing anything about it. I'm not telling you anything!"

"But Maura had no children with Harry – are you saying she has a child by someone else?"

"In a manner of speaking," said Catherine. She then gave Joanna a beatific smile. "Will you get me a chocolate biscuit – one with jelly on top?"

But Joanna wasn't giving up. "Could this child of Maura's be Colette's?"

Catherine looked upset. "I've already said too much. It's up to Maura to do what she sees fit."

433

Joanna sighed in frustration. It was pointless trying to get information from her mother. She herself was spending lots of money – albeit Tom's money – employing Ronan to scour the streets of London in pursuit of this offspring of Harry Sweeney, and to search further afield if the need arose – and Catherine was blithely claiming that Maura had visited her!

Joanna sighed deeply. She was now utterly confused herself – maybe Alzheimer's was catching! While she could believe that her mother had hidden documents on Agnes's behalf, and that Ivan wasn't Tom's father, she drew the line at believing that Harry Sweeney's wife had just dropped in to visit her mother!

"I must go, Mam – see you again soon." Joanna hugged her mother tightly. God, how she loved this woman! Tears filled her eyes, as she clung to her mother's frail little body.

"Goodbye, love," said Catherine, then she stood up and looked out over the manicured lawns of the nursing home. "Now I really must do something about those flower-beds – how did my garden get into such a mess?"

Joanna left her mother wandering in the garden and re-entered the nursing home in order to reach the front door exit. As she walked along one of the corridors, she felt so frustrated that she wanted to scream! Dealing with Catherine's Alzheimer's was a nightmare – her mood and her concentration could change so quickly, and it was impossible to know what was truth and what was merely Catherine's imagination. But one thing made sense – if Harry and Agnes were lovers, what was more likely than that Agnes would become pregnant? Besides, contraception hadn't been freely available in Ireland in the late sixties and early seventies, so an accidental pregnancy was always a possiblity.

Joanna groaned inwardly. She'd now have to tell Tom what her mother had said – if he could tear himself away, that is, from the raptures of Sasha's Miller's arse! Here am I, she thought angrily, dealing with *his* problems, and he's off somewhere, shagging that tart!

Her mind was filled with even greater misery when she thought that Tom was probably doing it with Sasha in his house in Ballsbridge – maybe even showing Sasha Miller the pond at the bottom of the garden, where he and she used to have their long discussions as kids. That's *my* pond, she thought with impotent fury, how dare Sasha Miller wheedle her way into other people's lives like that!

But Joanna had to accept the unpalatable truth – Tom was not hers to order about as she wished. Besides, she had Ronan now – no woman could ask for a better lover. Or a more attentive man. He was gorgeous, and she was in love with him, wasn't she?

"Joanna – hang on a moment, will you?"

Joanna came out of her reverie to see one of the nurses hurrying towards her. "Oh, hi!"

"Look, I meant to have a word with you the last time you were here – "

"Is Mam OK?"

"Oh yes, she's fine. It's just about that visitor she had."

"A visitor?" As far as Joanna was aware, only she and Tom, and previously Agnes, had visited her mother.

"Yes, an elderly lady – about the same age as your mother. They had tea in Catherine's room and your

435

mother's friend dropped a cross and chain we later found." The nurse smiled at Joanna. "I was wondering if you could return it to her?"

"Yes, of course," said Joanna, slightly in a daze. Had her mother really been telling the truth? Had Maura Sweeney actually visited her?

"It's in the office – hang on a moment and I'll get it for you."

Returning with the cross and chain, the nurse handed it to a bemused Joanna. "The lady rang back that afternoon to see if she'd left it here, but we hadn't found it by then," said the nurse apologetically. "You see, it was underneath the coffee table and somehow we missed it – it wasn't found until the following morning, when the cleaning staff did their rounds."

"Thank you," said Joanna, taking the cross and chain. "I don't suppose she left a phone number?"

"No, I'm afraid not. I assumed you'd have it yourself . . ."

"Yes, of course. I just don't have it with me. Thanks."

Joanna turned the cross over in her hand, noting its weight and the hallmarks on the back of the cross. It certainly looked expensive.

Joanna slipped the cross and chain into her pocket, said goodbye to the nurse and headed back to her car. As she walked, she fingered the cross anxiously, as though it could tell her something about the woman who had dropped it. Since it was undoubtedly valuable, perhaps she should place an ad in the "Lost" column of the newspapers, in the hopes that Maura might turn up to claim it? It was a long shot, but nothing ventured, nothing gained.

Joanna started the car and began driving home. So Maura Sweeney had really visited her mother. Did this mean that Maura was actually living in Ireland? Or was she just on a short visit and possibly already back in England – or wherever else she might be living now? Joanna sighed. She was still no nearer to a solution.

CHAPTER 75

Agnes hurried into the busy café where Catherine was already waiting. "Sorry I'm late, Cat — couldn't get a parking space anywhere!"

"Hello."

Agnes looked quizzically at her friend as she sat down at the table. "What's this all about? Why on earth did you choose to meet here? We've never been to this place before —"

"That's precisely why," said Catherine quietly. "I had to pick somewhere we aren't known but somewhere public, so that I couldn't make a disgrace of myself."

Agnes looked at her closely. "What on earth do you mean?"

"Well, if I started to cry, I doubt if I'd be able to stop. But I can't really do that here, can I?"

"Cat — what on earth is wrong?"

"I'm pregnant, Agnes."

For a split second, Agnes's face lit up with joy. For years, Cat and Bill had longed for a child . . . Then reality hit home. According to the hospital tests, Bill was infertile.

"Oh, Cat – oh, God, no!"

"I'm afraid so. What on earth am I going to do?"

"An abortion – it's your only option. I'll organise everything, Cat. We'll go to England – we'll tell Ivan and Bill that we're going on a shopping spree. Ivan won't dare object."

Catherine nodded gratefully. "Thanks, Agnes – I knew I could count on you."

"It's the very least I can do – I've just got this month's allowance, and I've saved a bit from the housekeeping, so we'll have no money worries."

"When can we go?"

"As soon as you like."

* * *

The phone rang in the Kilmartin house later that evening, and Agnes picked it up.

"Hello?" she said.

"Agnes – it's me. Is Ivan there? Or that lackey of his?"

"No, Ivan's out – probably with one of his floosies. I'm here on my own."

"Good – Bill's out as well, so I can talk to you freely. Remember our conversation earlier today?"

"As if I could ever forget it."

"Well, I've been having second thoughts, Agnes. Bill has always longed for kids – even more so than me – so why should I deny him the chance of a family?"

"But the hospital tests – won't he suspect?"

Catherine sighed. "Bill's never really believed what the doctors told us. Besides, what they actually said was that we were unlikely to ever have children. It was only later, when I badgered my own GP and begged him to prescribe some other form of treatment that might help us, that he finally admitted it would be a waste of time and money. Bill's results showed he was infertile. Needless to say, I never told Bill – it would've been too cruel. The poor man still keeps hoping that we'll have kids some day."

Agnes digested this news. "So Bill will accept this child as his?"

"Yes," said Catherine. "He'll be thrilled to know I'm pregnant."

"So this story may yet have a happy ending."

"I hope so, Agnes, I hope so."

*   *   *

"Bill – I have something to tell you."

"Yes, love?" Bill looked up at her, concerned.

"I'm pregnant."

"W-what?"

"I'm expecting a baby – I'm two months gone."

Bill's face lit up with delight, and he leaped from his chair and hugged Catherine. "My God – that's wonderful news, love! So we've proved the medics wrong – I never did believe all that mumbo jumbo they told us anyway!" He gazed in delight at Catherine and led her to a chair, as though she was some exotic bloom in need of tender care.

Catherine smiled at him, but she was crying inside. It had been easier than she'd expected – too easy. Poor Bill! It would never cross his mind that she'd be unfaithful to him. And she hadn't! She would never, ever, do that to him. She loved him dearly. She clenched her fists tightly by her sides. Now, all she could do was put that awful event to the back of her mind, and let nature take its course. After all, she was making Bill happy, wasn't she?

CHAPTER 76

Joanna picked up the phone on its first ring.

"So who is it this time?" said Orla chirpily. "Has Ronan dragged you off to his lair or has Tom finally got his act together?"

Joanna laughed. "Cheeky cow! I don't think I'll tell you anything."

"Aw, go on – put me out of my misery! Although it wouldn't surprise me if you'd found somebody else altogether!" Orla laughed. "After all, I haven't spoken to you for two whole days – that's long enough for anything to have happened, where you're concerned!" She snorted. "And to think I once thought you needed a social life!"

"I gather your own private life is going well," said Joanna dryly.

"It's amazing! Gary and I can't believe we wasted so much time –"

"I'm glad that you two are finally together," said

Joanna, smiling, "but can you tear yourself way from Lover Boy long enough to meet me?"

"Of course – now that my love life is sorted, someone else has got to supply all the scandal and gossip."

"Sorry – I don't have much to report on the scandal front, and even less on the love front, since Ronan's away. But I can tell you about my visit to Mam the other day –"

"Oh, God – you've just remined me of my own mother – she's been on the phone again, pestering me to call round –"

"Then why don't you just do it?" said Joanna, laughing. "Have you told her about Gary yet?"

"No, I haven't – but you're right, I'd better go and visit Mum. My only problem is that I've no time to spare. Gary keeps dragging me back into bed!" Orla gave a mock groan of ecstasy. "Sorry, what were you saying about your mam?"

"I said I'd tell you about my visit to the nursing home the other day."

"Well, begging your pardon, Jo, that's hardly likely to be earth-shattering news, is it? I think your mother's great, but she's not exactly at the cutting edge of things, is she?"

Joanna laughed. "You might be surprised – just meet me and see."

* * *

"Wow!" said Orla. "And you have the cheek to tell me that you're not having an exciting life? Are you going to tell Tom about Ivan not being his father?"

"Of course – I've no other option."

"And that Harry is probably his dad?"

"Yes, I must. The sums add up. Agnes had to be pregnant at the same time that Harry went to prison, given Tom's birth date. It's all a big mess, isn't it? Do me a favour, Orla – please don't ever ask me to be your solicitor, or executor of your will."

Orla laughed. "So you think that I'm going to die first? I have no such intention – I'll see you out, Brennan – in fact I intend to grow old disgracefully!"

Joanna smiled. "I'm sure you will. But, listen, that's not all I have to tell you."

"No?" said Orla in mock surprise. "You're telling me you have another bombshell?"

"Well, I don't know what it really means. But my mother also told me that Harry's wife Maura had been to visit her recently."

"And you believe her?"

"I didn't at first – until I discovered that an elderly woman had been in to visit her!" Quickly, Joanna explained what the nurse had told her about finding the cross and chain on the floor of her mother's room.

"My God," said Orla. "This will of Agnes Kilmartin's gets odder and odder. Do you really think it could have been Harry's wife?"

"Well, it seems to tie in with what my mother's been saying."

Orla pursed her lips. "If it really was Harry's wife, then surely there's no point in Ronan searching for her in England? She must have come back here."

"And brought Colette's baby with her."

"And reared it as her own child."

Joanna smiled. "On the other hand, she might just have been here on a visit and gone back to England afterwards."

"Or America. Or China. Or India."

"In fact, she could be anywhere."

The two women looked despondently at each other.

CHAPTER 77

Joanna stretched herself languidly and got out of bed. She and Ronan had just finished making love in her big double bed in Blackrock. Ronan had arrived back at Joanna's house around seven, and they'd sent out for a Chinese takeaway. Then they'd retired to bed – where they seemed to spend an inordinate amount of time anyway.

They'd fallen into a relaxed and easygoing relationship, and Joanna began to wonder if maybe this was the way married life would be. Ronan was passionate, a great lover, humorous – and he never left dirty dishes lying around and was happy to do his share of the cleaning. How many men were like that? Joanna had to confess to herself that she'd never met anyone as decent and caring as Ronan.

Joanna sighed as she stepped into the shower. What was she looking for? She had a handsome man who was great in bed and was kind, generous, loving. And he

445

wanted them to live together. He accepted that she was a professional woman in the course of establishing her own practice, and he was fully supportive of her need to have her own career. Where else would she find such a paragon? Was she expecting too much from a relationship? Was she harbouring some childhood unrealistic dream of what a loving relationship was all about?

Perhaps she was being silly, but she didn't seem to feel the same ecstasy and certainty that Orla was experiencing in her relationship with Gary. *They* had no moments of doubt in their relationship, and they were both eagerly awaiting their engagement, just as soon as Gary could afford the ring. They were doing it the old-fashioned way and enjoying every moment of it. They'd even set the date for the wedding, and Joanna had once again been signed up as chief bridesmaid. "Or Matron of Honour," Orla said, grinning slyly, "if you and Ronan get to the registry office before we do!"

Joanna scrubbed herself with determination. She'd told Mary that Ronan was the one she wanted . . . but then why did she still feel that something was missing? Perhaps it was just other people's certainty about their own relationships that threw her. After all, she was a very different type of person from Orla, so maybe she was just more cautious. Or was there something wrong with her? Here she was, with the kind of guy that other women would kill for, yet still she wasn't certain of her feelings. Maybe she was just a stupid cow who needed a good kick up the backside.

Ronan adored her and wanted to move in with her, yet she was still delaying giving him an answer. Why haven't I said yes? she asked herself in frustration. He's educated, good-looking, comfortably off, fun to be with, caring and considerate – in fact, he's the ideal man. What every woman wants. But somewhere, at the back of her mind, a little voice was niggling her. Is he what *I* want?

Maybe Ronan was too perfect. Would she be happier if he wasn't quite so good-looking? And if so, was that because she lacked the confidence to keep him interested for a lifetime? Or was it the "lifelong" bit that worried her? She tried to visualise herself and Ronan as an elderly couple and failed dismally.

As Joanna emerged from the shower, Ronan peered out from beneath the bedclothes and gave her a wistful smile.

"Have you thought any more about me moving in?" he asked gently, now sitting up on one elbow and staring pointedly at her.

Joanna coloured. "Well, no – I mean, you're not expecting an answer straight away, are you?"

Ronan smiled sadly. "Obviously not, Joanna – otherwise I'd already have had my answer, wouldn't I?"

Joanna still said nothing. Suddenly, brushing her hair seemed to be the most important thing in the world, so she sat at the dressing-table and attacked her hair vigorously.

"What's the problem, Joanna? Are you just reluctant to commit because you're a cautious person or because you just don't want to live with me?"

Joanna turned to face him. "I don't know, Ronan – maybe I'm just scared by the idea of making such a huge decision. I need more time. I mean, I really care about you – "

"But do you *love* me, Joanna?" Ronan asked softly. "The way that I feel for you?"

"I don't know," said Joanna, looking confused. "I'm not sure that I know what love really is – "

"If you loved me, Joanna, I think you'd know," said Ronan sadly. "And I'm sufficiently egotistical to want my partner to love me, not just to 'care for' me, like the way you feel about your cat."

There were several seconds of silence, which seemed to Joanna like hours. So she continued brushing her hair as though her life depended on it. And she felt inordinately guilty, because when she'd thought about love, an image of Tom Kilmartin had crept unbidden into her mind.

CHAPTER 78

Sasha quite liked the idea of living in Ballsbridge. In fact, she'd already decided that she was definitely a Dublin 4 type. Seamus McGrath lived there, and she'd already fantasised about sharing his luxury penthouse apartment in the Sweepstakes when they got married. Alas, her interest in Seamus hadn't been reciprocated – he'd remained aloof and peeved about being smeared with cream from the *Celebrity* birthday cake, and so far no amount of come-on from Sasha had produced the desired effect. Well, that was that, at least for the forseeable future, Sasha reckoned, so she would move on to pastures new. And that new pasture was currently Tom Kilmartin.

Sasha always did her research before going to interview someone – especially if the interviewee was a male. Before meeting them, she would know their marital and financial status, their likes and dislikes, hobbies etc. If, for example, a man was interested in a particular sport, she would acquire a few stock phrases that would convince him of her fascination with the topic. And if he had a favourite team, she might even turn up in his team colours – in skimpy T-shirt form, of course – and profess undying devotion to the same team herself. That ploy had got her into many men's beds and wallets, but it hadn't yet produced what Sasha wanted most of all – a wedding ring. Still, she reasoned, the more she tried, the more the likelihood that one of them would eventually turn up trumps.

She surveyed herself in the mirror and hitched the waistband of her skirt into her knickers. For this second interview with Tom Kilmartin, she wanted him to be able to see her legs and lust after them. But Tom was proving a hard nut to crack, although Sasha was confident that he would succumb in the end. In a sense, he was all the more thrilling because of his reluctance. Which also meant that he might be easier marriage material, since the serious ones were easier to enslave when you eventually got them going. Unfortunately for Sasha, the ones that she *had* managed to enslave – like Declan Dunne and John Boyle – had just been hacks like herself. And a monthly salary cheque didn't suit Sasha's plans for the future. She wanted *carte blanche* credit cards with all the major stores and restaurants, and a Banklink card that always disgorged cash from the hole-in-the-wall. She was sick of the embarrassment of being told by the ATM, *"There are insufficient funds in your account"*.

Sasha had also done her research on Tom Kilmartin and liked the information that came to light. As his wife, she would never again have money problems, since his father had been a wealthy property developer. And since his mother had just died, there'd be no mother-in-law problems either. The old dear's will was currently being probated, so that would mean even more dosh before long.

Another bonus was that he was actually quite attractive – there'd be no hardship involved in trying to seduce him or making babies with him. He was a bit too serious, however, but then, no man was perfect. And his love of bloody penguins – in Siberia or wherever – would mean that while he was away on expeditions, she could spend, spend, spend his money – and maybe entertain a few male friends as long as she was discreet. It seemed like the perfect marriage to her!

But first things first. She had to snare him before any of these events could come to pass. So Sasha intended ensuring that Tom got plenty of glimpses of her famous rear-end when she went to interview him again.

In fact, a second interview wasn't actually necessary at all. But since she hadn't succeeded in getting him interested during the first interview, she'd claimed on the phone that she needed to see him yet again, because his subject had been so "fascinating". Bloody penguins, Sasha thought crossly. She couldn't even fake an interest in them since she wouldn't even know where to start. But she'd hung on his every word and tried to look totally absorbed in what he had to say, while surreptitiously hitching up her skirt when he wasn't looking, so that he could get a decent look at her thighs.

Sasha decided that a suit was best for this second interview. She'd read in some magazine that men were excited by the idea of stripping their prim, neatly attired secretary, who would then let her hair down – literally as well as metaphorically – and turn into a rampant sexpot. Well, today Sasha intended to play the demure, professional journalist, neatly attired in a formal suit, but with just a hint of sexuality on display. And by engineering the interview to take place at his house, when she'd got him all excited, the bedroom wouldn't be too far away . . .

Clearly, the brazen come-and-get-it approach hadn't worked with Tom Kilmartin, Sasha thought sourly. She'd noticed how, in the Morrison Bar, when she'd suggested a drink after the first interview, he'd tried to escape from her as soon as was decently possible. Well, she wasn't going to give up that easily on such a good catch. If a man like Tom Kilmartin wanted to feel that *he* was doing the choosing and making the running, then Sasha would happily let him play that role. She would play the demure little female until things hotted up and got really personal. Then, of course, she would conduct events with her usual consummate skill . . .

CHAPTER 79

"Oh, Cat – she's beautiful!"

Catherine smiled as Agnes appeared at her hospital bed, partially hidden behind the enormous bouquet of flowers she was carrying.

"She is gorgeous, isn't she?" said Catherine, looking down at the baby in her arms. "Bill is absolutely thrilled."

"I'm sure he is," said Agnes. "He's got a beautiful baby daughter. What are you going to call her?"

"Joanna."

"What a lovely name!"

Catherine looked closely at her friend. "Thank goodness she's got my red hair. So there won't ever be any questions asked."

Agnes planted a kiss on her friend's cheek. "My dear, we've both got to put the past behind us now. And get on with our lives – for our children's sake."

Placing the flowers in a vase, Agnes surveyed the cards and flowers that filled the small room, especially the huge floral *arrangement from Bill. "He loves you so much, doesn't he, Cat?" Agnes said softly. "You're a very lucky woman."*

"I know," Catherine replied, "and I love him too. And I'm making him happy with the baby, aren't I?"

"Of course you are."

Agnes began to pace the room. "Now that your child has arrived, I want to tell you of a plan I have in mind. And I want your help and support when the time comes, Cat."

Catherine looked quizzically at her friend. "What on earth are you talking about, Agnes?"

"Assuming Ivan dies before me, Cat, and I inherit the Kilmartin estate, I intend to ensure that Joanna also gets her rightful share in it."

"Agnes, there's no need – "

"Oh yes, there is – and I also intend to leave a share to the child of that unfortunate young woman, Colette Devane. Both of those children are offspring of Ivan's, and so they deserve to share in the wealth he built up. I hope to God Ivan will die before me, Cat, so that I'll be able to leave the money to those I choose. After leaving Tom the house in Ballsbridge, I intend splitting the rest of the estate three ways."

"Agnes, I wish you'd stop talking about death and your will," said Catherine in exasperation. "I've only just had a baby, and your child isn't even a year old yet. It'll be ages before you need to think of things like that."

"I know, Cat, but as soon as Ivan dies – and it can't be soon enough for me – I intend drawing up this will. But it will have to be sufficiently vague to prevent Joanna and Tom from knowing about their birthright, until you and I decide when the time is right to tell them." Agnes looked straight at Catherine. "Depending on whether Bill is still alive or not when I die, you

can decide whether to tell Joanna about her true birthright and allow her to claim her inheritance." Agnes sat on Catherine's bed. "I wish I knew what happened to Colette's child. I wonder if it was adopted in England, as Harry thought? And how will it ever be found when the time comes?"

"Well, you'll have plenty of time," said Catherine, laughing. "Aren't you thinking a bit far ahead?"

Agnes shook her head. "I'll just have to include the child along with Joanna, under the heading 'offspring of Ivan Kilmartin'," she said thoughtfully. "Anyway, if I die first, Cat — you'll know who the money's supposed to go to."

"Are you sure it's legal? You know, leaving an inheritance to people you haven't actually named?"

"Yes, it's perfectly legal — I've discussed it with a solicitor, and he's confirmed that since I'm naming the children's fathers, that's more than adequate."

Catherine laughed. "You haven't wasted any time — Ivan isn't even dead yet!"

"His death can't come soon enough for me! Anyway, Cat, I can't even make a will until Ivan dies! And even then, it'll only be an interim will — until we've told our children who their fathers are — then I can write a will that names each beneficiary clearly. Hopefully, no one will ever have to probate this will."

"I'm glad of that," said Catherine, "because it sounds like an inpossible job."

CHAPTER 80

Mary and Jim had fallen into a pleasant pattern of weekend outings. Each Saturday night, they would go to the cinema, theatre or for a meal. Then they would stop off for a nightcap in O'Malley's, Mary's local pub. And after walking Mary to her door, Jim would peck her on the cheek, get into his car and drive home.

After several weeks of this, Mary began to wonder if she'd totally lost her pulling power. She'd made every effort to look attractive – in fact, she'd spent Joanna's birthday money on two stunning outfits – yet it seemed to have no effect on Jim. Maybe he was still pining for his late wife? Would she ruin things if she tried to take things further?

Mary sighed. It was frustrating to listen to Joanna's antics with the two different men in her life and Orla's exploits prior to finding Gary. Neither woman seemed to have any trouble attracting men to their beds. Was there something wrong with her? Had she misread the signs –

was Jim merely looking for companionship? Perhaps she was so long out of the dating game that she was giving all the wrong signals.

As they sat in their regular spot in O'Malley's the following Saturday night, Mary resolved to invite Jim back for coffee this time. That way, she was placing the ball firmly in his court. He could say yes or no, and even if he did say yes, neither of them was committing themselves to anything more than that. But if he got used to staying for coffee, eventually some evening he might decide not to go home . . .

Mary jumped as Jim touched her arm. "Mary, I don't quite know how to say this, but . . ."

"Yes, Jim?"

Oh God, he's going to stop seeing me, she thought, her heart now pounding fiercely in her chest.

"Look, Mary – there's no easy way to say this . . ."

"Go on, Jim." We might as well get it over with, Mary thought miserably. He's probably met someone younger and prettier, and he's trying to let me down gently. But because he's such a nice guy, he'll offer to continue cutting the grass and keeping the garden tidy.

There was an enbarassing silence, and Mary felt she was at screaming point.

"Look, I never liked to mention it before – because of the children, I suppose."

"It's OK, Jim," said Mary, patting his hand. "I understand. It was fun while it lasted. And I'll always be grateful for what you did for Paul."

Jim stared at her, mouth open. "Oh God, Mary – are you giving me the bum's rush?"

"No, but I thought –"

"Have I said something to upset you?"

"No –"

"Then why don't you want to see me any more?"

"I thought *you* were ending it!"

Jim took her hands in his. "Of course not – look, all I wanted to ask you was if you could come away with me for a few days!" He looked sheepish. "I really like your kids, but I'd also like to spend some time alone with you!"

"Oh, Jim! That sounds wonderful!"

"Then do you think you could get someone to look after the kids?"

"Yes – I'm sure Joanna wouldn't mind."

As they reached Mary's door, Jim drew her into his arms. "Mary, oh my dearest Mary – I want us to be *more* than friends."

"But what about Sheila?" Mary whispered from the comfort of his arms. "I wouldn't want you to regret this, Jim. I'd rather wait until you feel that you're ready."

"Oh, Mary, I'm never going to be more ready than I am now. Believe me, I've been thinking this through for ages – in fact, since I first met you."

"And you're sure that you won't feel guilty about starting something new – I mean, after being so close to Sheila and all that?"

"I'll always love Sheila," said Jim softly, "and I'll never forget her, because she was a very special person in my life and my kids' mother." He gazed into Mary's eyes. "But I don't want to live in the past – I want to live *now*. And you are my here-and-now, Mary – I think I love you.

Do you think you could ever care for me that way? Even though I'm an old guy with a gammy leg?"

Mary laughed softly. "I already *do* care for you, Jim. I just never dared to hope that maybe – "

She got no chance to finish the sentence, since Jim had crushed his lips to hers, and they sat there, clinging to each other, kissing and smiling at each other alternately.

"My God, I can't believe this is happening," said Jim. "I'm the luckiest man on earth. Oh, Mary!"

Extricating herself from his embrace, Mary opened her front door. "Jim," she said, amazed at her own bravado, "will you stay the night?"

Jim looked both eager and apprehensive. "There's nothing I want more. But what about the kids?"

"Don't worry about them – they're probably fast asleep."

Suddenly, Jim was in her arms again, and there was no need for words any more.

* * *

The following morning, as she and Jim emerged from her bedroom, Mary felt embarrassed in front of Paul and Emma. But both kids grinned knowingly before asking Jim if he'd like tea or coffee with his toast and cereal.

The atmosphere in the house was one of barely suppressed delight – clearly the kids were pleased to see their mother so obviously happy, but it was also clear that they both liked Jim very much.

And Jim kissed her openly, in front of the children, and said proudly that he and their mother were now a couple. Then he asked the children if they had any problem with him being in love with their mother –

treating them like two adults whose opinions really mattered to him. For which Mary was deeply grateful. In fact, it made her love him even more, if that was possible.

The children assured Jim that they were both delighted about the turn of events, and dear old Paul even tried to give a man-of-the-house speech of welcome to Jim, but Emma embarrassed him by falling around the place with laughter at his attempts.

All in all, Mary concluded, it was one of the happiest mornings she had experienced in recent years. Not to mention the night before!

Now, her only problem was to find a child-minder! She knew Joanna wouldn't mind . . .

CHAPTER 81

Tom Kilmartin left the lecture theatre feeling thoroughly fed up. He'd just given what was probably the worst lecture of his entire career. Since it was only the beginning of the new term, his students probably hadn't noticed, he conceded, but he prided himself on giving his best at all times. Well, today certainly hadn't been one of those times. How could he possibly concentrate on the lifecycle of the South American fruit bat when his own life was in tatters?

Although normally a mild-mannered man, when he reached his office he threw his lecture notes onto the desk with an angry thud. He was furious with himself. Why hadn't he done something before now? How could he have been so stupid as to delay saying something? Was he a man or a mouse? Sadly, he concluded that he was the latter. Wearily, he sat down at his desk and surveyed the pile of letters that needed to be signed. Then he pushed them away. Right now, he couldn't concentrate on anything.

He'd lost her. Through his own stupidity, he'd let her slip away. To that private detective, with his charm and good looks. He'd seen it in her eyes when he'd come into her office to meet the guy. Joanna could hardly take her eyes off him, and he couldn't blame her – the man had looks, style and personality. What chance did a stuffy university lecturer have when he found himself in competition with someone like that? A man in such a glamorous, exciting job would always be able to attract women, Tom thought sourly.

If only he'd followed up on that dinner date. But Joanna's phone had rung just as he'd been about to kiss her. Then she'd run off, and what should have been a wonderful night turned into a disaster.

Afterwards, he'd been so depressed that he'd even wondered if she'd purposely asked a friend to ring, in case he came on too strong and she'd needed to escape. In retrospect, of course, he'd realised that was highly unlikely. After all, Joanna had been responding to his advances, hadn't she? If he'd followed up that occasion with another invitation, she mightn't now be in the arms of that private eye. He snorted. The man was probably thrilling her, this very second, with his banter and his smooth talking. No doubt he'd already thrilled her into his bed . . .

Angrily, Tom stood up. Thankfully, he'd no more lectures today.

As he was leaving his office to go home, he collided with the Department's secretary.

"Oh Tom – I've got a selection of dates from the travel agency, for your field trip in December –"

"Look, Jenny, can we leave it for now? I'll talk to you about dates tomorrow."

Jenny nodded, looking puzzled. She'd never seen Professor Kilmartin look so upset before. She knew his mother had died recently, but even then he hadn't been as tense as this. While he'd never be downright rude, he was very preoccupied today. She sighed as she watched him storm down the corridor. It was clear that he was a very troubled man.

CHAPTER 82

"Let's be honest, Joanna – you don't really need me any more, do you?"

"What do you mean, Ronan?"

The two of them had just got out of bed after a delightfully languid lovemaking session.

"Well, I've exhausted my contacts in England searching for Harry Sweeney's wife, and now you've confirmed that she may actually be back in Ireland."

"Yes, it's a distinct possibility."

"And on a personal level, I think we've run out of time as well."

Joanna wasn't sure she'd heard right. "What did you say?"

"You heard me, Joanna – and I think you know that what I'm saying is true. I'm not really the man you want, am I?"

Joanna said nothing.

Then Ronan gave one of his quirky little smiles that

always made Joanna's hormones race. Then he looked at her sharply. "It's Tom Kilmartin – isn't it?" Seeing Joanna's stricken face, he smiled whimsically. "Don't worry, Joanna, it's not evident to anyone, except me. But at least I've proved my own theory."

He smiled that slightly crooked smile of his, and Joanna wanted him to kiss her yet again. But in her heart, she suddenly realised that what she felt for him was primarily lust. And the comfort of being loved, when the one you *really* loved no longer wanted you. Neither of which was a good enough basis for a lifelong relationship. And it wasn't fair to Ronan either.

She felt guilty as she read the pain in his eyes as he looked directly at her.

"You see, Joanna, when you love someone, you watch their every move. I guess I was looking for a sign that your love might have been for me, but," he grimaced, "I know now that I never really stood a chance. You've been attracted to me, but your heart was given long ago – long before you met me – although maybe even *you* didn't realise it."

Joanna turned guiltily to face him. "Oh God, I'm sorry, Ronan – I never meant to hurt you. But – I think Tom is seeing someone else – a journalist from the *Trident*."

Ronan looked amused. "Oh, Joanna – my dear innocent Joanna, I doubt it. And if he is, it's no more than a meaningless fling. It's *you* he wants. Call it a man thing – but one man always knows when another man is truly in love with a woman. I knew from the moment I met Tom that he adored you. That day in your office, if looks could kill, I would have been dead on the spot! But since all's fair in love and war, I hoped *I'd* be the one to finally win you."

Ronan quickly dressed, then began tidying up his possessions – toiletries, toothbrush and razor – that lay scattered about the bedroom, and neatly packing them into his holdall.

"God, Ronan – you don't have to go immediately! "

"I think it's best if I go now. You see, I have feelings too, Joanna, and it's not easy to watch the woman you love wanting to be with someone else."

Joanna said nothing, but her eyes told Ronan everything he needed to know.

"Goodbye, Joanna –" he whispered, giving her a gentle – and final – hug.

Joanna felt the lurch of her hormones yet again, but she knew that what Ronan said was true. She was physically drawn to him – to his masculinity, his strength, to the animal passion that seemed to lurk within every fibre of his body. But life with Ronan would always be a rollercoaster, and that wasn't what she wanted.

As Ronan reached the front door, he turned back to face her. "I think you should let Tom know how you feel," he said softly. "Since he's not as hardnosed and go-getting as I am, I think he may need a little encouragement." Then he laughed. "But only a little bit, because it's evident to any student of human nature that the guy is crazy about you! A few well-chosen words should do the trick."

Joanna blushed and stood up. Reaching out gratefully to Ronan, she brushed his cheek with an affectionate kiss. "Maybe you know me even better than I know myself," she whispered. "Thanks, Ronan, I'll never forget you."

Ronan smiled gently. "I wish those words didn't make me feel so much like a loser."

"You'll never be a loser, Ronan," said Joanna, smiling through the tears pricking at her eyelids.

"Well," said Ronan, shrugging his broad shoulders, "I might be a good detective but I've just lost out on what I hoped would be the most important merger of my life."

"But we *will* meet again, won't we?"

"Of course we will – even though I haven't managed to find Maura Sweeney, *née* Devane, I'll want you to keep me up to date on developments. *I* want to get to the bottom of this mystery too!" He hugged her again. "But it may take me a little time to get used to the idea of seeing you and Tom Kilmartin as a couple."

"Thanks, Ronan," was all Joanna could say. "You're a man in a million. I hope life is good to you and that you find what you're looking for."

Ronan smiled sadly. "I thought I'd found it," he whispered.

Then he was gone.

As Joanna heard the front door close, she went to the bedroom window and watched as Ronan climbed into his car and drove away without looking up. And she was filled with sadness, because she knew he was more deeply hurt than he would ever want her to know.

For a long time, Joanna stood there, as though frozen in time – feeling sad that she couldn't return Ronan's love, yet feeling a bubbling happiness inside her at the possibility that Tom might really care for her. Ronan had said that Tom was crazy about her – could that possibly be true? Could he really care for her, love her, want to spend the rest of his days with her? Was he simply too shy to tell her? If so, then she would have to take Ronan's advice. Suddenly, there was nothing in life that she wanted more than Tom Kilmartin's arms around her . . .

She lifted the telephone and dialled his number.

"Tom?"

"Oh, hi, Jo – how are you?"

I'm in love with you, Tom, she wanted to say. Instead, she suggested a meeting, since she had some more information for him. She felt that, in fairness, she ought to see Tom in person when she told him about the likelihood of Ivan being Colette's murderer.

"Well, why don't you call round here about seven tomorrow evening?" he suggested. "I won't have time to cook anything, since I've an interview to do first, but we can send out for a takeaway or go round to the Lotus Flower for a meal. Is that OK?"

"Sounds great," said Joanna happily.

After she'd hung up, Joanna couldn't help grinning to herself. I really *am* a slut, she told herself with amusement. I've just been making love to one man – and now, only a few minutes later, I'm pursuing a different one! But nevertheless, she felt remarkably clear-headed. Because, finally, she was following the true dictates of her heart.

* * *

"Oh, hi, Jo – you're early," said Tom, opening his front door. "Go on down to the kitchen and put the kettle on. I'll be with you in a few minutes."

Joanna smiled happily. She was fifteen minutes early, because she couldn't wait to get to his house. And he seemed really pleased to see her. She was just about to head for the stairs to the basement, when the ground-floor toilet door opened – and out stepped a semi-naked Sasha Miller! Both women stood gazing at each other in shock.

Sasha was the first to speak. "Oh dear," she said, in her high-pitched girlie voice, "I didn't know that Tom was expecting visitors!"

"Evidently not!" said Joanna, gazing in horror at Sasha who stood there in just a satin bra and a thong, her enormous bum fully on display. Joanna felt rooted to the ground and completely tongue-tied. Her mouth had gone dry, and she wanted to cry. Tom had been about to get intimate with Sasha Miller, or had they been at it already?!

"Well, I'd better get dressed," said Sasha, annoyed that her plans to seduce Tom had gone pear-shaped.

At that moment, Tom came out of the drawing-room, and his mouth dropped open as he saw the two women glaring at each other. "Yes – I think you'd better," he said, looking extremely flustered as he surveyed the half-naked Sasha. He turned to face Joanna as Sasha flounced off to the toilet again. "Jo – that wasn't what you think," he said, looking both angry and embarrassed. "The woman came to interview me. She spilt tea on her jacket and skirt and went off to the bathroom to wipe it off. I didn't expect her to take the whole lot off – "

"It's none of my business what you do, Tom," Joanna replied stiffly. "I think I'd better leave."

"Oh, Joanna, please, don't – "

"Goodbye, Tom." Joanna strode out the front door,

hardly trusting herself not to cry. She needed to get away from Tom Kilmartin and that tart as quickly as possible. Otherwise, she might burst into tears and make a total disgrace of herself. She willed herself to slow down as she walked down the driveway, knowing that Tom's eyes were following her. At last she reached the gate, turned quickly and sighed with relief. Now she could give way to her feelings at last. Her eyelids felt as though they would burst, and she walked along the street with the tears dropping onto the pavement. She didn't care who saw her, because nothing else mattered any more.

CHAPTER 83

Agnes was exhausted and looking forward to putting her feet up in the café in Grafton Street. She'd been shopping in the city centre with five-year-old Tom in tow, and now her feet were killing her. Tom was starting school the following month, and he needed clothes that were practical and easy to wash. So far, he'd behaved well and hadn't complained too much when she'd made him try on several outfits, and pairs of shoes, before she was satisfied about the size.

Suddenly, as they walked by the Trinity College entrance, Agnes recognised the woman walking towards her. They'd only met once, several years before, but Agnes would never forget her. She was a little older now, and her clothes were shabby but clean, and holding her hand was a small child of about five or six.

They passed each other, Tom tugging impatiently at his mother's hand, then Agnes turned around.

"Maura!"

For a split second the other woman hesitated, then ignored the call and continued walking on, her steps now quickening and her grip tightening on the child's hand. But Agnes knew she'd heard her.

"Maura, please!"

With a grimace, Maura turned around but said nothing.

"I didn't know you were back in Ireland," said Agnes softly.

"Why should you?" was the curt reply.

"Is this your child, Maura?"

"Yes – so what?"

"But I thought – I mean, Harry said – "

Maura looked brazenly at her. "Yes, I'm sure Harry told you that I couldn't have children. And regrettably, it's true. But how is any of this your business?"

"How old is the child, Maura?"

"Six."

Quickly, Agnes did her sums. "Then how – is it a stepchild? Have you re-married?"

"No to both questions. But I don't see – "

"My God!" said Agnes, suddenly realising who the child was. "Harry said she'd gone to England, and you went over to her – "

"Yes," said Maura bitterly, "my sister was too far gone when your husband ordered her to get rid of the baby. She was six months pregnant, although she was hardly showing at all. So she pretended to have the abortion, then told Ivan that a friend of hers was ill in England and needed nursing." Maura looked directly at Agnes. "Needless to say, your husband wasn't happy about his mistress being away so long, but it meant that she could stay there until the child was born."

"Ivan has never cared about anyone but himself," said Agnes.

It was clear that the two children were longing to play with each other, and as the women's attitudes towards each other began to mellow, they let go of the tight grip they'd maintained on the children, who quickly seized the opportunity to escape and climb the railings outside the university.

"I'd always wanted a child," Maura continued, "so Colette and I arranged that I'd keep her baby and register it as mine, then Colette would come back to Dublin and continue being your husband's mistress." Maura looked sharply at Agnes. "You're not going to tell anyone what I've done, are you?"

"No, of course not," said Agnes.

Maura nodded in acknowledgment. "Poor Colette had only just returned to Dublin when she was killed."

"By my husband," said Agnes sadly.

"So it was him, the bastard!" cried Maura, shocked. "And to think that he's still free and my sister and Harry are dead." She hesitated for a second. "Does that mean that Harry didn't commit suicide like they said?"

"No – poor Harry was murdered. I don't think there's any doubt about that either."

Maura's face turned red with anger. "And you're still living with that bastard! How on earth can you?"

"I have no choice, Maura. My father left everything to Ivan."

Maura drew in a deep breath. "Oh my God! Life's not fair, is it?

The silence lengthened between them, then Agnes spoke again. "I want to thank you from the bottom of my heart for allowing me the time with Harry. You were unbelievably decent, and I appreciate it more than you can ever know."

Maura shrugged, but the tension left her shoulders. "We didn't love each other any more. So what would have been the point of hanging onto something that no longer existed?"

"You could have made things very difficult for us. Or gone to my husband."

Maura looked shocked. "What do you take me for?"

"An unbelievably kind person," said Agnes. "And it's so providential that I've met you today. Because I'd already decided that, as Colette's offspring by Ivan, assuming he dies before me and I inherit from him, there'll be a share of the Kilmartin estate for this child of yours when I die." Agnes's voice softened. "But in the meantime, I'd like to help."

Maura bristled. "We're doing fine, thank you."

"No, you're not," Agnes replied brusquely. "I only have to look at the clothes you're both wearing to see that times are hard. Don't deny your child its rightful inheritance, Maura, because of your own pride."

Maura looked at her feet. "OK, you're right. The insurance company wouldn't pay out because they said Harry's death was suicide. Which you and I know wasn't true. So it hasn't been easy . . ."

"Here, Maura," Agnes reached around her neck and took off the gold cross and chain she was wearing, "please take this. It's solid gold, and if you ever need to sell it, you can get quite a bit of money for it. It's —"

"No, thank you, Agnes," said Maura angrily. "I don't want your charity."

"It's not charity, it's a gift. Take it for your child, if not for yourself. Please, Maura!"

Maura reluctantly took the cross and chain. "Thank you."

Hastily, Agnes took a notebook from her handbag. "Please, Maura — let me have your present address as well. We don't ever have to meet again — and I know we're never likely to be friends — but I'd like to ensure that your child wants for *nothing while its growing up. Although Ivan controls the purse-strings, I get a substantial monthly allowance."*

Maura hesitated, unsure of what she should do. At last, she said, "I'll think about it." Then she frowned. "No, you're right – I can't deny the child its birthright. But you'll keep my secret, won't you? I'm this child's mother in all the ways that matter."

"Of course," said Agnes, "and to show my good faith, Maura, I'll tell you my secret." She gestured towards Tom. "This is Harry's child."

Maura's eyes opened wide. "My God," was all she could say.

The two women stared at each other in wonderment, each now privy to the other's most intimate secret.

Agnes was the first to return to the practicalities of the situation. "So tell me, Maura – do you still call yourself Sweeney?"

"Oh, no – I changed back to my maiden name and registered the child under that name shortly before Colette was killed."

"When did you come back to Ireland? I'd always assumed that you'd stayed in England after Harry died."

"That's what I wanted people to think. I didn't see any point in coming back when Harry was imprisoned – I knew he couldn't have done it, and I assumed he'd be released quickly – I never expected him to die."

"Ivan made certain of that," said Agnes bitterly. "I don't know how he did it, but one of his lackeys got to Harry somehow."

Maura nodded sadly.

"So when did you come back?" asked Agnes.

"After Harry died, I got an estate agent to discreetly sell our house, then I cleared the mortgage and used the money left over to buy a smaller house on the other side of the city – where I'd be unlikely to meet anyone from my past." She smiled at

Agnes. "I let people believe that I'm a widow with a young child, and by reverting to my maiden name, I hoped to give Colette's child a decent future, without the scandal of the past always haunting us." Maura's eyes filled with tears. "Poor Colette! She was dazzled by your husband's wealth. Harry and I tried to help but Colette wouldn't consider going back to school or getting a normal job. We were afraid, you see, that Ivan might get tired of her – then what would she do? She'd have no home, no training or qualifications . . ."

Agnes nodded. There was every reason to fear Ivan's disinterest. Anyone he could no longer use was dumped unceremoniously without a backward glance.

"What did you think when you heard that Harry had been arrested for Colette's murder?" Agnes asked.

Maura's eyes were sad. "Of course I knew he didn't do it. I assumed that his arrest was a stupid mistake and that he'd be released within days. I stayed in England because I was looking after Colette's newborn baby. Besides, I could hardly return to the glare of publicity with a new baby in the circumstances! There was nothing I could have done to help him anyway." She looked directly at Agnes. "Besides, I assumed you were doing your best to get him released. He was no longer mine to help."

"Well, I didn't manage to save him," said Agnes bitterly. "My husband made certain of that. Harry was with me on the night of the murder, but he was killed before I could get to the police to tell them. You see, I delayed too long, because Harry wanted me to protect our baby –"

Maura smiled sadly. "Yes – I can understand that. Harry always longed to be a father, and you finally made his dream come true."

"Now I have his child, but no Harry," said Agnes bitterly.

"I'm very sorry – really I am. I know how much you and Harry loved each other."

"It's good of you to say that, Maura. I did love him – and I never meant to hurt you."

Agnes took out a ballpoint pen, opened a notebook and handed it to Maura. "Now then, you'd better give me all your contact details."

"Thank you, Agnes," said Maura. "This is good of you. I don't think many women in your situation would do this."

"I'd be happy to pay the yearly fees for your child to go to a good school as well," Agnes added as Maura began to write, "and then, if your child is bright, there'll be university – but please contact my friend Catherine Brennan if you ever need me: don't phone the house in case Ivan's there."

When Maura handed the notebook back, Agnes wrote down Catherine's number and address, tore the page out and handed it to her. Then she tucked the notebook deep into her bag.

"Do you intend to tell your child about its real parents some day?" she then asked Maura.

"I don't know," said Maura. "Maybe." She looked directly at Agnes. "What are you going to do?"

"I don't know either. Maybe when Ivan dies – maybe when Tom's an adult – I'm not sure. It's a difficult choice to make, isn't it? I'm terrified that my son may hate me if he finds out while I'm still alive."

"But surely you'd want him to know about Harry some day?" asked Maura softly, looking across at the two children playing together, oblivious of their mothers' conversation.

"Maybe we have a duty to tell them the truth. But some day in the future – not now. When they're old enough to understand what we did and why we did it."

The two women stood in silence, until eventually Agnes spoke.

"You'll receive a postal order from me every month," she told Maura. "That way, there'll be no bank record of it, so Ivan won't find out. And when he dies – that is, assuming he dies before me – I'll make sure that your child is a beneficiary in my will." She darted a glance at the children. "But since we've all got so much to conceal at present, I'll make an interim will in which I'll simply refer to your child – and another child who is also Ivan's – as the offspring of Ivan Kilmartin, so that their identities are protected until such time as they've been told the truth. Then it will be up to you to tell, or not to tell, your child about its birthright and its claim on my estate."

"Thank you, Agnes," said Maura. "I really appreciate what you're doing for us."

By now, young Tom and his new playmate had abandoned the railings outside the university and were inside the grounds. Tom was climbing the statue of Oliver Goldsmith, in pursuit of the other child, who had already reached the top of the plinth and was trying to push him off.

"Goodbye, Maura," said Agnes, as she grabbed Tom, "I wish you and your child well."

The women smiled guardedly at each other.

Then Maura retrieved her child from the statue, and Agnes, dragging a reluctant Tom, walked away without looking back.

CHAPTER 84

Back in her house in Blackrock, Joanna paced the floor. I *hate* him, she told herself. He's an opportunistic shit. He deserves Sasha Miller – I hope she makes his life a misery! Then she burst into tears again, since she didn't want to hate Tom – didn't she really love him? But she was hurting like hell, and he didn't even know it. In fact, he was probably having sex with Sasha Miller at this very moment. They'd probably got down to business as soon as she'd left his house, laughing at being caught out by the daughter of his late mother's friend.

Joanna longed to ring Orla's mobile phone, but she didn't want to interrupt her friend's burgeoning love life. No doubt Orla and Gary were busy – probably frolicking naked around Orla's apartment – well, as much as Orla could frolic with a broken ankle.

And Mary – she was probably with Mick McHale at this very minute, too! She could imagine them together in Mary's kitchen, one of them cooking, the other setting the table. They would be laughing and having fun, basking in the joy of their new relationship. Joanna was happy for Mary, but being surrounded by friends who were happily in love made her feel so alone and isolated. The whole world seemed to be happily in love except her!

Joanna leaned down and patted her cat, who was circling at her feet, looking very pleased with herself. "Oh, Devil," she whispered, "you're the only one I can turn to, right now. I feel so alone and miserable. What am I going to do?"

Devil indicated that she thought a bowlful of catfood would be an ideal way for her owner to demonstrate her affection, so Joanna followed the cat out to the kitchen and tipped the packet of dried food into the bowl on the floor and put fresh water into the drinking bowl. She was just thinking how big the cat had become – almost overnight – when the phone rang.

"Hi, Jo – I'm not interrupting anything, am I?"

Joanna's heart flooded with relief. It was Orla. "Oh, Orla, I'm so glad you phoned. I'm absolutely miserable!"

"Why – what's happened? Is it your mother?"

"No – Mam's OK. At least, she's as OK as she'll ever be. No, it's me, Orla – "

"Well then – what is it?"

"It's Tom – I called round to see him, and – oh Orla, I really love him!"

"Jesus – I can't keep up with your love life, Jo. What's happened to Ronan?"

"He's gone – the one I really love is Tom. But when I went around to talk to him, that – that *creature* was there, half-naked!"

"What creature?"

"Bloody Sasha Miller! The trollop, the bitch!"

"Well, I agree with you there," said Orla. "Sasha Miller should be taken out and hung by her scrawny neck. But what do you mean by half-naked?"

"Well, she came out of the downstairs bathroom in her underwear minus her other clothes – and she claimed that she'd just spilt tea on them!"

"Well, that's probably the truth," said Orla, "but I'm sure the little tart did it deliberately, to try to seduce Tom. It's hardly his fault, is it? I mean, was he responding to her little ploy?"

"Well, how do *I* know?" said Joanna indignantly. "He's probably been screwing her for ages! I mean, we saw them together in the Morrison Bar – "

"But he wouldn't have invited you in if he'd known that she was stripping off in the loo, would he?"

"But I was fifteen minutes early – he probably intended to be finished with Sasha before I arrived! Or maybe the plan was that she'd wait upstairs until I'd gone! Then they could continue where they'd left off –"

"Look, I'm sure he wouldn't have asked you to the house at all if he'd known she'd pull a stunt like that."

"No, I suppose not," said Joanna grudgingly.

"Unless he fancied a threesome . . ." said Orla mischievously.

"Oh Orla, don't say that!" wailed Joanna. "I think I'm cracking up!"

"Look, it's not as hopeless as you think," said Orla. "That little tart tries to seduce everything in trousers – it doesn't mean that she always succeeds. I doubt if Tom is as gullible as that shit Declan Dunne was."

"Then what's she doing in his house? Oh Orla, what am I going to do?" Joanna wailed at her friend. "I really do love him – I think I always have. Do you think I've left it too late?"

"Not if Sasha Miller is the only woman in his life," said Orla. "But there's only one way to find out – go and talk to him. You've still got important family business to discuss with him, haven't you? Well, go and tell him about it. Apologise for walking out earlier – just say that you were embarrassed. Maybe it's time the pair of you did some straight talking. Personally, I wouldn't be surprised if you discover that Tom's fancied you for ages."

"Oh Orla, do you really think so?"

"There's only one way to find out – go for it, woman," said Orla in exasperation. "Don't get your wires crossed like Gary and I did. Do you want *me* to have a word with Tom?"

"God, no – I'd die!"

"Well then, go and sort it out yourself – if not, I *will* talk to Tom," said Orla, with a threatening laugh. "I'm now giving you an ultimatum, kiddo. I'll phone you again first thing on Monday morning, and you'd better give me the answer I want to hear! And I'm still expecting to be your bridesmaid – whoever the groom is!"

CHAPTER 85

Tom Kilmartin paced his kitchen floor in Ballsbridge. He'd hardly slept all night; he was still exhausted and in a foul temper. He turned on the kettle and stuck a piece of bread in the toaster, although he doubted if he could eat any breakfast. He was furious with that appalling bimbo Sasha Miller, who had come to interview him a second time. How could he have been so naïve as not to realise what she was up to? After all, she'd virtually propositioned him in the Morrison Hotel, and he'd got away from her as soon as was decently possible. So how had he fallen for her request for a further interview? With hindsight, he could see that a second interview had been totally unnecessary. But he'd been flattered, thinking that Sasha found his interest in Emperor and Chinstrap penguins as fascinating as he did. And his stupid ego had allowed him to get carried away with the notion of seeing his interview in print.

He kicked a chair out of the way. He'd been so keen to impress Joanna that he hadn't realised what that dreadful Miller woman was up to. Clearly she made a habit of trying to seduce her interviewees. Under normal circumstances, he would have been able to deal with that situation easily enough – after all, a university lecturer often has to deal with smitten students – but why oh why had Joanna appeared at precisely that moment? It had been his worst nightmare come true!

He'd only wanted to do the interview so that he could ring Joanna and ask her what she'd thought of the feature when it appeared in the paper. He was just a sad, pathetic love-struck idiot, and anyway, who was he kidding? She wasn't likely to give him a second glance now that the good-looking private eye was hanging about. He'd seen the way she looked at him. Why was it so easy to deal with other women, but when he was near the woman he adored, he could hardly string two sentences together? Maybe he should just stick to penguins and other forms of wildlife. At least with animals, you didn't have all these endless misunderstandings. Maybe he'd get himself a cat or a dog as a companion – they didn't play games, they were always glad to see you and they didn't expect sparkling conversation all the time.

Tom paced up and down. Maybe he should try ringing Joanna? She couldn't think he'd be attracted to that awful woman, could she? Her reaction had seemed a bit extreme, but then he had put her in a terribly embarrassing situation. He'd assumed that Sasha would have completed her interview and left long before Joanna arrived. And while he'd calculated that there wouldn't be time to get a meal ready for Jo, he'd intended to take her out for something to eat, and he'd hoped to bring the situation between them to a head. He'd planned to ask her outright about her feelings for the private eye – even if it meant she'd never feel relaxed in his company again. But it was just ridiculous that a grown man couldn't sort out his own love life. He wanted Joanna Brennan desperately – he *loved* her, dammit, so why couldn't he just come out and say it?

Just then, the phone rang. "Hi, Tom!"

It was Joanna!

"Oh, Jo, how are you?"

"I'm fine, Tom – I'm just ringing to apologise for rushing off yesterday – I was a bit embarrassed – "

Tom felt a small stab of disappointment. Ridiculously, he'd hoped that she might be going to tell him she'd been jealous of Sasha and that she loved and wanted him more than anything in the world . . .

"Jo – it's me who should be apologisng to you," Tom replied evenly. "I thought Sasha Miller would have left by the time you arrived – she was interviewing me about my trip to the Antarctic next December."

Suddenly, Joanna's sense of humour took over. "Well, she wasn't exactly dressed for the climate there, was she?"

Tom laughed and relaxed. "Oh, Jo – the silly woman was obviously coming on to me. But I have no interest in her, never had. She's not the kind of woman I'd ever be attracted to."

"And what sort of woman would that be, Tom?" The words were out before Joanna realised what she'd actually said. There was a moment's silence, and Joanna wanted to die with embarrassment.

Then Tom chuckled. "Come on over here, Joanna, and I'll tell you," he replied, hardly believing his own bravado. How would she interpret what he'd just said? What would she think he meant? Maybe she was only exchanging meaningless banter with him. He broke out in a sweat. She was probably off to have another bonking session with the private eye . . .

"OK, Tom," said Joanna, taking a deep breath, "I really do want to know. Besides, it's time I brought you up to date on the latest information. I think you really need to hear it."

"Sounds ominous. Can you be here by seven? Then we can carry on as we'd intended to do the other night – with either a takeaway or a walk down to the Lotus Leaf."

"OK," said Joanna, hanging up. "See you tonight at seven."

* * *

Joanna finished her lunch, fed the cat, then decided to have a final search of the house for the documents her mother had hidden for Agnes. Normally on a Saturday afternoon she'd be shopping for her weekly groceries. But right now, solving the mystery of Agnes's will was uppermost in her mind. After all, she could survive on takeaways during the week if necessary.

Would the documents be in some kind of container? If so, it would need to be large? On the other hand, paper items could be folded up tightly in a small space . . . She sighed. They could be anywhere!

Joanna carried a cup of tea into the drawing-room and sat down, pondering on Agnes's last words. "Cat'll have the documents." Nothing could be clearer than that, could it? Her mother had been put in charge of hiding the documents. Now where would be the perfect place, where no one but Agnes or she would think of looking?

Joanna sighed as she drank her tea. Was there any point in trying to ask her mother again? Last time she asked her mother had begun singing "Away in a Manger". It was so frustrating. What sort of weird logic would bring a Christmas carol into her mother's head? Especially since Christmas was months away! And she'd kept singing the same bit each time: *"The cattle are lowing, the baby awakes, but the little Lord Jesus no crying he makes . . ."*

Joanna put down her cup and stood up. "Cat'll have the documents," she said aloud.

Suddenly, she frowned.

"The cattle are lowing . . . Cat'll have the documents . . . cattle . . . cattle have the documents!"

Instantly, Joanna's eyes were drawn to her mother's collection of bronzes on the sideboard. They'd been there since her childhood, and she hardly even noticed them any more. But Ronan had admired one of them – the group of several cows leaning against a fence! And a group of cows were cattle! She rushed over and, with hands that were shaking, lifted up the heavy bronze and turned it upside down. Sure enough, there was a base screwed on – which could be unscrewed with a screwdriver. She shook it and, yes, she could faintly hear something move about inside.

So the nurse, Lisa Noonan, had been right after all – Agnes had actually said: "The cattle have the documents" – not "Cat will have the documents". Poor Agnes – how awful it must have been to know that she was dying, and that there was only time and strength to pass on the briefest of messages.

Joanna felt very foolish. She'd made the wrong assumption and gone to her mother, yet it was her mother who had inadvertently provided the answer in the long run!

In her own way, Catherine had been making the connection between the documents and the bronze sculpture in her drawing-room. And although she couldn't explain it properly, her brain had made the connection between the bronze and the words of the Christmas carol. And Joanna had nearly missed it!

Afraid to let the bronze out of her sight, and still holding it in her arms, Joanna rushed to the phone in the hall. As she placed it on the hall table, she gazed at it in wonderment. It was a beautiful piece of sculpture, and she felt guilty she hadn't appreciated it more. Then she was dialling Tom's number, her words tumbling out as he answered. "Tom – I think I've found where the documents are! Oh God, I'm so excited! Can I come over straight away?"

"Yes – of course!"

Then Joanna's sense of humour took over. "I presume Sasah Miller won't be there this time?"

"God, no – "

Dashing upstairs, she showered and once again stepped into her beautiful satin underwear – the bra and panties she'd bought for the night she first went to Tom's house for dinner. Gently, she caressed the satin. She'd always regarded them as "Tom's" knickers and bra. Now she hoped fervently that the next time she stepped out of them, it might be because Tom was taking them off to make love to her.

The one and only time she'd worn the satin

underwear had been on the fateful night that Mary had phoned about Paul's behaviour and effectively put any relationship with Tom on hold. But not after tonight, Joanna thought determinedly. Someone has got to push the boat out. Even if it means making a fool of myself, I'm going to say *something* to him. After all, that comment he made about telling her the kind of woman he was attracted to – that couldn't have been just a joke, could it? Oh God – maybe it was just an amusing throwaway reply that he'd made on the spur of the moment and it hadn't meant anything at all!

God, she was so excited. And nervous too. Hopefully, when they unscrewed the base of her mother's bronze, there would be information that would explain who the other beneficiary to Agnes's will was and would also confirm whether Harry or Ivan was Tom's real father.

Suddenly, Joanna remembered that she'd yet to tell Tom what her mother had said about Ivan not being his father. I'm a selfish cow, she thought, to be thinking of my own happiness when Tom's world is changing by the minute. Romance would undoubtedly be the last thing on his mind!

Nevertheless, she inspected herself in the mirror once more before leaving the house. She'd gone to an inordinate amount of trouble to create the right combination of laidback casual and drop-dead glamour. But had she succeeded? She had selected really tight jeans and paired them with a figure-hugging top that left little to the imagination. Maybe she looked too tartish, but desperate needs required desperate means . . .

CHAPTER 86

Tom was smiling as he opened the door, but he looked edgy too, and Joanna's heart sank. The poor guy wouldn't exactly be over the moon when she told him what her mother had revealed. His eyes were now riveted on the bronze sculpture she was carrying.

"Hi, Tom."

"Hi, Jo – you're looking very – eh, lovely this afternoon."

Joanna blushed. "Thanks, Tom – but these are just an old pair of jeans – " *Now, why on earth did I say that?* she asked herself furiously. Why can't I learn to accept a compliment? I bet Sasha Miller wouldn't act as stupidly as that. She'd probably have grabbed him by the scrotum by now! Joanna smiled briefly as that image came to mind, but she quickly dismissed it. She didn't want to let in *any* images of Sasha Miller canoodling with her beloved Tom!

"What on earth is that?" he said, pointing to the bronze sculpture in her arms.

"This, I hope, is the source of the documents we've been looking for. I think they're hidden inside it."

He led her downstairs to the cosy basement kitchen, put the kettle on and turned to face her.

"So, how do we open it?" he asked, pointing to the bronze sculpture. "Will a screwdriver do the trick?"

"Yes, a screwdriver will open it, but first – I need to talk to you about something else. I didn't get a chance to tell you this last time I saw you, because Ronan was present."

As if I could forget, thought Tom bitterly. "Well, tell me now."

Joanna took a deep breath. "Tom, I don't quite know how to tell you this – but it was Ivan Kilmartin who killed Colette Devane."

Tom's face turned white as he tried to absorb this new, and frightening, information. "Oh my God – who told you that? Is there proof that he did it? Did my mother know about it?"

"Yes, I'm fairly certain she knew," said Joanna shakily. "I'm sorry, Tom."

"Oh my God – where did you find this out, Jo?"

"A client told me," Joanna explained. "She knows what happened and she's willing to go public about it and help me to clear Harry Sweeney's name."

Suddenly, Tom's face crumpled, and Joanna rushed to hold him as his tears fell unheeded. "Oh God, Jo – I'm sorry for making such a fool of myself. But I'm finding all of this a lot to digest right now – first, it was my mother and Harry Sweeney – now this bombshell!"

Joanna gently wiped the tears from his cheeks. "Cry

all you want, Tom," she whispered. "This has all been a terrible shock to you."

She cradled him in her arms, and for a few minutes they stood locked in a silent embrace. Gradually, he relaxed, and she found herself gently smoothing back his hair in a gesture that one might use to soothe a distressed child.

"Jo, I'm sorry," said Tom at last. "I'm being downright stupid. And selfish. Because, apart from the shock, with each bit of information you give me I feel as though you're slipping further and further away from me. I'm afraid that because of what you've just told me, I've lost any chance I might ever have had with you."

Joanna's breathing almost stopped. "W-what do you mean, Tom?"

"Oh, Jo," he said miserably, "I'm making a right mess of this, aren't I? I'm burning all my bridges – maybe I'll even lose your friendship by saying this. But if you don't know by now, you'll never know. I *love* you, Joanna Brennan. But whatever chance I might have hoped for before, when I saw you with that good-looking fellow Ronan O'Farrell, I guessed he was much more your type. He certainly fancies you, Jo!"

Joanna buried her head in his shoulder so that he wouldn't see her red face. "Oh, Ronan's a nice guy," she said as casually as she could, "but he's not my type at all."

"Well, I'm glad of that," said Tom, squeezing her tightly. "But now that you've told me I'm the son of a murderer, you'd never want me now!"

Quickly, Joanna silenced him by pressing her lips to his. Then they broke away and stood staring at each other in astonishment.

"Oh, Tom," said Joanna, tears in her own eyes now, "I love you too. Who your father was doesn't matter to me in the slightest. It's *you* I want. Besides – I haven't told you everything yet – " she added, stepping slightly back from him, "and I don't know how you're going to take this next bombshell – but you're almost certainly Harry Sweeney's son."

Tom lower lip trembled. "I was beginning to suspect that myself – but I was afraid to acknowledge it. I mean, I was born a few months after my mother's lover died, so it all adds up, doesn't it?"

"Yes, it does, Tom. I don't know whether your father – I mean Ivan – knew that you were Harry's child, but you were protected by virtue of your mother and Ivan remaining married." Joanna laced her fingers through his. "The way I figure it, Harry wanted his son to have the protection of Ivan's name, and he wanted Agnes to remain safe and secure, in order to rear his son. He knew that Ivan had somehow stitched him up. But on the other hand, he must have got some grim satisfaction from knowing that Ivan was obliged to rear his wife's love child, as the price of getting rid of her lover and maintaining his own position in society."

Tom pulled her towards him and held her tightly. He was clearly shaken by the changing boundaries – not just to his identity, but also their newly professed love for each other. She tenderly kissed his cheek, feeling the delightful stubble, which made her feel so protective towards him. Ronan had been right – she and Tom were meant to be together.

"Well, this is just hearsay at present, isn't it?" said Tom. "How do we find out for certain?"

"Well, that's where this sculpture comes in," said Joanna, reluctantly leaving his arms and crossing to the bronze she'd left on the kitchen table. "I finally figured out what your mother's dying words meant. Now have you got that screwdriver?"

Tom got a screwdriver from the toolbox in the pantry and handed it to her. Joanna then turned the sculpture upside down and began to unscrew the bottom of it. Gingerly, she prised it open – and pulled out the assortment of papers that were wedged inside: documents, a few faded photographs and a bundle of letters.

"Oh, Tom – now we may finally discover the truth," said Joanna, gently squeezing his hand. "Are you OK?"

He smiled. "Well, I'm a bit nervous, I suppose – so much has changed in the last few weeks – even in the last hour. I just hope that there aren't too many surprises in store!"

On top of the documents was a letter, addressed to Tom. It didn't say "Tom Kilmartin" – just "Tom".

He took a deep breath and took the envelope in his shaking hands. The sticky surface had long since dissolved, so there was no need to tear the envelope to open it. Inside was a letter signed by his mother. Silently, he read it.

Dear Tom,

When you read this letter I'll be dead, but hopefully I'll have had the courage to tell you the truth before then and this letter will be redundant.

The story I'm about to tell you is the universal one of a man and a woman loving each other deeply, but each being married to someone else. It could, I suppose, sound cheap and tawdry to you, because every couple thinks their love is unique and extraordinary. But Harry and I really did love each other deeply, and you are the son of Harry Sweeney, not Ivan Kilmartin.

Harry Sweeney was on remand for a murder he didn't commit. No one knows this better than me, since he was with me on the night that the murder was committed. I know that Ivan arranged for Harry to be convicted of murder, and I could have given him the alibi he needed. But he was afraid Ivan would hurt me if I publicly disgraced him and because of his love for me – and for you, the child that I was carrying – he begged me not to risk my safety and your future, at least until he was freed. Because then, we'd planned to leave for Australia.

Since Ivan prevented me from visiting Harry in prison, Catherine went in my place, and brought my letters to him and his back to me. Since these few letters are all I have of Harry, I'm giving them to Cat to hide them safely for me, so that some day you'll be able to read them yourself. I can't risk Ivan finding them, since they'll provide confirmation that you are not his child, and if he destroys them, you may never know how much Harry – your father – and I loved each other.

Harry risked his life to protect you and me, because otherwise I'd have been ostracised by society for being pregnant by a man who wasn't my husband. Even though this was the beginning of the 1970s, women were still expected to play traditional roles, and marriage break-up was still a huge taboo. If I'd publicly cuckolded him, Ivan would have abandoned me without any support – and you, Tom, might have been taken away from me. The higher your position in society, the farther you can fall! Even if I'd been able to keep you, we'd have had no home or income, perhaps a social welfare payment at best. What choice did I have but to stay with my husband? And he, in turn, needed me to maintain his so-called respectability. So, we've continued to live together in an uneasy alliance. Hopefully, in your time, my dear son, things will have changed for the better.

I truly believe that Ivan Kilmartin killed that poor young woman, Colette Devane, although I've been unable to find any actual proof so far. There were rumours that a friend of Colette's actually saw what happened, but Catherine and I have searched for that woman without success.

Although my beloved Harry is now dead, maybe, with the passing of time, he'll eventually be proven innocent of the murder of Colette Devane, and if this written statement of mine can help, please use it. Harry and I were outmanoeuvred at every turn by Ivan, whose money could buy witnesses and alibis whenever they were needed. I also believe that Ivan had Harry murdered in prison. At that point, I lost all heart and will to fight on. Instead, I devoted myself to rearing the only living memorial to Harry – you, Tom. His son.

I wish I could have done more to prove Harry's innocence, but the businesses and the money have always been controlled by Ivan. Only when he dies will I, as his wife, receive any direct benefit. Ivan could disinherit us both, but I don't believe his pride will allow him to do so. Because even in death, he'll want to be remembered as a respected man.

But you, my son, may have greater strength for the fight than I have, and you may decide to pursue your real father's right to have his name cleared.

I also want to be buried beside Harry when the time comes. Even though we couldn't be together during our lifetime, at least we can be together in death.

LOVE CHILD

Ultimately, there will be three beneficiaries to my will – the will I'll make when Ivan dies. But since you, my son, may be the only one who knows your true birthright by now, I'll refer to you in my will as the offspring of Harry Sweeney and to the other two as offspring of Ivan's, since my husband had two other children, neither of whom he knew about. I will not reveal their names here, because they might not have been told of their birthright yet. Telling them is not up to me – that decision rests with others who know the truth, if and when they choose to tell it.

Hopefully, when I, and the other mothers of the beneficiaries, reveal the truth, I can destroy this letter. But if you're hearing this story for the first time, then I've failed to be the mother you deserve. Please forgive me, son. While I'm a proud woman, I'm not a very courageous one, and it needs courage to tell the child you love that his birthright is not what you've always led him to believe.

I wish you well, my dear Tom, and hope that your life is filled with happiness and success – that way, all my suffering and Harry's may have some ultimate meaning. I hope you'll find someone to love deeply, and who will feel the same way about you. Because money and possessions are nothing compared to love.

All my love forever –
Mother.

Silently, Tom passed the letter to Joanna, whose eyes filled with tears when she read it.

"Oh Tom – what a beautiful and profoundly sad letter," she said, slipping her arm around his waist. "Poor Agnes – what a tragic life she must have led, yet none of us ever suspected what she was going through."

"Except your mother," Tom pointed out, wiping tears from his own eyes. "Clearly, Catherine was my mother's greatest ally during the ordeal of Harry's time in prison. And, as we now know, Catherine hid all these documents for her."

"I wonder if Ivan suspected that you were Harry's son? He could never prove it, since there was no DNA testing back then."

Tom picked up his mother's letter and studied it again. "Yes, I'm right – I thought I might have imagined it – but the letter says there are *three* beneficiaries!"

"My God – we always thought there were only two – who on earth can the third be?"

Tom looked blankly at her. "I've no idea, but I'm getting used to surprises!"

He studied his mother's letter again, before putting it back on the table. "Do you think that my mother's letter will be able to clear Harry's name?"

"It will certainly help," said Joanna, "but Ellen Byrne's statement – and hopefully Jackie Byrne's, if he can be convinced to cooperate – should be enough on its own to get Harry's name cleared. After all, the testimony of a witness was enough to get poor Harry arrested in the first place, so now it will be enough to clear his name." She smiled. "Obviously, Ellen is the woman mentioned in your mother's letter."

Tom smiled back. "I don't know how you found this woman, Jo – you're a genius!"

Joanna accepted the compliment and said nothing, although she felt a little guilty, since the discovery of Ellen Byrne had been completely accidental. If it hadn't been for Gary's court case, Ellen and her connection to Colette Devane's murder might never have come to light.

There were several letters in the pile of documents, and Tom began reading the heartrending letters that his mother and father had exchanged while Harry was in prison.

Suddenly, Joanna let out a gasp. At the bottom of the pile was a letter addressed to her! "Oh my God!" With trembling fingers, she opened the envelope that bore her name in her own mother's handwriting. The letters were strong and firm, clearly written before her mother's gradual descent into senility.

Unfolding the page, Joanna's hand shook as she read. No – it couldn't be true!

"What's wrong, Jo?" Tom hurried to her side when he saw the colour drain from her face.

Silently, she handed him the letter. In it, Catherine stated that Ivan Kilmartin was her father.

I'm sorry Joanna, her mother had written, *but Ivan raped me in anger because I supported Agnes in her relationship with Harry Sweeney. The only consolation I can offer is that otherwise you'd never have been born, since your father and I were unable to have children together. But you brought Bill and me immense joy, and Bill has never known that he isn't your biological father. But even if he knew, he would love you just as much.*

"Oh Joanna – my God!" Tom held her to him.

"It's OK, Tom, but I think I'll just sit down for a minute." Joanna flopped into one of the kitchen chairs. It was all too much to cope with at once. Her poor mother . . .

Tears filled her eyes as she thought of the man who, as far as she was concerned, would always be her father –

Bill Brennan, the man who'd reared her. An image of his kind, craggy face filled her mind, and she began crying softly for all the pain her mother had endured. And poor Agnes, loving and losing the man who meant everything to her . . . and Harry, who'd lost everything because he'd loved Agnes . . .

Suddenly, Joanna began to laugh hysterically through her tears. "Do you realise, Tom – the man who was once your father is now mine!"

"Well, thank God we haven't discovered that we're related," he said, pulling her to her feet and kissing her again, "I couldn't bear to lose you, just after we've found each other!"

For a long time they stood in a silent embrace, both overwhelmed by the changing parameters of their lives and the love that had finally brought them together.

"Do you realise," he said at last, "that you must have a half-brother or sister out there somewhere?"

Joanna nodded, unable to speak. Everything was changing too rapidly for her liking.

"Now we've only got to find my father's – I mean Ivan's – no, I mean *your* father's child by Colette," said Tom, grinning at the changes in his vocabulary. "Do you think Ivan killed Colette because he found out about the child?"

"I doubt if we'll ever know why he did it," said Joanna, finding her voice at last. "According to my client Ellen, they were rowing in the car. I think he lost his temper and strangled her. He probably never intended to do it, but having done it, he had to cover it up or his career and lifestyle were over."

"But how did poor Harry get turned into the scapegoat?"

"I suspect Ivan realised that the situation offered him a rare opportunity to get rid of someone who was a thorn in his side as well. With Ivan's money, it would've been easy enough to get a guy like Jackie Byrne to swear he'd seen Harry do it. So with one fell swoop, Ivan got rid of the rival for his wife's affections and the troublemaker at his building sites. And neatly exonerated himself of the murder of Colette Devane by producing a convenient scapegoat."

They were both silent as they contemplated the horror of Harry's and Agnes's lives when they found themselves caught up in Ivan's evil plans.

"Come here," said Tom, pulling her into his arms. "At least now, we're back to square one and looking for just one more beneficiary. Tell me, Jo, how does it feel to be the second beneficiary of my mother's will?"

CHAPTER 87

"Mam, Dad – I want to study law," Joanna had said, her face wreathed in smiles. "I've been thinking about it for ages, and I'd like to become a solicitor. I hate to ask you, but do you think you could help me with the fees? I'll get a part-time job, of course – two of them if need be – "

Seeing Joanna's enthusiasm, Catherine's heart had been stricken with love for her only child, and equally stricken with fear as to how she and Bill could possibly get the money to cover all the costs involved. For what Joanna didn't realise – in fact they'd ensured that she didn't know – was that the nest egg they'd built up over the years had been decimated through unwise investments. Foolishly, they'd allowed the broker to assure them that the shares he was recommending were going to rocket in value, but something had gone horribly wrong.

As Joanna awaited their reply, Bill harrumphed, and resorted to his usual technique of ceding power to Catherine in matters relating to their daughter. So Catherine was left to voice their joint concerns.

"Well, Jo – we'd love you to go to university – it's just that money is tight right now –" Seeing Joanna's look of dismay, Catherine ploughed on, "But your Dad and I will have a talk about it."

"Thanks, Mam, Dad!" said Joanna, rushing to hug them both. In her own mind, they'd already agreed.

* * *

"Your face is as long as a wet week," Agnes said to her friend. "What's the matter, Cat?"

"Oh – nothing."

"C'mon, Cat, I always know when there's something bugging you. Spit it out."

"It's just that Joanna wants to go to university."

Agnes raised her eyebrows. "But surely you're pleased? What does the dear girl want to study?"

"Law," said Catherine dully.

"Then what's the problem? It seems like an admirable profession to me," said Agnes. "Does she intend to be a barrister or a solicitor?"

Catherine sighed, not wanting to tell her friend what was wrong but knowing that Agnes would keep on at her until she'd wheedled it out of her anyway.

"A solicitor, I think. But we can't afford to pay her fees, Agnes," Catherine admitted. "I never told you – but last year Bill and I made a few extremely unwise investments. We lost all the money we'd intended using for Joanna's education."

Agnes didn't hestitate. "Then I'll pay for Joanna to go through university," she said. "I may have many problems, Cat," she added dryly, "but money isn't one of them. Why on earth didn't you say something before now?"

Catherine shrugged her shoulders. "I don't know – I suppose I felt guilty and incompetent at losing all that money. And you've already been more than decent in paying her school fees every year. I knew that if I told you about this, you'd offer to pay her university fees as well."

"Being misled over investments isn't your fault, Cat – but don't let Joanna miss going to university over a silly thing like pride!" Agnes smiled. "I've usually been the silly, proud one, Cat, and you've made me see sense. Now it's time I made you see sense for a change."

"You don't have to do this, Agnes –"

"I know I don't," said Agnes testily, "but I want to. You know that I'm very fond of Joanna, and if I can give her a headstart in life, then so be it. But there's one stipulation – " Agnes looked fiercely under her eyebrows at Catherine. "Under no circumstances are you to let her know that I had anything to do with it." Catherine was about to protest, but Agnes silenced her. "Those are the terms, Cat – take it or leave it."

"I'll take it," said Catherine meekly. "Agnes, I can never repay your kindness – "

"Don't be ridiculous, Cat," said Agnes abruptly. "I can never repay the help and support you've given me over the years. I know that friends never count the cost of those things, but this will give me a chance to do something for you. Give me this opportunity, Cat – please."

"Thank you, Agnes," said Catherine at last. There was nothing more to say.

But Agnes wasn't quite finished yet. "Hopefully, by the time Joanna is qualified, I'll have made a will that actually names the three beneficiaries I've chosen." She looked closely at Catherine. "And hopefully, we'll all have been able to tell our *children the truth by then. But just in case I'm knocked down by a bus before then –" she smiled, "it might be useful to have a competent solicitor in the family."*

"Well, hopefully, our children will all know the truth before then," said Catherine. Then she looked distraught. "Oh Lord, that doesn't mean I want poor Bill to die before me – that sounds terrible!"

"I know exactly what you mean, Cat," said Agnes, "and we both know that if anything happens to the other, even after this new will is made, the remaining one will have to eventually tell the truth to two of the three children. It's up to Maura to tell the other child, if and when she sees fit. Because I can't make a will disclosing each child's name until you, Maura and me have found the right moment to tell our children who their real parents are."

Catherine turned to her friend."Will you tell Tom as soon as Ivan dies?"

Agnes gave a deep sigh. "I don't know, Cat – I should, of course, but will I have the guts when the time comes?"

"But surely you'd want him to know about Harry?"

"Of course," said Agnes testily, "but what if he hates me? Oh God, maybe the proverbial bus would be a blessing in disguise. Then Tom wouldn't know about Harry and me until after I was dead."

"Don't be daft!" said Catherine, smiling. "It's better that you tell him while you're still around, because there's bound to be lots of things he'll want to ask you about."

"That's what I'm afraid of – I think I'm too much of a coward," said Agnes sadly. "I like things I can control – you know that, Cat. But I have no control over over people's reactions, and that's what I fear most of all. I spent years of my

life worrying about what my father thought, now I have to worry about what Ivan thinks, and it's hard to give up the habit of a lifetime."

"Isn't it odd," mused Catherine, "that you're longing for the day when Ivan dies, yet I'm dreading the day Bill does. Yet when those two events happen, you and I have to do something we're both dreading."

"I just hope Ivan goes before me, and I inherit, so that this proposed will of mine will be valid. I want to see that the wrongs of the past are righted – even if only in money terms."

Catherine nodded. "I've just had a thought – in case I go before Bill, maybe I should write a letter to Joanna and hide it with Harry's letters. What do you think?"

Agnes nodded. "Good idea – as long as you're sure there's no chance of Bill ever finding it."

"Bill never notices anything. He's far too absorbed in his books"

Suddenly, Agnes frowned. "Wouldn't it be awful if something prevented us from telling the children – and they were left with a very vague will to decipher?"

"Then maybe you should write Tom a letter yourself," said Catherine sensibly. "I'll put it with my letter to Joanna and your letters from Harry. Just in case . . ."

The sentence hung in the air. Unfinished, like the mission that would take almost a generation to complete . . .

CHAPTER 88

Exhilarated and exhausted from their discoveries, Tom and Joanna decided to take a break over a cup of tea.

"How is Ronan getting on with his search for Harry's wife?" asked Tom, and suddenly realised that he was talking about his father.

"He's actually finished the search," said Joanna, hoping that Tom hadn't noticed her blush when Ronan's name was mentioned, "because it seems that Maura may actually be here in Dublin."

Then she told Tom about her mother's visitor in the nursing home and of the cross and chain that had broken and been found beneath the coffee table in Catherine's room.

"That's weird – isn't it?" he said. "Do you think Maura could really be here? And why would she be visiting your mother?"

"Well, it wouldn't be all that surprising, considering the links both women had with Agnes. And my mother said that Maura told her they must all tell the truth – obviously that meant telling us who our real fathers are."

"But who would Maura need to tell the truth to? It can only mean Colette's child, right?"

"Well, that's the last strand to the mystery," said Joanna, curling up in his arms, "and hopefully, we won't have to wait too long to solve it."

Suddenly, he smiled. "Can we go and see Catherine soon, Jo? I want to tell her that I'm going to marry her daughter!"

Joanna kissed him hungrily once again. "Is that a proposal, Tom?" she whispered. "If so, then the answer is yes!"

"Oh, Jo, I can't wait to make you Mrs Kilmartin – or will it be Mrs Sweeney?"

"I think I'll keep my own name," said Joanna, smiling. "So let's plan a winter wedding, love – then maybe we can turn your Antarctic trip into a honeymoon as well?"

Tom kissed her again. "There's only one small problem – you'll have to share me with a group of students and around ten thousand penguins."

Joanna gazed tenderly into his eyes. "I can cope – as long as I have you all to myself each night," she told him, smiling.

They grinned happily at each other. They were still both in awe of their long overdue declaration of love for each other. And with hindsight, each of them was wondering why such a wonderful and natural happening had taken them both so long to profess.

Suddenly, Tom looked at his watch. "Are we going out for this meal we've arranged, Jo – or am I finally going to make love to you?" he whispered. "You can't possibly imagine how often I've wanted to – "

"I'm not hungry any more, Tom – except for you," Joanna whispered back. "I know that sounds corny, but maybe we can send out for a takeaway later. Much later . . ."

At last, Joanna thought, as her body thrilled to his touch, "Tom's" special satin bra and knickers were finally about to fulfill their destiny – and she was about to fulfill hers . . .

CHAPTER 89

Joanna was happily daydreaming in her office. Ostensibly, she was going through a conveyancing contract, but in reality, her mind was on the events of the night before, when she and Tom had finally consummated their love. She couldn't wait to tell Orla, who'd be ringing soon to find out what had happened over the weekend. Now, Joanna could confirm that the bridegroom was definitely going to be Tom Kilmartin!

Suddenly, the phone rang. "Joanna? Mick McHale here."

"Oh, hi, Jim – "

"I've spoken to some contacts of mine about Paddy Byrne."

"Great – what's the story, Jim?"

"Paddy used to do all Ivan Kilmartin's dirty work – he'd threaten workers, blackmail people, buy off town councillors for favourable rezoning of land, hand over the brown envelopes and the like. Ivan wasn't exactly a knight in shining armour. But then, are any of them? By its very nature, making money necessitates walking all over the little guy.

"And it was the little guy that Harry Sweeney was looking after." Jim paused. "Then, of course, there was the fact that Harry had become friendly with Agnes Kilmartin. That spelled the beginning of the end for Harry. Whether there was anything more to that friendship I don't yet know."

"In fact, there was," said Joanna, "and I've lots to tell you as well. Maybe Tom and I could meet you and Mary for a drink some evening?" Joanna smiled to herself. She was letting Jim know that she knew about his relationship, and she was publicly announcing her own for the first time!

"Great – we'll look forward to it."

* * *

"I can't believe it!" said Orla, grinning. "You've finally managed to get Tom Kilmartin into bed!"

The two friends were having a lunchtime sandwich in a pub off Westmoreland Street, since Joanna had refused to divulge any information to Orla over the phone.

"And we've discovered who two of the three beneficiaries to Agnes's will are!" said Joanna.

"Did you say *three* beneficiaries?"

"Yes – but I'll explain that later," said Joanna, and she proceeded to give Orla the details of everything that had happened since they'd last spoken and how she herself was now one of the beneficiaries of Agnes Kilmartin's will.

"My God, some people have all the luck! I suppose

you won't want to know this poverty-stricken friend any more," said Orla, grinning insolently, "since you're a rich bitch now!"

"To be honest, I haven't really had time to think about the money," Joanna admitted.

"I know why!" chuckled Orla. "You've been too busy shagging Professor Kilmartin! Is he any good between the sheets?"

Joanna grinned back. "Is this a happy face – or what?"

"But," said Orla, "you said there are *three* beneficiaries to Agnes's will? I thought there were only two."

"Colette Devane's child hasn't been found yet," Joanna explained. "I'm the extra, unexpected one! And the key to finding Colette's child may rest with my mother's mysterious visitor. Ronan had no luck finding Maura in England, so I've dispensed with his services –"

"And you've dispensed with his *personal* services," said Orla, grinning. "Watch out, Jo – you're blushing!"

"– since she may well be in Ireland," continued Joanna, doing her best to ignore Orla's teasing.

"You think she could be *here*?" said Orla, arching her eyebrows.

"Well, Ronan found out that a Colette Devane gave birth in London, and her sister was with her. Then they both disappeared. Since we know that Maura was Colette's sister, she probably kept the baby when Colette was murdered."

"You said the woman dropped something – was that of no help?"

"Not really – it's just a plain gold cross and chain. Expensive, though. I was thinking of putting an ad in the papers in the hopes that she might turn up to collect it. Look – " Joanna delved into her pocket and produced the cross and chain. "I've started to carry it around with me, in the hopes that it might provide me with some inspiration . . . "

By now, Orla had picked it up and was looking at it.

"It's lovely, isn't it?" said Joanna. "It's solid 18 carat gold, so I think it's probably worth a lot of money. What do you think? Hey, Orla – you've gone very quiet."

Orla looked up and stared in amazement at her friend. Her voice, when she spoke, was barely audible. "Joanna," she whispered, "this cross belongs to my mother."

CHAPTER 90

It was with great relief, but with sadness for her son, that Agnes stood before Ivan's open grave as they lowered his coffin in. A heart attack had finally removed the greatest blight on her life, and now she looked forward to some years of peace and solitude. She'd seen Ivan's will, and at last the Kilmartin estate was under her control. Now, she could complete her own will — the will she'd long vowed to make.

The funeral had attracted thousands of mourners, and Agnes was tired of having her hand shaken and being offered an endless stream of condolences. She wondered how many of the people in attendance genuinely mourned for Ivan, and she suspected that, like herself, the majority of people were experiencing relief rather than any other emotion. But decorum still had to be observed and the motions gone through with dignity.

As always, Cat had been at her side, clinging to one arm while Tom held the other. Agnes's face had worn an expression of dignified sadness, but only Cat knew the relief that her friend was really experiencing. In fact, Agnes was feeling joyful for the first time since she and her beloved Harry had been making plans to emigrate to Australia.

She'd endured years of Ivan's insults and barbs in private, while playing the loving wife in public. She'd attended gala dinners, charity balls and given dinner parties. Always, she'd been the smiling hostess, laughing at his jokes along with the other guests, while waiting fearfully for the tirade that would inevitably follow as soon as the guests had left.

Now, at last, she was free. For Harry's sake, she had endured years of misery, so that his son could have the kind of life she and Harry had always wanted for him. She had honoured Harry's wishes, and he could be proud of the son their love had produced.

Agnes had arranged a reception at one of the city hotels for those who had attended the funeral. She'd quickly brushed aside a suggestion from Tom that the reception be held in the family house. Agnes knew that people would come simply to see what the inside of the Kilmartin house was like. And she had no intention of satisfying their curiosity.

"How are you feeling, son?" Agnes was standing at the bar in the hotel, while Tom was ordering refills for some of the guests at the reception.

He handed her a vodka and tonic. "I'm OK, Mum. A bit sad, I suppose, but I wasn't really close to Dad – as you know only too well."

"Well, I won't claim to be heartbroken myself," said Agnes dryly. "But from this day on, son, money will be no problem if there's anything you want to do. And that goes for you, too," she added, turning to Catherine and Bill, who had just arrived at the bar counter.

Bill smiled. "Thanks, Agnes, your offer is greatly appreciated. But I'm actually doing quite well at the moment – the books I've been buying lately are just flying off the shelves. Recently, I bought up the entire library from an old country house in Scotland, and no sooner was it in the shop than the Trinity students and their professors bought it all! At this rate, I might even be able to take Catherine and young Joanna away for a few days' holiday!"

Agnes looked at Bill with a lump in her throat. He was so genuine, so decent and just so perfect for Cat. And he absolutely idolised his daughter. Agnes was so happy that their marriage had worked out well – unlike her own. But then, that mistake had been her own doing. If only she'd listened to Cat all those years ago . . .

But as she looked at Bill's happy face, the secret of Joanna's birthright weighed heavily on Agnes's mind. It wasn't fair that they'd had to deceive such a lovely man as Bill. But he was happy, wasn't he? Through their little deception, Bill had got the daughter he'd always longed for. And young Joanna had a wonderful father.

Agnes drained the last of her vodka and tonic and was quickly handed another by the barman. Smiling her thanks, she excused herself from Catherine and Bill's company and wandered off to mingle among the other guests. But her mind was not on the pleasantries she would now have to mouth inanely – she was thinking ahead to her appointment with her solicitor the following morning.

It was so important that when she drew up her will Bill would be protected from the knowledge of his wife's rape, and Joanna's birthright would remain a secret until Cat felt the time was right to tell her . . . if ever. That was Cat's choice. As *was her own decision to tell Tom – some day – that his real father was Harry Sweeney. And there was someone else to protect too. Ivan's other child . . . She would have to word her bequests very carefully. Because the time wasn't yet right to tell any of those children the truth . . .*

Hopefully, she'd have the courage to tell Tom herself sometime soon, but she was also scared that he might judge her harshly for living a lie for most of her life . . .

CHAPTER 91

"Hello, Joanna," said Maura Rogan.

"Hello, Maura," said Joanna, hugging Orla's mother, as she stepped into her small suburban home. The home where Orla had spent her childhood.

In the living-room Orla was already sprawled out in front of a roaring fire.

"Hi, Jo," she said, getting up with the help of her crutches. "Come here, sister, and give me a big hug. I can still hardly believe it! "

As the two women hugged, they both had tears in their eyes.

"Sit down there," said Orla gruffly, for she hated any display of sentiment, "and I'll make us all a cup of tea."

Joanna took Orla's place beside the cosy fire, and Maura sat down opposite her.

"So it *was* you who visited my mother?" said Joanna.

Maura nodded. "When I read about Agnes's death in the newspaper, I wondered if she'd managed to tell Tom about his father before she died. The only one who might have been able to tell me was Catherine."

"And was she able to?"

"No, she wouldn't or couldn't say. But she told me about some secret place where letters were hidden, though I couldn't make much sense of it. So I decided I'd tell Orla about that when I was telling her that Ivan and Colette were her real parents. I didn't know that you were administering the will, Joanna, or I would have come forward earlier. But while I could tell Orla about her father, I had no right to tell Tom Kilmartin about his. And I didn't know anything about your connection to Ivan Kilmartin either."

"Nor did I, until the other day," said Joanna.

Maura leaned over and threw a log on the fire. "So I was hoping that when I spoke to Orla, she'd know, through your friendship, if Agnes had managed to tell Tom." She grimaced. "Catherine also managed to tell me bits of her own sad story, which I hadn't known before." She inclined her head. "I presume you know what happened, Joanna?"

"If you mean about Ivan raping her, and me being the result – then yes, I found out the other day, when Tom and I opened the hollow bronze sculpture where Mam had hidden Agnes's letters, and her own letter to me, all those years ago." She paused. "And it was you who took your sister Colette's child."

Maura nodded. "Colette left it too late for an abortion, but she didn't want to keep the baby, because she wanted to continue being Ivan Kilmartin's mistress. On the other hand, I'd always longed for a child, but hadn't been able

519

to have one. At that point, my marriage to Harry was over, and he and Agnes had become a couple, so I'd decided to start a new life posing as a young widow with a baby." She grimaced. "I never expected that I'd really become a widow – when poor Harry was murdered. He and Agnes loved each other so much, you know."

"And you weren't upset about that?"

"About Agnes and Harry? Well, I did love him, of course, but Harry wanted Agnes so I wasn't going to stand in their way. When one person in a relationship wants out, there's no point in the other person trying to hang on. But what I wanted most of all was a baby, and Colette – God rest her soul – gave me what I wanted. We'd planned that she'd adopt the role of 'Auntie' Colette, and she'd be able to see her child anytime. But sadly, that never happened . . . "

"Why did you both disappear from the London flat just after the birth?"

Maura smiled. "Isn't it obvious? With Colette's full agreement, I was registering the birth, with me as the child's biological mother. She was returning to Dublin, to be with Ivan Kilmartin. We couldn't risk having the midwife poking her nose in or maybe offering to register the birth for us. It was safer to just disappear."

"But Maura, why didn't you come back when Harry was charged with murder?"

"If I'd come back to Dublin then, since I was Harry's legal wife, I'd have been immediately in the spotlight, wouldn't I? And how would I explain away a newborn baby, registered in my name?" She bit her lip. "Besides, I assumed that Harry would be released as soon as the authorities realised that they'd made a huge mistake. The next thing I heard was that poor Harry was dead."

Joanna reached out for Maura's hand. "I had a private detective searching all over London for you, but we couldn't find any trace of either Maura Sweeney or Maura Devane!"

Maura smiled. "Well, as Orla will have told you, Devane was actually a kind of 'stage name' that Colette adopted when she left home. It was just her attempt to distance herself from the parents she hated. She thought that by changing her name, they wouldn't be able to trace her and bring her home. And she wanted to dissociate herself from them because they were really tough on her. Both Colette and I were Rogans, and that's the name I reverted to when I came back to Ireland with Orla."

Joanna smiled. "Luckily, fate intervened, or we might never have found you."

"Yes, I was under your nose all the time," said Maura, "but I would have come forward eventually, if only because of Orla being a beneficiary in Agnes Kilmartin's will. I couldn't deny her that opportunity. And if you and Tom Kilmartin hadn't found out about your parentage by then, I suppose I'd have had to tell you too."

Just then, Orla shouted from the kitchen that tea and muffins were ready, but that anyone who wanted them would have to come and collect them, since she was too infirm to carry them.

Joanna hurried into the kitchen. "Poor old you," she said, giving her new-found sister another hug. "Just as well most of your activities are horizontal these days!"

Orla grinned back. "I can't wait to get off these

damned things, but Gary says I should be able to do without them very soon."

"Well, not every woman is lucky enough to have her own private physician!" said Joanna.

Soon, all three of them were sitting around the fire, mugs in their hands, the two young women grinning at each other in wonder from time to time, since they were both thrilled and excited at finding out they were sisters.

Joanna turned back to Maura. "How did you survive financially over the years?"

"After the first few years, with Agnes's help. From the time Orla was six, Agnes sent me a postal order every month. And, as you now know, it was she who gave me the cross and chain – she thought that I could sell it if things got really tough. But I could never bear to part with it. Besides, with Agnes's help, things were never so bad after that. And she paid for Orla's school fees and university fees too. I also discovered from Catherine that she paid for your school fees and university education too, Joanna."

"My God," said Joanna, "that explains the regular postal orders that were listed anonymously in Agnes's household accounts! What a kind, generous woman Agnes was!" She smiled at Maura. "I often wondered how you and my parents managed to send Orla and me to university – I mean, neither of our families were exactly well off, were they?" She looked sad. "I used to wonder how Agnes and my mother could possibly be friends, but now I know." Then she suddenly remembered she'd something to tell her friend's mother. "By the way, Maura, there's mortality benefit for Harry still waiting for you at his trade union!"

Maura grimaced. "I was afraid to contact the union all

those years ago – in case any gossip got out about Orla and me. I wanted to protect her and give her a childhood that would make her confident and strong."

Joanna chuckled, looking across at Orla. "Well, you achieved that all right, Maura – you raised a brat! Did you know that she used to tie my pigtails to the desk in school and flick pellets of used chewing gum into my hair?" Joanna ducked as a cushion came flying in her direction.

"Why did it take you all so long to let us know about our fathers?" asked Joanna.

"I was scared," said Maura humbly, "and I know that Catherine and Agnes were scared too. I suppose we were all afraid you mightn't love us any more if you discovered we'd been deceiving you – even though it was always meant for the best." She smiled sadly. "Besides, it was easy to put off the day of reckoning – I could always find excuses why tomorrow would be a better day for telling Orla. Then the years went by, and there never seemed the right time. Besides, it didn't really matter to Orla until Agnes died – then I had to do something about it." She looked over at her daughter. "Especially now that she and Gary are getting married."

"So that's why you kept nagging me to visit you!" said Orla.

Maura smiled back. "Yes – I felt it was time to tell you, but you were always too busy with your hectic social life to bother!"

"Well, I found Gary," said Orla, "so I wasn't entirely wasting my time." Then suddenly, she started. "Oops! I've just realised that I haven't told Gary about the money yet!" She grabbed her crutches and hobbled out to the phone in the hall.

Joanna smiled at Maura. "And does Orla love you any less, now that you've told her everything?"

Maura looked down at her feet. "No – she says it makes no difference. I'm still – and always will be – her mother." Tears began to slide down Maura's weatherbeaten face, and Joanna silently squeezed her hand.

"I feel no different about my mother either," said Joanna, "nor does Tom. If anything, we love you all more. I just wish, for your own sakes, that you hadn't all suffered in silence for so long." She smiled. "So tell me, Maura – what was Harry really like? He's been on my mind and in my dreams for ages, but he's still such an elusive figure!"

Maura's eyes misted over. "Harry was a lovely man. I wish all of you could have known him. I was lucky to have been his wife – even for a little while." She looked earnestly at Joanna. "You'll be able to clear his name now, won't you?"

Joanna nodded. "That's the next job to be tackled, although Harry was never actually charged with murder. He was only on remand."

"But people thought he'd murdered Colette," said Maura. "I'd like people to know the great man he really was."

The two women sat in silence, thinking of the man whose life had been cruelly cut short by the greed and evil deeds of others, and ultimately because he fell in love with the wrong woman. Eventually Maura spoke. "So is your work on Agnes's will finished now, Joanna?"

"Well, there are various legal formalities still to be

sorted out. For one thing, I need to advertise, just in case there are any other beneficiaries out there!"

"How long does that take?"

"Normally about three months. If no one's applied by then, Tom, Orla and I share the entire estate."

"Well, let's hope that old Kilmartin wasn't putting it about any more than we know he did!" said Orla as she came hobbling in from the hall.

"You've a cheek!" said Joanna, laughing. "Haven't you heard of the Fourth Commandment? You shouldn't be speaking so disrespectfully of your father!"

Another cushion came flying in her direction.

"Well," said Maura, "I'm sure Agnes would have made a point of keeping track of Ivan's later conquests, and if there'd been any more offspring, she'd have included them in her will. She was a very decent woman."

"She was," said Joanna. "And Harry Sweeney was a decent man. I have one more trip I want to make, Maura – to the old house where you and Harry used to live. The young woman who now lives there is positively revelling in the idea that Harry was a murderer. I want to see her face when I put the record straight." This recollection also made her think of Ronan, and she found herself blushing yet again. In fairness, she'd need to bring him up to date too.

Orla settled herself by the fire, grinning from ear to ear. "Gary says he's glad he proposed to me while I was a pauper – otherwise I might think he'd only wanted me for my money!"

CHAPTER 92

"Mam – this is Tom, Agnes's son. You remember him, don't you?"

Catherine nodded. "Of course I do. How nice to see you again, Tom. How is your dear mother?"

Joanna and Tom shared an anguished glance, and Joanna tried to distract Catherine as quickly as possible. I'm becoming quite adept at this, she thought sadly. But she and Tom had decided that there was no point in upsetting Catherine by any further mention of Agnes's death. Her mother seemed unwilling to accept the news, despite having been told about it several times.

"Mam – Tom and I are getting married."

"How lovely!" said Catherine. "Agnes and I will have lots of fun going shopping for new outfits." She leaned forward confidentially. "I'm going to ask her to help me choose my outfit – she's got wonderful taste." She smiled at Joanna. "By the way, how is your father, dear? Will he be coming to the wedding?"

Joanna lowered her head to hide her tears and gripped Tom's hand in her distress.

"It's just going to be a small wedding, Catherine," said Tom, taking his future mother-in-law's hand in his, "but we hope that you'll be there. Unfortunately, Agnes won't be able to be there – "

"Well, I suppose she has to go to school, hasn't she? Prefects can't take time off, can they? But I'll tell her all about it afterwards," said Catherine happily. "Can I be bridesmaid?"

"Well, not really, Mam," said Joanna, her heart almost breaking, "but, as Mother of the Bride, we'll have to get you something really special to wear."

Joanna and Tom exchanged a quick, pained glance. But Catherine seemed happy in her world of confusion and delusion. Whether she would be well enough to attend their wedding would depend on how her Alzheimer's continued to develop. But Joanna longed to have her mother with her, to share the most special day of her life. I want to have some photographs of her – maybe they'll be the last ones we'll ever take of her, Joanna thought, feeling a lump forming in her throat.

Trying to think of more cheerful things, Joanna focused her thoughts on her forthcoming wedding. She'd definitely invite dear old Freddy O'Rourke. In fact, she thought suddenly smiling, Orla should, by rights, invite him to hers too, since indirectly he was responsible for her meeting Gary! If Freddy hadn't passed on the dog-bite case, her friend might never have met the love of her life, and she herself would never have found out about Ellen's connection to the Harry Sweeney affair. Freddy, I owe you big time, she thought.

"Mam – remember you told me you were minding letters and documents for Agnes?"

Catherine looked wary.

"Well, it's all sorted. There are no secrets any more. Agnes told us the truth at last."

Which, in a way, she did, thought Joanna. And Catherine, too, had told her daughter of her true birthright in a letter. Although now, it seemed, Catherine had long forgotten about the letter she'd once written.

Catherine smiled back at her daughter. "I'm very glad," she said.

Then she got up and wandered out into the corridor, and was quickly distracted by meeting another elderly patient. The pair began a conversation that was totally unintelligible to anyone but themselves, so Tom and Joanna decided that it was an opportune time to slip away from the nursing home.

"I wish I didn't feel so guilty each time I leave her," Joanna said sadly.

Tom slipped his arm around her. "I think that in her own way, Jo, Catherine is happy enough. It's obvious that she thinks she's in her own home – at least most of the time, anyway." Tenderly, he kissed her hair. "Don't let all the worry and guilt sit on your shoulders, love. Now, you've got me to share it with you."

* * *

Back at Joanna's house, Tom put the kettle on, while Joanna spooned out cat food for Devil. As she filled the cat's dish, Tom leaned over and planted a kiss on her cheek.

"I'm doing very well in the family stakes, aren't I?" he said, "Very soon, I'll be acquiring a wife, a mother-in-law – and a pregnant cat as well!"

Joanna laughed, sliding comfortably into his arms. She felt safe, cherished and incredibly happy as he held her tight. But also more than a little guilty, since she'd neglected to get Devil spayed.

"Oh, Jo," said Tom huskily, kissing her hair, "I'll be the happiest man on earth when we start our own family. But I think we really should get Devil neutered as soon as she's had her kittens."

"I agree – I feel so guilty for not taking action earlier – "

"Well, you were working on my mother's will, love. You just didn't have the time to take her to the vet."

Joanna snuggled in his arms so that he couldn't see her face go red. Ronan O'Farrell had also been taking up a lot of her time!

Tom smiled. "We'll keep all Devil's kittens, won't we?"

"Of course! I wonder that colours they'll be?"

"Who cares? They'll all be gorgeous. I'm looking forward to having a full house, complete with wife, cats and children!"

Devil meowed loudly, and Joanna guiltily placed the cat's dish on the floor. Joanna herself could hardly think of food – she was far too happy!

"I presume we'll live at my place?" asked Tom.

Joanna nodded. "And we'll sit with the children beside the pond at the bottom of the garden and teach them all about nature. Like you taught me, all those years ago –"

"Hold on – that's a few years away yet!" said Tom, grinning. "But before then, I intend to take you on a long honeymoon to the Antarctic – if you can spare the time from work, that is. Of course, you know that you needn't ever have to work outside the home again, if that's what you want – between us, we've more than enough money, you know."

"I know – but like you, I enjoy my work, Tom. I intend to continue as a practising solicitor, but now I'll be able to do a lot more *pro bono* work."

Tom smiled. "I knew you'd say something like that. That's one of the million reasons that I love you, Joanna Brennan – because you care about others. You're good, kind – and damned sexy too!" He kissed her again. "Well – can you manage to come on honeymoon with me?"

"Isn't it usual for wives to go on the honeymoon? But two weeks is probably as much time as I can spare." Joanna suddenly had an idea. Maybe she could return the favour and offload some cases onto Freddy O'Rourke!

Tom kissed her again. "I see – already I'm taking a back seat to your career."

"Well, you might as well learn your place early on," said Joanna, kissing the tip of his nose. Then she laughed. "You know, Tom, I learnt more about the birds and the bees from *you* than I ever learnt from my parents – they used to get all embarrassed and mumble on about how babies grew in their mothers' tummies, but they never told me how they got in there!"

"I presume you know by now?" said Tom mischievously. "If not, I can give you an immediate demonstration – "

"Don't worry," said Joanna, laughing, "you've already

explained to me how it happens with frogs – back in your garden, when I was seven. For years after that, I actually assumed that people produced some kind of frogspawn!"

"You didn't!"

"Yes, I did – but eventually Orla sorted me out! When we were twelve, she found a sex book and brought it into school – so we all passed it around the classroom, one afternoon during French."

"Hmm – I like French kissing," said Tom, pulling her close and sliding his tongue into her mouth, "and there's a lot more that I can tell you about the birds and bees if you're interested – "

And before Joanna could answer, he had swept her up in his arms and was carrying her upstairs.

CHAPTER 93

It was early morning, and Declan Dunne was sitting in his tiny bedsitter, eating toast and drinking a cup of tea before heading off to the *Evening Dispatch* office. The morning paper had just been delivered – the only bloody luxury he had left, he grumbled – and he skimmed through the headlines, then turned to the smaller features, to see if there were any stories worth nicking and rewriting for his own column. He'd once managed to write up a whole "exclusive" based on a story that had been in a previous day's rival newspaper – and he'd got away with it too. The author of the original piece had been too timid to complain, and the paper's editor had been away at a conference that day. So the whole thing had worked perfectly to Declan's benefit. Maybe today would also be his lucky day.

Nothing caught his attention, so he turned to the Births, Deaths and Social Notices page. The deaths were always entertaining. They made him feel superior to all those dead people, because at least he'd managed to survive another night of aimless drinking and still wake up – albeit with a hangover – the following morning. He knew he was drinking far too much, but that was what happened when a man's fiancée was so hardhearted that she was making him pay dearly before she'd agree to take him back.

Suddenly, for no logical reason, his eye was drawn to the Engagements column.

"No – it can't be!"

But it was. There were two entries in the column, and Declan's heart sank as he surveyed the first entry.

CULHANE and ROGAN

Dr Gary Culhane and Ms Orla Rogan, together with their families, are delighted to announce their engagement.

Declan cursed as his toast landed buttered side down on his freshly dry-cleaned trousers. Orla – the love of his life – had really and truly left him this time! He'd always felt certain that once she'd realised what a good catch he was, she'd come to her senses and beg him to take her back. He'd even imagined her sitting lonely and bored in that big apartment they'd once shared – in fact, he'd derived sadistic pleasure from those thoughts – and all the time, she'd been cavorting around with some medical moron! Declan felt cheated and severely put upon.

He was just about to abandon the paper in disgust and self-pity when the second entry in the Engagements column caught his eye. Bloody hell! He knew half of this duo too! Everyone was getting engaged, yet he didn't even have a date for the weekend! To compound the indignity of it all, he'd heard that Sasha and John Boyle were a serious item again. Christ, he thought indignantly, next thing *they'll* be announcing their engagement in the bloody newspaper too!

Declan glowered with rage that all these people were achieving this rite of passage before him. Especially since he'd been engaged himself long before any of them! And if it wasn't for hardhearted Orla, he'd still be engaged! His eye scanned the second entry in the Engagements column. Yes, it was that bloody solicitor friend of Orla's. That woman had always been a bad influence on Orla. She was just the meanspirited type who would never forgive a man for a simple little lapse – she'd probably encouraged Orla to drop him! He'd never really liked her ... And who was this poor guy that she'd got her miserable claws into? He scanned the entry avidly.

KILMARTIN and BRENNAN
Tom, son of the late Harry Sweeney and Agnes Kilmartin, and Joanna, daughter of Catherine and the late Bill Brennan, are pleased to announce their engagement.

Harry Sweeney? That name rang a bell. Declan furrowed his brow and tried to think where he'd heard that name before. And quite recently too. Got it! Wasn't he that chap who'd been on remand for murder all those years ago, but who hadn't actually done it? Some witness who'd lied back then had finally come clean and confessed to fitting Harry Sweeney up. By confessing, this guy – Jackie Something-or-other – was hoping to get a reduced sentence for some other crimes he'd commited.

And some woman had apparently seen the crime being committed by a millionaire property developer back in the early seventies, but it was impossible to charge a man who was dead.

There had been substantial coverage of the story in all the papers, but Declan had been so busy nursing his own wounded pride, and trying to win Sasha back, that he'd failed to pay attention to the details.

Declan perused the column once again. Tom Kilmartin, son of Harry Sweeney. Why didn't they have the same name? Could it possibly be the same Harry Sweeney? Probably not. On the other hand, maybe there *was* a story here. Declan's newshound nose was suddenly twitching. Under the guise of ringing Orla to congratulate her, he would also ask her for the Kilmartin chap's phone number.

And he could also broach the subject of the redundant engagement ring . . . she'd hardly want to keep it, now that she'd squeezed a second sparkler out of another poor sucker, could she?

He grinned. Maybe the day wasn't going to be so bad after all . . .

THE END

If you enjoyed *Love Child*, don't miss out on Linda
Kavanagh's debut novel, *Love Hurts*, also published
by Poolbeg.com.

Here is a sneak preview of Chapter one . . .

www.poolbeg.com

LOVE
HURTS

LINDA KAVANAGH

POOLBEG

PROLOGUE

The woman sat down at her computer and began typing. The words formed swiftly as her fingers flew over the keyboard, and before long she had filled the entire screen. Oblivious to the darkening room as evening set in, she continued typing as though possessed. Vitriol poured onto the screen, as though a dam had burst inside her. She typed on and on until her fingers began hurting, her hatred spurring her on.

Finally, she stopped typing, exhausted but relieved. This was just the beginning. There was still so much more that she needed to write before her story was told. This was the sad story of her life, and her justification for what she had done to Ciara. No one would ever see her words, but letting out her anger was a cathartic experience. She pressed "save", then closed down her computer. Tomorrow she would continue with the next stage of her story . . .

BOOK 1

CHAPTER 1

"It was a beautiful service," said Ciara's mother Annie, as the first of the guests began arriving back at the house after the funeral. Ciara nodded numbly. Since her husband's sudden death four days previously she'd been walking around in a daze.

At first she'd been hysterical, then unbelieving. She and Niall had been so happy together! They had a lovely home, no money worries, good friends and an enjoyable lifestyle. Niall ran a successful public relations company, while she earned a good income from her painting. They'd enjoyed each other's company, shared many interests and had a healthy, if somewhat volatile, teenage daughter. Ciara gulped. They'd even been planning to take a holiday together the following month!

At the thought of the holiday that would now never be, Ciara's eyes filled again with tears. It just wasn't fair! She felt cheated of that last idyllic time they might have shared together. In some ways, anger was a more

545

manageable way of coping with the pain. It briefly eased the terrible ache inside her, which kept welling up and threatening to choke her.

There were times when, she realised, Niall's death hadn't yet registered with her at all. Momentarily her mind would play tricks. She would look up and expect to see him coming through the door. He was too young to die. It was simply too devastating to accept that this man in his mid-forties whom she'd adored since her schooldays would never walk through the door again.

Hastily, she took around a plate of sandwiches. It was comforting to see so many friends, neighbours, family members and work colleagues of both hers and Niall's. Yet the situation all seemed so unreal. At gatherings like these Niall had always been there in their midst, cracking jokes and filling up glasses.

"Are you all right, Ciara?"

Her old school-friend Kate was at her elbow, looking concerned and caring. "Here, let me take those."

Kate tried to take the plate of sandwiches, but Ciara clung on as though the plate was a life-raft in a raging sea. "I'm all right, really. It's better if I have something to do."

"OK, love. But don't tire yourself out. It's been a tough day for you."

Ciara nodded her thanks through eyes brimming again with tears. Any show of concern from friends or family overwhelmed her. Maybe handing round the sandwiches wasn't such a good idea after all. Quickly, she abandoned them to the sideboard and headed out to the sanctuary of the kitchen.

Gazing unseeingly out the kitchen window, Ciara recalled all too vividly the events of that fateful evening just four days ago. She and Niall had just finished dinner and were considering what to do for the rest of the evening. They'd debated the merits of watching television, or walking down to the local pub for a leisurely nightcap.

"I think I'd rather stay in tonight," Niall had eventually said. "I'm not feeling too good. Maybe I'm just a bit tired. If you don't mind, I'd rather unwind with a movie. Is there anything decent on?"

Ciara suddenly wondered how Sarah, her daughter, was coping. Many of Sarah's friends had come to the service and graveyard, anxious to give Sarah support but embarrassed and uncertain of what to say. Most of them had never had to face death at such close quarters before and were unsure of how to behave. Ciara had been deeply touched, knowing that their presence had required greater effort than many of the older people, some of whom positively thrived on funerals. So as they'd left the graveyard, she'd given Sarah a wad of notes to buy drinks for her friends at the local pub.

Annie had been shocked when she'd discovered that her granddaughter was in a pub on the day of her father's funeral, but Ciara dismissed her mother's misgivings. This day, of all days, Sarah belonged in the bright world of the living. The child would have to do her grieving soon enough.

Startled from her reverie, Ciara turned as Charlie Somers entered the kitchen. Charlie had been Niall's best friend since schooldays. Without saying a word Charlie put his arms around her, holding her tightly, both of them united in a fresh wave of grief. Sobbing together, there were no words needed. They had both lost someone they loved dearly.

Dee, Charlie's wife and one of Ciara's closest friends, joined them and they all stood together, arms linked and holding each other in wordless communication. Over the years, they had all shared so many milestones. It was impossible to accept that Niall would not be there to build more memories in the years ahead.

Gradually, the kitchen began to fill up with people bringing in food. Delicious hams, cold meats, salmon and salads had appeared on the kitchen table as if by magic. Ciara realised with gratitude that her neighbours and friends must have organised it all. Fires had also been lit in both dining-room and drawing-room, creating a cosy and welcoming atmosphere. She was now angry with herself for being so self-indulgent. Niall would have expected her to look after the guests properly. After all, these were the very people who had come to pay their respects to his memory.

People were still arriving back from the graveyard, and Ciara heard the deep booming voice of Liam Golden in the hall. Leaving the kitchen, she hurried outside to greet him, needing to feel the warmth of his embrace as he enfolded her in his huge arms.

"Ciara, love . . ." He held her tightly, smoothing her hair as one might soothe a small child. No words were necessary. They had known each other for years, and Ciara found comfort and solace in his affectionate embrace.

Since her art college days, Liam had been her mentor

and friend. As owner of the Domino Gallery, Liam had spotted Ciara's talent and given her a solo exhibition when she was still an unknown. It had been a wonderful opportunity for a young art student, and to everyone's surprise but Liam's her work received rave reviews and the entire exhibition sold out within a week. Since then, despite offers from bigger, more impressive galleries, Ciara had continued to work exclusively with Liam and his gallery. She might have made more money elsewhere, but to Ciara money wasn't everything.

Suddenly, Ciara became aware that there was a woman standing just behind Liam smiling sympathetically at her. Simultaneously, Liam released Ciara from his embrace and turned to introduce the woman to her.

"Ciara, this is Ita. She wasn't sure if she should come, but I said . . ."

"You're very welcome, Ita," said Ciara, extending her hand. "Any friend of Liam's is a friend of mine."

Ita smiled shyly as they shook hands. "Thanks, Ciara. I'm very sorry about your husband."

"Maybe you two can get together some time," said Liam eagerly. "Ita just loves your paintings."

Ciara felt a sudden surge of affection for Liam. He was transparently anxious that she should like this woman. She now recalled that Liam had casually mentioned a new woman in his life. When he'd mentioned her there had been a gentle smile at the corner of his lips, and Ciara had thought, "Uh-oh, this one might be different."

Ciara would have willed herself to like any woman who was important to Liam, but in any event she didn't find it difficult to like this tall, beautiful and effortlessly elegant woman. Ita seemed to have an empathy about her, and Ciara was pleased to think that Liam had found someone he evidently cared for.

Just at that moment, Annie edged her daughter aside.

"Are you all right, love?" she asked, "would you like a cup of tea? I'm just going to make a fresh pot."

Ciara shook her head. For as long as she could remember, a cup of tea had been her mother's answer to all the woes of the world, but Ciara felt in need of something stronger. As though anticipating her need, Dee appeared with a brandy.

"For medicinal purposes," she whispered, winking, as Ciara gratefully took the glass.

"Are you OK?" Dee asked, giving her arm a squeeze. Ciara nodded. At least she had managed to keep her composure so far.

Ciara was glad to see that people were enjoying themselves. Having shaken off the sombre atmosphere of the church and graveyard, they were all relaxing now and sharing jokes, chatting about their families and careers as though the morning's event had never happened. In fact, Ciara observed dispassionately, there was the makings of a good party underway already. Yet in the midst of all the chat and camaraderie, Ciara felt terribly alone. Everyone else seemed to be with their lover or partner, whereas hers was gone forever.

She now recalled how tired Niall had looked that night. She'd noticed the first streaks of grey in his previously black hair, and his skin had an unhealthy pallor too. Not unreasonably, he'd been unusually quiet since Eamonn Merrigan, his friend and contemporary from the golf club, had died of cancer a few weeks earlier. Therefore she'd assumed that Niall's lethargy was a reaction to the loss of a friend, tempered by fears about his own mortality. Now, memories of that unnatural colour haunted her. If she'd realised its significance, she might have acted faster and been able to save him . . .

Why hadn't some sixth sense warned her? Surely after living with a man for years, there would be some form of telepathic communication between them? Yet when she'd brought two cups of coffee in from the kitchen after dinner, Niall had been lying on the floor, groaning and clutching his chest.

The next few hours had passed in a daze. She vaguely remembered ambulance personnel asking her a series of meaningless questions, Niall being taken out on a stretcher, the interminable drive to the hospital with the sirens wailing. In the hospital, she'd just stood there twisting the buttons on her cardigan as the clamps were applied time and time again to Niall's chest. His body had shuddered like a rag doll as the electrical charges went through him.

Then suddenly, the emergency team weren't trying any more, and a hush had descended over the room. Then they had all turned to face her, with pity in their eyes. And she'd felt like an outsider, watching a ghastly play in which she had no part.

As she now crossed the room aimlessly, she was welcomed into a small group that included her younger brother Cillian and his wife Betty. Ciara and her younger sibling had little in common, but she was glad he'd been able to get here. As a busy surgeon, he'd probably had to rearrange his entire schedule.

Thanking them for their solicitations, she glanced around the large room at the cousins, aunts and uncles from both sides of the family. Many of them she would never see again, or at least not until the next funeral. She shivered as she remembered seeing photographer Alan Moore at the church. He had a nerve turning up, after all the harm he'd caused her! How she hated that man, with his insolent grin and knowing eyes. Thank goodness he hadn't come back to the house – that would have added insult to injury!

Her heart pounding, she headed towards the drinks cabinet. Perhaps another brandy would help her to keep going.

"I'll get that for you . . ."

Ciara's brother Kevin had spotted her empty glass and seen her moving in the direction of the drinks cabinet. Ciara nodded gratefully. Kevin was the eldest of the family and home on leave from Africa. As a priest, his work involved travelling over hundreds of miles of rough terrain each week to places where there were no roads, where water was always scarce and where electricity and flush toilets were non-existent. Added to that was the never-ending horror of hunger and disease and the hopelessness of people living constantly on the edge of disaster.

Ciara watched her brother as he poured the brandy into her glass. It was lucky that Kevin happened to be at home. He'd been a tower of strength over the last few days. Although she'd been surprised when he'd declined to say the funeral mass, arranging for a distant cousin in Niall's family to do the honours instead. Perhaps there was some kind of priestly etiquette involved. She would ask him about it some time.

"Thanks, Kev," Ciara took the drink gratefully, "and thanks for all your help over the last few days. I don't think I could have managed without you."

"Glad to help, love, but you'd have done fine, even if I hadn't been here." He squeezed her arm affectionately. "That was a marvellous tribute you paid to Niall in the church this morning."

Ciara smiled, her lower lip trembling at the memory. It had taken all her physical and mental strength not to break down and cry when she'd stepped up onto the altar to read one of Niall's favourite poems before the assembled congregation and to pay her own brief tribute to the man she loved before he was finally taken away from her and laid in the cold earth.

"Oh, Niall . . ." she thought, "if only I could hold you one more time."

She stifled a sob, knowing that she was only torturing herself. Niall was gone, never to return, and she was now a widow. What a horrible word! Suddenly, it all proved too much for her, and the tears began streaming down her face.

Direct to your home!

If you enjoyed this book why not visit our website:

www.poolbeg.com

and get another book delivered straight to your home or to a friend's home!

www.poolbeg.com

All orders are despatched within 24 hours.